Cedar Crest Books
Natick, MA USA
www.cedarcrestbooks.com

I0611189

The Other Side of Everything
by Linda Ruth

The Other Side of Everything takes place in the fictional town of Riverboro, NH. This setting is inspired by the real town of Peterborough, in southwest NH; however, this is a work of fiction. Names, characters, businesses, places, events and incidents are the products of the author's imagination. Any resemblance to actual persons, living or dead, actual places, or actual events is purely coincidental.

Piper Hadley, while a compulsive quoter, has no intention of plagiarizing her fellow artists' works, and any reader who finds an unattributed quote is invited to post the discovery on author Linda Spitzfaden's Facebook page so we can correct the oversight.

Cover and Book Design: DuCiel

First Printing – January 2017

ISBN: 978-0-91029-114-9

To the two Davids. Then and now.

Praise for *The Other Side of Everything:*

"A smart, larky entertainment, Linda R. Spitzfaden's debut novel is chock full of vividly realized characters beset by a memorable winter storm. As they hunker down in a very cold, wonderfully shabby house, they must deal with a variety of familial, social, and emotional predicaments, unexpected and startling, which force them to rethink the stories of their lives. This is an impressive novel, wise in the contradictory ways of the human heart."

Martha Cooley, best-selling author of *The Archivist* and *33 Swoons*.

"The plucky New England regional magazine *Riverboro Rocks* is hanging in there – barely – as most plucky print publications are these days. Plucky owner-editor Piper Hadley Hammond starts a blog to chronicle daily life in her small town and perhaps increase interest in the monthly magazine. Author Spitzfaden weaves the blog posts and their comment sections together with the narrative of that crucial November in Riverboro. When an unexpected (except to the magazine's mysterious Weather Oracle) early winter storm raises the river banks and knocks out power to much of the town, an ashram of six monks takes shelter at Piper's ancestral home, adding to the magazine staff, family members and friends who always seem to be dropping by. I confess I spent some time wondering where we were going with all this – when we got there, though, the payoff was tremendous and I realized the signposts had been placed in plain sight all the way through. I had been taking a leisurely stroll through the book, but I raced through the last 100 pages or so to a satisfying conclusion. *The Other Side of Everything* is a quirky, clever and captivating look into complicated relationships and their impact."

Warren Bluhm, author of the *Myke Phoenix* and *Imaginary Era* series.

"It's like the great English author Anthony Trollope, is alive again. Portraying a vibrant web of human relationships in all their beauty and complexity, the book is a giant puzzle of people loving, hating and loving each other again. Quite a read!"

Tony Anthony, award-winning author of *Long Before the Next War*

"With a cheerful voice that addresses sometimes heartbreaking realities, [Spitzfaden] seamlessly blends literary themes with modern life. This book draws on the fundamental strength of women to explore the question, what happens when there are obstacles we cannot overcome?"

Cathy Utzschneider, Professor at Boston College, sports columnist, and author of *Move!* and *Mastering Running*

THE
OTHER SIDE
OF
EVERYTHING

PART 1

NOVEMBER LIES

PIPER'S PEBBLES

Musings from the Editor of *Riverboro Rocks, the Voice of Our Town*

by Piper Hadley Hammond

~~Hello World! (Use this space to write your first post).~~

Day 1, November 1: The November in Our Town

Dan took a fall this morning, his feet flying out from under him on a patch of unseasonably-early ice in the parking lot at the depot downtown. He had dropped Donny off at preschool, and had stopped in at King's Market, as he does almost every day, to get coffee. Picture him, a bluff, bearded, Nordic-looking man coming out of King's, bellowing cheery greetings to passers-by. In his hands are two extra-large cups of coffee, one for him and one for me.

He starts across that wide-open area toward the footbridge. His foot hits a patch of black ice; he skids. At first he manages to stay upright, balancing coffee, surfing the ice. He picks up speed, rocketing forward, his upper body lurching back and forward, arms windmilling, coffee sloshing. A group of our town's white-robed monks stands unmoving. They watch, with their Zen-like calm, as he shoots toward them.

Then, a bowling ball into a group of standing pins, he careens into them, a flying tangle of arms and legs. Strike! The remains of two Columbian dark roasts (no cream) come arcing out of those cups (I imagine this part of the scene in slow motion) and splat! A pile of human beings. And coffee stains all over those nice white robes.

Meanwhile, a crowd has gathered to help—a humiliation worse, for Dan, than if he'd had to lie there for hours, in pain. Some of the people group around the monks, setting them upright, straightening their robes, dabbing at the coffee-stains; others collect around Dan, pulling and hauling him to his feet. That part isn't so easy—Dan's a big guy! In the end it takes two or three to get him up. Let's imagine that as part of the comic scene—getting him partway to his feet, him trying to brace on the ice, another skid, more people going down, and finally, when Dan is upright, a helpful soul handing him his extra-large paper cups, an inch or so of coffee and snow in the bottom of each one.

Dan stormed in a few minutes ago, relating the entire embarrassing episode while I split a gut laughing. Dan was beside himself, swearing he was going to move us all to Florida this very year.

November is officially here.

As all my local readers know, and so does anyone in the rest of the country that follows the news, Nature has welcomed November in New Hampshire with the most snow ever on this day. A shock to all except to the *Riverboro Rocks* Weather Oracle who warned us to expect something extraordinary on this date.

Those of you who keep a close eye on the goings-on at my magazine will know that the Weather Oracle, the great seer of *Riverboro Rocks*, has retired. After so many good years of astounding predictive successes and occasional (and always-entertaining) failures, we bade him goodbye and looked to our new and (till now) untried Oracle, who assured us we need only gaze up and we would see something falling from the sky. There were no specifics exactly what to expect—it could have been pianos for all we knew—but one thing we could count on: it was going to be big. And here we are, with over two feet of the white stuff. A good beginning for both our new Oracle and the November in our town.

It was already coming down thick and fast last night, evocative and moody for Halloween. The sky was blurred with snow; it fell in bright pools near the streetlights; the calls and laughter of the children were engulfed by that muffling silence. The trick-or-treaters were indistinct shapes appearing and disappearing in the storm; up and down the street the little (and not-so-little—Coral Lane, I saw you there in that Princess Zelda costume, so not cute, not cute) pirates and zombies and witches came slipping and sliding up to the doors with snow on their hats and hair and eyelashes. Cherry noses and wind-bussed cheeks! And Riverboro, what's with the animals—someone was leading a goat, and a man was carrying a goose…a coincidence, or a new trend?

A few days ago I did a Google search for depressing November quotes—I've been planning this blog launch for several weeks, and I thought I might as well be ready with some seasonally-appropriate references—and I found plenty of great downers. But Nature is out there this morning with something else in mind. The sun is coming up and glinting on the snow, which covers still-bright autumn leaves: think crystals, think diamonds, think prisms. Kaleidoscopes almost, it dazzles so much. The pines are shagged with ice, the spruces rough in the distant glitter of the sun; Sasha (my cat; I'll post her picture for you later today) is draped over my lap, purring loudly; and out my window our town sparkles, its converted mill buildings Dickensian in the snow. The rising sun glints a path down the steep slope to the river, across the footbridge to the old depot (now full of boutiques); its rays dance across to where the Riverboro Ashram rests peacefully, its meditation center and shop more white-robed than its monks, who now chant and pray with great tan coffee splotches spreading like camouflage over the fabric of their garments.

This blog is part of an overarching plan—we're always involved in some exhilarating project here at *Riverboro Rocks*—and that is to save our own sorry hides. *Riverboro Rocks*, unique in so many ways, does have something in common with every print publication in the country, or in the world, for that matter. We're all teetering on a brink—you know that, I know that, everyone knows that. My magazine's advantage is that we've been teetering for years, so we're able to keep our balance better than most. We've had practice. We know what we're doing. And we always get yanked back from the edge by some miracle or other. Dan tells me that this time we need a bigger *machina* to be wheeled on stage, complete with *deus*, to save our butts—a stronger tourniquet, if you will, to stanch the hemorrhaging of the green stuff—in short, a bigger infusion of cash. But not to worry, Riverboro! Let's put our noses to the grindstone, our shoulders to the wheel, our hands to the plow (for many of you here in town that means to buy advertising), and by the first of December we'll be up on our financial feet and walking off with barely a limp, as Dan did from King's this morning.

I'm enabling comments, so drop by and let me know what you'd like to see here, or be my roving reporters and add your own bits of news. There is going to be moderation, so watch your language if you expect to see your posts go up. I'll see you here tomorrow. Now there is a winter wonderland to go out and enjoy.

Piper's List: Top Five Dismal November Quotes

5) *November always seemed to me the Norway of the year.* (Emily Dickinson) Did she mean both are cold and expensive? Which should be flattered—Norway or November? Which offended?

4) *Because of an adulterous affair I will leave office in November.* (James Mc-Greevy) But what governor doesn't have adulterous affairs? If only this former political figure had left it at that. I recall quite a package of exploits rolled up in that affair, not excluding patronage, or whatever you call it when you give high-paying jobs to your special friends. At *Riverboro Rocks* we also employ our friends, but you can't call it patronage if you can't afford to pay them. Ah, November: the best of times, the worst of times for politicians.

3) *Nothin' lasts forever and we both know hearts can change/ and it's hard to hold a candle in the cold November rain.* (Guns and Roses) Hearts can change at any time, even, as I have reason to recall, in the merry month of May; but if we're going to be miserable, was ever there a better month than November to indulge?

2) This goes one better: *The gloomy months of November, when the people of England hang and drown themselves.* (Joseph Addison) Our neighbors across the pond don't mope, they take action—doing November up in grand English style.

1) And my favorite (and yours too, I'll bet)—Ishmael from Moby Dick, saying: *Whenever I find myself growing grim about the mouth; whenever it is a damp, drizzly November in my soul; whenever I find myself involuntarily pausing before coffin warehouses, and bringing up the rear of every funeral I meet; and especially whenever…it requires a strong moral principle to prevent me from deliberately stepping into the street, and methodically knocking people's hats off—then, I account it high time to get to sea as soon as I can.* The problem and the solution in one lovely passage; so if you are pausing before coffin warehouses and knocking off people's hats, get yourself to sea without delay. Nestled as we are in the mountains two hours from the sea, it will be a bit of a haul, but hey, no one said it would be easy.

Tags: Riverboro Rocks magazine, NH local weather, King's Market, November quotations, Piper's List

COMMENTS:

MollyHH: Mom? You really coming out? Want to walk me to school? (*Comment declined*)

Private Message to MollyHH: Molly sweetie, it does help to comment, and thank you for the support, but it looks lame for the first one to address me as "Mom." Can you do a more general comment? Something about how ridiculous it looks for grown women to dress up as comic book characters and go house-to-house on Halloween, for example?

Private Message from MollyHH: Mom, I've told you, like, a zillion times, Zelda is from a videogame, not a comic book. And Coral had the kids with her, give her a break. Also you said you were going to say something about November Lies. It's the first day!

Private Message to MollyHH: I'll do it tomorrow, I promise. I've maxed out this blog post. Plus, I've got to start work on the February issue of *Riverboro Rocks*. Any ideas?

Private Message from MollyHH: I give you ideas and you don't use them. Anyway I've got to get to school now. Bye!

Private Message to WeatherOracle: Please post a comment. I've got no public comments, only private messages. I'm desperate.

WeatherOracle: November's offerings are meager;
As it begins, we're hardly eager.
The dark, the cold, the widespread freezes
Will pull from you your last 'bejesus!'
Beware the smile of false elation—
And brace for more precipitation.

PipersPebbles: This is dark stuff. Weather Oracle, I admit to setting a bad example with my banter about the magazine's financial peril, but surely you know that that was all in good fun. At *Riverboro Rocks* we try to uplift. Do you want to start your predictive career out so gloomy?

Weather Oracle: For news less dire but more perjurical
Go find a different Weather Oracle.

PipersPebbles: You heard it here, Riverboro—we're not going to sug-ar-coat our predictions, and we haven't seen the last of it. Be it rain or snow, something wet is coming down. Visit this blog for the latest Oracle updates.

(*Comments approved*)

Private Message from DanTheRiverMan: Piper, this blog isn't going to turn into an ongoing comic sketch, with me as the butt of every joke, is it?

Private Message to DanTheRiverMan: Don't worry, it won't. There will be many more butts of many more jokes!

Private Message from DanTheRiverMan: That's a relief. I think. Now that you've started this blog, I expect I'll wake up each day to a new surprise. What fun. Who or what are you targeting for Day Two?

Private Message to DanTheRiverMan: How about your favorite politi-cal leaders, who are puppets for creatures from outer space, and who plan to release cholera into our drinking water?

Private Message from DanTheRiverMan: Piper, your wit is, as always, knife-sharp, and never more so than when it's at my expense. But you should know by now that the thinking of the outer-space-aliens conspiracists does not overlap with the drinking-water-contamination body of thought. They are two entirely separate studies.

Private Message to DanTheRiverMan: So remind me: who exactly is releasing cholera into the drinking water?

Private Message from DanTheRiverMan: No one—who do you know has cholera? If you want to find out what thought leaders in the drinking-water field believe the government is doing, I address it in my study group for twenty-first century conspiracy theories. Throwing around unfounded accusations only serves to draw unwanted attention.

Private Message to DanTheRiverMan: As opposed to well-founded accusations that will be ignored?

Private Message from DanTheRiverMan: All I'm saying is, better we each keep to our own area of expertise. I'll cover the conspiracies. You stick to the low comedy, if you must.

* * *

Piper was still chuckling when she clicked out of her blog and opened up her list of ideas for *Riverboro Rocks'* February issue. Three months in advance, that was the world of magazine publishing; you always had to think a season ahead. It was going to be a nice change to write this blog, to focus on the fleeting, the day to day. So much was happening in Riverboro this month alone: the local elections, the campaigns for next year's primary, the opening of the new franchise restaurant, Hey! It's Thursday, down at the plaza. The protests that were sure to ensue—one of them scheduled for this very day.

And the weather, always a rich source of conversation and fun. Today's snow was a special gift, making the third floor of the Hadley House glow with the muted light of the wintry world outside.

The reflection of the changing seasons contributed to Piper's sense of this part of her house as a sanctuary, and indeed it was a haven of rescued space, salvaged from the attic. The reclamation was a partial one, as the other side of the third floor was still slope-ceilinged and cobwebby and filled with forgotten relics. But on this side, she and Dan had built out their master suite: the bath with the old-fashioned claw-footed tub, the bedroom with the big sleigh bed—now with a little mattress on the floor for Donny on those special nights he was allowed to sleep there—and Piper's office.

Piper liked to think of her office as Command Central. From here she watched over her domain. From the window you could see the people on the streets far below, walking their dogs, going in and out of shops, waving greetings or stopping to chat. When the air was clear and still you could hear their distant voices, their laughter. Overhead the big skylight in the gabled ceiling reflected the changing weather, glimpsed through the summer leaves or winter branches of the huge oak tree that towered over the house.

Piper's shelves were lined with all the years of the magazine, tracking its evolution from saddle stitch to perfect bound and, now, back again. A few old guidebooks anchored the magazines, books they had used over the years to plan that once-in-a-lifetime trip to Japan. It was Molly who had fallen in love with Japan through its anime and manga, she who had begged for the trip. But the hours spent looking through the magazines, reading the guidebooks, and learning the culture had been precious to the three of them. Those hours had created their own special enchantment, a rich store of memories made without even stepping out of the house. Not every adventure could go exactly as envisioned. Yet that didn't have to take away from the pleasure of travel, so much of which was to be found in the planning.

This office fairly hummed with memories from those years, years when she and Dan started and built their magazine and their family. To the Hadleys and the Hammonds it must have felt like a dynastic alliance, this union of the two oldest Riverboro families. Oh, the Hadleys and Hammonds had a long history of friendship and enmity, alliances and betrayals, marriages and even (apocryphally) murders. Piper and Dan's marriage was the first such union of the two clans in this generation and neither family was likely to let *that* pass unnoticed. Piper and Dan, the house, the magazine—the building of their life together was a project for both the Hadleys and the

Hammonds. And, by extension, the entire town.

Dan called the office the beating heart of the magazine. What would make you happy, he had asked; what would make you productive? Nestled under these eaves along with her old-fashioned brass floor lamps, her ancient Persian carpet, and the cozy wing armchair that sat ready for any visitor that might stop by, she had the state-of-the-art technology she needed to create her magazine. Plus, a miniature refrigerator and a coffeemaker, for those busy mornings when she just didn't want to venture down to the kitchen.

The rest of the house was another story. They'd thought of it as a fixer-upper when they'd negotiated its purchase from the Hadley family co-op, but somehow they'd never gotten around to much fixing-upping. Walls and floors were scuffed, paint on the woodwork was peeling, and it wasn't only paint it needed. There were mice in the unfinished part of the attic (she hoped only the unfinished part), and they were chewing the wires, if the nighttime noises were any indication. The windows were drafty, the floors crooked, some of the doors hung oddly on their hinges, or got stuck opening, or wouldn't close at all. The wiring needed an overhaul, and forget about the insulation.

But to Piper, the Hadley House was as special now as it had been when she was growing up, a Hadley kid in a town where the big house represented something solid and enduring. And, even today, the house looked great from the outside. The Hadley family co-op had put on some kind of permanent siding— tacky, Dan said, a consequence of management-by-committee—but it kept the exterior from collapsing into the faded-glory look of the rest of the place. Piper and Dan rarely entertained, so few people in town knew how bad it was inside. Between the look of the house, big and grand on the hill teetering over the town, and the fact that Dan and Piper had their own business, everyone in town thought they were well off. Rich, even. Leading citizens and all that.

It was kind of a joke, because Dan had spent a good bit of what nest egg he'd had on the house and the magazine launch. As for Piper, if she had any of the Hadley family money coming, it would require more than one family member to move on to the next plane before it fell to her. Not that she was waiting, not that she was hoping! But in the meantime Piper and Dan were always being asked to serve on boards and vestries and rotaries and chambers of commerce. Dan was usually happy to oblige. Oh, he kept his fingers in the various town pies. His involvement with the River Place alone was enough to get him involved in virtually every commercial, social, or community project that went on in town. Piper, herself, had plenty to do just raising a family and keeping the magazine going and trying, somehow, to keep her head above water with the house, the bills, and that Coral Lane...

It made Piper tired to think about. To be honest, she was a little tired anyway. Every now and then she'd be awakened in the middle of the night by a hot flash and kept awake till she breathed herself cool again. Sometimes she awoke in anticipation of one. Who knew? You could wake up at 2 am feeling normal, perfectly calm, perfectly still; but somehow you *knew* that one was coming, bearing down on you like a freight train, like a tidal wave. And funnily? Those were the good ones. At least you saw them coming. You could prepare for them. You could begin to relax your body, breathing in and out, in and out, and when they began, seconds or minutes later, you'd be halfway through already.

Like they said, getting old wasn't for sissies. And here she was, not even forty and already starting to feel it.

Still! With her body providing an early alarm system, a publisher could pop into her office and have half her day's work done before the clouds turned pink or the sun edged over Abbey Mountain. By now Piper had already assigned the article on maple sugaring (a perennial favorite with her readers), modified the calendar of events, and planned the photo-essay of non-migratory birds. And now, with her morning well underway, written and posted her first-ever blog entry. Everything had an upside.

As if to underscore that thought, the sound of the kitchen door banging brought a quick, almost Pavlovian lift to her heart. Piper had wanted, before lunch, to contact the rec department for its schedule, check in with the historical society, and call the head of the school board about the upcoming meeting. But when was anyone's to-do ever done? And now Dan was back.

Piper was wearing her off-the-shoulder raspberry tunic and dark leggings: comfy enough for a day at the computer, cute enough for lunch with Dan. She wouldn't have to change. She lassoed her hair up into the high ponytail that Dan liked best, and ran down the two flights of stairs, pausing at the kitchen doorway to hook in her earrings.

Dan was unpacking groceries as she entered, but he turned to greet her, his blue eyes bright in a face reddened by the cold. "I thought I'd better stock up on provisions, what with the Weather Oracle's latest prophecies," he said, smiling. "Tonight's going arctic, widespread power outages, folks freezing in their beds."

"It never hurts to be well-provisioned." Piper, spontaneously reflecting back Dan's welcoming smile, slid into a seat at the round oak kitchen table. "Weather Oracle or no."

"The scary thing is that after all these years it's come to seem normal, planning our days around the pronouncements of a half-daft end-of-the-world farmer without a trace of a meteorological background." Dan set a loaf of seeded rye in front of Piper and handed her the bread knife. "I mean, who's crazier, him or us?"

Piper felt that inner buoyancy, like rising giggles, that came when, in the sunshine of Dan's infectious good humor, they shared simple, everyday tasks. "This from a guy who thinks the weather comes to us courtesy of the Trilateral Commission?" she teased, slicing the bread.

"I never said that. I just like to keep an open mind. Unlike some." Dan shrugged good-naturedly.

Piper buttered the crusty slices, passing them to Dan as she finished. "Our *former* Weather Oracle was the half-daft one," she reminded him. "Our new one…who knows?"

"I'm going to miss the old guy." Dan layered cheese onto the bread and slid the slices onto the grill. "Let's hope your new one does as good a job. Riverboro plans weddings, parties, and outings a year in advance based on those rhymes of his."

"We'd do it with our funerals, given half a chance."

Dan, who had always understood how happy their banter made her, sent the conversational ball back her way. "Remember the year the town moved the Spring Festival based on the Oracle's forecast?"

"Remember! I can still see the vendors in their booths, staring morosely out at the empty, rain-drenched streets."

"While the original date—"

"—was the most gorgeous weekend that spring," Piper finished. "I thought the local businesses would tar and feather us for that stunt."

"They should have stripped us of our weather predicting rights for all time," Dan said.

"I thought we'd never predict weather in this town again," Piper added, eager to keep the conversational ball in play.

"But Riverboro loves its Oracle." Dan peered into the refrigerator and brought out a jar of mustard. "His predictions are our goldmines."

"If only…"

Piper, her ebullience dampened by the reminder, forced a little laugh, but Dan caught the tension behind it. "Come on, Pipes, you know ad sales spike whenever there's a prediction. The more outrageous, the better."

Piper reached for a casual tone. "That should make today a good one to sell ads."

"Silas is on it. He'll make the most of those couplets of doom." Dan turned back to the stove to flip the sandwiches, pressing them down with the spatula. "So tell me about the new Oracle. Who did you hire?"

"Wouldn't you like to know?" Piper teased.

"Are you setting out to drive me crazy?" Dan waved his spatula comically. "Or is that a side-benefit?" He turned back to the sandwiches. "Please! I'm begging you—a word, a hint—"

"Give me a few days," Piper temporized. "Let's see how it goes."

"As soon as he gets his first paycheck I'll know. Why not tell me now? We may keep him a secret from the town, but not from each other. Never from each other."

"You did let Tommy's identity slip—"

"I didn't let it slip! I told the one person—"

"—with the biggest mouth in town—"

"—who has a financial interest—"

"—she does not—"

"All right, all right. Let's not fight about it. Anyway, your new guy's made a good start," Dan said pacifically. "Although his luck might not last. WMUR is predicting a thaw, soft breezes, balmy weather. And here's your guy promising another weather event. The supermarket's jammed—lines snaking back through the aisles, carts piled high with staples. I got milk for hot chocolate, eggs and bread for French toast. Plus two five-gallon cans of gas for the generator." He shook his head. "All on the word of an Oracle. A big, *secret* Oracle. Still, better safe than sorry. You'll thank me later."

"I thank you now," Piper said. "So, what's doing downtown? Any news?"

Dan flipped the sandwiches one last time and slid them onto a plate. "Jacques Marquand's in town. He's planning one of his flash mobs." He turned to set the plate on the table. "The guy has a genius for staying relevant. From publisher to performing artist to politician. Keeping us guessing."

Piper's stomach clenched. "Are you going?"

"One of us should." Dan poured coffee into a mug, set it in front of Piper, and reached to give her shoulder a reassuring squeeze. "Something wrong?"

Piper opened her mouth to deny it—but what was the point? Dan knew her too well. "It's just, Jacques started a contest," she said. "He's calling it November Lies. The person who tells the biggest whopper wins." She helped herself to half a sandwich. "He announced it on his blog. You must not have checked it today."

"How could I?" Dan pulled out a chair and lowered himself into it. "Getting Donny off to school, stocking up for the weather, providing fodder for your bloggery—who has time to keep track of Marquand?" He pulled the plate of sandwiches toward him. "So now it's November Lies? He must be grooming a new generation of political aspirants, Marquand-style. Where's the problem?"

"Molly." Piper nibbled at the edge of cheese oozing from her sandwich. "She thinks she's going to throw a party, a masquerade—"

Dan looked blank. "A masquerade?"

"For her November Lie. It was Coral's idea—Coral and her costumes!"

"But working with Jacques—you have to see that's a great opportunity. So what if Coral gave Molly the idea? You can't latch on to trifles—"

"Dan. *Listen.* Jacques says he's going to film the entries and put them on his cable show. He says he'll take the winners overseas, have them do flash mobs in Japan, Thailand, all over the world—"

"All the better," Dan said. "Jacques dreams big. No wonder Molly wants in."

But Piper was shaking her head adamantly. "Dan. Think. You know Jacques, we've known him for years. Do you think he'll keep his word on this? Of course he won't. Molly's not going on his show, she's not going with Jacques to Asia—even if she wins. Which she won't, of course. Most of New England follows Jacques' blog. He's going to be flooded with entries."

"And you think Molly shouldn't enter a contest because she might not *win?*" Dan sounded incredulous.

"Not because she won't win. She'll get lost in this." Piper felt rising frustration. Why couldn't Dan understand? "How will she keep up with her schoolwork while she's putting it together? She's a junior, she needs to focus. And the cost! She's thinking open invitation. Who's going to chaperone? Where will she hold it? She can't have it here—it's not safe. Strangers in cosume? This is a home *and* a business! We can't have a bunch of random people in costume strolling through."

Dan nodded, thinking. "What if she held it at the River Place? Have a small cover charge to pay for the food?"

"Then there's Jacques himself," Piper continued, ignoring Dan's suggestion. "The people he attracts run the gamut. Senators to hobos."

"Hobos? There are still hobos?"

"You know what I mean."

"So she'll do it at River Place. Chaperoned."

"And Molly and Japan—I can't even think of those two in one breath. You of all people should understand."

"You can't let old resentments—"

"Easy for you to say!"

Dan and Piper's eyes met; for a beat Dan said nothing. Then he reached for the carton of milk and poured himself a glass. "So she won't go," he said. "It'll be fine. Seeing as she's already been."

Piper looked at Dan in disbelief, but he was piling sandwiches onto his plate, refusing to engage. She opened her mouth to speak, then closed it. What was the point? Pick your battles. "OK," she said. "It's on you. She can have her party. You take responsibility."

She tried to mean it, to let it go, to get back to the space where she and Dan were at their best, where they could be quick and verbal and clever and playful. The Piper and Dan Show, Jacques used to call it. On a good day, it was still there for them.

She gave a comical eyeroll to signal it. "Molly wants me to announce the contest on my blog. Never mind it's one day old and has, what, half a dozen readers? Compare that to *Damn Lies*. Marquand must have a couple hundred *thousand* readers."

Dan accepted with relief the change in tone. "Yours will build. How do you think *Damn Lies* got its start? All it takes is a great voice and some controversial topics—"

"Written in code, if *Damn Lies* is any indication. I could never manage to be that unintelligible. Should I do a bit on his flash mob?"

"Good idea." Dan's smile glimmered. "Will you go down?"

"I might. If I make my afternoon deadlines. Take notes for me just in case, OK?"

"Come on," Dan urged. "You've already put in a day's work. Weren't you piping at the gates of dawn?"

Piper reached for her mug of coffee. "A hot flash woke me up—I figured I might as well get something done."

"Hot flashes! Look at you—still practically a kid."

Piper raised a shoulder. "It happens."

"You need to get to the doctor for a full physical workup," Dan said decisively.

Piper made a dismissive sound. "Doctors! They'll pathologize anything uniquely female."

"I'll schedule an appointment." Dan took an enormous bite of his sandwich, a swig of milk, and continued talking while he chewed and swallowed. "We're having a meeting here today."

Piper felt her fingers tighten around her coffee mug. Carefully and deliberately she relaxed them. "Who," she asked, "is coming?"

"Silas. Advertising pages are in free fall for January. Down for December too, year on year. Ten pages an issue—a fool could sell that in his sleep. Silas is good, but he's cobbling it together with classifieds and personals. We need more display ads to even print February."

Piper nodded. Only Silas. OK. She could manage that. "When?"

"Any minute. Stay. We need your ideas."

"The house…"

"You know that Silas is immune to the disorder here," Dan said. "Or any disorder, for that matter."

Piper nodded, resigned. "Okay," she said. "Ideas it is." She reached for a pen and notepad from a stack on the table, her brain beginning to tick through possibilities. "How about this: we give our advertisers links from the blog? I could mention them in it?"

"Excellent," Dan said, and Piper felt a glow of pleasure. "Great start. What else?"

By the time the door opened and Silas slouched in, all shaved head and tattoos, clomping melting snow from his heavy boots all over the kitchen floor, Piper, Sasha back on her lap, was jotting her third page of notes. Even so, she felt her teeth clench. *Do not say 'yo,'* she thought grimly. *If you say 'yo,' I will scream.*

"Yo," said Silas.

* * *

Damn Lies
By Presidential Candidate
Jacques Marquand

WTF—Why the Facts? Set the record awry—today you start your Lie. Our candidates are doing their damnedest to make political history with their prodigious prevarication. Are we going to let them show us up? Not if I can help it. November Lies demands that you beat the best B.S. those shucksters can shovel. Submit yours here. I'll post anything, regardless of how pathetically inadequate it is.

November 2: Bleak Month

Snow everywhere. Snow up the river. Snow down the river. And people on the bridge barely visible in a nether sky of snow, as if they were up in an air balloon, half-hidden in billowy white clouds.

Actually, that was a paraphrase of Charles Dickens. In truth there are no people on the bridge. But it did snow again, and quite a lot, last night. I can see, looking down from my tower office, that the streets are deserted, or almost so. Sam King is out on the sidewalk scraping with a shovel, and it looks as if he's going to open the market. I feel a real satisfaction about that. King's corner market (www.KingsofRiverboro.com) opens more reliably than the post office, regardless of weather. And the reason? Like a character in a Dickens novel, Sam King lives right over his store; and a true old-fashioned grocery it is.

This, for me, is one of the great joys of small town living. Sam King knows me by name (full disclosure: we dated in high school), and I (or you) can sign a slip for a purchase and pay at the end of the month, no questions asked. *And* he delivers. If I were to call him now, even in this weather, and ask him to drop over a dozen eggs and a loaf of bread, he (or one of his clerks) would be at my door within the half hour and all I would need to do is sign a slip. And that's not only for ex-girlfriends; that's for the whole town.

Dan stocked the fridge yesterday—as did everyone else who reads our Weather Oracle. Who, in addition to the usual forecasts in the magazine and on the website, will make unannounced appearances in my comments section to provide up-to-the-minute doom and gloom.

Which few of you came by yesterday's Hey! It's Thursday demonstration? You may be sorry you missed it when you hear that Riverboro's own Jacques Marquand, New Hampshire's most idiosyncratic activist and most celebrated blogger (having received the coveted Golden Cursor award for his daily blog *Damn Lies*) showed up in person. He apparently decided to kill two birds with one stone (Jacques is familiar with throwing stones from his sixties youth): to support those of our citizens who denounce the planned opening of a chain restaurant in our town, and at the same time score free drinks from the restaurant. Yes, Hey! It's Thursday obligingly brought drinks to the protestors in the parking lot.

If you follow Damn Lies, you already know that Jacques has begun structuring his campaigns—political, environmental, social, and economic—around flash mobs, those pseudo-spontaneous uprisings where all the people in a filmable area simultaneously break into song and dance. There's always a kid on a dad's shoulders, entranced by the spectacle (Jacques has enlisted Donny and Dan from time to time); there's always a street musician or band providing an upbeat oldies song; there are always people who meet one another's eyes, laughing in wonderment. There's always a sponsor.

Jacques loves the flash mob. It appeals to his sense of irony since, originally intended as a joyous expression of the masses, it was so quickly co-opted by the establishment for corporate and political purposes (mostly advertising). The bubble of flash mob fever having burst, Jacques is determined to wrest the narrative from those profit-hungry hands and deliver it back to the people. He intends our flash mobs to reach the same dizzying heights of storytelling, of mythmaking, of plain old lying, that our leaders have achieved.

So says Jacques, and I say: may New Hampshire never lose its role in hosting the nation's first primary. It brings us wonders such as he. Dan calls Jacques' eternal campaign "platform presidency meets performance art." He says we could do a lot worse, and I am sure he is right.

As yesterday's flash mob started, another storm was settling in, and our town's activists found the fires of their indignation dampened by bad weather. Jacques did his best to keep everyone's spirits up. He chained himself to a shopping cart, waving a placard with one hand and shouting slogans. "Live free—or die in the chains of megacorporate greed!" Or: "Break the balls and chains of corporate America!" While he was having fun with the concept of corporate chains, he held, in his unchained hand, his anarchistic free drink from the restaurant, from which he took fortifying sips between shouts. A few people from his retinue were there in support. (Jacques travels the country in a $200,000 General Motors campaign bus, customized by the Pierce Crossing Body Shop (located just south of Riverboro; see our display ad for contact information), and he holds political protests cum flash mobs cum performance art parties in it as often as he can come up with reasons). But in the hard, driving snow huddled a spontaneous mob of (I kid you not) *five people*, shivering miserably and holding tightly to their free drinks.

Between shouting slogans, Marquand narrated, in that New-England-inflected, gravelly voice that a Hollywood actor might trade his trophy wife for, an instructive historical vignette from his protesting days in the 70's, explaining to his little audience how to cover their faces and zigzag out of the way should police armed with tear gas or Tasers show up. He managed to get a few people tearing back and forth across the parking lot, arms over their heads, leaning into their turns like baseball players rounding the bases, while stirring music blared from Hey! It's Thursday's open windows. (I understand the manager had asked Jacques if he and his hearty band needed anything beyond a drink, and Jacques had shamelessly requested the music in the interests of morale).

The protesters ignored the fact that the police chief himself was actually present. I've known Hap LeClaire since pre-school, and I have to say he is one of the nicest guys in the world. In second grade I stole a cupcake from his lunch bag, (my mother would never pack me a cupcake, only apples and pears), and he cried and cried while I, greedy thing that I was, swallowed his cupcake in two bites right in front of him. I like to think it was this gross injustice that set him on his path as a crime fighter. But he didn't rat me out, and, even though I know he remembers, he has never given me a traffic ticket, not once; and whenever someone in town wants to sell a truck, car, or boat he tells them to forget Craig's List and put a classified ad in *Riverboro Rocks*. (Pay for one issue in print or one week online and we will keep the ad running until your item is sold).

But getting back to Marquand: he orated and gesticulated, shopping cart clanging at his side, as he exhorted the group to take the lessons he was offering and use them as tools for a lifetime of protest. Maybe they will do so. Who knows? But early indications aren't promising. After ninety minutes of braving the snow and cold, yesterday's dissidents and police—including both Hap and Jacques—decided to go into Hey! It's Thursday and warm up over a nice cuppa.

We will be seeing many more presidential candidates in our town over the coming months, and my hope is they are all as creative and funny as Marquand. We did get pictures, and will post them soon.

There are, by the way, about half a dozen of you out there, according to my site statistics. I refer to readers of Piper's Pebbles. And no one, other than our Weather Oracle, has commented, and that only because I begged.

My loyal Molly did try to post but I turned her away, ashamed that the first comment came from my daughter. I regret that now. For all I know, every visit to this blog so far has been from a family member. After all, I've asked at least a half a dozen friends and family members to read and comment. You know who you are! Since the conversation in the comment section is considerably less lively than I had anticipated, I cannot afford to refuse any contribution.

It seems a lot of work, writing this daily (for the second day in a row) for just the few of us. On the other hand, if I were writing letters in old-timey correspondence, each letter would only be for one person. So we're a cozy group, the seven of us, and I am sharing my thoughts with you and asking you, in turn, to share with me. We'll be a club, a book group maybe, as I have long wanted to join a book group. I have a suitable stock of quotations all handy in case we need them to stimulate conversation, and if I use them without proper attribution, you may call me on it and I'll give you a point. The one who ends the month with the most points will get a prize, though whether it is to be a mention on my blog or an all-expense-paid trip through Asia will remain, for the moment, unannounced.

But that leads me to an announcement I did want to make, as I promised my daughter that I would: November Lies.

How to explain Jacques Marquand and his Lies? In the 1970's, when Jacques was a young iconoclast launching *To the Barricades*, he said he would rock America with them—and for a brief time, he did. He said his Lies would explode the truths of the war-mongering, the greedy, the humdrum and the mediocre—all the banshees of 1970's America. History does remember Jacques' splash. Back issues of *To the Barricades* sell on Ebay for prices that make those of us who publish free-circulation magazines woozy.

But we, along with many in Riverboro and throughout New Hampshire, continue to support his Lies and read his blogs and vote for him wherever and whenever he runs for office. Yes, he is outrageous and unreliable and shamelessly attention-seeking. He is also creative and funny and as close to a real-life hero as any of us are likely to see nowadays. Who hasn't seen that photo of him from the 1970's, a young man at a Rolling Stones concert at the Boston Garden, saving a nameless young woman's life? That photo—snapped as, surrounded by security and buffeted by the crowd, he carried her to safety after administering CPR—was picked up by media outlets all over the world, and became the iconic image for that era. Even today, if you watch a 1970's retrospective on the History Channel or google the decade, you are likely to see it. I have a mug in my office with that image on it. (Jacques himself gave it to me, as a matter of fact).

So, when Jacques tells us that he wants us all to start new stories—idiosyncratic, conflicting, impossible ones; that he wants to see a new generation of Liars shake off the dull trappings of quotidian thought to fly free into the aetheric realms of What Might Be—well, we are on board. Molly, who grew up on stories of Jacques and his exploits, is joining in, and she's gathering a group to join, too. She is fascinated by the idea that through disguise we discover or reveal our inner selves, and her whopper is going to be a costume party.

Jacques says that he will post pictures of her party on his blog and show them on his cable TV show. Jacques, I hope you are not going to disappoint my daughter! If you do, you will have me to answer to—along with, if I can help it, the entire town of Riverboro. As for that trip to Japan you've been talking about, what can you be thinking? You and I will have to take that conversation offline.

But for the rest of you: Molly wants volunteers. She can't do it all herself. So please rally round. Help throw the party, or tell a whopper of your own. Make your voice heard! And re-invent the world by so doing. No idea too trivial, no idea too wildly outrageous.

And all the November Liars, and Molly and I, and you, dear reader, will make this entire month an exuberant party, a frolic through the fields of truth and illusion. And at month's end we few, we happy few, we band of Liars will sit together in my cozy tower office (you, my dear reader, can have the wing chair), sipping our coffee and watching the sun come up over the mountain and glint on the river; and Riverboroans still abed will think themselves accursed to have missed it.

Piper's List: Top Five Reasons to Support Jacques Marquand

5) His swanky campaign bus is always open to visitors, and it might actually be more comfortable than your (or my) living room.

4) His November Lies challenge keeps us from sinking into the November blahs and gives us a party to look forward to.

3) Who among us hasn't dreamed of participating in a flash mob?

2) He has promised to return for the opening of Hey! It's Thursday—though it isn't for me to say whether that's for the joy of protest or the free drinks.

1) He is taking out a full-page campaign ad in the January issue of *Riverboro Rocks*, and has promised to put *Piper's Pebbles* on the *Damn Lies* blogroll. Thank you, Silas, for closing that sale! And thank you, Jacques, for your support.

Tags: NH local weather, First in the Nation, Jacques Marquand, *Damn Lies*, St. Crispin's Day speech

COMMENTS:

BookLover603: Hi. Love the blog…great start. I'm not a Liar, but I think I caught a whiff of an un-credited quotes on Day One…a hint of Dylan Thomas…maybe a soupcon of Wallace Stevens?

PipersPebbles: Oh, very good! I will rely on you to keep me on my toes. You'll have to be an honorary Liar, like me.

BookLover603: You're honorary too? I thought for sure you were full-fledged…such good social satire. I thought November Lies must be your idea.

PipersPebbles: That's flattering, but Jacques is one of a kind. And much as I envy Jacques his audience, you will hear no Damn Lies from me. As chronicler of this town, I need to stick strictly to the truth to maintain my credibility.

RiverCoral: Jacques is a hoot, alright. He wants us to lie every chance we get. ☺

PipersPebbles: I'm sure it comes naturally for some. For my part, I will lie only when the truth is too unlovely to be told.

MollyHH: Mom, wait till you hear this, I've got big news. HUGE news. Hey! It's Thursday wants to co-sponsor my party. They're going to let us use the space for free, and provide free snacks. Plus people will order food off the menu and drinks from the bar. H.I.T.'s even going to give us free publicity!

PipersPebbles: How on earth did you organize it?

MollyHH: Amazing luck. Yesterday at the protest, Silas and I got to talking with the manager. He said he wants to get the town excited about the opening. The protests are a start but they only go so far.

PipersPebbles: The ironies are building on the ironies.

MollyHH: The manager thinks my party will build awareness for the restaurant. And you know how we cosplay anime characters? Well, he has a kid in middle school who's into that too. And GUESS WHAT? Jacques Marquand thinks it's a great idea and he said he'd come HIMSELF to it. To my party! Could you announce that, Mom?

PipersPebbles: I think you already did, Molly. But to clarify for our readers: anime is when your costume represents both your female side, that's anima, and your male side, that's animus, so you'll notice that some of the costumes are quite androgynous.

Molly HH: Mom, anime is short for animation. You know, like cartoons? It doesn't have anything to do with anima or animus.

PipersPebbles: Then where does the androgyny come in? From the cosplay? For our readers: cosplay means you wear costumes (that's the cos) and have a good time (that's the play). So dress up as your favorite cartoon character and join the fun. Coral Lane, you already have a Princess Zelda costume, so you're all set.

MollyHH: That isn't the exact definition of cosplay, either, but I guess it will do. And Zelda would be a good idea for Coral for sure. She's like Coral's alter ego, isn't that right, Coral? I was thinking of going vintage, but Coral suggested dressing up as someone from Final Fantasy.

PipersPebbles: Though Jacques might say that life itself is the final fantasy. Have you set a date?

MollyHH: Yes, it's official: after school on the 29thth. It's a Tuesday, and they officially open on Thursday, December 1st, so it gives them a day to clean up. My party is going to be the Grand Opening event—Mom, can you believe it? Let's announce it lots more times—every day! Mom, mention it on your blog every day. Or I will here in the comments. I hope lots of people come. What if nobody comes?

DanTheRiverMan: Molly your party sounds fantastic, and of course people will come. I'll be there. Piper, you'll be there?

PipersPebbles: Wouldn't miss it.

DanTheRiverMan: In the meantime, caffeine calls. King's Market is open, and Sam is brewing a fresh pot of coffee—organic, fair trade, medium roast. He's inviting the Happy Few, the band of Liars, down for coffee and pastries.

PipersPebbles: I need to edit the Christmas calendar as we're going to press with the December issue and there are some changes that came in. Bring some up for me, OK? And cat food for Sasha, too, please.

SamKing: The band of Liars can stop by King's for their breaks. We'll set them up with hot drinks suitable for any age group.

ZombiePatrol: This Marquand guy. The one who wants to be president. Will he set up a Department of Zombies in case he gets elected?

MollyHH: So the government can protect us from zombies?

ZombiePatrol: Or maybe the government can protect the zombies from us. Make sure they aren't persecuted.

MollyHH: Oh my God a political discussion on my mom's blog, I can't wait to tell Jacques. You guys have to join the Lies.

ZombiePatrol: I'll be there.

TheGeekster: Me too.

WeatherOracle: Lay in supplies, all Riverboro;
                  What lies in wait is dark and sorrow.
                  Joy from the fleeting moment borrow;
                  What's here today is gone tomorrow.

MollyHH: Are the zombies lying in wait?

WeatherOracle: Ask nothing frivolous or rhetorical.
                  "Are zombies weather?" asks the Oracle.

DanTheRiverMan: Right. Let's all of us stick to our own areas of expertise. We have a Weather Oracle, not a Zombie Oracle.

MollyHH: Well today we have a snow day from school, and that doesn't make me sorry at all. Hey Dad, how about you, me, and Donny make a snowman? He can stand guard against the zombies.

(*Comments approved*)

* * *

A thump overhead: Sasha dropping from the oak tree onto the shingled roof of Piper's office and padding over to the skylight. Looking up, Piper could see her whiskered face peering in. She reached up and unlatched the skylight. Sasha leapt through into her arms, bringing with her a shower of snow. Piper brushed the snow away and settled back into her chair with Sasha tucked in next to her; and there the cat purred, staring at Piper's computer monitor as if weighing the merits of her work.

Piper opened the spreadsheet of outstanding stories and ran through the list, checking statuses. Yesterday she'd assigned the one on maple sugaring to a freelancer. She also needed to check over the reader-submitted photos of the storm. The best had come from Silas; surprisingly (astoundingly) he had real talent with a camera. *Riverboro Rocks* documentation would likely end up in the archives of the historical society. She needed to get this on record before it was gone. And gone it would be, if the National Weather Service was to be believed, by the end of the week. The Weather Oracle's dire predictions aside, Saturday was expected to be sixty degrees.

Last night something had disturbed her sleep. She'd heard—she *knew* she'd heard—a noise from the shed that linked the kitchen to the barn. Empty except for stacks of cordwood, rickety, not well-secured, that old passageway was the most vulnerable part of the house. Piper shivered. Like any town, Riverboro had its derelicts, its lowlifes. Could someone be sneaking into the house by way of that old shed? And if so, what were they looking for? What did they want?

Keep kitchen light on at night, she jotted on her list for the day. *New deadbolts kitchen door?* The best she could do right now. Later she'd bring it up to Dan. He'd have ideas what to do.

Next in her litany of worries was Molly. What mother wouldn't worry about her daughter, verging on womanhood, so often gone from the house? And now this party of hers, this Jacques thing—Molly thought he would come to her party, and of course he wouldn't. Or worse, he would—it was hard to know which outcome was more to be dreaded. When Jacques showed up you couldn't anticipate, couldn't manage what was going to happen. And now, Japan: how could he? Oh, how *could* he? This whole thing was a catastrophe waiting to happen. It would be Piper's Damoclean sword all month long, and she wasn't sure she could deal.

But deal she must, and she'd better start now. Molly was strong. She would survive. Surely it would all shake out. It would be a learning experience. Molly needed to learn, and Piper needed to let her get on with it. Molly's lessons couldn't all come from her mother anymore. It was hard, but it was life. Nowadays Piper sometimes felt as if she experienced her relationship with her daughter more as separation than closeness. When Molly was small, it was as if she and Piper were one person, sharing the same bubble of being. The growth into two separate universes was bound to be hard. Molly had grown closer to her father in her teen years. Dan was a wonderful dad, but Piper missed that closeness, that almost-exclusive closeness a mother and a daughter could share. It was almost like grief, the intensity with which she missed Molly, or what she had once had with Molly.

Still! It was no different from what any parent went through. Piper knew she was lucky, very lucky, to have raised such a kind and loving daughter. And now she had Donny to shower with love. Not the same as a daughter, of course, but he was a great joy, a great consolation.

So what else?

Silas. Another whole worry. Yesterday Silas had stayed all afternoon, sitting at the kitchen table, making calls, booking classified ads. That kind of thing can't be easy, but for all the rejection, there had been moments of triumph. He had begun talking to their advertisers about the online partnership ideas they had brainstormed together over lunch. Local businesses were interested. The feed store wanted a full presentation. All good.

But then school had gotten out and Molly had come in, and Piper had realized that no wonder Silas had stayed so long and worked so hard. Because when Molly came into the kitchen in her tapestry vest and quirky fedora, all dark silky hair and vintage finery, Silas had looked and looked. And Molly? What girl her age wouldn't respond to that kind of attention?

So that was a definite point of anxiety. But there was more, deeper in her mind, a wake-up-in-the-night-and-fret point, and she was just now getting to it. It had to do with Dan. Piper always wanted to please Dan, she tried hard to please Dan; but Dan, it turned out, was not pleased to-day—and there it was, she could tell by the intensification of anxiety as her probing thoughts turned this one up—he wasn't pleased with her, with her blog post yesterday. He wasn't pleased about her comment about Coral Lane in the blog. The one about Coral Lane trick-or-treating in that prin-cess costume.

Why not? Piper thought. *I mean, lighten up.* Why was he making a big deal of it? Only half a dozen people even read that blog. Six people in the whole town of Riverboro, and they were probably—who? Molly, Dan, Coral, and…a few others. Hardly anyone! And what did he expect, anyway? After everything, after all!

Thinking about it was agitating. Piper got up, spilling Sasha into a com-plaining heap on the floor. Coral Lane with her stick-thin legs in her skinny jeans; Coral Lane with her sharp features, wearing all that dark makeup around her eyes! Now *she* was supposed to be nice to *Coral?* God help us all, the clowns were running the circus, the animals taking over the zoo.

And how was Piper supposed to bring people to her blog, to bring money to her magazine, if she wasn't amusing and irreverent and maybe just a tiny bit mean? It was voice, it was tone, it was playful and lighthearted verbal sparring, and what oh what would happen to *Riverboro Rocks* if she didn't shake things up a little? It wasn't to be considered, it wasn't to be borne—and it didn't have to be. They were fine, just fine, she and Dan and *Riverboro Rocks.* They had survived till now, they would continue to survive, they just needed to be smarter, more creative. They would be lean, mean, publishing machines, and somehow the gods of those who buy ink by the barrel would smile on them.

Downstairs the door swung open and Dan bellowed up the stairs (why couldn't he come quietly up and tap at the open door?), "Piper? Molly, Donny and I are going to make a snowman in the front yard. He'll be HQ security guard, OK?"

Donny's voice piped up, "We got a hat! Come see it!"

Piper picked up her coffee mug, put it down, collected her pens and pencils, put them in the lopsided mug on her desk (Molly had made it for her when she was in middle school; it was both totem and icon for Piper), sat in a chair, uncurled her fingers, and delicately took a tissue out of the tissue box to wipe the perspiration from her palms. Molly's voice floated up. "Mom?"

Piper leaned out the door of her office to call as loud as she could down the back stairs to the kitchen two floors away. "Just a jiff, darling. Hot flash. Be right down." She sat down in the wing chair and closed her eyes. Now breathe, she said to herself. In. Out. In. Out. Long breaths. Deep breaths. Soothing, cooling, oxygen-filled breaths.

Breathe.

* * *

Damn Lies
By Presidential Candidate and Political Gadfly
Jacques Marquand

The scorpion stings its head, the snake swallows its tail, and the seat of capitalist oppression becomes the cradle of Riverboro's revolution. First to the bar, then to the barricades! Riverboro's November Lies had its birth in the chain and will spill into the streets in a costumed carnival of animated anarchy, burlesque Bolshevism, capering caprice. And come the revolution, everyone will drink strawberry margaritas at Hey! It's Thursday—and by God, we'll like them!

November 3: A Heartbreaking Blog of Staggering Genius

It goes beyond the cold; it goes beyond the dark; it goes beyond the eerie, muffling silence. This morning brings a sense of isolation, an unsettling knowledge that all is not right in our world.

It brings, in fact, a state of emergency—literally. *The power is off.* No lights, no running water, no heat, in Riverboro, in all of New Hampshire, and throughout Maine, Vermont, Massachusetts, and even Connecticut. A massive, region-wide ice storm descended like a curse from the gods, and our world is cut off from power.

The storm began yesterday afternoon as another snowfall in the series of weather events we've been having, but early in the evening the snow turned to sleet, then to freezing rain. It covered the trees and houses and roads and power lines with glaze ice. Our power went off before we were even abed—how about yours? Were you braced for more precipitation, as our Weather Oracle advised? Or did this outage pull from you your last "bejesus?"

We bundled ourselves off to bed as soon as we decently could, and all night long we could hear the freezing rain rattling on the rooftop. By morning we were hearing the sounds of branches snapping like gunshots, and periodically, like cannons, the sound of trees crashing down. Trees tore through power lines; power lines sprawled over the roads;

and even now, with the occasional snapping and popping of ice-encased branches and trees, it sounds like the Riverboro Militia must have sounded in the final moments of one of their epic battles.

And underneath and surrounding all that, silence. As if in a countryside that has been touched by war, the ordinary noises that we are accustomed to hearing have vanished. The furnace, the refrigerator, the water in the pipes—all have gone silent. The rattle of the sleet and the creaking of the house and the moaning of the wind all combine to emphasize the uncanny silence beneath.

It makes me uneasy; it makes me restless. I am up to the window to peer into the dim outdoors. I am back to my keyboard, checking my backup battery life. I am wrapping myself in blankets and shawls, shivering as the cold creeps stealthily into my house. I type my blog, searching for connection, my fingers growing cold.

Riverboro, are you out there? Are you all right? Are you rejoicing in the adventure or freezing in your beds? It's time for us to rally round, to pull together, to help one another.

How strange that, on the third day of my blogging adventure, a real adventure begins—an adventure of this kind, of this magnitude. It's ironic and poetic: Truth has broken in on our month of Lies with a lot of matter-of-fact about ice storms. The inner dome of Heaven has fallen. It's a dream come true for the diarist or memoirist: something big comes to you without you even leaving your chair. Fire, flood, family dysfunction—things fall apart, the center doesn't hold. Grist for the writerly mill, a windfall for the chronicler of the day to day.

Only—not for me. I started this blog to showcase Riverboro, our sweet town with its animals on Halloween, its pratfalls at the coffee shop, its shopkeepers, innkeepers, and entrepreneurs, its teachers, artists, musicians and monks, and the river—structure, metaphor, or plain old river—running through it all. Also to link through to advertiser sites, I'll admit that to the three people or so who are following me (twelve actually as of this morning, but I think some of them were me, clicking to see if there were comments). You write a blog and you talk about local businesses and people read and advertisers are happy. And people say how clever you are, and how you have saved *Riverboro Rocks* with your creative genius. A real adventure happening was not part of the plan.

At least, it wasn't part of *my* plan. But for our new Weather Oracle, it's an intriguing—an astonishing—beginning, the loss of power following those "dark and sorrow" prognostications. Maybe we can avoid the sorrow (a girl can dream), but while the sun is now beginning to send a bright edge of light over Abbey Mountain, the dark this past night has been pretty complete.

So now our world is covered in ice, and we're going to have to figure out how to manage. And the ice and snow and loss of power are not the whole of it, not for me. Somehow I've already managed to make people angry. The fate of the social commentator!

Tell me: how is it possible, with only a couple of blog posts and half dozen readers, I've already ticked people off? Coral Lane: really, you made a lovely princess, and I'm sure you delighted all the families when you trick-or-treated at their homes. Next year go as a princess, go as the tooth fairy, trick-or-treat in your birthday suit on the streets of Riverboro if you like, you won't hear a word out of me. So. That's out of the way, and we shan't ever mention it again, shall we?

Looking out across Riverboro last night, it was like a big hand had come down and rubbed out the picture—the darkness was so much darker, by contrast to the light that should have been there. Here at the Hadley House we lit candles and played Scrabble at the kitchen table—our tradition for power outages since Molly was little. Then Molly, all 17 years and five-foot-three of her, climbed into the big bed (as we always used to call it when she was a child and did visit us there from time to time) and we shivered each other warm till morning, Sasha draped across our feet like a living, breathing hot water bottle.

Today we hear—via battery-powered radio—that it could be a very long time before the power comes back on. Weeks even. The power company has been taken by surprise—unlike our Weather Oracle, who is quickly adding notches to the old rain stick.

To be fair, with power lines down all over New England, curling like spaghetti on the roads, blocking traffic, and branches strewn like rough carpet on the ground, the cleanup and repair is going to be astronomical. Crews are converging on our disaster-ridden region. School is called off, now and for the foreseeable future.

While electric is down, the phones are not. Between the battery in my computer and 3G for the Internet, I have my connection to the outside world. But does the world have a connection to me? Are you out there, Riverboro? Checking your email and reading my blog though our power outage has darkened your home?

The sun has heaved itself over the mountain now, and outside my window every single thing, whether twig or branch or automobile, is outlined in glittering ice. The rising sun is splintering on the ice, dazzling the eye. Everywhere is crystal and white and sparkling gleaming glints of beautiful, breathtaking destruction.

SO. Stay in. Stay warm. Don't venture outside without a hard hat. Eat your perishables or put them on the porch to stay cold. And be of good cheer, because we're in for a thaw and it will be spring all over again this weekend. At least that is what the ordinary weather people say. We'll have to consult our Oracle to see what *really* is going to happen.

Here's hoping our Oracle can get behind the thaw. Because without our power, we will need all the spring we can get.

Piper's List: Top Five Bad Weather Quotes

5) *In America the ice-storm is an event. And it is not an event which one is careless about. When it comes, the news flies from room to room in the house, there are bangings on the doors, and shoutings, "The ice-storm! the ice-storm!" and even the laziest sleepers throw off the covers and join the rush for the windows.* (Mark Twain) We are known. We are recognized. We have not changed in all the intervening years.

4) *America needs to get over it. We can't control the storms.* (Russel Honore) Although Dan might say that's what They want us to believe. In fact, he might say, maybe They are controlling the storms, and using the storms to control us…

3) *The trouble with weather forecasting is that it's right too often for us to ignore it and wrong too often for us to rely on it.* (Patrick Young) Maybe that's true for WMUR, but our Weather Oracle is off to a most auspicious start, don't you think, Patrick?

2) *New-England weather - it is a matter about which a great deal is said, but very little done.* (Charles Dudley Warner) Talk to Dan, Charles Dudley! More might be being done than you think.

1) *Summer up there is pretty short. It usually falls on Tuesday.* (Mike Morley) I think it fell on a Thursday this year. We decided to open a franchise restaurant to celebrate…

Tags: NH state of emergency, state-wide power failure, survival tips, winter weather quotes, Robert Frost, *Birches*, WB Yeats, *The Second Coming*

COMMENTS:

RiverCoral: Really funny! Thanks for keeping us all cheered up! Love the blog! Great quotes! Great tips! ☺

Private Message from DanTheRiverMan: Piper, enough with the Coral shtick—whatever small bit of humor it might have had is overdone.

Private Message to DanTheRiverMan: Coral thinks it's funny—and who else is reading, really?

Private Message from DanTheRiverMan: Marquand for one, and don't pretend you aren't aware that he posted a link to that trick-or-treating swipe in Damn Lies. He's going to be watching your blog for local tidbits, and I don't want him making a spectacle of Coral.

Private Message to DanTheRiverMan: As she doesn't need his help—she does a perfectly good job making a spectacle of herself.

SamKing: King's Market is selling its perishables at a loss. We'll have to discard anything that isn't sold in the next few hours—so, customers, if you can make it, visit the market this morning. If you're shut in, we'll deliver. And if there's going to be a shelter, we'll donate the groceries.

RiverCoral: Why Sam that is so nice of you! The town is setting up a temporary shelter at the middle school for people forced out of their homes. There'll be generated power and showers, and people can use the school computers to log in to Piper's blog. I'll let them know to come get your donations, Sam. ☺

MollyHH: Kids from school told me the road to Pierce Crossing is closed. Trees are completely shaved down along the sides of the road, almost like someone was logging it. I'm checking in by phone, by the way. Anyone can, if they can charge their phones.

DanTheRiverMan: The pines in the park came down. This storm is re-sculpting the town. Why didn't we move to Florida when we had the chance?

RiverCoral: Dan, you like to talk about Florida but you know nothing could make you leave this town. Anyway, the weather calls for a thaw, so some of this will melt off. ☺

WeatherOracle: If you in thaw expect to frolic
               You'll find this warning melancholic:
               Build your ark. Add food to your hoard.
               Get ready to welcome the stranded aboard.
               Your bobbing boat, your pitching coracle
               Reported here by Weather Oracle.

RiverCoral: Oh God, here we go. ☺

(*Comments approved*)

* * *

The oak branch creaked; Piper glanced up through the skylight. Sasha strolled out on the icy branch, nonchalant, protected, no doubt, by the superpowers of balance and surefootedness that she shared with her kind. Piper stood for a moment to watch in admiration.

"My little panther," she said affectionately. "Is there nothing you can't do?"

Perhaps Sasha heard her through the skylight. She turned her head. As she did, there was a loud cracking noise. Sasha scrambled for footing as the large branch over the roof crashed into the skylight, then a streak of gray and black tabby hurtled by in a shower of breaking glass. Piper glimpsed her shocked face, her legs outstretched, claws extended as she scrabbled to get her footing on her way past the keyboard. For a moment a claw snagged, a key rattled, a long scratch of letters appeared on the monitor. Then with a thud Sasha hit the floor, turned faster than Piper could register, and streaked out the door, leaving wreckage in her wake.

* * *

"Molly, you may not bring that dog into the house," Piper said. Donny's puppy, Ralph, a shaggy black and white border collie mix, yipped and wriggled his way into the kitchen. Sasha crouched on a chair, hissing. "It will pee on the floor, and it scares Sasha. Poor baby—she's still traumatized by her tumble through the skylight."

"Sorry, Mom." Molly opened the door and nudged the puppy into the shed, where it set off to explore the wood pile.

"That dog is going to drive me crazy. Donny, love, did your snowman survive the night?" Piper folded the boy, stiff in his snowsuit, into his booster seat and dropped his hood back. She kissed the top of Donny's head and paused for a moment to breathe in his sweet, small-child smell before turning to shove Sasha, who was eying the shed door mistrustfully, off her chair.

Sasha landed with a thump on the floor and stalked toward the living room, hair bristling, growling in her throat. Piper took Donny's small hands, rubbing them between her own. "You're cold." She leaned forward to breathe on his fingers. "It's cold in here, isn't it?"

"Warmer than outside." Molly shifted her backpack onto the floor to free up a third chair at the table. "Who wants French toast?"

"Me!" said Donny; and then, to Piper, "Snowy's hat froze on his head. Daddy says he's one cold dude."

"We all are today," Piper said. "Cold, that is. Not necessarily dudes." Though the kitchen still held some residual heat, it couldn't be expected to last. Cold air was seeping through the glass of the windows and from around the door.

"You can be a dude, Donny. We'll be dudettes." Molly took eggs and milk out of the dark refrigerator and began cracking eggs into a bowl. "Donny, I have an idea for a costume for you to wear to my party. You know Link from that game we play?"

"Yes!" Donny bounced in his chair.

"Donny's too young to go to that party," Piper objected.

"Mom, he's got to come. Dressing in costume is his favorite thing."

Molly poured water from the jugs by the sink into an assortment of pots on the stove, then lit a match and held it to the gas range.

"He could wear his cowboy outfit," Piper said thoughtfully.

"He wears that all the time." Molly set a cast iron pan on the gas burner and dropped a chunk of butter into it. "He needs something new. Don't you, Donny? Something special for my party?"

"Something special," Donny echoed. "Does Link have a cowboy outfit?"

"He's got something better." Molly began dipping bread slices into the egg mixture and arranging the slices in the sizzling pan. "A green tunic. You'll love it." She paused, listening to the sounds of clanging and cursing coming from the barn. Then she turned to put a stack of French toast in front of Piper. "Dad's setting up the generator."

Piper poured maple syrup over her French toast, then reached over to cut Donny's into bite-sized pieces. "No, love," she said, fending off Donny, who was reaching for the syrup. "We want to keep the sticky off the snow suit. I have a feeling you're going to be wearing it for a while."

"It's warming up." Molly was pouring hot drinks from an assortment of pots on the gas range—warm milk for Donny, hot coffee for Piper, and hot cocoa for herself. "Good thing, too. Riverboro looks like a ghost town. Completely deserted. Even the stoplights are out." She poured warmed milk into a saucer and set it on the floor. As if by magic, Sasha reappeared, apparently mollified; she lapped the milk, her tongue flicking in and out rapidly. Molly turned off the burners and pulled a chair up to the table. "Mom, you've never seen anything like this. Let's take a walk down into town and see it together. You don't want to miss this. It's once in a lifetime."

"I've been keeping tabs from my office." Piper was using her napkin to wipe Donny's fingers. "It's a great place to watch the world go by. Still, an outing sounds fun."

Molly smiled. "Remember how people used to think you were my big sister, back in middle school when you walked me to the bus stop? Now that I'm bigger, we look so much alike I bet people think we're practically twins."

Piper laughed. "Really Molly," she said lightly, "you are shameless. Twin sisters. As if."

"Come on," Molly coaxed. "What do you say we take the Molly and Mom show on the road today?"

"It's tempting." Piper said. "Maybe after—"

The roar of the generator cut off whatever Piper was going to say. Sasha looked up from her saucer and froze, milk lining her mouth. The lights flickered on in the kitchen. The refrigerator hummed. Dan came banging in through the shed door, which swung shut on a disappointed Ralph.

"I had to rassle that beast to the ground." he announced, scooping up a delighted Donny and swinging him high into the air. "The generator, that is. Made it cry uncle."

"Dan," Piper said, over Donny's giggles, "can you get someone to replace my skylight? I can't work with that hunk of cardboard taped to my ceiling. Also, I think Sasha totaled my keyboard. Working from a touchscreen's going to slow me down."

"Got it covered," Dan promised. "Meanwhile, we've got one hour to run the generator and that's it till the end of the day."

He handed the boy off to Molly and picked up a waiting cup of coffee. "Delicious. Molly, love, get Donny to the bathroom while the toilets are flushing, will you? Piper, Coral is stopping by. She needs to talk to you."

"*Coral?*" Piper started to stand up, turning to Molly, looking for support. But Molly was ducking out, Donny on her hip, murmuring, "Come on, baby bro, time for potty and bath."

"Coral?" Piper repeated. "But…I apologized. She thought it was funny. It was funny! Why are we making a federal case of it?"

"It isn't that, Piper," Dan said, going to the stove for a refill on his coffee.

"She's on again about the magazine, isn't she?" Piper said rapidly. "She's always pestering to help. She thinks she's so brilliant that she can do something none of the rest of us can. Doesn't she have enough to do at the River Place?"

"No, no, no." Dan was shaking his head as he stood at the counter putting sugar into his coffee. When had he started acting so elaborately casual? Piper felt behind her for the chair and sank into it, breathing. "What is it, then," she heard herself say.

Dan sat down across from her and leaned toward her, finally meeting her eyes. "The emergency shelter at the middle school is filling up," he said. "The River Place is looking for spillover housing."

"It's getting warm! People won't need heat. They can stay in their homes—they'll want to be in their own homes—"

"Yes, it's warming up. That's part of the problem. With all the melt-off, the river is rising." Dan reached across the table and covered Piper's small, cold hand with his large, warm one. "We're evacuating the houses closest to the river. We have to move people to higher ground. We have to find them places to stay. And we all have to help."

* * *

Damn Lies
By Presidential Candidate and Sustainability Missionary Jacques Marquand

Citizens, awake! Today's power outage is a shot fired across the bows of the world by the parasitic power mongers responsible for this multi-state mega-corporate mockery. This oligarchical outrage is orchestrated so they can tighten the grip of their technological tentacles. Shall we bow our heads till these grasping gods say, "let there be light?" Never! To the barricades! Free yourself from the IV drip of disastrous dependency. Graduate from the grid. This affliction is our opportunity. Seize it!

November 4: Too Much River, Not Enough Burrow

Winter's rains and ruins are just beginning, and already the light is losing, the night is winning. The season might be bringing the snows and sins of poetry or the gods and goddesses of mythology, but you couldn't prove it by me. What I am getting are…monks.

Yes, dear readers, you heard me: monks. Not one monk, or two. Multiple monks.

What do you call a group of monks? A monastery of monks? A mountaintop of monks? A miasma of monks? Given the succession of events—snow, ice, darkness and flood—a plague of monks might be the word.

How to begin? One of Dan's favorite phrases has always been, "Lord willing and the creek don't rise." As in: we'll do a massive spring cleaning—Lord willing and the creek don't rise. Or: we'll get that room ready for Christmas—Lord willing and the creek don't rise. Well the Lord might have been willing and the creek didn't rise, not *then*, but we never did that makeover, that repainting, or any of those other projects, and now I am paying the price. The creek is rising and displacing the lowliers, including our town's Zen monks, whose ashram is right on the water. The monks are coming here.

Yes, our helpful, social-work-y type friends from the River Place (www. RiverboroCommunityPlace.com; see also the new display ad on the *Riverboro Rocks* home page—thank you, River Place, for your support) have identified the Hadley House as roomy enough to accommodate and also east-facing —which for some reason seems to be an important consideration for this group. Since the disappointing cancellation of a long-planned trip to Japan, monks have not exactly been my cup of tea, and unexpected houseguests are always a challenge. Still, we all must do what we can. So thank you, good neighbors from the River Place, for looking out for our town. I will bow with good grace to my fate.

This bombshell was dropped on me yesterday, and I should have spent the afternoon cleaning and airing and opening bedrooms and making beds. Instead, Molly and I wasted the entire afternoon, blasting out 1950's music from her freshly-charged iPod and dancing about the kitchen till we collapsed in chairs laughing till we hurt. I was almost able to forget the broken skylight and keyboard, the peeling walls, the stained bathroom fixtures, the no heat—and the impending descent of those monks. Almost.

Meanwhile, Riverboro is a ghost town: *no one* on the streets. Stoplights out, streets unplowed, gas stations shuttered and dark. Beauty, poetry, devastation. And over the mountain at the Home Depot, no generators to be had for love or money.

We got fifteen unique "hits" on yesterday's blog post—quite the groundswell for us. Our company has doubled in size! Please be sure to click the link to the River Place (above) as it will make them happy, and God knows we don't want them unhappy. Today they are happy with me and I'm getting monks! What will they do if they aren't?

Now I'm off to see what some open windows and clean sheets might do in the spare bedrooms. Ironic, isn't it, that the rising of the creek seems to be *causing* the cleaning frenzy that we always imagined it would prevent?

I hope those monks aren't allergic to cats.

Piper's List: Top Five Flood Quotes

5) *The flood waters will recede, the sun will shine, and I will always be here to take care of you.* (Charlie Brown to Snoopy) We might not all have a Charlie Brown to take care of us, but we do know the river will go back down again. The sooner the better for the refugees. And their hosts.

4) *What's the proper salutation between people as they pass each other in this flood?* (Prince Gautama Siddharta, the founder of Buddhism) This ancient question is remarkably relevant to me today. I expect to pass many people right here in my own house due to this flood, some of them no doubt Buddhists (or something of the sort). It would be helpful to have the proper greeting.

3) *We must build dikes of courage to hold back the flood of fear.* (Martin Luther King, Jr.) Flood as calamity to be faced.

2) *There is a tide in the affairs of men, which, taken at the flood, leads on to fortune. We must take the current when it serves, or lose our ventures.* (Shakespeare) Flood as opportunity to be seized.

1) *There is a tide in the affairs of women, which, taken at the flood, leads God knows where.* (Lord Byron) And flood, for some of us, as a surprise hidden in a box behind a game show curtain.

Tags: Riverboro Ashram, Riverboro flood, flood quotes, cat allergies

COMMENTS:

RiverCoral: Piper, you are such a hoot! And a great sport, too! Thanks for opening your house! You get the Good Neighbor award! ☺

HarvardProf: Historically, the phrase "Lord willin' and the Creek don't rise" was a reference to the Creek Indian tribe. But in modern usage most people do think of a river or brook.

RiverCoral: That is much less offensive, isn't it? ☺

BookLover: I'm sure I spotted a Swinburne. Do I get a point?

PipersPebbles: You do indeed, and so far you're the only one who has any.

MollyHH: I'll give a point to anyone who joins my November Lies group. Post a comment or PM me to let me know. Mom, you don't mind if we have our sessions at Hadley House, do you, since there's lots of room and a generator?

ConArtist: You mean to plan the party?

MollyHH: That's right, plus other projects too. Jacques says he's looking for a fever of creativity.

PipersPebbles: Let's hope that fever keeps us warm till the power comes back on.

(*Comments approved*)

RiverCoral: I have an idea! Why don't you post an invitation for volunteers to come over today and do a massive cleaning to get ready for your guests? Say, 10 am? ☺

(*Comment declined*)

* * *

"I feel," Piper said, "that it is, after all, my house; and that all sorts of people think they know what I 'should' be doing with it and how I 'should' be managing it, and I resist that kind of pressure from well-meaning neighbors."

If you could call Coral Lane well-meaning, Piper added mentally. She felt a virtuous glow that she hadn't said it aloud—though, knowing Jake, he probably knew what she was thinking. She flashed a sly smile at him. He raised an eyebrow in return.

She measured the loose tea into the pot—lovely organic tea straight from Darjeeling, it was—and poured just-finished-boiling water over it. Jake liked tea better than coffee, and she wanted to make him comfy, to make him feel welcome. She and Jake had several years to make up for, years she hadn't seen him at all. A rift had come between them, one she didn't like to think about; but now he was back in her life. That was the important thing. He was back in her house, in her kitchen, and despite the years of estrangement, it felt easy and natural having him here. Or at least, as natural as it could be to entertain a guest in a house where the air was so cold you could see your breath, where you had to make the tea while wearing a knitted hat and gloves. Jake was still in his outdoor coat, and so was she. You couldn't take them off at all nowadays, could you? But he looked right at home, leaning back on the counter, watching her move about the kitchen. It made her feel housewifely and domestic, despite the outdoor clothing.

"Should we talk here or in the living room?" Jake asked.

"It's better here. There all I can think about is all that's left to do."

"What's left to do?"

She handed him his cup of tea, steaming into the cold kitchen air, then poured out coffee for herself and a saucer of milk for Sasha. "Mountains of work. Oceans of work. Vast untouched reaches of interstellar space of work."

She shifted a stack of *Riverboro Rocks* magazines from a chair to the table. "Here you go, sit here."

Jake accepted the seat. "Do you plan to tackle it alone?"

Piper sat too, lacing her cold fingers around her warm cup. She shivered. "Dan set up this monk-o-ree. I think he's going to have to figure out how to make it happen."

Jake nodded. "I was interested in that comment on your blog, about the trip to Japan. You must feel as if Dan let you down about that."

"Oh!" said Piper. "That was a long time ago. This whole ordeal with the monks—it's a reminder—and now your dad's contest—sometimes it all comes down at once, doesn't it?"

"You and Dan spend a lot of time together. More than most married couples do," said Jake. "Disappointments, reminders of disappointments, must bubble up from time to time."

Piper stiffened, then relaxed. Even after these years apart, Piper felt, she could accept this kind of personal question from Jake. Piper had always been comfortable with Jake. Being around him was natural and effortless. Dan was the star around which her entire adult life had orbited, but when you were with Jake, she now remembered, it wasn't so much about him all the time. It was more about you.

Jake had been born right here in Riverboro, a few years ahead of Piper; he had grown up here, too. He'd stayed in New Hampshire for his education, first at Exeter, then at Dartmouth. It amused Piper to think that Jacques Marquand, counter-cultural relic and self-professed iconoclast, would raise a son with such an iconic education. In reality, Jacques had not had much to do with it—or, indeed, with any aspect of Jake's upbringing. Jake was a mama's boy, through and through, from his last name to his way of combing his hair, as different from his itinerant father as it seemed possible to be. What a lovely man he was! Slim and straight and country-elegant, with his understated ease of manner, his silver hair, his diffident good manners. Piper thought about Dan, always talking, riffing on this or that: philosophy, history, conspiracy theories, aliens. Half the time she didn't even know what his topic was; she let it wash over her. Dan knew her better than anyone in the world. But how would life have been different, Piper wondered, if she'd married someone like Jake instead? Jake asked questions. Jake listened. With Jake, there always seemed to be more *air* in the room.

And now Jake was wondering how things were working out with Dan.

"You think Dan and I need space from each other," Piper interpreted.

"I didn't say that," Jake replied mildly. "Actually, I was interested in knowing what *you* felt."

Piper leaned forward. "Dan needs to be more present," she said. "I know he has responsibilities with Coral and his precious River Place, but he's got responsibilities here, too—business responsibilities, family responsibilities."

"He mentioned business worries," Jake said. "He's afraid they'll undermine your peace of mind."

"Who isn't worried about business?" Piper tried for a light tone, though the thought of business worries felt like a dark cloud drifting in front of the sun.

"What else?" Jake asked.

"For one thing," Piper said, "I'm concerned about Molly. Jacques is going to let Molly down, isn't he?"

"It wouldn't be out of character," Jake replied. "Not intentionally, of course, but I'd hate to see the stakes get too high."

"I think they already are, between her party, and Jacques' TV show, and Japan. Blast Japan! I wish people would stop talking about the wretched place."

Jake smiled at the attempt at levity. "She's putting a lot of eggs in the Jacques basket."

"And Dan and I will be left to pick up the broken shells." Piper sighed. "It's always something, isn't it? Some drama. November Lies might end up being the least of our worries."

Jake waited for a moment, giving her space to finish her thought. When the moment stretched, he asked, "What alternative drama do you see? Something to do with Molly's father?"

"No, not Molly's father. Molly and her father are *fine*. I'm thinking about Silas."

"Because…?" Jake prompted.

"Because Silas is obviously noticing how gorgeous Molly is! And there would be nothing, nothing appropriate about a relationship there. Silas is four years older than she is. He hasn't finished college. He's covered in tattoos. And Molly is going places, and she doesn't need…plus, there is a noise that's been happening at night. Right out there—right out in the shed.

"A noise?" Jake asked gently, accepting the change in subject unquestioningly. His tea was cooling on the table but he didn't pick it up.

"A kind of stealthy creeping and scraping sound. As if someone is moving around."

"Have you mentioned it to Dan?" Jake asked.

Piper nodded. "He checked the shed. He says it's nothing. He thinks my fears are groundless. That is what he says: my fears are groundless. And that is how he is beginning to think of me: as a person with groundless fears."

"And you?"

"First, I didn't say I fear the noise," Piper said. "Let's not call it a fear; let's call it a concern. And whatever I might think of it, the noise is real. I would think, for the sake of his family, it's something Dan would want to look into."

"What do you think it is?" Jake asked.

"Oh! Who knows?" said Piper. "It could be anything. Kids—a raccoon—anything. Anyway, what about you? What do you think of this weather?"

Jake smiled a reply. "It's OK to talk about you for awhile, you know," he said. "We don't have to take turns. Let's have this visit be your turn. All about you."

"You might regret that offer, once I really get going."

"I'll take that chance."

Piper laughed happily. "You are too good to me, Jake. What have I done to deserve you?"

"You deserve more than you think," Jake said.

November 5: Good People, Head for Higher Ground

The snow is melting and for most of the day, when the sun is out, you can hear the drip-drip-drip from the eaves and see rivulets running down the street, joining other rivulets and pouring down, down, down. The river is rising. It's almost up to the footbridge and lapping close to the road at that dip by the library. At the Riverboro Ashram, at the Cutty Sark Hotel, and in the homes that line the river, people are moving their possessions from the lower floors upstairs and getting ready to evacuate.

I had hoped to spend the morning cleaning and preparing for our "guests," but the printer called with a question about the December issue. They are working through the weekend there, shifting files electronically from here in New Hampshire to a sister facility in Pennsylvania. How can I refuse to do as much? It turned out that some pages needed color correction, which I was able to fix right from my office. Thanks to technology and an hour of generator time, I never had to walk out my door.

You will all thank me for that when the December issue is delivered on time. Look for favorite holiday recipes from our readers—click through to www.facebook.com/RiverboroRocks for Sam King's own spiced cider recipe; so delicious. While you are there you can sign up for our newsletter to receive a recipe each week. They are all tested in our own kitchen, and I can vouch for all of them. (Don't forget to "like" the page while you are there.)

February will be our storm and flood issue. Keep diaries, take pictures, Riverboro! Hopefully by then we'll be back to normal and able to enjoy these weather events as memories, shared anecdotes, and family stories. And for March, how about stories from Riverboro families? I have lots from the Hammond and Hadley families, and I'm hoping for good ones from you, my readers, and your families as well.

Here's one to get you started: the Hammond family used to own the old coaching inn between Riverboro and Pierce Crossing. Dan's uncle loves to tell how the Hammond boys—rascals even back then—used to ply their guests with drink and then win money from them in cards. Some-time in the 1800's, newcomers called Hamon came to town. Now, you'll notice that, while the name is very different in spelling, *it is pronounced the exact same way*; and as those upstarts insinuated themselves into the life of this town, they seemed to imply by their very presence that they were part of the founding Hammond family.

One dark night, a Hamon came into the inn and joined the game of cards. But this Hamon did the unthinkable, the unforgiveable: he *out-cheated the Hammonds*. By three in the morning Ethan Hamon had won the inn and most of the Hammond fortune. Oh, was there ever an uproar. Now, the Hadleys and the Hammonds were on the outs back then, as they have frequently been over the years, but these newcomers with the motley name could not be allowed to upset the natural order of things. So the Hadley fellows and the Hammond fellows took out their weapons (how we love our guns here in New Hampshire) and accused Ethan Hamon of cheating—which, naturally, he was. Never mind that Isaiah Ham-mond had been cheating as well. A few chairs were broken, a few teeth knocked out, a few shots fired, and *voila*! The inn and the fortune were back in the hands of the Hammonds, both somewhat the worse for the wear.

No Hamon was ever allowed in the inn again, and in subsequent years, any out-of-town Hammond who showed up was required to prove that he spelled his name with the requisite double "m" and final "d".

There are many other anecdotes I could tell about the Hadleys and the Hammonds, and when, all those years ago, Dan caught my eye at Sam King's college graduation picnic, both families couldn't have been more pleased. Dan had grown up in Philadelphia but his name passed the spell check, and he was in town visiting his Great Aunt Becki and his assorted cousins. And, true story, the young man who brought him to that fateful picnic was Jacques Marquand's son, our own Dr. Jake Rosen. Jake was Dan's roommate at Dartmouth, and Dan and I have stayed close to him over the years. He is, in fact, Donny's godfather, and takes a godfatherly interest in our Molly as well.

Jake came by yesterday and we sat in the kitchen sipping hot drinks and talking our hearts out. He didn't leave until quite late. Later I paid the price for that treat as I tossed and turned all night—I was up by three awaiting the sunrise. I am still waiting! I am going to have to switch to decaf past noon, and I don't think I can wait till the New Year to do it.

Piper's Index of Hadley and Hammond Hauntings and Happenings

1739: William Hadley and James Hammond first appear on the scene, casting about for a town to establish. They find their spot in the curl of the river and began staking out the lots, claiming all but three of them as their own. Their first snag, it seems, comes when they try to get their friends to buy plots for settlement. Their friends decline.

1745: William and James return to check out the site of their town-to-be. They camp in a rock-strewn clearing. Or so says the plaque at Riverbend Park. Auntie Polly says that their actual bivouac was the place where the Hadley House now stands. The misdirection (my auntie says) is due to the family's desire for privacy. So let's review. We have an event no one ever heard of. An event to which no one wishes to draw attention. And a plaque—put in the wrong place. Whether or not they are laughing at us from the afterlife, William and James have made their mark by confusing us all.

1753: The Hadley House is built, complete with an attic for the various ghosts later to move in (they've shifted, now, to accommodate my office) and a barn to hold all the junk that will accumulate over the years—it doubles as a garage today. In it is an ancient carriage seat, said to have transported some of the original Hadleys to this town (now it is the home of a family of mice); an old school desk carved with many layers of initials of students and lovers over the years (in more recent years it has become a ritual for young lovers in the family to make a pilgrimage to the barn to find the desk and add their initials: DH and PH can be found on it somewhere); and many half-forgotten relics of the Hadley clan.

1775: Battle of Bunker Hill. Extraordinary because, according to town history, fully one fourth of the town's inhabitants march to Massachusetts to fight (this one's on a plaque at the historical society). This includes every man and boy in the Hadley and Hammond families. We say so, ergo it must be true!

1840: Isaiah Hammond and Ethan Hamon, both courting the fair and fickle Abby Ann Adams, get into a dispute at the coaching inn (this was shortly before the cheating-at-cards debacle), and Ethan whacks Isaiah with a shovel. No lasting damage is done except, perhaps, to their standing in Abby's eyes. Abby ends up marrying the Reverend Silas Manford, and I believe (I would have to check my genealogy here) the two of them are ancestors of Riverboro's branch of the Fontineau family.

Tags: Holiday recipes, spiced cider, the Hammonds of Riverboro, the Hadleys of Riverboro, Dr. Jacob Rosen

COMMENTS:

Guest: How well I remember that picnic where you and Dan first met. You and Sam King had been inseparable since you were small children—we all thought you were surely going to marry—but from the moment you and Dan met, you had eyes only for each other. We used to joke that he swept you away with his smooth-talking, big-city ways. Felicity Fontineau King can, by the way, trace her lineage on her mother's side back to that shovel incident, as you indicate in your somewhat tongue-in-cheek recounting.

PipersPebbles: Is that you, Auntie Polly? How are you holding out in this power outage?

Guest: That's right, Piper, it is I. My condo is FREEZING cold and as you know I have no live-in family to keep me warm, but I will survive. Here at the library we have neither power nor generator but I am proud to say that we are still open. We have an almost-party atmosphere as people come together and exchange stories (in low voices). I would love to see both you and Molly here. I'm bringing in baskets of those fingerless gloves, so if Molly and her fellow Liars (as you call them) want to gather here to work, we are happy to receive them.

PipersPebbles: We run our generator for a couple hours a day, Auntie Polly, so if you need to get warm come on up. We're getting monks, and we can certainly have you—blood being thicker than Buddhists.

Guest: Praise the Lord for that, but I will be all right.

HarvardProf: Hadleys and Hammonds were in the Civil War, and Hamons too. In New Hampshire's Company C, a Hamon fellow had friends on the Confederate side. Not unheard of, even this far north—brother against brother, remember—but, as an interesting bit of local history or legend, he saved his regiment (and betrayed his friend) with inside information about troop movements. In later years he insisted that he obtained his insights clairvoyantly.

Guest: Isn't that just like a Hamon, claiming second sight. They seized on that and turned it into a cottage business. We have the letters at the library—town women would go to them to find out if they were able to conceive, or when to have their weddings, or to talk to relatives that had passed on. Those Hamons tried to meddle in everything, they did.

HarvardProf: They were lucky they were never accused of witchcraft, as they might have been if they'd stayed in Massachusetts.

PipersPebbles: At least if the Hammonds had anything to say about it!

Guest: But the Hammonds never forgave those Hamons for trying to usurp their name, and for cheating at the coaching inn, and of course for that shovel incident. Hamons might fool some newcomers to town, but any family that's been here right along can tell the difference between a Hammond and a Hamon.

PipersPebbles: Auntie P, we're talking family stories from hundreds of years ago.

Guest: Josh Hadley came back from the war as respected as when he left for it—and as generous. You don't find any Hamon scholarships in town—not even any night classes on mental clairvoyance or whatever they claim to have. But our library's Josh Hadley scholarship helps a local boy or girl go to college every single year. Piper, you or Molly should give that presentation this year—it's coming up in just a couple of weeks, and you know a family member always presents.

PipersPebbles: Lacking the Hamon gift of second sight, I can't tell if I'll be able to get away from the office that day, but I'm sure Molly would love to do it. I'll at least join you for a cup of coffee after.

DrJake: Since you plan to cut down on caffeine, you might try switching to tea in the afternoons.

RiverCoral: Great idea! At the Ashram they love tea! Try herbal—caffeine-free! ☺

DanTheRiverMan: I'll pick some up at King's this morning.

(*Comments approved*)

* * *

People seemed to be everywhere—all over the house. Calling to each other, banging doors, thundering up and down stairs. Sasha fled beneath the wing chair, peering out with round, watchful eyes—hyper-vigilant since the incident with the skylight, she jumped and skittered at every sound. Piper thought she knew how Sasha felt. The best thing to do was to keep your office door closed and your head down. Focus on other things. She had, God knew, plenty to focus on: the February storm issue to finish lining up, the January issue to finish editing, and the December issue, on press now. Plus all those comments to moderate on the Facebook page and on her blog. And last night, another hot flash.

If this power outage went on much longer, Piper thought, she might start *welcoming* these hot flashes. Right now she could see her breath. She had to tuck her hands into her armpits to warm them up. Despite the thaw, and the generator, the ambient temperature was *cold*. How could people be so active with the temperature so low? Everyone should burrow into a corner and hibernate.

Every time a door slammed, Piper imagined dirt, dust, and dead bugs drifting down from wherever they had been shaken loose, silt settling. But up here in her office, Dan had put the pane back in the skylight and the shards of broken glass had been vacuumed away. Once again she had a quiet space, a door that closed, projects that needed to be accomplished. Those were the important things. Keep an eye on what mattered.

Shivering over her tablet screen, Piper tapped to the *Riverboro Rocks* page on Facebook and posted an invitation: "Tomorrow from 1:00 to 3:00 we're having a party here on Facebook. Come and post weather and family stories, and the best story will win a prize—a free breakfast for two at the Riverboro Sugar Shack."

Not bad, she thought, *for a spur-of-the-moment idea. Now we need to see if the Sugar Shack will pay for it.* She reached for her phone to dial Silas's mobile. She heard the ring, an unpleasant squawking noise—Silas's idea of a joke—go off somewhere downstairs. It cut off, then: "Yo."

"Silas, I have an idea. Can you call the Sugar Shack and see if they will give away breakfast for two as a prize for a *Riverboro Rocks* historical vignette contest? We'll mention them on Facebook and give them a link."

"Sure thing. I can come upstairs and call."

"No. I'm sure you can find a quiet place somewhere. What's going on?"

"Coral's organizing. They're…let's see…dusting, sweeping, mopping floors. Washing walls. You sure you don't need help? I'll put in that link."

"No. I'll post the link myself. Call me as soon as you get an answer. I'm thinking if Sugar Shack doesn't grab it, we'll go to King's Market with it. In fact, I'm thinking you should call Sam anyway. Let's get all the breakfast places involved. Call me back with who's in and who's out."

"Call you." Silas' voice was flat with disbelief. "From downstairs. In your house."

"Silas. You heard. Now go." Piper hung up and turned back to her screen.

Sometime later, there was a tap on her door. With some reluctance, she opened it and was unsurprised by the unwelcome sight of Silas, a knit cap pulled over his shaved head, a tattered sweatshirt zipped to his chin. He slouched past her without waiting for an invitation and dropped into the wing chair.

Resigned, Piper shut the door and went to sit in her desk chair. "What?"

"Sugar Shack's in. Marty's Café is in. King's is in—special batch, morning coffee."

Not bad. Silas, say what you would, was not a total loss. "What else?"

"Your monks. Coral says you need to come down and meet them."

"Coral says so, does she? Since when is she hostess in my house?" Piper reined in her temper; with these thin walls, if she raised her voice she would be heard downstairs. "You go back down and tell Coral Lane that I've got an important deadline—actually, *three* important deadlines—to meet, and I'll be down *after* I've put out all the fires up here."

"'Kay." Silas stood.

"Wait," Piper said. Silas sat down. "Who...who is here?"

"Three men. Shaved heads. Wearing long kind of white robe-y things. Three women. Ditto shaved heads. Ditto white robes."

"*Six people?* Where on earth will we put them?"

"The three dudes go down at the end on the second floor, the room with the sloped floor? And the women get the big room with the double bed. They say they can all sleep together. Then they say they sleep on the floor anyways. Whatever."

"They're going to be crowded."

"Right."

"That little room by the bathroom..."

"Crammed with junk. Molly says they can use her room."

Piper shook her head. "Molly is too good. There is no way that we're going to inconvenience her in that way. No one is to put anything or anyone in her room."

"She says—"

Piper interrupted sharply. "Silas, you tell Dan and that Coral Lane that if Molly's room is going to be part of the deal, they can take their monks elsewhere. They should know better. They should know I would not tolerate that. End of story."

"'Kay." Silas gave a brief nod.

"And what are they going to *eat?*"

"They brought lentils and rice and stuff. Bags of bananas. Huge pile of chard. A juicer. Plain yogurt in big tubs. Dan said they had to put it all away out of sight. They want to know what times they should cook and eat."

"How can I tell them that? I'm in and out of that kitchen all day!"

Silas shook his head. "Dan brings coffee at eight. You have lunch at one. You're up here most of the rest of the time."

"Oh," Piper said.

"I told them to have their morning meal before eight. Open access from ten to one, then they need to be out of there till three, in case we have to meet. After three they can do as they please."

"Bathrooms…"

"Eight to nine in the morning. Dan will run the generator. The monks will use the second floor bathroom and the half bath on the first floor."

"Dinner," said Piper faintly.

"Molly brings it up to you."

"Just now and then…"

"Every day," Silas said firmly.

"Just lately…"

"Every day," Silas repeated. "Every day since summer began."

* * *

Damn Lies
By Presidential Candidate and All Round Good Guy
Jacques Marquand

Some of the philosophic philistines that follow my work tell me that their proclivities are philanthropic rather than political. No problem. Send me your email address and I'll personally make sure you're on the Damn Do-Gooders mailing list. It's your license to run around doing good. Start by supporting the Marquand Fund for Re-Election and Japan Friendship and Trade Junket. Checks, cash, money orders, bitcoins—we accept all forms of currency, real or fake. I will not sell your name to the FBI, CIA, or any of the multi-national corporations that want to find out what you do so they can put you in jail or sell you things. Or both. Trust me!

November 6: Monks and Mayhem

Day four of our power outage. Lights are flickering on in some parts of the state, but not here in Riverboro. In our town, most of the shops that cluster at the depot are open for business, powered by generators or doing business in the dark, run by hardy New Hampshire folk who don't let things like states of emergency keep them down. Sam King got rid of his perishables but he's still open, admitting people in twos or threes to pick up basic necessities. They roam the dark store, feral shoppers with flashlights, and at checkout the boys tally their purchases on calculators and jot the totals on paper.

The bookstore and library are also dark but open for business, and the more literary-minded among us thread through the stacks wearing coats and mittens, peering at books in the natural light filtering through the windows, breathing out puffs of steam. People collect to exchange news, to tell jokes, to offer help. Yesterday evening I looked down from my window to see the brave lights shining at Marty's, the drugstore, and the diner, and I picked out throughout the town a few homes whose generators were running. Overall, though, our town is dark.

I have grown to love, these last few days, sitting in my tower office in the early morning, before the sun rises, before doors start opening and closing and coffee starts brewing and the questions and challenges of the day start to take shape. Before anyone is awake but me, doing my blog, and Sasha, purring on my lap (but startling from time to time at small sounds). It is silent and solitary and still and I have the structure of my purpose and the freedom of my voice and the coziness of my little audience (although we broke two dozen yesterday; and Jake, you were one of them. It made me happy to see your comment).

This morning, though, something feels different. Even as I settle in and turn on my tablet and stare at the awakening screen, I can feel a low rumble throughout the house. The generator? Too early for that; Dan will give us our first blast of heat, lights, and hot water at eight. And this sound is different, a low vibration that's gathering and growing, almost a hum, the still, sad music of humanity…

It's those damn monks. They must be greeting the day by chanting. They've got one *hell* of a nerve waking the house with their caterwauling!

I. Am. So. Not. Pleased.

Just like that, the solitude and serenity of the morning has vanished. Molly (who snuggled in the big bed again last night; the power outage has brought some sweet gifts) comes into the office in her PJs, tousled and yawning, a heavy quilt around her shoulders. She curls into the wing chair and stares into space. I get up and tuck the quilt more cozily around her, into the edges of the chair. I put water on my camp stove for her hot chocolate. She peers out of the folds of the quilt, her enormous eyes gradually coming into focus.

I ask her if she's gotten any responses to her invitation to join November Lies. She says she got commitments from her closest friends from school, Jilly and Peter and Colby. Jilly's big sister, Miranda, has promised to join. Miranda stayed with us for a while when she was younger, and she and Molly remain close.

Molly would like to add a few people to that core group. So, Aspiring Liars, gather at the Magic Mushroom Bookstore (as the library is closed Sundays) at noon today for a working session. You'll help Molly plan her party, you'll invent whoppers of your own, and you'll inspire and support one another.

This will give the kids a place to go while there is no school, and Sam King will brew up coffee and cocoa, and I will set up a November Lies forum where you can come and let us know how you are doing. We'll focus on our Lies, and keep our minds off the dark and cold.

The brilliant works that will come of it! Riverboro will become like Paris in the 1920's: a hub of art and culture and iconoclastic thought. Molly will be at its center (unless Jacques takes all the credit—I've got my eye on you, Jacques), assembling the intellectuals and hosting the salons. Tourists will flock into town to buy from the shops, whose owners will be grateful to *Riverboro Rocks* for our role, and they will buy lots of advertising.

So waking the house worked out after all. Thank you, monks!

Molly's List: Top Five Costume Ideas for the November Lies Party at the H.I.T. (Molly posting on Piper's Blog)

5) *Jacques Marquand.* Wouldn't it be funny if EVERYONE came as Jacques? Imagine a whole room full of Marquands, wearing those French explorer hats or chained to shopping carts or carrying young women out of dangerous mobs. You wouldn't be able to tell who was the real thing! Bonus points for anyone who does this.

4) *Anyone who might have inspired Jacques Marquand.* That will please him I bet. Since Jacques is super old—back in the day he was like a big brother to my Great Auntie P, if you can imagine—we might have to open our history books, or go through old issues of *To the Barricades.* (No offense, Jacques!)

3) *Anything that can shock and awe.* We're talking superheroes. How about Buffy or Lara Croft or Iron Man or The Doctor? I bet you could buy most of those costumes online, so you wouldn't even have to make one.

2) *Vintage is always great.* Rummage through your closets for something you haven't worn in years. It might have achieved costume status. How easy is that?

1) *There are some super easy anime costumes.* And no, Mom, they don't have to be androgynous. I'm thinking of ones like Ouran High School Host Club: just blazers and pants. Or L from Death Note: baggy pants, dark circles under your eyes. Make sure you get the details right (like the patches and glasses), or you'll look like a generic dweeb, or worse, some-one who didn't want to bother with a costume. You can be a dweeb (over here we are all dweebs) but not generic, OK? But beggars can't be choosers, and since I am begging you to come to my party, you get to choose the costume.

Tags: William Wordsworth, *Tintern Abbey*, Riverboro Ashram, Magic Mushroom bookstore, Riverboro Public Library

COMMENTS:

RiverCoral: Piper, you've got to get down there to meet those monks. You can't stay up in your office all day! The house looks great, I know you'll be so happy when you see it! ☺
(*Comment declined*)

RiverCoral: I think the comment thing isn't working. I tried to post and it didn't show up. Piper, I think there's a bug or a virus or some-thing— ☺

RiverCoral: Oh, here we go, it's working now. So, I was going to say, why is it so many costumes include weapons? I think we all should do costumes of peace. ☺

ConArtist: Weapons rock.

The Geekster: You need weapons to bring down zombies.

ZombiePatrol: And zombies don't use them—it's our prime advantage.

RiverCoral: That six-shooter of Donny's, for example. Is that the best message we want to send our kids? ☺

PipersPebbles: Coral, you know that studies have shown that a toy gun with a cowboy costume does no harm and actually makes a powerless child feel safer in the face of the *invisible* bad guys. It has nothing to do with later gun violence.

RiverCoral: Here at the River Place we don't allow weapons. ☺

PipersPebbles: Then you are denying your kids the chance to feel powerful in a very innocent way. So let's drop the subject.

MollyHH: Before you two start using weapons on each other!

PipersPebbles: Very funny, Molly. Readers, I invite you to send in your own ideas for costumes, along with any pictures or cute stories to go with them. We'll set up a site page to display them. Let's spend the month getting ready for the party and working on our Lies, shall we? It will give us something fun to do while we wait for the power to come back on—although, from what I hear, that could be any day now.

WeatherOracle: Despite official understatement

Your woes show no sign of abatement.
And when your Lies are celebrated
Dark Truths will be illuminated.
Your innocence is not restorable—
Thus proclaims your Weather Oracle.

Private Message from DanTheRiverMan: I want to meet this Oracle. His dark and eerily accurate prophesies give me a shiver. Time to spill, Piper. Who is he?

Private Message to DanTheRiverMan: I love being the only person who knows...

Guest: Everyone at the library is abuzz about your Oracle, Piper. It's Andy Hadley, isn't it? He serenades his gardens and dowses for water on his patch of land on Hadley Pond Road, and he takes joy in scaring the pants off his guests with stories of local ghosts and demons.

MollyHH: I'm sure you're right! Last time I visited Cousin Andy, he gave me sun tea and sent me home with a recipe in verse.

DrewHadley: Hey, that's my dad you're talking about. He can't even figure out what I want for Christmas, never mind the weather. If he's the Weather Oracle, I hope Uncle Dan is paying him well, lol. And don't expect him to be the dark truth at your party, Mol. You know he's not one for parties. Or costumes for that matter, lol.

MollyHH: Though he does give out great treats on Halloween.

DrewHadley: He's good at that. He thinks that anyone who comes all the way out to the farm should be rewarded, lol.

ImmaterialGirl: Hi...can I join in? You all sound as if you know each other. It isn't private, is it?

PipersPebbles: Not at all. This is the community voice of Riverboro. We welcome all comments.

BookLover603: A newbie…happy you're here…

ImmaterialGirl: Oh, awesome. I have a question: I found out I'm going to have a baby and I thought I might want a doctor. Could I get Dr. Jake?

PipersPebbles: Congratulations, dear, and I wish you a world of happiness. Why don't you have a doctor?

ImmaterialGirl: I don't usually get sick or anything. Is everyone supposed to have one? I'm as healthy as a horse. But now, you know, pregnant and all.

RiverCoral: That's such good news, we're all so excited for you! Have you thought about a midwife? ☺

ImmaterialGirl: I was wondering about Dr. Jake, since Piper likes him so much.

PipersPebbles: Dr. Jake is *not* an ob/gyn.

BookLover603: He's super hot, though…

ImmaterialGirl: But doesn't Dr. Jake work in family planning at the River Place?

RiverCoral: The River Place isn't for family planning per se, although we do have great resources. ☺

PipersPebbles: The Riverboro Community Place coordinates the social outreach for the community, and Dr. Jake provides their psychological support services. There's an excellent medical group with offices at the community hospital. I'll look up their number and private message you.

ImmaterialGirl: Thanks for clarifying!

RiverCoral: My midwife was wonderful, you should think about using her. I'll send you a PM. ☺

(*Comments approved*)

* * *

The kitchen was empty, as Silas had promised it would be at this time. The air seemed to crackle with cold. Piper puttered around, Sasha puttering with her. They prowled about peering into cupboards and peeking around corners.

"Doesn't it feel," Piper complained to the cat, "as if you and I are guests in our own home?"

Sasha gave a trill of agreement.

"It doesn't feel normal," Piper elaborated to her willing audience of one. When had the kitchen been so stocked with food? How would she keep track of what was hers and what was the monks'? And what if one of them came in while she was here? She would feel caught in the act—as if she were doing something wrong!

She jumped at a sound coming from the shed. Sasha jumped too. The two of them stood, side-by-side, poised and tense, looking toward the sound. The outside door opened and closed. Feet stamped and scraped. Then, a tap on the kitchen door.

Jake looked in. "Mind if I join you for a few minutes?"

"Jake!" Piper cried. "Welcome! I wasn't expecting you today." She and Sasha broke formation, she heading to the stove, Sasha lifting a hind leg in front of her face to lick it rapidly.

"I thought I'd stop by to see how you're doing with your new guests," Jake said, pulling off his gloves and stuffing them into his coat pockets. "It isn't every day you get a cadre of monks."

"A cadre—is that what a group of monks is called? They might be a regiment, the way they fill up the house." Piper picked up the jug by the sink and poured water from it into the teakettle. "The place feels like it's bursting at the seams. They're swarming out of the woodwork."

Jake pulled out a chair and dropped into it. "How do you like them as people?" he asked.

"Actually," Piper admitted, lighting a gas burner with a match and setting the kettle on it, "I haven't met them yet."

Jake raised his eyebrows and tilted his head. "I didn't feel quite ready," Piper said defensively. "I thought if they settled in it would make the transition easier. For them and for me."

She piled cookies on a plate and set it on the table, scooped tea into a pot. "A pot of tea takes on a whole new meaning when the power is out. But overall we're managing surprisingly well."

"As I had every confidence you would."

"Your confidence exceeds my own. Between the monks, the power outage, and all the money worries, I feel as if I'm holding up a teetering house of cards. It could all crash down at any moment." The kettle began to rattle and whistle. Piper lifted it and poured the hot water into the pot.

Jake helped himself to a cookie. "Where's Dan?"

"Out somewhere." Piper gestured vaguely. "Being useful. Doing good."

"There is a lot to do." Jake broke his cookie and put a piece into his mouth. "The gym at the middle school is packed with people displaced from their homes. There are cots and sleeping bags all over the place. They've got a huge diesel-powered generator and it's going round the clock. The school cafeteria is filled with volunteers cooking big meals—pastas, soups, sandwiches."

"You should see my refrigerator," Piper said, pouring out the tea. "It could feed a mountaintop of monks. In fact, it practically does. Thanks to you kind folks at the River Place."

"Dan thought it would all work out," Jake said peaceably, taking his cup and sipping.

"He'd better make sure it does," Piper replied irritably.

Jake glanced at Piper, concern in his warm brown eyes. "Piper," he began, "Is Dan—"

On cue, the door banged open. Piper froze; Dan stood there with a load of wood in his arm. A beat while he registered the situation; another beat while everyone waited for someone else to speak.

"Did I interrupt?" he asked.

Jake drained his tea and stood up, smiling. "It's OK," he said easily. "We were just finishing. I'll be on my way."

* * *

"I didn't know you were expecting Jake today," Dan said, returning to the kitchen after dropping the wood by the fire.

Piper felt something tighten inside her. "He was just checking in," she said offhandedly. She picked up the teacups and stacked them in the sink to wash later, when the generator was running. "Making sure everything was alright."

Dan forked his fingers into his hair. "Piper, you know I don't mind him coming to the house, I've said as much. But I'm not comfortable with—" He broke off. "What?"

Piper had raised a hand to cut him off. "Shh!" she hissed. "Listen!"

Because there it was. The sound.

The sound from the shed, the noise she heard late at night, the proof of her suspicions, the smoking gun.

And this time there was a witness—one other being who heard that sound as she did, who recognized its danger, who reacted in the same startled manner.

Sadly, it wasn't Dan.

"Dan, listen! It's the sound! Look at Sasha!"

Because Sasha heard it. Sasha was standing, ears laid back, tail bottle-brushing, staring toward the shed, toward the sound. Then she turned, hissing and spitting, and streaked out of the room.

"I didn't hear anything," Dan said, infuriatingly.

"Sasha did! You saw her, didn't you? You saw how it freaked her out!"

"I saw something frightened her," Dan agreed. "But lately, doesn't everything?"

* * *

It was quiet in the afternoon. Silas opened the office door and peered in.

"Yo. Ms. H. Time for the tour."

"Silas," she protested, "I don't need you to take me through my own house."

"Mandatory," he said, with enough conviction that she put down her tablet and followed.

On the second floor, Piper stopped to peek into Molly's room. Thankfully, it had not been disturbed. The bed was neatly made, spread with Molly's old patchwork quilt. Her first stuffed animal, an ancient blue dolphin, was propped against the pillows.

The room looked as if the past few years had barely brushed it. On the wall by the bed, the paint was marred by pencil drawings Molly had doodled when she was twelve or thirteen—cartoon waifs with big eyes, awkward depictions of Hello Kitty, sketches of the Pokemon creatures that Molly loved. The drawings, now almost unrecognizable, made dark gray smudges on the wall. They should probably be painted over, but Piper didn't see how she could bear to have it done. Pinned to the bulletin board were photos: Molly in the first costume she'd ever made, a marvel at the time, though eclipsed by subsequent efforts; Molly with Miranda at the bookstore, their heads together over a comic, newly in, already coveted; Molly and her father posing in front of a Japanese temple on that long-ago trip. Piper felt something clutch at her heart. The room was unchanged, but that skinny girl in pigtails and braces was gone.

Grown into a beautiful young woman, Piper reminded herself. *Helping clean rooms down the hall.* She started down the hall, looking for her daughter.

Without question the house looked brighter from the heroic efforts of the past couple of days. Bedroom doors were ajar and Piper was startled to see buckets of paint sitting on newspapers spread on the floor.

"The monks got inspired," Silas explained. "No matter how much we washed them, the walls got dirtier and dirtier. They found some buckets of paint in the basement. Dan told them it would be OK."

Someone, Piper thought, *should have checked with me.* Clean, freshly-painted rooms were a good thing. This feeling that outside forces were taking over the ship she should be captaining was not.

"Dan said so, did he? Still," she added, thinking out loud, "there might be something here. Displaced monks, a home makeover—this could be a story, Silas. What do you think?"

"Sure thing," Silas agreed easily. "*Monks Go Nuts in the Riverboro Rocks HQ.*"

"A.k.a. *my home*," Piper emphasized. "Where, I remind you, they are here as guests. Still, a story might work. Before and after shots. Silas, at the rate these monks are going, you had better get going on the before. And lots of pictures of the monks in their robes, hard at work. They do work in their robes, don't they?"

Silas nodded. "Careful, Ms. H, don't step on that newspaper. You'll track paint."

They found Molly in the little room near the bathroom. Old furniture and cardboard boxes were crammed into the center of the room. In the cleared space around the pile, Molly was scraping woodwork and Dan was prying up a rotting floorboard. Donny had a scraper in his hand and was working away at a bit of wall, an expression of intense concentration on his face. "Make sure you find some hidden treasure or invaluable historical papers while you're doing that," Piper called in to them. "We could use the cash."

Molly and Dan emerged into the hallway, wiping their hands on rags and tossing them back into the room. Donny dropped his scraper and followed.

"Don't think we haven't thought of it," said Dan. The three of them fell in behind Piper and Silas like an honor guard and followed them down the hall.

"We should do the floors next," Piper said. "They all need sanding and staining. Dan, did you hear my idea about the feature? Silas will take the photos."

"Sure thing," Silas said again. "All over it." He guided her down the next flight of stairs. They paused at the entrance to the living room.

Piper froze. The essence of control she had been grasping for, that she had been trying to pull around herself like a blanket, began unraveling, dis-solving, a dream where you find yourself naked on stage. She suddenly felt how cold it was in the house.

The room was *full* of people—monks, it seemed, were everywhere. One over on the window seat, and two on the sofa, and three standing in a cluster near the fireplace: that's right, half a dozen, a blur of faces. With the white robes and shaved heads there was no telling them apart. Piper wasn't even getting a clear sense of which were the men and which the women—they all looked bald and drapey and, yes, paint-splotched too, though even the splotches looked intentional.

They turned toward Piper—she had a sense that they were *converging* on her—and joined their hands and began to murmur something in a foreign language. Was it Japanese? Hindi? Swahili? Piper supposed it was some kind of greeting, or blessing, or invocation. Or, what did she know? It could be a curse to rid the house of its current occupants and deliver it to the monks for their new ashram.

There were tables set round the room—her tables, actually, or anyway the end tables and coffee tables that had always been in the house—*where* had they put the magazines that were usually stacked on them? The tables were draped in cloth now and covered with flowers and candles and fruits. Little lamps were set all about, on the tables and the mantelpiece and the floors. All the candles were lit and the lamps were burning, though it was the middle of the day, and in a way it was quite beautiful; but what Piper saw was confusing and overwhelming, a blur of light and color.

The monks were joining their palms and bowing toward her. Piper reached out and grasped Silas's sleeve, and he patted her hand in a way that she actually did find a tiny bit reassuring. He led her to the deep chair by the fire—the monks moved politely to one side—and handed her a cup of tea, which appeared to have been passed to him by one of the monks. Silas took an afghan that had been folded on the back of the chair and put it over her lap, as if she were an invalid. But the gesture was comforting, and the room *was* cold.

Then all the monks found seats for themselves and murmured amongst themselves; and one by one they stood and came up to her and each gave her a few silk flowers, until her lap was quite full of them. And each stood quietly near her chair and said things like: Thank you for your generosity toward us.

And: We are so very happy to be here.

And: What a blessed place you live in.

And: You have a beautiful soul.

November 7: Chop Wood, Carry Water

Picture this, Riverboro: Yesterday afternoon, break time. The generator is on. Dan and Donny are downstairs, washing up. Molly and I are on our way upstairs to the luxury of our private third floor bathroom. We pause in the second floor corridor, where the monks are gathered outside their bathroom in their white robes, talking peacefully, waiting patiently. Inside the bathroom, someone is moving around. We hear the swish of the shower curtain, the rattle of the toilet lid, the light thump of feet on floor. Molly and I pause to admire the harmony of six people waiting so patiently for their turn in the bathroom.

Wait. Six people? Molly and I glance at each other, turning back for the head count. Yes, we have six bald, white-robed people standing in line outside the closed bathroom door, talking in low voices, chuckling at murmured jokes. All appear serenely unconcerned that a selfish person is clanging around in the bathroom with no apparent intention of coming out.

Did a draft pull the door closed? But if so, who is in there? Did those monks bring in someone *else* to live with us? Do they have an imaginary friend?

"Um…" says Molly, and six pairs of eyes turn to look at her. "Is anyone in the house besides us?"

Now you can see each monk looking at all the others, counting. Six people. Six on the outside of the bathroom. What is going on? Brumi reaches over and gently pushes the door. It swings inward.

And out strolls Sasha, every inch the princess, tail high in the air and looking fresh and clean indeed.

When we all could speak again for laughing, Molly said, "That's it—I'm making a schedule." She is going to do so today and post it on their bathroom door. A girl after my own heart! Whether the monks follow it or not is up to them. Given their advanced spiritual state—who else would give a cat a turn?—it's hard to tell what they might do.

But in these trying times we must all make accommodations. At the middle school, the gym is filled with sleeping bags and cots; volunteers cook meals in the school kitchen and serve them in the cafeteria as people wait for their homes to become habitable. It's historic, a community event, with refugees and volunteers pulling together to survive, stay fed, stay warm.

Here at the Hadley House we are making our small contribution to the effort by hosting this cadre of monks.

How I will bear the next few days (or, heaven forbid, weeks) I do not know, as I am not what you might call an overly social person. Not for me the parties and teas, the hoopla and folderol! My circle is small and precious to me. But say what you will about those monks (and whatever you do say, say it in the comment section, because we will all want to hear it) those monks know how to *work*.

They are buzzing about my house like a hive of bees, a picture of purpose in action, and we emerge, bit by bit, from layers of dirt and grime and neglect. Who knew it had gotten so bad? The monks, in their Eastern-thought-induced state of productive harmony, go about their business in the chill and (formerly) silent house. From time to time the electric sanders and other rechargeable tools begin to run out of juice.

Then Dan fires up the generator and calls a break for bathroom and washing up and changing the soapy water in the buckets and warming up the house, and all sorts of jollity and good fellowship (cat-related or otherwise) take place. Then the generator is shut off and wham! Back to work.

Every family in Riverboro should have its own cadre of Eastern monks (and oh, how happy I would be to offer you mine…).

Now here's an interesting thing about these so-called Eastern monks: *they are all American.* And although at first glance they all look alike, they are all different from one another. They appear to be a pleasant enough bunch if you go for that *om maha shantih* sort of thing (which I don't).

In case you are ever contemplating hosting monks in your own home, let me introduce them to you.

Ananda is somewhere in her late twenties or early thirties, and let me tell you, with those high cheekbones and brilliant green eyes, she'd be a stunner if she grew out her hair. She's quite tall—at least five ten or five eleven—and model-thin, and the way she moves makes that plain white cloth she drapes herself in look like the robe of a queen. What is she thinking throwing all that away at this stage in her life?

Cassandra is younger—she looks barely older than Molly, and she's a bit of an elf, lively and sparkly. Dark eyes, caramel skin, smiling all over all the time.

Lisette must be in her sixties. She has the kind of strong facial bone structure that wears well. And what a lot of jewelry she wears for a woman of her age! A row of gold hoops along the rims of her delicate ears, a jeweled dot between her eyebrows, a diamond nose stud, enameled bangles on her wrists, toe rings and belled ankle bracelets so she jingles when she walks. How to reconcile all that with her shaved head and plain robes? Maybe she began wearing jewelry when she was a young devotee and never stopped? Maybe it's her way of personalizing her outfit, the way girls will add personal touches to their school uniforms? Or is it significant of her rank in the order?

That last makes sense to me, as Lisette is clearly the Mother Superior of that group. She seems to be in charge of both the men and the women. I don't know if she instructs them, per se, in their Eastern arts, but on the level of day-to-day activity, she's the boss. Not that it's always apparent. She moves quietly in the background. But I have seen her, with look and gesture, direct each member of that group—and believe me, whatever she indicates is what gets done.

As for Pasco and Brumi, they seem to be in their early thirties, and I wonder if either is taking his calling as seriously as the women. It isn't such a big commitment for men, is it, shaving their heads? I mean, look at Silas. And I can't help thinking Pasco seems to like Cassie more than he should. Yesterday they always seemed to be working together, joking and laughing the entire time, and I thought I caught a few scuffles in which tickling and daubing with paint were involved.

Leon is the one who most meets my preconceptions of what the people in this group ought to be. For starters, he doesn't have to try to be bald; it comes naturally to him. Plus he's got a bit of that Buddha thing going. He's got a look about him that's sort of merry and serene at the same time. I've got big plans for Leon. I've decided he is going to be the Wise Man in our saga (if you can call a daily blog a saga). I'm imagining conversations wherein I wholly-unintentionally let slip this or that seemingly-innocuous detail of my life, and he sees its deep significance, and with a few brief and life-changing words puts my entire existence into its proper cosmic perspective.

Though come to think of it, if Lisette is the one in charge, she'd be the person for that, wouldn't she? We could do a Wise Woman kind of thing—very archetypal, very Drawing-Down-the-Moon-ish.

In other news, the November Lies group got started yesterday with ten members. By the end of the afternoon, there were only seven, and based on a couple of comments that were made, it looks as if today we can expect only five. But five aspiring Liars—it's a start. And if any of them writes a sizzling philippic, we'll publish it in *Riverboro Rocks*. Post in the *November Lies* forum, and if you have a great idea for an article in an upcoming issue, let me know and we'll see if we can fit you in. Of course, we can't afford to pay you, but think of the experience and visibility you'll get.

Idea for today: a page on the site called *Riverboro Recommends* to promote our local businesses.

Piper's List: Top Five Monk Quotes

5) *Artists are the monks of the bourgeois state.* (Cesar Pavese) I have no idea what this means, do you?

4) *You haven't partied until you've partied at dawn in complete silence with Buddhist monks.* (Cameron Diaz) I have heard my monks at their early-morning parties, and I must say that complete silence does not describe it. But, Cameron Diaz, you have laid down the gauntlet; you have challenged those of us who have monks to party at dawn with them. We shall see.

3) *What is the sound of one hand clapping?* (Zen koan) I don't know, but I imagine it's quieter than the sound of six monks doing a home makeover. Is it quieter than that party at dawn?

2) *After Enlightenment, the laundry.* (Zen proverb) I fear if I were to arrange things in that sequence I would wear many unwashed garments.

1) *We cannot survive without human affection.* (Dalai Lama) I hope I am never called upon to try.

Tags: Wise woman archetype, Eastern wisdom, Riverboro Recommends, November Lies

COMMENTS:

MartysCafe: Piper, as you mentioned, thanks to our generator, we are open for business, so, for anyone who wants a nice hot breakfast these cold mornings, we have eggs and coffee and our water is running and toilets are flushing. We're proud to be part of November Lies and to have sponsored the first day with free hot drinks. And Piper, if you do go ahead and publish one of their screeds, you can count on a quarter page from Marty's.

SamKing: King's is also open, though dark, and we're starting accounts for all the November Liars. Today our special is Pumpkin Pie Spice Latte, served from thermoses. Stop by before your working session or call and we'll bring your coffee to you.

PipersPebbles: If you text the keyword 'KingsMarket' to #1052 you'll get a coupon right there on your phone. Then bring your phone in to King's and show him the screen to redeem it. Also, Sam is taking suggestions for coffee flavors, the more unusual the better.

MollyHH: How about Raspberry Coconut English Trifle?

PipersPebbles: Very creative, Molly; however, I should have said: the more unusual the better, *within reason*.

AuntieP: I logged in to this comment section with a name and it isn't so difficult. I encourage everyone posting as a guest to get "handles" of their own. Today the library will host a forum (a real live three dimensional one with people standing around talking to other people) to share stories of their adventures to inspire the Liars. We'll start at three sharp. I intend to show slides from my latest trips to Outer Mongolia and Uzbekistan.

HarvardProf: I am sure few people would want to miss that, as your philanthropic work with schools and orphanages abroad is well known in this town, Auntie P.

AuntieP: It is the proud tradition of our Hadley family, and I hope to see Molly carry it on. My next trip is scheduled to be to some Hadley grade schools in Rwanda, and I harbor the hope that Molly will be persuaded to join me on it.

HarvardProf: The experience of travel is greatly enhanced when you share it with a protégé. I myself traveled in Africa with my godson and it was enriching to both of us. I look forward to seeing your slides.

AuntieP: And perhaps you would be willing to share a story or two with the group, as well?

HarvardProf: I would be honored, Auntie P.

AuntieP: I'll be the one behind the front desk.

HarvardProf: I'm the one in the tweed jacket with leather elbow patches.

(*Comments approved*)

* * *

It was early—too early for anyone to be stirring. Well, let's be honest, it was more middle of the night than early morning by most people's standards. Three am.

Cold as the nights were, Piper had, ironically, been awakened by a hot flash. After she had taken a few minutes to breathe herself cool, she had gotten quietly out of bed, pulled her robe around her and headed across to her office.

Stepping from the bedroom carpet to the wood floor of the office had made her wince. That floor was *cold*. She'd felt her way back across the bedroom to her bureau, pulled out a pair of thick socks, and put them on. Still, it would take a few minutes for her feet to warm up. She padded silently back to the office in the dark.

The office was even colder than the bedroom. Piper felt the cold inside her nose as she breathed in and out. Under her robe she was bundled in layers of clothes: long underwear under pajamas under a big bulky sweatshirt and sweatpants. Still, she shivered.

In her computer chair she wrapped herself in a blanket, tapping at her laptop, squinting at the glow of her monitor, the only light in her office. Once she had finished her blog entry, she was at a loss what to do. It was so dark; it was so cold. How cozy it would be if she could turn on the lamp, if she could turn on the heat. Her early-morning blog sessions were going to be misery until they got the power back on.

Should she go back to bed? She'd never sleep…but it would at least be warmer. Maybe she could light a candle and read by its light? But she never found that illumination quite sufficient for comfortable reading.

How their lives depended on electricity! Should she get Dan to start the generator? She hated to disturb him in the middle of the night; besides, it would make him cranky. Very cranky. Men and their sleep! Best thing would be to try and do some work.

Then she heard it: the noise. That sound from the shed. Was it footsteps? Who could it be? Piper froze, fists clenched. *Make them go away,* she thought. *Make them go away.*

Piper crept to her office door and stood listening, barely breathing. She could hear it in the shed: that creeping, stealthy noise. But tonight was different. Tonight it wasn't staying in the shed; it was moving.

Someone easing open a door? Intermittent creaks, as if someone was deliberately silencing heavy footsteps; a muffled thump, as if, in the dark, the intruder had bumped into a wall.

It was happening: the thing that Piper had feared most. The noise had moved from outside to *inside the house.*

I knew it! Piper thought. *I knew they would come into the house!* That was a floorboard creaking; that was a person, creeping about her darkened house, looking for something to steal, looking for damage to do.

She felt around in the glow of her monitor for a weapon. A pen to stab the intruder's throat? Compressed air to spray in his eyes? Her fingers touched something hard and closed around it. Her disabled keyboard, victim of Sasha's fall through the skylight. A keyboard: flimsy, lightweight, not as good as a brick; but, clutching it, Piper felt slightly more powerful. It would have to do.

Silent as Sasha, Piper slid out of the office, across the hall, down the stairs, clutching the keyboard in her icy fingers. She slid, step by careful step, in her thick socks along the wooden floor of the second floor hallway, the fingers of her free hand trailing along the wall to guide her, lightly touching the bedroom doors as she crept by. Past Molly's room, the door closed tightly, deep silence within: thank heaven for that. Past the other bedroom doors, all closed, the monks sleeping peacefully, with hours to go until their pernicious morning wailing.

Down the stairs to the first floor, moving silently, barely breathing, the darkness so complete that Piper, clutching the banister, closed her eyes and it made no difference. Halfway down the stairs she paused. She opened her eyes...

A light. A pinpoint beam moved across the hallway from the kitchen, nearing the stairs, passing the stairs. Directly below Piper.

What followed Piper would always remember as one of the bravest, if most foolish, things she had ever done. She didn't think; she didn't plan; she felt. And what she felt was not panic; it was not terror; it was not anxiety, or weakness, or defenselessness. It was rage: sheer rage. Rage at the invasion of her home. Rage that her security, and the security of those under her roof, might be compromised. Rage that someone might feel that she, unprotected, could be vulnerable.

Piper screamed. Not in fear, not in retreat. Her scream rent the night, a cry of attack, a war cry. Raising her keyboard over her head, she leapt.

Out into the air, into the dark, she leapt. Off the stairs and toward that light, toward whomever was holding that light. She collided with the intruder and brought her keyboard down with all her strength. He staggered. The two crashed to the floor.

What happened next? Cries and thumps, the keyboard torn from her hands, Piper striking with her fists, her nails. Someone holding her wrists, Piper writhing, kicking, screaming, icy water splashing. Shouts echoing throughout the house, footsteps running. A light from a lantern, flashes of faces: Ananda at the bathroom door, staring, eyes huge in her thin face, clutching her robe at the throat; Brumi, fingernail scratches down his face, dripping wet, apologizing over and over; Cassie and Pasco mopping at the floor, soaking up the water; Lisette holding Piper while she sobbed.

Those goddamn monks.

Ananda had been up in the night, feeling queasy, thinking she might throw up. "She's delicate," Cassie explained. "All the moving and the no heat and all upsets her equilibrium."

Ananda had made her way to the first floor bathroom, the better to hurl undisturbed. "She didn't want to wake us," said Cassie. "She thought it would be quieter if she went downstairs."

The helpful Cassie, flitting to the men's room to rouse them. "We put buckets of water in the kitchen in case we needed to use them to flush the toilet in the night. They're kind of heavy…I thought Brumi…"

The chivalrous Brumi, lugging the bucket in from the kitchen; the sounds of Ananda retching; and Piper, flying shrieking through the dark.

"Piper, you are the most courageous woman I have ever met," said Cassie, and the other monks murmured assent.

* * *

By midday it had warmed up. All the windows were open on the first and second floors. A soft, springlike air wafted in. Outside, the sound of water—dripping, trickling, rushing down the hill to the very bottom, from whence came the powerful steady flow of the river itself.

Indoors, the hive of monks buzzed, carrying buckets of paint, climbing on stepladders, unscrewing light fixtures to clean out the dust and bugs and screwing the lightbulbs back into their sockets.

Piper, feeling like an outcast in her own home, crept out to find them. What to say to them—she who had, only last night, thrown herself down upon them, a screaming bolt from the heavens? Would there be a long ordeal of mutual apologies, reciprocal explanations? The thought made her cringe. But it had to be done. The longer she hid upstairs, the worse it would become.

In the living room, no one seemed to notice Piper peering in at the door, poised as if to flee. A fire crackled in the fireplace. Lisette was kneeling before one of the tables. At first Piper thought she was praying—right there in public, for the world to see! Then she realized that the older woman had a basket filled with apples, oranges, mangos, and pomegranates. From her position at the door, Piper watched, fascinated, at the ceremonial way Lisette touched the fruit, cradling each piece in a beringed, blue-veined hand, piling it on the table around a devotional picture, scattering sweets on the table, creating a pool of beauty. As she finished the table she was working on, she pulled herself to her feet and moved to another to repeat the process, using these ordinary items to set up focal points of rich abundance.

Molly's voice diverted Piper. Molly sat on the window seat next to a pile of books, handing them up one by one to a young monk who teetered on a stool, dusting them and returning them to the shelves. Molly had her tablet on her lap and was intermittently tapping out her promised schedule.

"For you, five minutes," she was saying. "In and out. That's 8 to 8:05 for you, 8:05 to 8:10 for Leon, 8:10 to 8:15 for Brumi. That leaves the rest of the hour for Lisette, Ananda, and Cassie."

The monk on the stool was the dark one, the one that Piper had thought seemed interested in Cassie. Pasco. "Fifteen minutes for the three of us? And the women get forty-five? You're worse than our Guruji at the ashram in Vermont, and he's as tough as nails. Did they hire you to negotiate for them?" he protested.

"You boys don't need more than five minutes each in the bathroom," Molly said brutally. "Look at you."

"Hey, the hair, the hair! It takes time to get these gleaming pates. I cry foul."

Molly handed up another book. "Share, then. You shave while Brumi showers and Leon brushes his teeth."

"We need someone to plead for our side," Pasco said. "Can we buy you off?"

Well, really, thought Piper. That Pasco—he was a bit of a flirt, wasn't he? Would Lisette say anything? But Lisette continued peacefully in her work, only standing, with a bit of an effort, when a table was organized to her satisfaction, to move and start on a new one.

Pasco passed Molly down a hand-drawn book. "Look at this," Molly squealed. "It's a picture book Mom and I made when I was little." Molly set her schedule aside to page through the book. "I told her the story and she wrote it down, and I drew the pictures. I almost forgot about this. Look, there's Pikachu, and that one is supposed to be Squirtle. I used to think I was such an artist. Can you believe it?"

"Be careful with that, Molly," Piper said, drawn from her cover, stepping into the room. "I thought I had put it safely away."

"It's safe," Pasco assured her. "I took those books from the very top shelf, and from the dust on them, no one has touched them in ages."

"Come join us, Mom," Molly coaxed. "We're having so much fun. Sit here by the fire and I'll make you a cup of tea."

So there was that moment, that moment when everything hung there, as if every element of life was harmonious, and people could all be together laughing, and life was, as Piper had always wanted it to be, a big friendly sitcom filled with quirky but lovable characters; that moment when everything could be different, what you always hoped it would be. But then, of course, there came an immense crash from upstairs, and everyone froze, and after a moment of unnatural silence Donny began screaming (which was a good thing, you wanted that scream at the end of the silence, Piper remembered that from when Molly was little), and Dan came downstairs carrying the boy.

Donny's face was white except for the blood pouring over his forehead and cheek. He had a gash over his eye. What had they allowed him to do? Why had no one been watching? Piper rushed over. "Donny! Baby! Are you alright?"

Somehow Lisette was there with a small vial filled with a flower remedy; somehow she was putting a few drops in Donny's mouth, then turning to Piper. In the uproar, in the confusion, Piper found herself accepting some.

"It's OK, it's all right, it's only a cut," Dan was saying calmingly. "Do not worry. He climbed up a ladder to try to scrape higher on the wall and fell off. I have to take him to the hospital. He might need a few stitches."

Molly had dropped her books. "I'll drive," she said. "Oh Donny, you are so brave. Daddy, you carry him out. I'll get the keys."

"He's going to need—" Piper began.

"—his mother," Dan said. "Please call her. She's at the River Place. Tell her to meet me at the hospital."

It was a good thing the River Place was on speed dial; Piper's hand was shaking so she didn't know if she could have dialed all seven numbers.

"I need to speak to Coral." Piper said. "Coral Lane. It's about her son."

"Coral Lane?" The person who answered sounded like a child.

"Yes dear, the social worker. The grown up who supervises playtime."

"Oh, Coral," said the child, and Piper could hear an adult voice in the background asking for the phone. "Coral Hammond. You want Mrs. Hammond. She's right here. Hang on, I'll give you to her."

* * *

Damn Lies
By National Presidential Candidate and Good Will Ambassador Jacques Marquand

I bring a melancholic memo to my political pals, the Damn Liars, and to my philanthropic followers, the Damn Do-Gooders: despair! A splinter cell seeks alternatives to anarchy. They ask: Is there something to be said for compromise? Of course there is! You just can't say it in polite company. Still, we accommodate all. If subversion isn't your style, watch for my correspondence course for diplomat wannabes. I'm calling it Damn Suck-Ups. Write in. I'll post the good stuff here. Also the crap.

PS: Tomorrow is election day—one of the boring ones. No big jobs to be filled. So what? Consider it a practice election. Vote to keep your hand in, you'll find plenty of job openings on the ballot. Vote for your school boards, your selectmen and women, vote for the dogcatcher or the garbage man, but vote. Remember, Communists are everywhere—so vote for some of them! Next year's the primary, so I'll be popping by the polls, shaking hands, slapping backs, and kissing babies. My schedule is, as always, subject to radical and unpremeditated change.

November 8: Taking the Gravy Train to Easy Street

Making another too-close-for-comfort call by our Weather Oracle, the river continues to rise and spread. Looking down into town this morning, I see men in waders pushing a stranded SUV that an over-confident resident tried to drive through downtown. One of our local wags has found a rowboat and is pulling it up the street—some kind of joke? No, on second look I see that the boat is loaded with jugs of milk and plastic bags full of something—canned goods maybe. It must be the volunteers from the River Place taking food to the elderly and shut ins.

Our town is kind.

Here at the Hadley House, we regard forty degrees as warm. We dress as for the outdoors; we wear fingerless gloves to type on battery-powered devices; we line up for the bathroom at specified hours and jockey for position with monks and cats.

Regardless of any monk's (or cat's) claim to the bathroom, Ananda is sure to get dibs. I've seen it in action several times already. Though Lisette with her greater years (and hence, no doubt, greater wisdom and maturity) is their chief administrator, Ananda in her beauty and delicacy is their gentle queen. They bend over backwards to accommodate her; they cater to her every need. To be fair, Ananda rules through love, not fear; she asks for nothing but is given everything. People are always running off to fetch her shawls and pillows and treats of one sort or another. The power of beauty! From grade school on, who hasn't seen what the pretty girls get? Though in Ananda's case, no doubt, her beauty is spiritual as well as physical. These are monks. We expect more from them.

The guys, with their shaved heads, are not so gorgeous, but they have their uses. Brumi is the most skilled handyman. He was messing with the windows all day yesterday, using planes and drills and electric sanders and putty and caulk, while Pasco and Cassie (who continue to move as a team) followed with paintbrushes. Later came Lisette with cleaner and rags, and room-by-room it was as if they turned the lights on, it was so much brighter.

It turns out there has been a convergence of spiritual and material in the monks' intentions. I had thought that their cleaning and repair frenzy had to do with gratitude for the bivouac, coupled with the need to get the place habitable. And I am sure that both those motivations have played their role. But they were also getting ready for an event in their own esoteric calendar. Their ouster from their ashram coincided with the beginning of an Eastern festival (I've been informed by Lisette) that is heavy on the light-overcoming-darkness thing. Part of the celebration involves cleaning your digs top to bottom, out with the old and in with the new, and getting it all set up nice to welcome the spirit of goodness, light, and (incidentally) prosperity that will come. And here I thought it was all to welcome me, coming down from my office to greet them.

Candles and oil lamps and fruit and silk flowers are part of it too. Last night this house was ablaze with light, top to bottom, rooms heaped with flowers and windows lit with candles—all night long. You'd think it would be annoying, but I actually found it comforting, since I am often awake when it is black dark and all the world is sleeping. Last night my lights were on and somebody, I felt, was home.

This morning in the small, small hours, Lisette tapped on my office door with a cup of herbal tea (so Jake, I have begun to take your very good advice), and she said that the spirit of abundance has descended and entered my home, and she left a plate of fruit here for me to nibble at till coffee comes.

So Riverboro can expect halcyon days, if the monks are to be believed, and my house is gleaming and lit and filled with beautiful altars. Outside the sun is shining brilliantly, sparking off the river in patches so bright it looks as if it is catching fire, and I've got a new project for those monks. What if next year for their festival the whole town participates in overcoming darkness by floating burning fires on the river?

Imagine the beauty and drama of hundreds of tiny barges with candles and flames and twinkling lights floating down the river while townspeople and tourists watch from the bridges and banks. Imagine the artists and buskers and jugglers and vendors lining the banks and setting up in the park, selling their wares and drinking in the beauty. Imagine the paper lanterns set throughout the town, in streets and in the public buildings (wherever the Just/exchange their messages), everything bright, everything ablaze. We will stand up against the engulfing darkness. And those of us who (like W.H. Auden, like me) are uncertain and afraid, who (like W.H. Auden, like me) are beleaguered by negation and despair, we will hold aloft our points of light. We will show an affirming flame.

Piper's List: Top Five Light Quotes

5) *If you are in a spaceship that is traveling at the speed of light, and you turn on the headlights, does anything happen?* (Steven Wright) The first of life's great imponderables. I have often wondered about it myself.

4) *There is a crack in everything, that is how the light gets in.* (Leonard Cohen) He must have spent time in my kitchen…or my laundry room…or pretty much any room in my house.

3) *The sole purpose of human existence is to kindle a light in the darkness of mere being.* (Carl Jung) Thank goodness someone cleared that one up. Where

would we all be without Jung to tell us what our sole purpose is? And, incidentally, since when is Being 'mere'?

2) *At times our own light goes out and is rekindled by a spark from another person. Each of us has cause to think with deep gratitude of those who have lighted the flame within us.* (Albert Schweitzer) I think with deep gratitude of Molly and Donny, spark re-kindlers extraordinaire. Who has rekindled your spark?

1) And my favorite (and yours too, I'll bet), from Shelley's eulogy to Keats:

The One remains, the many change and pass.
Heaven's light forever shines; earth's shadows fly.
Life, like a dome of many-colored glass
Stains the white radiance of eternity. (Percy Bysshe Shelley)

I'm getting Percy's point, with the stained glass making a cathedral of all of life. And the fact that a stain is also a smudge makes this a rich image, and layered in meaning in a way I usually find seductive. But today I can't resist asking: is "stains" what we want to say? What about decorates? Embellishes? Enhances? Dances on the face of? Gives depth and texture and meaning to? What would our monks say? And would they choose, for themselves, the many-colored glass of life or the white radiance of eternity?

Tags: Festival of Lights, WH Auden, *Adonais*

COMMENTS:

RiverCoral: What great ideas! And what intellectual quotes! You are so smart, Piper, how can you think of all those things? ☺

BookLover603: I would never have thought of questioning Shelley… but since you've begun looking for a word to replace "stains," what about "frames?" Like, "frames the white radiance of eternity?"

ImmaterialGirl: Although could something as big as eternity be framed by something more limited, like life? Wouldn't the big thing have to frame the little thing? Or is that where the "mere" comes in?

BookLover603: And what about L. Cohen's crack...is it in the dome of glass?

DrewHadley: Who but my Aunt Piper would even consider re-writing a famous poet? Auntie Piper, you'll be taking a red pencil to Shakespeare next, lol.

The Geekster: It might be tough to choose between many-colored glass and white radiance, both of them sound fine to me. But for my money there's no contest between flying shadows and light forever shining. Who wouldn't pick the light?

HarvardProf: The timing of what we know as the Festival of Lights is determined by the lunar calendar. The celebration, which typically includes the giving of gifts, is in some ways similar to the western celebration of Christmas, with some resonance, as well, in the light-in-the-darkness imagery.

WeatherOracle: Halcyon days, your flowers all abloom?
                   A Gravy Train to wealth? Best not presume.
                   As days grow shorter, more foul weather looms.
                   Your Gravy Train's next station stop is doom.
                   The dire signs are not ignorable—
                   Not when you have a Weather Oracle.

PipersPebbles: Weather Oracle, are you going overboard with all these predictions?

AuntieP: They do seem somewhat strongly-worded.

PipersPebbles: No, no, no, I don't mean that. I just don't want my Weather Oracle to use up the best predictions on the blog. Not enough people read it, and we have the print magazine to think about. Weather Oracle, save some good stuff for the January issue—the deadline is today.

WeatherOracle: When you your Oracle handpicked
                    You learned how well I could predict.
                    And though not of the cognoscenti
                    Good rhymes this farmer has a-plenty.
                    My words might not be oratorical
                    But have some faith in Weather Oracle.

DanTheRiverMan: The weaponization of weather is nothing compared to these prophesies. I think we need to meet to hammer out some guidelines for the Oracle. Maybe later today?

PipersPebbles: Great idea—except, now that I think of it, there's that January deadline I mentioned.

ZombiePatrol: Somehow I know this is about the zombie apocalypse. Don't worry, Auntie P, we'll all ride it out together.

TheGeekster: Can you ride out a zombie apocalypse?

WeatherOracle: Although the path ahead is blurry
                    And unclear omens are a worry,
                    Unriddling rhymes is not permitted.
                    But if befuddled (or dull-witted):
                    No auguries are allegorical
                    Come on! I'm just the Weather Oracle.

ImmaterialGirl: It sounds to me as if the Weather Oracle is beleaguered by negation and despair, like W.H. Auden and Piper. But

Weather Oracle, don't worry, we'll ride our gravy trains right past that doom stop to whatever comes after, and I'm sure it will be better.

RiverCoral: That is such a wonderful thought, Immaterial Girl, and I'm positive it's really metaphorical, too! Or maybe allegorical, I get mixed up between the two. Whichever. Piper, Donny is fine, by the way. I'm surprised you didn't mention his fall. ☺

PipersPebbles: For my part, I'm surprised no one called to let me know how he was doing.

RiverCoral: We were at the hospital till late, so we knew you'd be in bed. He's doing great. He got three stitches! I do want to talk to you, Piper, when you have a minute, about the time that he spends up there. That's a big rambling house and he needs to be closely watched. There are lots of things that could go wrong, and he's only three after all. ☺

PipersPebbles: Coral, he was in the same room as his father when he fell off that ladder. Don't talk to me about it—talk to Dan. I would never have let him climb that ladder, and I think it's absolutely beyond the pale that you're implying this was my fault.

RiverCoral: OK, OK, I didn't mean to make you mad. I just mean it's not as child-proof as our house or the River Place or Donny's preschool. ☺

MollyHH: That reminds me, I was going to have November Lies at the Hadley House this morning, ten to noon. Is that OK, Mom? And Coral, I was going to ask if Donny could come too, and hang with me and the monks. We'll watch him every minute. Is that OK?

DanTheRiverMan: I'll bring bagels.

(*Comments approved*)

Piper's To-Do Today

5) Contact Board of Selectmen re: Riverboro Festival of Lights

4) Talk to Auntie P re: family vignettes

3) Finish editing January issue

2) Call Silas re: ad placement lineup

1) Go out and vote

* * *

By the time Piper had completed four out of the five tasks on her list, she was getting restless. The murmur of voices coming from downstairs made her feel like a prisoner chained to her computer, and she smelled bagels toasting. She needed to stretch, and she was hungry.

On her way to the kitchen, she paused to look into the living room. Molly was tucked into the corner of the battered sofa with Sasha curled beside her, one white paw in the air, looking up at her through slitted eyes, a wheezy purr rumbling in her throat in time with her breathing. Silas was leaning over the back of the sofa, looking at something on Molly's screen.

And all around were people, a world of people crammed into one living room.

Who was there? Three from Molly's class: Jilly and Peter and Colby. They were an attractive trio: Jilly with her pale, delicate skin; lanky Peter, a long ponytail down his back, circling the room like a pirate on the deck of a frigate scouring the sea; Colby with his soulful eyes, now directed at Molly. Colby was a preppy type, good looking enough if you went for that show-offy kind of thing, but he had broken Molly's heart when she was only fifteen, and Piper would never, ever, forgive him.

Jilly sat with her half-sister, Miranda, in the big chair by the fire, the two of them tapping on twin touchscreens. Why couldn't Silas date Miranda and leave Molly alone? Miranda was more his age, and she might not be a great beauty, but, with her lightly-freckled skin and swirl of copper curls, she was pretty enough. Certainly pretty enough for Silas. And if Miranda's personal style was idiosyncratic (those embroidered overalls; those tissue paper carnations; that matching teardrop—today a hot pink—painted on her cheekbone), well, look at Silas. Silas had a tattoo on his *head*.

Miranda, Piper thought now, had been given so little her entire life: those long winters in that mildewed cabin with an alcoholic father, scavenging for her meals; those years in foster care. The Hadleys had seen it happen and done their best to help—Auntie Polly could still give you an earful about *that*. But Miranda was always giving, and what she gave—a smile, a paper flower, a cheerful compliment—seemed unencumbered by bitterness. Hers was one of the many stories tucked into the long tangled tale of this New England town, stories that begged to be told.

But not today. Today the issue was Molly, and the issue was Silas, and the issue was how a mother could protect her young. There appeared to be no hope on the Miranda/Silas front—Silas seemed immune to Miranda's quirky charms.

Dan's voice boomed from the kitchen, filling Piper's space with comfort and familiarity, creating a place within this over-crowded room where she could breathe more freely. "There are no small elections, Donny, only small politicians. Remember that."

Then, Donny's piping voice: "Is Jacques Marquand a small politician?"

"Only in height, Donny," she heard Dan reply. "Never in stature."

"Jacques was at the town house?" Piper asked the air. "What was he getting up to?"

Miranda replied laughingly, her hands poised over her touchscreen. "When he finally showed, like, two hours late, he did one of those flash mob things. High school band playing marches, people dressed as farmers marching around with pitchforks, Jacques darting around singing and shouting. Bonkers."

"Exhausting," said Piper.

Peter paused his pacing to join in. "Forge your destiny, not your chains!" he cried, flinging a hand into the air in a wicked mimic of Marquand in oratory mode. He pointed, straight-armed, at Piper. "You, no-show, no-go, no-glow, no vote; flash-mobster manquee, maker of flash-monologues; you are the Hamlet of this hamlet."

"What does it mean?" Piper asked. "Are you sure you got it right?"

"It was Jacques' message to the no-shows," Miranda said.

"But Peter could have gotten it wrong," Molly added. "How would anyone know?"

"You, my lovely young friend, shall write a manifesto on malfeasance." Peter, channeling Marquand, pointed at Jilly. "Begin at once!"

"Who is Malfeasance?" Jilly asked, falling into the re-creation.

Peter/Marquand waved his hand airily, cutting Jilly off. He swung round to Colby. "Young man, your talent for public service shines through. For your Lie, you will write my official biography."

"He took to me," said Colby smugly. "The great Jacques Marquand said I'd go far."

"All Marquand's biographies are 'official,'" Piper said unkindly. "And Jacques might be good, but what's with the great?"

"I'm working on an honorific for him," Colby explained. "Suitable for history, his bio, his press releases. Like 'the distinguished Jacques Marquand.' Or 'the esteemed Jacques Marquand.' Or 'the renowned Jacques Marquand.' I'm trying out different ones."

"How about: 'the late Jacques Marquand?'" Miranda suggested, mirroring Colby's air quotes.

"Go with that," Piper advised. "It'll work for his tombstone, too."

"And you," Peter-as-Marquand pointed at Miranda. "What do you do?"

Miranda tipped her head to mime a curtsy. "I make paper flowers and write poetry, sir."

"The Pablo Neruda of origami. You will politicize the masses through Paper Flower Haiku."

Miranda handed her tablet to Jilly and stood, pulling a sheet of tissue paper from her overalls pocket and beginning to fold it into a flower with her quick, freckled fingers while she spoke. "Bright paper flowers/neither blooming nor dying/as fleeting as life."

"So that's Paper Flower Haiku..." Piper said, thinking about blog possibilities.

Miranda nodded. "Jacques said to start thinking about origami haiku flash mobs. Stuff to do on the streets of Japan."

"He said he'd take you?" Piper asked sharply.

"Maybe. He likes me and Molly the best."

"And me," said Colby.

"And me," said Silas. "To film it."

"Jacques has been promising the moon to people since long before any of you were born," Piper said. "Don't get your passports yet."

Miranda tossed her paper flower to Piper, who had to jump to catch the drifting bit of color. She said, "Paper flower Lies/A month of wistful dreaming—/don't count on Japan."

"What does all this have to do with Jacques and his politics?" Piper asked.

"Jacques says that anything the true artist creates is a work of politics," Miranda replied. "That's the beauty of it, isn't it? I can do a scathing exposé and no one might ever know."

"But if no one knows, how is it an exposé?" Piper asked. "Isn't that so—"

"—so Marquand," finished Dan, coming in from the kitchen with a cup of coffee in each hand. Donny followed, clutching a bagel in both hands, cream cheese smeared on his mouth, his bandage peeking out from under his cowboy hat like a grimy white sweatband. "Maybe we should call this whole thing November Obfuscation." Dan handed a cup to Piper. "Mocha Mint today."

"Donny, come sit here and give me a bite of your bagel." Molly pushed Sasha to the floor and patted the sofa. "Dad, Jacques talked to me, too. Peter, show him."

Peter tipped an imaginary hat and made a sweeping bow to Molly. "You, my dear, will make heroes of the masses, one costume at a time. Your Lie will reflect back to your people what is and what might be."

"Our Costume Oracle." Dan leaned over and kissed his daughter on the top of her head.

Molly smiled up at her father. "He says my costume party will be the most *searing* of political commentaries. He says if people truly understand my Lie, they'll be totally radicalized. They won't be able to hide from themselves until they begin the revolution."

"My biography is going to focus on Jacques Marquand's personal revolution," Colby said, eager to get back into the conversation. "He says it's going to change the world."

"He says my party is going to change the world," said Molly.

"He says Miranda's haikus are going to change the world," said Peter.

"He says my manifesto…" Jilly trailed off.

Piper sipped her coffee. "How about you, Peter?" she asked. "What does Marquand decree for you?"

Peter gestured with his recorder. "I'm writing a script for a videogame. Starting a whole new world from scratch."

"Hard to top that," Miranda said. "Isn't it?"

"Impossible," said Peter. "And of course it's going to—"

"—change the world," finished Piper. "Why settle for less?"

"Big job," said Molly. "Do you need help, Peter? Maybe Pasco—"

"Dude, I'd love the help," Peter said. "And from a monk!"

"But—" Pasco began.

"No buts," said Molly. "You're on Peter's project."

"—but there will have to be zombies," Pasco finished.

"There are always zombies," Peter assured him. "We're going to have a whole effing zombie apocalypse, trust me on that."

"Better and better," Pasco said. "It's the prospect of the zombie apocalypse that gets me through my day."

"Not your spiritual practice?" asked Piper.

"The spiritual practice gives me something to fall back on," Pasco said cheerfully, "if the zombie apocalypse falls through."

"Guys, enough with the zombies," ordered Brumi. "Move the meeting outside."

Peter turned and headed for the kitchen. Pasco followed, still talking. "Do you know how to tell the difference between a monk and a zombie?" he was asking as they left the room. "The monks are the vegetarians."

Molly snapped her laptop shut. "Mom, look, we've got three new members for November Lies."

She gestured and Piper looked around, registering the oddity. At various places on chair and floor, behind laptop screens or tapping on tablets, were three of the most unlikely additions to the Liars group that Piper could have imagined.

Three bald, white-robed monks looking up at Piper with smiling faces and fingers poised over their keyboards.

Lisette, Brumi, and Cassandra.

* * *

"I'm here for the big guy," Silas said. Piper and Donny were sitting together on the floor, paging through his picture books. Donny was telling Piper about preschool.

"I don't like it," Donny said. "They won't let me bring my puppy. And if you get sad and cry, they put you on a teacher's lap to cry it out."

"Harsh," Silas observed.

"Harsh," Donny echoed.

"Kind," Piper corrected. "Why do you want Donny, Silas?"

"The monks. They're going to work some voodoo on his cut."

"What does his father say?"

"He said OK. He and Coral like the natural approach."

"I know what *Dan* likes," Piper said. "I was married to him for fifteen years. And if Coral is going to send her son up here for me to look after, she's going to have to trust my judgment on some things."

"So I can have the dude?" Silas, unruffled, held out his hand for Donny, who got up to join him. Piper made a motion to stop them. Silas obligingly stood still and waited.

Piper looked at him, standing there with Donny. Where to even begin? "Silas," she asked, "what is it that you want to do in life?"

"Dunno," said Silas.

They looked at each other in silence for a few long moments. *I will wait him out*, thought Piper. *I will not speak.*

"It's only," Piper said, "Molly is going places. As a person."

As soon as she saw the smile begin on Silas' face, she realized her mistake. "I don't mean," she added in a hasty attempt to slam shut the door she had so unwisely opened, "that she's going anywhere with *you*. Actually, never mind. Forget I said a word."

"She said something?" Silas asked hopefully. "About me?"

Piper shook her head emphatically. "No. No she did not. No, no, no, no, no."

"So that's a no," Silas said.

"Yes, a no."

Silas stood, thinking. "I'm working on my con art," he finally offered.

Oh, for God's sake. "*You're* the con artist? In the comments?"

Silas nodded. Piper looked at him. There were so many things wrong with that, it was hard to know where to even start. "Silas," she said, "you *cannot* be a con artist."

"Why not?"

"Because you can't. You just can't. For starters, you have to be good-looking and a smooth talker to be a con artist."

"No way." Silas shook his head emphatically. "None of the con artists I know are either."

"You know other ones?" Piper asked, startled.

"Of course I do. Miranda, for one."

"Miranda isn't a con artist," Piper protested. "She just needs something of her own to do. Something with meaning. Where she can use her talents. Something with a future. It won't be cons."

"OK," Silas agreed easily.

"And Miranda is good-looking. And very articulate. And you said con artists aren't."

Silas laughed, a rare moment of pure amusement, and turned to go, putting out his hand again for Donny. Piper watched the two of them, Silas slouching toward the door, Donny's hand engulfed in his.

God, what a bust. "Wait. Silas." Silas turned back to her. "Are you bring-ing Donny back?' she asked. "Or not?"

"Not. Chanting class with the monks."

"For Donny?"

"They taught him a few riffs."

"Riffs?"

Silas looked at Donny, who obligingly started to sing some strange sounding words in his treble voice.

"But—why?" Piper asked.

"For fun," Donny explained. "Ananda says I have a good voice."

Piper laughed. All the men liked to please Ananda, even the three-year-old. "OK Donny. Go with Silas."

Silas paused on the way out the door, turning back to address Piper once more. "Anyways," he said, "I think Molly likes Colby now."

"Oh, God," Piper said. "You're not going let that happen, are you?"

"I'll do what I can," Silas promised. His eyes met Piper's in an appalling instant of utter complicity, then he turned back to Donny. "Come on, big guy. Looking forward to the jam session?"

"On the inside, I'm excited," said Donny, taking Silas' hand again. "On the outside, I'm quite calm."

"You nailed it, dude," Silas was saying as they left the room.

* * *

Damn Lies
By Presidential Candidate and Patron of the Arts
Jacques Marquand

Even if, for you, great lying is only aspirational, you can develop your talent and hone your skills with November Lies. Start small—lie about what you had for breakfast. Baby steps. In no time you'll delight your family and amaze your friends with your miraculous mendacity. Your extraordinary equivocation will open wondrous worlds of work and play; it will prepare you for professions rooted in pretension—and what professions are not? Rise to the top in politics, history, science, the arts. Click to download step-by-step instructions.

November 9: What Monks are Good For

Did you make it to the polls yesterday? While the line wasn't snaking around the block, as it will on the big election days, there *was* a line—the reason being that, with no power at the town house, we had to take it slow. We're one of the few places left where the voting and tallying is done by hand; we haven't sold out to the machine, not here in Riverboro. So yesterday wasn't that different from a normal election, except that the town house was unusually dim and silent-feeling. And cold.

Still, we had a nice turnout of civic-minded people and the usual handful of protesters—the Occupiers, the Free-staters, the Libertarians—all the representatives of independent thinking that we are proud to boast in our little town. They clustered in front of the town house clutching their signs, and the Libertarians provided hot chocolate for all, regardless of political persuasion.

Jacques Marquand himself was there to lead and inspire, showing how our stories can be overlaid, one upon the other, poetry upon paper flowers, like the delicate sheets of crystal in mica, so that each stratum illuminates and reflects the one below; and thus we build, layer by layer, a beautiful, shifting composition of perception and imagination which becomes, quite simply, reality.

No local election would be complete without a Hamon (or a Hammond, or a Hadley) participating. Jamie Hamon is running for Selectman with an eye to bigger things on the Libertarian ticket, and I've been thinking that if the Hamons really do have a family talent for seeing the future, we might do worse in our elected officials. And if their talent is, instead, family mythologizing, then they (along with the Hadleys and the Hammonds) are also well suited for local politics, at least as far as I am concerned. The main job of our politicians should be to reflect our story back to us in heroic ways, and many of them do that very well.

Our monks were there, doing their civic duty, along with the many other duties they perform on a daily basis. I'm beginning to think the Riverboro Ashram and its inhabitants are the best-kept secret in Riverboro—till now, anyway. Since they moved into the Hadley House they have become fair game to all of us.

Now we know several things about this group.

Piper's List: Top Five Things We Know About the Riverboro Monks

5) They vote in our local elections.

4) They are not Eastern (not really). But,

3) They do celebrate Eastern festivals.

2) They can do a complete home makeover in a matter of days.

1) They are aspiring Liars.

Perhaps aspiring is too strong a term. Perhaps it's more a case of see the job: do the job. They came into a house that needed a makeover; they gave it a makeover. They came into a room that was dedicated (for the morning, at least) to telling whoppers and, wouldn't you know, they set right to it.

Unless…is that what monks do anyway? Is that their role in the greater scheme of things—taking apart a world and putting it back together in a more satisfactory way?

Either way, they are now official members of November Lies. Cassandra says that Marquand told her to write a polemic, and she's ready to give it a try. She had, however, no idea what a polemic is. So Molly texted Jacques Marquand, and he replied suggesting Cassie read Jonathan Swift's A Modest Proposal. Do you remember that one? The great social satirist makes a case for selling the children of the poor to the rich—as food! Cassie was looking greenish by the time she was well into it. To be honest I was afraid she might be sick (and how many monks do I need throwing up in my house?). But Cassie says she's grasped the concept and is ready to give it a try.

Brumi's métier will be a music video. He started yesterday by pulling video clips and songs off the internet. I heard snatches of Day-O, Sixteen Tons, Song of the Volga Boatmen—what images are to go with the music, I wonder? What will the protest be? I imagine a soundtrack celebrating the hard work of brawny men overlaying images of monks in white robes, sitting in lotus, eyes closed, completely still.

And Lisette? She intends to write an entire book! It will be based on her experiences when she was a young adult converting to monkhood. I asked her what about the political angle, and she said (sounding like a cross between Jacques Marquand and the Dalai Lama) that nothing is more political than the completely spiritual.

Even Pasco will be involved, helping Molly and Peter with their Lies. Not Leon, though. Leon has other fish to fry. Yesterday he spent the entire day out in the barn, heaving things about. I didn't see Ananda around anywhere, and I'm guessing she was out there with him. In consultation with Dan, they started to shift out masses of things. Now, in the paling darkness of the very early morning, I can see the crouched shapes of those piles of junk on the sidewalk. I suppose I should feel nervous because they are making so free with my possessions, but in reality the possibility of a bright clean barn (a.k.a. garage) appeals.

I do know some of those rusting tools out in the barn are antiques. I asked Dan and Leon to bring the things they aren't sure about to an antiques dealer to get evaluated. Or, who knows? Take them to the Antiques Road Show to sell for a gazillion dollars, make our fortune, save *Riverboro Rocks*, massive happy ending. Although in truth? Getting rid of that junk is its own reward.

So, excuse me, cancel that bit about junk because I just heard that this Saturday, November 12th, *Riverboro Rocks* is hosting its own barn sale right here at the Hadley House from eight to noon. We'll get rid of anything get-rid-of-able, and if you have things that you can't stand to throw away but know you'll never use again, come and sell from here. Warning: could this sale of a barnful of old junk be the real November Lies?

Idea for the day: a web page highlighting old, whimsical, unique items brought by townspeople for the sale. Riverboro Recycles?

Tags: Riverboro Barn Sale, Antiques Road Show

COMMENTS:

AuntieP: As you say, Piper, there are Hamons running in most local elections, way back to their earliest days in this town, and unwary residents sometimes vote for them, thinking they are voting for a Hammond.

BookLover603: And vice versa...I keep voting for Hammonds by mistake, thinking the family gift of foresight will be useful...always a disappointment, since none of the Hammonds have it...

DrewHadley: No one mixes the Hadleys up with anyone else. Whenever my dad runs for Town Clerk, he gets edged out by a Hamon or a Hammond. They get twice the votes since no one can figure out which is which, lol.

HarvardProf: Ethan Hamon and Isaiah Hammond of shovel-whacking fame were bitter opponents in local politics. If you check the historical record you'll find that it was their political differences, more than their amorous rivalry, that led to the shovel incident.

WeatherOracle: Those Hamon boys will curse and grovel
And whack a Hammond with a shovel
To win their moment in the sun
And tell this town how it should run.
Note: sun is weather, not historical
Thus in the purview of the Oracle.

RiverCoral: That is so cute! And why shouldn't the Hamons get their moment in the sun and help run things? What with their second sight and all that. ☺

WeatherOracle: That gift is not worth fig or feather
To those who can't predict the weather.
And those smug claims are not endurable—
Not to the one true Weather Oracle.

AuntieP: Yes, Andy dear, what you do is very important, and you know how we all appreciate it. Piper, about that sale of yours. There are likely family heirlooms there and some of them could be cleaned up and donated to the Hadley Room at the library.

HarvardProf: That barn itself is a piece of history. It still has the original framework from the 1700s.

AuntieP: I well remember the dance you and Dan had in that very barn, Piper, for your wedding reception—lanterns strung up and down the block, Andy Hadley's string trio playing and Andy himself calling out the dancing, Hammonds and Hadleys from near and far spilling out into the street. You and Dan made such a sight—he so big and blond, you dark and slender and vivid. And despite all the unexpected twists that life has put—and will always put—in our paths, it is a moment I still treasure in my memory, and I hope you do too.

HarvardProf: The horseshoes nailed above the entrance date back to the original barn.

AuntieP: The two of you were a part of history as well, woven into the history of that old barn—how many wedding parties, I wonder, have been held there over the years? How many Hadleys, how many Hammonds? Sam King gave the toast—I remember it to this day. He said that you, Piper, would always live in his heart and he wished you all the happiness in the world. And he said how right it was that the two families, already connected at so many points, should be connected through the two of you. And then he stood at the side and watched the dancing and he looked as if his heart would break. I thought my heart would break for him. But then his father, Douglas Samuel King that was, came across that barn with Felicity Fontineau on his arm and told Sam to be a gentleman and ask the girl to dance. Sam King turned to her as sweet as a man could be and asked her for the next dance, and they danced together the rest of the night.

HarvardProf: If there are any items you have questions on, I'd be happy to take a look at them and give my opinion.

AuntieP: Would you? We do appreciate that. Piper, Harvard Prof and I will come to the barn this afternoon to take a look at what you've got. Would that be alright?

PipersPebbles: That's fine, Auntie Polly, and take whatever you want for the library, or to have in your own condo, for that matter.

SamKing: Stop by the market on your way over. The specialty coffee today is Caramel Crème Brule and we've got raisin bran muffins.

ConArtist: Yo. Ms. H. Can I have that old jukebox that's in the barn?

PipersPebbles: As long as you show up to help on Saturday. And you also can be in charge of selling the table space.

ConArtist: I'm on it.

(Comments approved)

* * *

Lately her office had felt like Grand Central Station with its steady stream of people coming and going, so Piper was not surprised when, around mid-afternoon, someone tapped at her door. And she shouldn't have been surprised when Jake stepped in. Still, she was. She had forgotten they had agreed to meet today. It was brilliant of him to find her.

"The hordes have invaded my house," she greeted him. "There isn't much opportunity for privacy."

"I thought we could sit and talk here."

"It's the only sanctuary." Piper gestured Jake to the wing chair. He made a joke about "the comfy chair," and she laughed, and somehow she ended up in the wing chair and he ended up sitting in her desk chair, swiveled around and lowered so he wasn't towering over her. Once they were settled, she had to get up again to pour them both tea from the thermos she kept by her desk nowadays, and then there was the business with the spoons and the sugar, and then they were squared away, cold fingers laced around warm mugs, blankets over their laps (despite the thaw, it was chilly), and Piper felt comfy and good.

"How are things at the River Place?" Piper asked. "Keeping your heads above water?"

"If you mean literally, at least we haven't drowned." Jake sat with his elbow on the arm of the chair, one leg crossed over the other, and stirred his tea thoughtfully. "We're lucky. The Cutty Sark Hotel had to close, temporarily. We took in a few of their long-term guests. It feels like camping, with sleeping bags spread over the floors, but the generator is keeping the lights on and the water warm."

"Sounds…cozy."

Jake laughed. "You could say that. We're bumping shoulders as we pass in the hallways. We have to stand in line to use our few bathrooms."

Piper murmured sympathetically, and Jake added, "The breakfast and after-school programs could use a few extra hands. Are you interested?"

"What, me? Help at the River Place?" Piper snorted. "Like that's going to happen."

Jake looked disappointed. "If you got involved with those kids, Piper, I think you'd get a lot of satisfaction from it."

"This isn't about the kids, though, is it? It's about Coral Lane. Who, by the way, is not my problem."

Jake replied gently, "No, Coral isn't your problem. And she is not the issue, either."

"What's the issue, then?" Piper asked, more belligerently than she had meant.

"You might want to think about challenging yourself more. Socially, I mean. Get out and face people you might not want to face."

"Face people?" Piper set her mug on the corner of the desk with enough force that the tea sloshed. "Jake, I have a house full of monks, for God's sake. Not to mention that this house serves as the offices of a magazine. And that's not even factoring in the November Lies group. Do you know that they were here all morning?" She gestured expansively. "There are probably more people in and out of my house than at your precious River Place."

Jake, unruffled, sipped his tea. "And you see them and talk to them?" he asked.

"Of course I do. Where do you get the idea I don't see people in my own house? You read my blog, you see the stories!"

"I do. I love your anecdotes. I'm just not sure how many of them are first-hand observations and how many are passed on from Molly or Dan. Or Silas, for that matter. Am I wrong?"

Piper tried to still her rising agitation—not so easy to do when carrying on a conversation at the same time. This was part of the difficulty: at a certain age, when you felt a hot flash coming on, it was better to be alone to ride it out.

"Jake, let me ask you something. In a whole town full of houses, plenty of places to put people, plenty of people in need of housing—old people, young kids, people who can't get around well and who can't sleep on floors—which, by the way, this bunch can do comfortably, thank you very much—why do I have a house full of monks?"

"It seems a good placement to me," Jake said fairly. "They don't seem demanding. In fact, from what you say, they're a big help. They support each other. We wanted to keep them together, and you've got space to allow for that. Taking it all into account, the River Place thought it would be a good match."

"You mean Coral Lane thought that, don't you?" Piper could feel the washes of heat start up her body. "Don't you see what a meddler she is? She cloaks it in that goody-good routine but how good do you think she is? Did she think that she could take my husband and make it up with monks?"

"Did she take Dan, Piper?"

"She did—you know she did! You were there, you saw it happen. Little Coral Lane and how she admires the big smart man with his scary theories. And isn't she such a giving person, looking out for all those kids at the River Place, and isn't Dan such a help, giving the boys a role model? And doesn't she love Molly, aren't they like sisters, the two of them? Heads together, giggling over clothes and boys, and Molly in and out of the River Place at all hours?" Piper got up and began to pace agitatedly. "I mean who does that? What kind of person uses a child to get to the parent, to destroy a parent's marriage? And next thing you know Dan has blundered into her web and oops! He is snared."

"If by 'oops,' you mean Donny, I sometimes think you love him as much as his own parents do. It's an inspiration to see how something as shattered as your marriage can be re-formed into something so strong and positive."

"Ask Coral about the influence I've been on Donny—her going on and on about that toy gun I gave him. And trying to pin his tumble off that ladder on me! Anyway, Donny's a child, you can't blame him. It isn't his fault; he didn't do anything. His mother did. And now she won't leave me alone. And you—you're taking her side." Piper sat down, stood up, sat down. Breathe, she told herself. Just breathe. She drew her breath, let it out. She could get through this. She could.

"I'm on your side, Piper. You know I am," Jake said. "But I think you are allowing yourself to blame Coral because it's easier than blaming the person you're really angry at."

"I am *not* angry at Dan. We run the magazine together. We are raising a daughter together. Or trying to—because Coral Lane can't keep her hands off that either, can she? Why does she have to try to parent Molly? Giving her advice on growing up, telling her to be there for dinner, telling her to come 'home' to bed! And wheedling Dan to let her help with the magazine—who does she think she is? She won't leave *anything* alone that's mine. And Dan is...he's *leadable,* and Coral Lane turned out to be better at *leading* him—"

And here it was, rising inside her, the white-hot searing anger, the sheer rage and powerlessness and, yes, fear too—fear of what might happen, fear of it all falling apart, fear of herself, even, if she were to give in to it. Jake stood up. She fended him off, palm upraised.

"It's OK," she managed. "Hot flash. Give me a minute."

"A hot flash?"

Piper gripped the arm of her chair. "It helps if I...breathe." She closed her eyes, breathed; Jake waited, quiet and still.

Her hot flash receding, Piper opened her eyes. "See? All better," she said brightly. "They come, they go."

"Since..."

"Oh! I don't know. A while, I guess. It's my age...it's a woman thing..."

Jake was shaking his head. "It's not your age. You're too young for hot flashes."

"How would you know?" Piper cried. "You've never had one. You're not a woman."

"You don't have to be a woman to understand your problem."

"What are you saying?"

"I'm saying plenty of men feel fearful and panicky."

As if in confirmation of what Jake was saying, a new kind of dread started creeping up Piper's spine. "It could be hot flashes," she insisted. "Sometimes women my age get them."

"Whether it's possible or not isn't the point, because you aren't having them." Jake sat down again, leaning forward to meet Piper's eyes. "What you are having," he said gently, "are anxiety attacks."

"And doesn't that put the icing on the cake," Piper said, sagging back and closing her eyes wearily.

* * *

Jake had left. Piper was still in her office, alone. The light was gone, the room dark and cold.

Her phone beeped: a text from Cassie. "Camomile tea? Gr8 4 sleeping." A coincidence? Or had Jake, on his way out, asked Cassie to bring her a hot drink?

Whatever. Piper wanted to say goodbye to Donny and kiss him goodnight. She texted back: "Be right there."

Downstairs, Donny was careening toward out-of-control. The center of attention, a half dozen pairs of eyes on him, he was waving his six-shooter screaming, "Bang bang!"

"Give that gun to me, Donny," Molly demanded. He threw it at her and started to whirl around, peeling off layers of clothes and leaving them scattered on the floor.

"Donny, come on. Mommy wants you back home." Molly's voice was becoming sharp. "Get over here this instant or no Hadley House tomorrow."

Donny tore past, shedding clothes. "Bath! Bath!" he cried.

"No, Donny, there's no hot water. Stop—it's too cold to take off your clothes. Donny, *put your clothes back on!*"

Donny, stripped to his undies, slipped through her reaching hands, laughing, and ran out of the room; a moment later he came zooming back in, stark naked, shrieking in the cold. Molly tried to head him off but he evaded her easily.

Silas and Colby stood watching, both apparently waiting for Molly. Colby looked amused, Silas nonchalant. Molly stamped her foot. "Donny, stop it!" she screamed as Donny streaked by.

Silas glanced at her, then moved into Donny's path. Donny came tearing toward him, swerved to avoid him. Silas put out an arm and snagged him around the waist, lifting him from the floor where he hung, naked, feet peddling frantically, little fists pummeling air.

Donny's shrieks of laughter turned into screams of protest; he writhed and kicked, sobbing loudly. Lisette hurried over. "Donny, would you like to try on a little robe, like ours?" she asked.

Donny nodded, fisting his eyes. Lisette fitted a pair of white drawstring pants over his feet and pulled them up while he hung, now unresisting, in the crook of Silas' arm. Cassie brought over a little white tunic. "Arms up," she said, and he obediently put up his arms so she could pull it over his head. "Lisette made them for you, Donny," Cassie said. "She finished them today."

"Nick of time," said Colby.

"Mini monk," said Silas.

"Want to wear them home?" asked Lisette. Donny nodded.

"Blanket," said Silas. Piper wrapped a shawl warmly around Donny, murmuring "'Night, baby. See you tomorrow."

Donny didn't reply. He was beginning to go glassy-eyed. In a moment he was slumped, limp, over Silas' shoulder, eyes closed, mouth open.

"You'll carry him home, Si?" Molly asked.

"Sure thing," Silas assented.

"I can carry him," Colby offered. "Didn't you want to stay to meet with Piper, Silas?"

"Tomorrow," said Piper.

"Dude's down for the count," said Silas.

"You can come, too," said Molly, reaching for her coat and starting out after Silas.

Colby hesitated, then followed them out.

November 10: Becoming the Change

It's cold this morning, very cold. I shiver over my blog and await with impatience Dan's arrival to start the generator and warm us up. Do you know, Riverboro, that over 100,000 people have been without power in New Hampshire this past week? Teams have come in from Florida, North Carolina, and even Canada to repair the lines. I think it's clear that Riverboro has not been the priority—not that we complain! We know we're small and out of the way. We're grateful for whatever help can be spared.

If you stop by the River Place, you will find the guests that were ousted from the Cutty Sark Hotel. They sleep in bedrolls on the floor. Guests and staff line up for food and bump shoulders waiting for the bathroom. We are all doing our part for our town.

Yesterday we did see some men here on Hadley Street, up in the utility poles fixing the wires. Molly took them muffins and a thermos of coffee. They said that people give them things to eat all day, wherever they are working, but they accepted gratefully anyway, and asked which was our house, and promised to do all they could to get us our power as quickly as possible.

People can be good to one another.

Few people are as good to me as Jake. He was here yesterday, full of (unnecessary) concern. He's worried I'm overworking myself with these early-morning blog posts, in addition to the magazine. I told him I was never better, but he wants me to make some changes in my routine. So unnecessary! But he pressed and I acquiesced. Nothing he wants me to do can *hurt*, and in fact they sound like great prescriptions for everybody.

So, Riverboro, let's get on a health kick and change our lives together. I pledge to adopt strong measures and you must too. Go to our Facebook page and sign the pledge, then check in now and then to let us know how you're doing. Here's what we need to do:

Piper's List: Top Five Jake-Mandated Lifestyle Changes for Us All

5) *Sleep more.* That means go to bed before ten, Riverboro. I'll bet with this power outage most of us are doing that anyway.

4) *Exercise more.* Half hour a day is good, plus maybe some yoga. A walk is best. That is no problem for me. I use a treadmill on the days I can't get out, but if you don't have one and the weather prevents you from leaving the house (as it has all of us, I imagine, these last few days), going up and down stairs or doing some vigorous housework is helpful.

3) *Cut down on the caffeine.* That's harsh—very harsh. You have to have something to live for! Even Molly, who isn't a fellow addict, says that caffeine is an almost religious part of November Lies. But, Riverboro, here are some inspirational words for you: I'm going to make a permanent switch to decaf after noon. If I can, you can.

2) *Pay attention to what you need.* At least that's what Jake says—but I question the wisdom of this. I have my doubts about the entire concept. We all pay attention to what we need, don't we? It seems to me that focusing on what we need is what gets us to the place we are now—that same place we want to get out of.

Plus, we can't always get what we need, can we? Sometimes what we need depends on other people. And if you can't get it, that thing that you need, because it is in the power of another person, and that person can't or won't give it to you, then what good is paying attention to it? No good, is what I say. The more you pay attention to it the more stressed out you are likely to become. Why upset yourself, thinking constantly about what you need? So I say: pay no attention to what you think you need, or feel you need! Forget about it! Lose yourself in work!

But Jake says it's important to take a break from work now and then, to stretch or get some fresh air or take a long, hot bath (when you have hot water, which we don't), or pamper yourself in some way. Even if, like me, you are happiest when you are working, producing, accomplishing, you still have to stop from time to time. So I'm going to change Jake's "pay attention to what you need" to:

1) *Take breaks from time to time and do something different.* And I will do that, and so will you.

Now how about this: suppose we all do this together as a pre-New-Year's resolution, and on New Year's get together on Facebook and compare notes on how it improved (or worsened) the holiday season? Give me your thoughts on this—do we start this program now or later?

Tags: New Hampshire power failure, tips to survive the holiday season, New Year's resolutions

COMMENTS:

TheGeekster: I resolve to find out who the Weather Oracle is. Ideas, anyone?

DrewHadley: I asked my dad, and he said it's not him. But I can't always tell if he's telling the truth, lol.

AuntieP: Of course Andy's the Oracle. It's obvious. And I can't face taking on all those resolutions now. The attention and the breaks sound OK, but the rest of them? I'll do them, but after the New Year.

ConArtist: I stand with Dr. Jake. Do it now.

RiverCoral: Piper, if Jake says start now, you've got to start now. I'll start too and post on your Facebook page! ☺

DanTheRiverMan: What's all this about starting after the New Year? We're starting now. This morning I'll get the half-caf at King's.

PipersPebbles: Then make sure you get twice as much.

SamKing: Today we have Frosted Gingerbread Latte. I'll have two extra-large half-cafs ready when you come.

ImmaterialGirl: I think I do all that stuff already. What should I do?

PipersPebbles: Have you been to the doctor? They might want to put you on pre-natal vitamins.

ImmaterialGirl: I mean on the Facebook page.

PipersPebbles: Let us know how your pregnancy is going and post pictures when the baby comes.

ImmaterialGirl: Thanks! By the way, Dr. Jake is cute. Is he your boy-friend?

PipersPebbles: Any romance you will find here in this blog will be with the true love of my life: *Riverboro Rocks*.

(Comments approved)

* * *

"I don't think I'll ever get warm," Molly said. "My *bones* are cold."

"At least we have the fire," Piper pointed out. "You don't have one at your dad's house."

"But that house is smaller. It doesn't take much to warm it up." Molly crouched next to the fire, sweatshirt hood pulled over her head, clutching Donny for warmth. "And it has better insulation."

"Should you and Donny have stayed there this evening?" Piper worried. "I don't want you getting sick."

"Mom, the cold won't make us sick. We wanted to hang with you."

"We've got earmuffs in the mudroom," Piper said. "Let's find a pair for Donny. Did you put on your long underwear?"

"We never take it off. Anyway, Mom, don't worry. It isn't your fault this house is big and drafty."

"This power outage can't go on forever," Piper soothed.

"Your lips to God's ears," Leon said. He was standing with the other monks. Piper thought they looked rather like penguins in Antarctica, clustered together for warmth. They all were looking in one direction—toward the kitchen, from whence would come the first sounds of the generator.

When the familiar roar came, the huddle of monks broke. Cassie and Lisette each put an arm around Ananda and started with her up the stairs toward the second floor bathroom. Pasco and Brumi made a break for the first floor bathroom, but Leon flung out an arm to stop them. "Ladies first," he said, gesturing to Molly.

Molly stood up. "That's OK, I'll go up to third floor," she said. "I have got to wash my hair or I will pull it out by the roots."

Cassie ran back down the stairs. "I'll take Donny," she said. "We'll change his bandage and get him in his pjs."

As Molly started for the stairs, Pasco and Brumi bolted for the first floor bathroom. Pasco shouted, "Dibs!"

Brumi grabbed his shoulder and pulled him back. "No way, you got dibs last time."

Pasco shook him off; the two careened toward the bathroom and collided at the door. There was a brief scuffle as each tried to heave the other out of the way to get in first. Leon caught Piper's eye and smiled. "Watch this," he said. He walked past the young men into the bathroom and closed the door.

Later, in the kitchen, with the generator humming in the background, Dan dealt Scrabble tiles to Piper, Silas, Pasco, Cassie, and Molly. Coral was giving a class for parents this evening, as she did many evenings—so here, once again, were her husband and child with the ex-and step-family. It was ironic, one of many ironies in a situation that, Piper thought, looped like the river through their valley in a twisted flow of interwoven paradoxes.

Pasco and Molly had agreed to play as a team, so Silas turned to Cassie for a partner. That left Dan and Piper to team up. "Which," Dan said, "is hardly fair, as we're the megagaltasts of the group."

"What's a megagaltast?" asked Cassie.

"Don't give him the satisfaction of asking," Molly warned.

"Someone who makes up words," said Silas. "Like he just did. I call shenanigans"

Piper glanced over to catch Dan's eye. "That's not how you use 'shenanigans'," they said together.

"Not an auspicious start for a Scrabble game," Piper teased, laughing happily.

"Big words can backfire," said Pasco, stacking his tiles. "Go for little words with lots of points."

"That's true, you can't squander points for an impressive word," said Cassie. "Not when you're playing for bathroom minutes."

"Too much to lose," agreed Molly.

So many great moments to record in her blog. *As Dan says, we're the megagaltasts, he and I,* she would say. *But the monks know that simplicity brings the results.*

"Bring it," said Silas.

"Silas seems to think I never leave my office," Piper said, buoyant from her moment of synchronicity with Dan. "He thinks I do nothing but work."

She caught a glance pass between Molly and Dan but ignored it and went blithely on. "Like Eloise, I am apt to be on any floor at any time, here at the house. For example, here we are now, all together. You see, Silas, you aren't here all the time, and just because I've had to work through dinner quite a lot lately doesn't mean I have set times for coming and going."

Silas looked up from his tiles. "Nothing wrong with a schedule," he said helpfully. "What are we using for a ref?"

"Reference or referee?" asked Pasco.

"In this case, one and the same," said Dan. "I like the OED."

"Oxford English Dictionary," Piper put in. "For you Scrabble newbies."

"Dad, ours is so old," said Molly. "Too many words have been invented since they wrote it."

"Which is why we're using a dictionary," Dan said. "We want to weed out the riffraff of common usage."

"Is 'riffraff' a common-usage word?" asked Pasco.

"Is that like a common-law wife?" added Cassie.

"I always feel comfortable," said Piper, continuing to pursue her point. "In or out, here or there. Also, I am the eyes and ears of the town." She drew a tile and glanced at it. "B. Low tile. We go first."

Molly murmured, "Mm hmm," and kept her eyes on her tiles.

"And speaking of eyes and ears," Piper continued, "has anyone heard that noise at night? Kind of a creeping, scratching...as if someone is trying to get in?"

"Raccoons?" Cassie suggested, and Pasco added, "A bear?"

"Brumi?" Molly said, adding, in the beat that followed, "I mean, I thought it was Brumi—"

"That one time it was Brumi," said Piper. "We still have the noise."

"Libations," Dan said. "For us, that is. In keeping with our resolutions, herbal tea for all." He stood up to make the tea but paused to point at their Scrabble tiles. "Seven letters. Fifty bonus points."

"I saw it," said Piper. She arranged the tiles on the board. "H-i-r-s-u-t-e: hirsute."

"Shenanigans," said Silas.

"Challenge," said Pasco.

"Pasco, never challenge my dad," Molly said. "He's always right. He knows all the words."

"Those types get overconfident and start making up words," said Pasco. "They know no one will challenge them."

"You challenge, then?" said Cassie, a challenge in her own voice.

"Nope," said Pasco. "I can see by the look on your face you know what that word means."

Cassie answered, her voice bubbling with innocent triumph. "It means 'hairy.'"

"Come on, Cass, how do you know that?" Pasco protested.

"I looked it up," Cassie replied with satisfaction. "When we shaved our heads, I went to a thesaurus and looked up words for 'hairy' and 'bald,' and I learned them all so I'd have lots of intelligent things to say." She beamed at the group. "I *knew* it would come in handy."

Silas rubbed the tattoo inked on his shaved scalp. "Handy for non-monks, too."

"But more for monks," Pasco said. "People think we wear hair *shirts* but those of us who are really dedicated go for the entire hair *suit*."

"*Hir*sute," Cassie corrected him.

"The *her* suits are for the lady monks," Pasco shot back.

"You gotta take a break now and then," Silas said, tilting his chair back and stretching out his legs. "Get out. Breathe the air. Even Dr. Jake says so."

Piper said sharply, "He said that? To you? When?"

Silas glanced at her, eyebrows raised. "To you. Your blog? You mentioned it."

Piper exhaled. "That's right. I did. And here we all are, taking a break. Isn't it fun?"

"Very nice indeed," Dan said heartily. He had filled the kettle at the sink (such a luxury), and now he was re-filling the plastic jugs they were using for water storage.

Molly murmured, "I need a 'g'."

"We've got one," Silas offered. "We'll trade, won't we, Cass?"

"Sure, if they've got a 'j'."

"Collusion between teams is not permitted," Dan said. "Ginger or orange tea?"

"Ginger for me," said Silas. "I don't see you around town that much, do I, Ms. H?"

"I'm apt to be anywhere at any time," Piper repeated coolly. Why wouldn't Silas let this go? And why had she started this stupid line of conversation, anyway? She jotted down her score and drew seven new tiles.

"You know that in today's virtual world our readers do a lot of reporting for us, and I take the bird's-eye view. But for the really important things, there can be no substitute for feet on the ground. For example, when they had that fire at the middle school, I made it a point to get down there to check it out myself."

There were a few beats of somewhat-echoing silence. Then Molly said, "Mom, that was over three years ago. *I* was in middle school then!"

"Oh! Well. It was just an example. A time an editor might want to get out and check out a situation personally. That kind of thing," Piper continued airily, "happens more often than you might think."

Molly's eyes met her father's again. Silas watched speculatively.

Cassie said, "Is 'fuddy' a word? Like in 'fuddy duddy'?"

"Do you want to play it?" Dan said. "If someone chooses to challenge, the OED has the final say."

"Would 'fuddy' be the adjective for 'duddy'?" Molly asked. "As in: he is a hirsute fuddy duddy?"

"Is hair suit fuddy duddy another word for monk?" Pasco asked.

Molly broke into a laugh. "I thought monks were supposed to be cool."

"Cool doesn't begin to cover it," Pasco said. "Freezing, more likely. It's why we need hair suits—the zombie version of long underwear."

"Now we're zombies again?" Cassie asked.

"Who, us?" Pasco said. "Completely chill. Not of this world. A witness to life. What does that sound like to you?"

"Zen zombies. Blood dripping from their teeth," said Silas. "Don't play fuddy, Cass. These brain eaters will go for you. Play 'fudge'. Here, on the 'e' from hirsute."

"There goes our 'g', Molly," said Pasco. "Silas gives with one hand and takes with the other. Anything for our Molly—unless points at Scrabble are involved. He doesn't even need to scrabble for bathroom minutes with the rest of us. Sad. Just sad."

Silas made a rude gesture and reached to pick up his tiles.

Cassie said, "Is 'anile' a word?"

Pasco said, "What's anile?"

Molly said, "It's a fuddy kind of fish."

Silas was arranging his tiles. "So Ms. H, you get out every day?"

Piper forced a laugh. She was starting to feel prickles in the back of her neck. Not a good sign. "Not every day. Guilty as charged. Who does? There are always those days when one is too busy, or lets time slip by, or the weather is too discouraging."

Silas responded with a non-committal "Mmph," and Piper continued more rapidly, "Don't you find that to be true, Silas? With your job here you have to be out and about weekdays, but don't you sometimes find on a weekend you get caught up in a book or the TV or a videogame and it's evening before you know it?"

"I suppose," said Silas.

Piper's face was beginning to get hot; she was starting to get that queasy feeling in her stomach. She rubbed her hands on her sweatpants, focusing her attention on the Scrabble board.

Molly said, "Si, you should think of a project for the Lies. Jacques says we need every voice."

"I'm more of a man of action..." said Silas.

"We have plenty of guys in the group," Cassie said, flashing her mischievous smile. "Pasco, Brumi, Peter. And, of course, Colby..."

"...but I'll join," Silas finished firmly.

"We knew you'd see its value," Cassie said, her smile bubbling into laughter. Silas turned red.

Molly, who'd also turned pink, was trying not to join in, but Cassie's laughter was contagious. Soon one of those random fits of hilarity (all out of proportion, Piper thought, to the meager humor in the conversation) was sweeping the room. Molly and Cassie leaned into one another, giggling. When they recovered (still regressing into sporadic giggles) the conversation turned to flash mobs, and Molly's party, and tips for keeping warm. Dan handed round the herbal tea and resumed his place at the table. Donny, who'd been sleeping in the next room, came in, wearing earmuffs and rubbing at the bandage over his eye. He climbed onto Piper's lap and leaned against her shoulder, letting his eyes droop closed, and Piper put her arms around him and leaned her cheek on his head and closed her own eyes and breathed. Just breathed.

"Yep," said Pasco, "a lot of fuddy things can happen in this game we call Scrabble."

November 11: To Light a Single Candle

Riverboro is coming alight at last. The power hasn't come on all at once, but in sections, like a giant ballpark: up by the bowling alley, over around the elementary school, north to the middle and high schools, and in the center of town, Main Street and the depot, lights have flashed on. Here at *Riverboro Rocks*, we're still on generator power. Molly has been told by friendly utility workers that our placement high on the hill, with a separate line running to us, has created difficulties. It is the tenth day.

The floodwaters have mostly receded, but the damage is so great in some of the buildings that it will take time to make them habitable again. The buildings so damaged include (but are not limited to) King's Market, the Cutty Sark Hotel, and (wouldn't ya know) the Ashram.

So the monks are still here with us, one big happy family. We have grown almost military with our schedules. Our timetables are posted all over the house: in bedrooms, in the kitchen, on the bathroom doorways. Bathroom time has become the currency of the day, and almost anything is eligible for bartering.

Cassie made an apple pie the other day, with local apples. She timed it so she could have it in the oven and do the washing up while the generator ran. That meant it came out of the oven in the late afternoon, well after lunch and before the monks' afternoon prayers. She waited until the apple-cinnamon smell had permeated the house and our monks were starving, crowded into the kitchen, begging for a slice, and then what did she do? She told that group that no one would get so much as a taste unless they traded in some of their afternoon bathroom time. Five afternoon minutes for a piece of pie!

By that time, even a monk would sell his soul for a piece of that pie. And when she had collected half an hour of bathroom time, you know what she did? She gave it to Ananda! For a bath. She went in there and ran a bath (she used up all the water in the hot water heater, but she had cleared that as part of the barter), and she dumped in some lovely aroma oils and she led Ananda to the bathroom and presented it to her. Ananda cried, she was so touched.

Bathroom minutes are used as points in games and winnings in wagers. Pasco bet Brumi that he could get every single person in the house, separately, to laugh at a joke before Brumi could, and of course he won easily—Brumi is, after all, not that funny. And so Pasco got a nice long shower that morning and Brumi couldn't shave at all. And last night for Scrabble? When Pasco and Molly came in ahead of Silas and Cassie (of course Dan and I won the game), Pasco cashed in on further bathroom minutes, which he very generously presented his teammate. Molly didn't need them, as she can shower and wash her hair at her Dad's house. Cassie begged for those minutes, but Pasco said she would have to come up with something worth trading, and she said he should wait, she'd show him.

She and Pasco are two imps, full of mischief and humor. Last night they were challenging our very speech as if it were part of our Scrabble game. Scrabble games lead inevitably to wordplay, and Dan loves to flex his language muscle as an athlete loves to train. He started accusing the group of indulging in meretricious persiflage, and I replied, 'It might be persiflage but it is anything but meretricious.' Then Pasco said "Challenge," as if we had played a word, and we laughed until we were giddy.

Of the group only Dan and I know the source of this quote, and it is one of those inside jokes that people like us, who share a history and a magazine, will always share. The very-literate followers of this blog know whom he was quoting; and if among my readers there are any so busy doing good that they can't find time to open a book, it's DH Lawrence, *Women in Love*. If you haven't read it I recommend it; and in fact, Riverboro, what do you think of starting a book group online?

To learn to read, said Victor Hugo, is to light a fire, with every syllable a spark. Here in the November in our town, so dark so much of the month, we need light both literal and metaphorical. We have crews working night and day to get us our literal light; and for the lamp of the soul, the light of knowledge, the fire of reading (and so on), let us Read a Book. Or perhaps, like us, your actual lights are still not on? If your candles cast insufficient light for extended reading, if your generator is only on for an hour or two a day, if your e-reader battery life is short, let us share something brief but brilliant—a short story, an essay, a poem.

We'll start with those of us who gather here. Our numbers grow by the day—can you believe that there were over fifty of us yesterday? Fifty people dropping by my blog (and most of you are local, according to Google Analytics). And each of us will suggest a work of genius to read, and we'll share our thoughts

All I know to do, said Mr. Rogers (he of the Neighborhood) is to light the candle that has been given me. So let us open our books and light our candles and post on our blogs, and in this way winter will pass and spring will come.

Piper's List: Five Long-Form Suggestions for our Book Group

5) *Women in Love* (DH Lawrence) For those of us who love meretricious persiflage.

4) *Moby Dick* (Herman Melville) Because I love Ishmael and the November in his soul.

3) *A Study in Scarlet* (Sir Arthur Conan Doyle) Introducing Sherlock Holmes and written in only three weeks, an inspiration to our November Liars, who are trying to create something very great in a very short time.

2) *Peyton Place* (Grace Metalious) The goings-on, both licit and illicit, in a small New Hampshire town.

1) *The Da Vinci Code* (Dan Brown) Written by a New Hampshire native who made good. Perhaps some day he'll do a mystery for us—the Riverboro Code?

Idea for today: Riverboro Reads—a forum for us to discuss the great books we're reading and post suggestions for new ones.

Tags: Great books; great authors, Victor Hugo, DH Lawrence, Mr. Rogers' Neighborhood, Herman Melville.

COMMENTS:

BookLover603: I vote brief but brilliant, since our light is limited... *The Old Man and the Sea*, or *Catcher in the Rye*...or maybe a book of poetry...

RiverCoral: Piper, I know that *Women in Love* was a standard back when you went to college, but no one in my generation reads DH Lawrence. I'm in though if we start with Peyton Place. ☺

MollyHH: I can't start reading till December, I'm too busy with the party. And if we're going to read Lawrence can we do *Lady Chatterley's Lover*?

ConArtist: Does it count if we saw the movie?

BookLover603: I came by the barn with some paperbacks to do-nate...there was a guy in tweed with elbow patches...was it Harvard Prof? I wanted to say hello but came all over shy...

TheGeekster: Was he hot?

DrewHadley: Hey Geekster, guys don't ask if other guys are hot, lol. Auntie Piper, tell the Geekster to keep it G-rated, lol.

BookLover603: Remember your social skills, Geekster...but he was pretty cute. If I were a few decades older I might go for the type... love the elbow patches...pure vintage. I was the strawberry blonde in skinny jeans and clonky workboots with the big pile of paperbacks...

ConArtist: Megatons of donations coming in.

AuntieP: I saw that, too. Piper, if you are trying to get rid of stuff this barn sale might not be the best way of doing it. It's a magnet for all the unwanted items in this town. Not that we don't thank you for the paperbacks, Book Lover. I was there with Harvard Prof, taking inven-tory, though you say nothing about seeing me, and I didn't see you. People kept coming up the road with boxes of stuff. It will take hours to sort through it all.

MollyHH: I saw a rusty kid's bike, an aquarium with a crack running through it, a bent birdcage, some random croquet mallets, a box filled with what looked like the t-shirts of the entire Riverboro High wrestling team of 1988, and a Viking-style helmet. Plus costumes from the performance of Peter Pan that the River Place put on when they were trying to get that drama group off the ground, and a half set of chipped china plates. Next thing someone's sure to drop off a box of String Too Short To Save.

RiverCoral: Those costumes will be perfect for some family's dress-up box. ☺

AuntieP: And the birdcage is a one of a kind, all you have to do is straighten out the sides.

PipersPebbles: Auntie P, you can't have dropped off that old birdcage—your cockatiel died in it. And Coral, you've been trying to talk the River Place parents into taking those Peter Pan costumes off your hands for months.

DanTheRiverMan: Well, as you say, Piper, beggars can't be choosers. That Viking helmet was part of an initiation ceremony for a frat at Dartmouth. It's got some history.

ZombiePatrol: A good helmet could keep the zombies from getting to your brains.

TheGeekster: Maybe with all those donations there's some other stuff that helps with zombies, too. The mallets, maybe? For zombie croquet?

ZombiePatrol: I hear zombie heads make great croquet balls.

WeatherOracle: After the sales and celebrations,
                   The bargains, steals, well-meant donations,
                   The gimcracks, knickknacks, bric-a-bracs
                   That stop the zombies in their tracks
                   We must re-enter night's dark portal
                   Remembering we're merely mortal.

ImmaterialGirl: Are we merely mortal? Or are we more than merely?

HarvardProf: When you speak about night's dark portal, are we to take that literally or metaphorically?

WeatherOracle: If weather could be metaphorical
                   Where would that leave your Weather Oracle?

ConArtist: This barn sale sounds intense.

Private Message from DanTheRiverMan: Piper, some of these Weather Oracle predictions verge on terrifying. The Oracle isn't Auntie P, is it? She likes to play the dear old lady, but you know that what she's really after is to stir things up.

Private Message to DanTheRiverMan: You've got her right—she's Auntie Polly with a capital P that rhymes with T that stands for Trouble.

Private Message from DanTheRiverMan: Kind of like her niece, you think?

RiverCoral: School starts again on Monday. Enjoy the weekend! ☺

PipersPebbles: And I hope to see all of you at the barn sale. Remember, we still don't have power, so visit the bathroom before you come.

(*Comments approved*)

* * *

"I can't wait for the power to come back on," said Molly, gathering her dark glossy hair into a handful and twisting it into a knot at the top of her head. She was wearing her sweats, her only adornment a pair of vintage earrings she'd picked up at a thrift store. "I hope those linemen outside have good news."

There were men in electric company uniforms out on the street, up in the wires. Brumi, at Molly's direction, had gone out to take them cookies and get the news.

"I don't know," Piper answered, reaching up and bending down in a series of flexes. "It's inconvenient not having the treadmill, but in some ways it's been fun." She windmilled her arms and went into a set of jumping jacks. "On the other hand, that barn sale doesn't seem to be going according to plan. All day long people come tramping up the street to leave things in the barn. I see them from my office window, going past with bags and boxes—one guy was even pushing a load in a wheelbarrow. They look like refugees in reverse. Some look positively furtive."

"But people like big barn sales, don't they?"

"Let's hope so. The junk is flooding in like water into the ashram. Coral Lane and her Peter Pan costumes—can you believe her? That comment about me being the older generation?"

"Mom, please." On the rug in front of the fire, Molly was mirroring her mother's jumping jacks. "You take swipes at her every day in that blog."

"I've only been a little playful," Piper protested.

"You've been trying to get a rise out of her. You should be happy you succeeded at last."

"At last? The blog has been up less than two weeks." Piper allowed herself a satisfied smile.

They were all in the living room together—Molly, Piper, and (Piper did the head count) five monks. Pasco and Cassie sprawled like puppies on the floor. Leon and Lisette sat decorously upon the sofa as befitted their advanced years. Ananda, swathed in blankets against the chill air, had the big chair near the fire, a purring Sasha on her lap. Woman and cat looked snug and contented. When Ananda said, "I think in some ways this is how people should live," Piper gave a "mmph" of surprise.

The thing was, Ananda wasn't around much. On a day-to-day basis, the six monks were rarely in the same place at the same time, although a changing few of them always seemed to be around. In the swirling mix of monks, you could easily lose track of which monks you'd seen and which ones you hadn't. Pasco and Cassie were around a lot; clearly social creatures, they were often in the living room or kitchen or wherever people gathered. Piper still thought that something (what?) was going on between the two of them. Or was it Molly Pasco had his eye on? There seemed something very un-monk-like in the way he related to people, especially to women. But Ananda was usually invisible. Off by herself praying or chanting or reading sacred texts, presumably—so young, yet so devoted to her practice. Not usually in their midst, participating in conversation.

"Simplicity?" Molly suggested helpfully.

Ananda considered. "There's something very communal about it, the way we all help each other. It's like the Ashram in that way but even better. The way we have to change our routines to deal with the outage makes it special."

"Festive," said Pasco.

"That's it!" said Cassie. "Like a party! Like a long-term sleepover."

"I like the way the cold brings my mom out of her office," said Molly. "Like a chipmunk from its hole in the ground."

Piper laughed. "That's a good image, Molly."

"You're welcome to it," Molly said generously. "Use it in your blog."

"Today is Friday," said Ananda. "We came last Saturday. We've been here a week."

Lisette got off the sofa to join Molly and Piper in their toe touches, long underwear peeking from beneath her robes at her wrists and ankles, grunting as she bent and stretched but surprisingly limber for her age. Molly and Piper started to jog in place. Molly began to hum and Piper picked up the tune—an old jukebox favorite of Molly's. They started to sing: "Well, she *got* her daddy's car and she's cruising through the hamburger *stand* now…"

"I love this one!" Cassie exclaimed, and jumped up to jog in place and sing with them: "Seems she *forgot* all *about* the *library* like she told her old man now…" Lisette lifted her slippered feet one after the other, pushing them out in front of her in little kicks, her ankle bells jingling. Pasco sprang up to strum an imaginary guitar, rocking around the living room as if on stage.

"Is there no end to your talents?" Molly asked.

"Hey, air guitar is the best exercise there is," said Pasco. "Works every muscle in your body."

Cassie pantomimed a drumroll and started to march; the others fell into step behind her, a parade of people playing imaginary flutes, recorders, maracas, singing, "she'll have fun, fun, fun…"

"Look at you all," said Ananda. "This has been one of the best weeks of my life."

"I know what you mean," agreed Molly, in complete disregard of her own earlier statement. "I could go on like this forever. I don't really care if the power ever comes back on."

"That's exactly how I feel," managed Lisette, shaking and slapping an imaginary tambourine and gasping from the exertion.

"Nor I," said Piper.

"Me too," said Pasco.

At that moment—because Nature will have its jokes—Brumi came into the room, followed by Silas.

Silas took in the scene and said, "Whoa. Flash mob. Practicing for Japan?"

And Brumi said, "Good news from electric."

And a moment later, as if to finish his sentence, there was a dinging sound—a clock resetting itself—and the lights blazed on in the living room.

And wouldn't you know? Pasco and Leon and Cassie and Lisette and Molly and Piper broke into cheers and applause and began dancing around shouting "Hurray!" and "The lights are on!" and hugging one another, while Ananda sat in the chair and laughed and clapped.

PART 2

THINGS HIDDEN AND REVEALED

Damn Lies
By Presidential Candidate and TV Personality
Jacques Marquand

Was there ever a cause more *celebre* than I? The cable TV version of my internationally-acclaimed *vox* of the *populi*, which you are presently perusing, has been scouted for syndication by Campaign Only Network (C.O.N.). The C.O.N. producers, those Souls that Try Men's Times, have tapped me to host the coveted pre-prime time (or post-daytime-TV) slot. So gather round, children, every day at 5 pm, and together we will foment a fantastic and fantastical future. We will purge our patrimony of pusillanimous parasites. We will think the unthinkable, conceive the inconceivable, elucidate the ineluctable, and cognize the incognito. We will examine events great and small. We will find meaning in the meaningless and meaninglessness in meaning. Wherever chaos is brewing or a butterfly is flapping its wings, our reporters will be there. I will make or break kings or princes on one day and be a king or prince or president of this great land on another. Liars, Do-Gooders, and Suck-Ups, reconcile yourself to a life lived in the limelight. Learn to accept, as I have, the plaudits of a grateful nation. And watch me on TV.

November 12: The Monks' Plot Thickens

Today brings a big plot twist, an enormous revelation—a revelation that came as a direct result of our power coming back on.

Here at the *Riverboro Rocks* HQ, we are widely agreed that the power outage was good for us, bringing us face to face with our true selves in an existential way and all that. Still, it's hard to regret the return of what I have lately concluded is the greatest convenience of modern civilization.

EXCEPT. The return of our power led to conversations with the monks about the longevity of our arrangement (short and expected to end any day, except that their building is badly water damaged, and what to do? They have, apparently, nowhere else to go); and there were parlays and powwows among the houseguests, who now appear to believe that they should be thinking in a longer-term way about their current stay with me, as even with the power on they can't find a way to move back home as yet. And the upshot is: my humble Hadley House is to remain their temporary residence and they want to reshuffle their living arrangements like a deck of playing cards. They want to move out on their current roommates and move in with new ones: Pasco wants to room with Cassie, Brumi wants to co-habit with Ananda, and Leon wants to move in with Lisette.

The reason being: *they are all married*. To each other! In the configurations that I have outlined. Everything I believed I knew about these monks is crumbling and right now they are down there moving furniture around and whistling while they work.

Even more shocking (to me) is this: the venerable Leon and Lisette have been married only four years. I got the story out of them yesterday afternoon, and I count myself remiss not to have done so sooner.

Leon, the man I had identified as the archetypal Buddha (as he looks both merry and serene), has only been a part of this community for the past four years. He used to work as a homebuilder in Vermont with a crew of men, and on that same team of homebuilding men was another future monk—our own Brumi. These anchorites-to-be were living the life of independent carpenters: spending their days on-site, stopping at the end of the day for a few beers, watching sports on TV, going fishing, visiting the bars on weekends. Not dissolute, but neither was their lifestyle particularly spiritual.

Brumi was dissatisfied. He was looking for a deep and permanent change. So he started attending the séances, or the covens, or whatever they hold, at his local ashram. There he was initiated into whatever mysterious esoteric rites they practice. And there he met the angelic Ananda.

Ananda, luminescent and lovely, had grown up in that community. That's right—she was born there and raised there and educated there. I *knew* she was special. What must it be like to be Ananda? Does she perceive herself as an impulse of the Divine, a glint on a wave on a vast ocean of Being? Does the life around her appear as insubstantial, as evanescent as gossamer veils tossed over an unchanging, absolute Reality? Is her world, in short, that dome of many-colored glass staining (enhancing, embellishing) eternity's bright radiance?

So I would like to believe. But then, until yesterday I believed that Leon was the Buddha, so what do I know?

From the moment he first saw Ananda, Brumi was a goner. He gave up everything to join the monks and marry her. But while he was still working with the crew and dating his true love, he introduced Leon to an older woman, full of grace and maturity, who had been a spiritual seeker (or finder, or whatever they call it in that group) her entire life.

Or so, once again, I would like to believe.

Lisette was that woman. She was three years widowed. Yes, you heard me right. Lisette had been married for three decades. Not only that, she had borne and raised two children in her ashram—a girl and a boy. The boy found his way back to Boston and the real world, where he lives and works as a computer programmer and has a family of his own.

The girl is Ananda.

Lisette, of whose grandmotherly skills I have marveled, given that she had (I thought) chosen the life of an ascetic and had no children of her own, actually learned them the old fashioned way—by having and raising children. No wonder she is so good with Donny. And with all the rest of us, for that matter.

No wonder Leon loves her so.

Leon, for his part, had been looking for nothing. Never having sought, he somehow ended up finding. Because after he met Lisette, he knew that what he wanted was to be with her. Whether it was in an ashram as a monk or living in a house as a carpenter was a matter of indifference to him. He is as happy one place as another. So it was no sacrifice to leave the crew and the world for the ashram, and I suspect he could move back out as easily if Lisette were to decide they should do so.

How is it possible that I haven't known all this? I who report on all of Riverboro and its 6,000 inhabitants have missed the big news flash in my own house, under my own nose.

After the power came on, Dan came by to help Pasco and Brumi move furniture around and open up the small bedroom, the one that was full of stuff and generally un-usable. All that stuff is going in the barn sale (you'd better head on over if you want to see what was there), and the room has had its own makeover.

So Leon is going in with Lisette into the room with the double bed, Brumi and Ananda are going to get the room at the end where the men were, the one with the sloping floor, and Cassie and Pasco are going to move into that little room that we opened up. I picture them nesting like cute animals in a burrow, poking their heads out to twitch their noses and view the world with their bright eyes.

I admit to being taken aback, not only by the big revelation (*how*, exactly, are they monks?) but also by the shift of the sleeping arrangements. Certainly as married couples they should be together, but also the shift seems to indicate that they intend to be here for quite some time. Otherwise why bother?

I hasten to say that they are welcome! Always welcome.

I expect to see all of you, Riverboro, at the barn sale today. Dan, Silas, and Leon are running it, as it looks like another working weekend for me—a conference call with our paper supplier somehow scheduled itself for this morning. But I will be in and out among you. Auntie Polly, if you come by and don't see me, stop up here to my office as I need to talk to you about these ideas you've been floating about Molly talking at the library and going to Rwanda with you.

Dan says we'll have a meeting about the status of these monks later today, as soon as the sale is over, and I do intend to find out what they mean by "monk," as well as many other things I probably should have asked early on. It's all been such a blur, and perhaps I made a lot of assumptions...well, Riverboro! Between the barn sale and the big meeting,

I expect I'll have plenty of material for tomorrow's blog.

See you then.

Tags: Riverboro monks????? Riverboro Ashram?? barn sale

COMMENTS:

RiverCoral: Honestly, Piper, I thought you knew that they were couples. Anyone who knows them knows it! Didn't you ever see them coming into Marty's together, or walking around town in couples? Haven't you noticed that Ananda and Brumi use the same last names? You've got to show more interest in the people around you. There's more to life than work! ☺

(*Comment approved*)

(*Comment declined*)

(*Comment re-approved*)

PipersPebbles: One of the natural laws here in New Hampshire is that people mind their own business and allow their neighbors to mind theirs, and Coral Lane, those of you who have moved here from Massachusetts don't understand that. I'm not saying that one way is right and the other one's wrong, but you should take the time to learn the ways of the place to which you've moved.

ImmaterialGirl: I think you notice all the important things about people! For example, I love the way you describe Pasco exactly as he is, warm and affectionate and playful. You seem to capture the essence of someone with your words.

BookLover603: Not necessarily plot twist... more a surprise? It has to change the direction of the story to be a twist…

MollyHH: Yeah, Mom, a surprise. This "revelation" isn't seriously going to change the direction of anything, is it?

PipersPebbles: That depends on the outcome of the big meeting, doesn't it?

ImmaterialGirl: You aren't going to kick the monks out because they are married, are you? That would not be a good plot twist.

PipersPebbles: On what planet, in what universe, could they possibly be monks?

HarvardProf: The Riverboro Ashram group is neither monkish nor excessively ascetic. It would be more accurate to call them yogis. We have a strong tradition in America of people adopting a lifestyle that incorporates yoga, meditation, and a spiritual orientation and still maintaining the responsibilities of a householder. The Riverboro Ashram represents an idiosyncratic yet locally vernacular marriage (if you'll pardon the inadvertent play on words) of these extremes.

ConArtist: Ms. H, about that jukebox in the barn.

PipersPebbles: Is it worth anything?

ConArtist: Might be, if you could fix it up.

PipersPebbles: Can you?

ConArtist: Maybe. I'll ask Brumi what he thinks.

(*Comments approved*)

* * *

The yard was a churned sea of mud from all the people tramping around. People had been in and out all morning, looking at stuff and buying it and hauling it away. In and out of the barn, that is. Piper had locked the door to the house.

Silas kept Piper updated with a steady flow of texts:

Sold: High school wrestling t-shirts, circa 1988, $1.00 for the lot.

(Sam King had worn one when he'd won the state final for his team so Riverboro High could go to regionals. Piper had felt like the female lead in an old movie when he lifted her in his arms and spun her around while people screamed and cheered and she and Sam laughed and hugged).

Sold: Lovin' Spoonful original LP, Do You Believe in Magic, *$3.00.*

(Dan wore glasses back then. His hair was long enough to brush his collar. The fast-disappearing analog sound could not be duplicated with digital technology, he said. He took Piper away from the picnic to bring her to Jake's house and play analog music, track after track on record after record; and when he put on the vintage Lovin' Spoonful album and took her in his arms to dance her around the room, she felt the magic, not only of that moment, but of all the possibilities of all future moments with Dan).

Sold: Complete set of To the Barricades *magazine, 1972 to 1978, $1.00 for the crumbling, mouse-eaten bundle.*

(Jake had been with Dan and Piper that day. They'd been exploring the old barn when they'd come across this breathtaking piece of history: a youthful effort by Jacques Marquand, feted for a half a dozen years, forgotten by most, a startling treasure for Jacques' son and Jake's two best friends. The three of them had sat together in that old carriage seat for one entire afternoon, turning the pages, laughing at the outdated styles, exclaiming over photos of a tiny Jake in the arms of now-dead or long-forgotten activists and anarchists. What about that afternoon had made Dan turn to Piper and say "We'll start a magazine of our own, shall we?" Whatever it was, it had felt completely right).

Sold: Painted wooden carousel horse, $50.00.

(Dan and Piper had combed the antique stores of New England look-

ing for that horse and finally found it in Vermont. What a triumph to discover the thing they were looking for, to bring it home and sand and paint
it a glossy enamel and to set it up in the living room near the tree. "Santa's
been here," they told the two-year-old Molly, and her eyes flew wide and she
gasped in astonishment and delight).

Sold: set of gilt hairbrushes, 25 cents.

(Piper and Dan divided up the two most difficult parts of Molly's day:
putting on her socks and brushing her hair. Either could lead to tears. Dan
invented the sock game to cajole the child, and on a good day could have
her laughing happily as he eased the socks onto her feet. Piper told stories
about Princess Molly, a heroine with magical tresses that, when combed,
gave her the power to ride dolphins and rescue princes. Every birthday
Molly got wonderful, whimsical socks covered in stars and princesses and
dolphins, and, for her sixth birthday, a special big-girl brush and comb set
just for her).

*Sold: 21st Century Conspiracy Theory—study group syllabus and hardcover
books, $1.00 for the lot.*

(It had been Coral's idea to set up the study group at the River Place.
Dan would be up till all hours going over lesson plans or reading student
papers, or down at the River Place talking to the members who lingered
after, asking questions, trading conspiracy theories and alien abduction
stories. He'd lumber into the bedroom at one or two in the morning and
sit heavily and creakily on the bed to take off his shoes, muttering about
controlled demolition and dark helicopters and secret autopsies. One day,
sitting at the counter at Marty's, searching through her purse for coins for
Molly to feed into the jukebox, Piper froze, hearing Coral's voice coming
from a nearby booth: "You know Stonehenge and Easter Island and Mac-
chu Picchu and all, don't you, Jake? They were really built with the help of
visitors from outer space." And Piper had felt her heart pounding hard and
her breath coming short and that squeezing, squeezing pain in her chest. All
of which would become familiar. But that was the very first time).

Sold: Cotton yukata, slightly mildewed, one size fits all, $1.00.

(Molly had brought it back, a gift for Piper, from her trip to Japan with
Coral and Dan. She had returned buoyant from the adventure of travel, the
romance of Japan, eager to share her pictures of temples and manga stu-

dios, her stories of hilarious misunderstandings and wrong turns leading to magical destinations. Piper twirled in the robe; hands tucked in the sleeves, she took playful geisha steps, modeling for her delighted daughter. And she privately vowed that Molly would never know that she would never again put it on, that she could never bear looking at it ever, ever again).

* * *

"I thought maybe Jacques Marquand might come," said Miranda. The garage sale was winding down. Miranda, her teardrop lime green today, sat with Piper at the kitchen table, paging through a recent edition of *Riverboro Rocks*. "For Found Art and all. I wanted to talk to him about the Lies."

"I wanted to update him about my party." Molly was wearing a false nose and glasses. She had her cell phone out and was scrolling through the messages. "I've got a voice message here from him."

"What does it say?" Miranda asked.

"I can't really tell," Molly admitted. "My voice-to-text program transcribed it and it came across all buggy. It wrote that he was going to trounce my hearty and plea to fail. But I think it means he's going to announce my party and see us at the sale."

"Unless he's going to renounce his malarky and flee by rail," Miranda suggested.

"We can only hope," Piper said.

"Wait till we're dancing in unison down the streets of Japan." Molly adjusted her black plastic glasses and squinted through them at her text screen. "Voice-to-text might be Jacques' true medium."

"Maybe it's how he writes his blog," Miranda suggested. "Unedited dictation."

"We all expected him," said Silas. He wore the Viking helmet, big horns jutting out on either side of his shaved head.

"Everyone else was there," said Miranda. "Total mobs. Did they make a dent? Last I looked, there seemed to be more stuff than when we started."

"Not anymore," said Silas. "Dude wants to buy what's left."

"What?" Piper exclaimed. "Who?"

"Little guy with a big truck," Silas said.

"Why?"

Dan had come in from the shed, carrying Donny. "He gave us $250 for the lot," he said, passing Donny to Piper. "Who knows what he'll do with it?"

"I snagged the pet carrier for Donny's puppy," Molly said. "Also that old Peter Pan outfit. It'll be perfect for Donny's party costume. It's exactly like the tunic Link wears in *The Legend of Zelda*. It'll make for a super easy costume."

Piper sat Donny on his booster seat. "I'll give him lunch. Donny, don't you want to be a cowboy for Molly's party?"

Molly objected. "Mom, I told you—"

"OK, OK," Piper conceded. "Molly, sit down and have some soup with us."

"We're heading out." Molly took a saucer of soup from Piper and set it down for Sasha. The cat sniffed it delicately and, crouching, began to lap. "Where did Pasco and Cassie get to?"

"We're here." Pasco and Cassie stopped at the door to scrape the mud from their feet, Cassie steadying herself with a hand on Pasco's shoulder. Pasco was speaking. "I've got an inspiration for Cassie's polemic: monks, revealed to be married, are evicted from their temporary refuge and end up homeless as winter sets in."

Cassie hit him on the arm and glanced at Piper. "Pasco!"

"I'm glad to see you read my blog," said Piper composedly. "How are your Lies coming?"

"Great. Pete and I have it all: ninjas, vampires, a zombie apocalypse. Cassie's floundering, though."

"It's hard for me," said Cassie. "Whenever I try to write, something different comes out from what I meant to say. I end up doodling recipes in the columns. Not for cooking children," she clarified hastily.

"Children! Why—"

"Jacques wanted me to be thinking along those lines, remember?" Cassie explained. "Something edgy, like cooking children? But I'm not the edgy type. Miranda, how about you?"

"I might be the edgy type," Miranda said. "I've written about as much paper flower haiku as I can stand. What's edgier? Bad weather haiku? Tooth-ache haiku? Roadkill haiku?"

"Slam haiku," offered Molly.

"Zombie haiku," suggested Pasco.

"I munch on your brains/and find I no longer care/that you didn't say goodbye," Miranda said immediately.

"Quick," approved Piper.

"Edgy," said Molly.

"No wonder you're bored with flowers," said Silas.

"What about you, Silas?" Piper asked. "How is your project coming?"

"Good. Cross-genre. Got it here." Silas held up his cell phone. "Text message language. Intense political satire in abbreviation."

"Like Jonathan Swift," said Miranda. "If he could tweet."

"Biting," Silas agreed.

"But," said Piper, "the *whole thing* is text? And all on your phone?"

"How long is it going to be?" Molly asked. "What's your word count?"

"I go by character count." Silas made a circling motion with his hand. "Goes faster."

"Creative," Molly approved.

"I think it's been done before," said Miranda.

"Everything has," Silas said. "No new ideas. It's all in the execution."

Dan broke into the bemused silence that followed. "I'm out of here," he said. "Piper, the big monk summit is at four. You'll be available? We'll have it in the living room. I'll make a fire. Pasco, who from your group is coming?"

"Lisette does all the organizing. The rest do as we're told. Will we need Coral?"

"No," said Piper. "We will not need Coral."

"Lisette then. Also Mr. King."

"Mr. King?" Piper repeated blankly. "Sam King? What's he got to do with it?"

And Sasha, who was sitting there looking and listening, said, "Mraow?"

* * *

Sam King was standing by the fire talking quietly to Dan. He turned when Piper entered and smiled.

"Pipes." He crossed the room, casual in his flannel shirt, jeans, and sneakers, and kissed her on the cheek. Piper felt wrong-footed. How do you kick monks out of the house (not that they *were* monks) when their spokesperson was your high school boyfriend and he appeared to have already reached an agreement with your ex-husband?

Not that I mean to kick them out, Piper thought. *But I'd at least like the illusion that it's my decision.* To Sam she said lightly, "What are you two conspiring about?"

Sam's face creased into his easy smile. "Patriots," he said. "How 'bout 'em?"

Piper was opening her mouth to protest, but Sam took her hands in his and eased her down onto the sofa beside him. "Now," he said, "let's talk monks."

Piper's List: The Top Five Things to Worry About Now (Not for Publication)

5) Little dude with the big truck: what is he doing with the junk?

4) Sam King and his monks

3) Silas and his con art—and Molly

2) Noise from the shed: serial killers? Or maybe outer space aliens have made contact with Dan and he's holding out on me…

1) Money—a new batch of bills, and insufficient money to pay them. On the bright side, it absolves me of any stigma about anxiety…with that looming, who wouldn't worry?

November 13: Of Monks and Men (and Women)

Who doesn't want to believe they are piloting their own ship, in charge of their own destiny? Fools that we are. When I started to brew my destiny in that kettle we call life, I never in a million years would have thought to cast a cadre of monks into the pot. But somehow, in a little town like ours, everyone's life wraps around everyone else's. The threads part and come back together, sometimes in unexpected ways.

After the Monk Summit, Lisette came by my office on the third floor to tell me about her first encounter with the King family. Over forty years ago, young Lisette Beauchamp, a girl in her twenties, left her home and family in Boston, traveling all by herself to start a new life as a spiritual aspirant at an ashram in Vermont. (People were doing that kind of thing a lot back then). On her way through Riverboro, she went into King's Market after hours (the door was still open to accommodate late-comers) to cash an out-of-state third-party check. A courtly gentleman (Sam King's grandfather, it would have been) was kind enough to give her, a complete stranger, cash for it—something probably no one else would have done. How ironic that, years later, Mr. King's grandson would become the secular organizer of a spiritual community in town, and that Lisette would be the leading member of it.

Lisette tells me that means that there is a karmic connection between the families.

My own karmic connection, as you know, is that I might have been Mrs. King of King's Market, living above that store, if life had taken a different turn. Or if I had made different choices. If I had done that, where would the monks be living now? With me and Sam above King's Market? Like sardines in a can? (Do people still eat sardines? Must ask Sam).

Sam ended up marrying Felicity Fontineau, whose family owned the soda shop, and they had a couple of kids. And in a fabulous stroke of karmic coincidence, Sam and his family, seekers all, got involved in the very ashram where Lisette lived. Weekends, when other families were at scouts or on the soccer field, Sam and his family would be in Vermont, praying or chanting or...well, to tell the truth, I really don't know what they did there, or why. But Sam liked it well enough to decide that we Riverboroans could do with some monks of our own. So he convinced the main monk to send some monks our way.

This big kahuna of theirs agreed to share a few of his married monks with us. Not, Sam assures me, because the guru thinks of couples as dispensable. To the contrary, he decided that, away from the main collective, married couples would make for a more stable group. So Sam settled our monks into the ashram by the river, where they lived until the river forced them to evacuate to my place.

Sam says that, married or not (only they all are), my monks are the real deal—that is, they spend a good part of every day in monk-like activities. And whatever it is monks do, Sam means to keep them doing it. And that, he tells me, is where I come in. These monks have a few sources of income—their little store, some classes they give—but they don't have buckets of money to buy a new place. They might have some flood insurance coming to them, but who knows when or how? Meanwhile, they need a place to live.

I told Sam they can't set up their shop here. I've got a magazine to run and enough people coming and going at all hours to keep me on the edge of crazy. But Sam told me that the Riverboro Drugstore offered to clear out a section for them to put up their merchandise. That's what people are like in Riverboro, and why it is so rewarding to be the chronicler of its day-to-day. It's also the reason I was unable to say no to Sam. When so many are pitching in to do their part, how can I do less? In any case, I don't seem to have much choice. The men pretty well have it settled between them that, for their living arrangement, stay at the Hadley House those monks must and shall.

Sam did say that, who knows, since the Riverboro Ashram is non-profit we might be able to find some tax break in there somewhere. That alone makes me nervous—wouldn't they have to be here an awfully long time to merit a tax break? What is Sam thinking? A Marquand-esque do-gooder fund-raiser for the kind but temporary host of indigent monks seems more likely to yield something.

But either scenario seems to me a very faint hope. Still, given the fact that the single largest expense on this house is the property tax (oh Riverboro, thou knowst of which I speak), even a faint hope is worth checking.

So for better or worse I now have monks, or yogis, or anyway men and women in white robes with bald heads, living and moving and having their being here at the Hadley House until further notice.

Tags: King's Market, Riverboro Ashram, Riverboro tax code

COMMENTS:

ImmaterialGirl: Thank you, Piper! You won't regret this!

PipersPebbles: Wait a minute…who's that? Ananda?

ImmaterialGirl: No, it's Cassie.

PipersPebbles: Cassie—you are Immaterial Girl? And have been all this time? Why didn't you tell me?

ImmaterialGirl: I'm sorry, I thought you knew.

PipersPebbles: Then who is Pasco? Is he Zombie Patrol?

ImmaterialGirl: Of course.

PipersPebbles: And you and Pasco are having a baby??? How can you do that? You're monks! And you live here! And what do you know about babies?

ImmaterialGirl: Don't worry, we took your advice and went to River-boro Family Care, over by the hospital. They gave us a doctor. It's all good. The baby is perfectly healthy.

PipersPebbles: Oh lordy lord, what to do?

ImmaterialGirl: Cheer up, it'll be fun!

PipersPebbles: Fun? You can't call a baby fun. Fun is a game of Scrabble!

ImmaterialGirl: It's just a baby…People have them all the time.

(*Comments approved*)

* * *

Damn Lies
By Presidential Candidate and Political Party-Goer
Jacques Marquand

November Lies' first Political Party is just that: a real party. In a masterstroke of subterfuge, the Party will be held at Riverboro's H.I.T. restaurant, and if you show up in costume you are entitled to provide a plank. Preferably pine. Pop quiz: Can we expect a gubernatorial guest to drop by, hoping to meet his Riverboro constituency and the lovely Piper Hadley? Will he ask her to chair his State Council on Literacy? Or is it a Captain of Industry who will come with a creative funding idea? Truth or fact or dirty lie? The invitations are out. Come to the party to learn the answer. Come in costume—it creates deniability. Bring wads of cash—Party is also a Jacques Marquand fundraiser. Bring your Lie. Live the Lie. Be the Lie.

* * *

"Where is Molly?"

Piper, mastering her impulse to flee, stood on the lowest step and looked around. Molly was nowhere to be seen.

Unfortunately, Molly appeared to be the only person on the planet who was missing. The rest of the whole damn world was milling around in Piper's house.

From where she stood, Piper could see that the living room, library, and dining room were crowded with the November Lies gang. Although Piper felt she was almost getting immune to the chaos, today it was compounded with the explosion of costume-making paraphernalia. Floors were covered with bolts of fabric, pattern pieces, and spools of thread. Surfaces were strewn with pairs of scissors, tubes of paint, pieces of cardboard, and sheets of Styrofoam.

Piper wondered if she could stand it.

Donny and Ralph were in the midst of the uproar, tussling over a strip of leather. "At least get that dog out of here," Piper said, trying for one small bit of order.

"Ralph needs to be here," Donny begged, sensing weakness. "Please don't make him go—he's supervising!"

Piper sighed. "Donny, where is your sister?"

Miranda, her cobalt-blue teardrop bright against her copper curls, put down a pair of scissors and stood up from the floor. "None of us know where Molly is. She's not answering her phone—she must be on her way."

Piper took a tentative step into the room. "Then why are all these people here?"

"She posted the invite on Facebook." Miranda came forward to take Piper's hand, to coax her further into the room. "Costume-making party. Seven o'clock at the Hadley House. So we all came."

"Fun," Piper said, unconvincingly, following Miranda with tentative steps.

Miranda smiled. "It's a party apocalypse, isn't it? Molly's worried we won't be ready. Especially now, since Jacques announced it."

"No one knows what he announced," Piper said, a little desperately. "That stuff was like voice to text. It could have meant anything."

Miranda glanced at her sympathetically. "I know what you mean," she said. "Why can't he just say you are all invited to a party? What's with the governors and captains of industry and what all?"

Piper had been trying to forget about that; the reminder sent prickles of dread down her spine. "That's just Jacques trying to get us in a tizzy over this," she said with an assurance she didn't feel. "He likes to play those games. Why would important people like that come to Molly's party? Jacques thinks if he throws enough spaghetti against the wall some of it will stick."

"I think some of it already has," Miranda said. "He's got us going, for sure."

She flung out her hand at the mob in the living room: ta-da! Despite herself, Piper's eyes followed the gesture; she almost couldn't bear to look. Without Molly here—how could Molly do this to her?—the disorder threatened to close in. Piper took a breath. She focused. Identify the people. Identify the activities. This was her house, her space. She could calm herself by seeing the method underlying all this madness.

Her eyes sought the people she knew, people she trusted. Not Molly (where was Molly?), but others. Cassie, kneeling at one of the low tables, running cloth through a sewing machine. Pasco, cutting out pattern pieces. Silas, Viking helmet looming, a corsair with a camcorder. Lisette was scrolling through some images on a laptop screen, pointing out details, showing Cassie how the stitches should go. They greeted Piper and beckoned her over to show their progress.

Piper moved into the room, a Dante with Miranda as her Virgil. "You'll love these costumes, they're from Final Fantasy," said her guide. "Bad guys draining the resources of the planet, rebels and outcasts fighting them. Very Marquand-esque."

"Good guys against bad?" Piper bent to examine the images on the screen.

"Yes and no," said Miranda. "It gets complicated."

"Like politics," said Piper.

"Like life," said Silas.

"Like TV," said Donny, dragging Ralph over to join them. "I'm going to be on TV."

Piper straightened, looking at him. "What? When? Who says so?"

"Jacques Marquand," Donny replied. "He's going to put me on TV."

"Donny, Jacques is not going to put you on TV." She took Donny's hand and the two of them followed Silas and Miranda into the dining room. "Jacques and his TV, and his governors, and his committees, and his rogue financing ventures—" she broke off. "What's this?"

"Weapons lab," Silas said.

Jilly and Brumi were at the table, measuring out lengths of plastic pipes. Peter walked among them, his voice rising and falling as he explained how to convert these innocent pipes into weapons. *Toy weapons*, Piper reminded herself, picking up a piece to examine, turning it over in her hands, feeling herself breathe. *Like Donny's six-shooter. Plastic weapons. Like my keyboard. Illusion. Like a string you mistake for a snake. Art. Like November Lies.*

"Plowshares into swords," she said, trying for a joke.

Donny climbed onto a chair and leaned over the weapons. "Will they make a noise?" he asked.

"We make the noise, dude," Silas replied.

"A loud noise?" Donny asked. "It has to be loud. If you make a loud noise you get to go on TV."

"Donny, you will not—"

"Jacques Marquand said if we make a noise he'll put us on TV. I jumped and shouted—very loudly. And he said he'd put me on TV."

"When was this?" Piper demanded.

"Yesterday," Silas said. "He said: 'Donny, I'll make you famous. Tomorrow.'"

"Tomorrow! Does he think Donny has no concept of tomorrow?" Piper snapped. "Kids don't forget promises, even if they're only three—" She broke off, listening. Noises were coming from the kitchen. "What's that?"

"Door," said Miranda. "Should I go?"

"No, I'll go. It's Molly. Finally!" But as Piper started for the door she realized she was hearing the scraping of more than one pair of feet, the sound of more than one voice. Molly was not alone.

Worse: Molly was not happy. Piper could hear it in her voice; she could hear it quaver. What was wrong? Who was with Molly? Why was she near tears?

Piper, clutching the pipe, charged into the kitchen. Seeing Molly shrugging out of her coat, toeing out of her shoes, she tried to stop, sliding in her socks on the wooden floor, skidding into a crash against the other person standing there. Hap LeClair.

Hap LeClair, nicest guy in the world. Hap LeClair, from whom Piper had stolen cupcakes as a child.

Hap LeClair, Riverboro's Chief of Police.

Hap caught Piper and steadied her, keeping her on her feet. He took the plastic pipe from her hand and calmly set it against the wall as if disarming people of artificial artillery was an everyday occurrence. Piper, barely noticing, turned to her daughter. "Molly! Are you hurt? What happened, why are you—"

Molly clung to her mother. "I went to the bus—there was a crowd—" In the safety of her mother's arms Molly began to sob. "Jacques wasn't anywhere—there were some kids from West Riverboro—I got mashed against a wall—the police came—"

"What bus? What kids? What wall?" Piper glared over Molly's head at

Hap. "What's this?" she demanded.

"Marquand's campaign bus." Hap looked almost as miserable as Molly. "Parked at the plaza. Lot filled with cars. One of these flash mob things—someone tweeted or posted the invite. Got out of hand—"

"Not in Riverboro—"

"Not just Riverboro—outside, too. Manchester, Nashua, Worcester, Boston—all over. Looking to party. More a riot than a flash mob."

"Molly!" Piper was aghast. "You went to a riot?"

"It wasn't supposed to be a riot!" Molly sobbed. "Jacques wanted the core group—"

Piper was white with rage. "*Everyone* is Jacques core group! I've been trying to tell you—"

Piper broke off. Molly, choked with sobs, was starting to hiccup. Piper led her to the kitchen table and sat her firmly down, then turned to fill the kettle and bang it onto the stove. She gestured to Hap to follow. He took a step further into the kitchen, then stopped, looking ill at ease.

"Hap, come in," Piper commanded, and he took another step. "And please explain to me what happened."

Hap cleared his throat, shifted from foot to foot. "Someone called it in—I went by in the cruiser—"

"And arrested *Molly*?"

"Mom, he didn't arrest me—"

"Just bringing her home," Hap said. "Sent everyone on their way. Dropping a few of the town kids off. Before they get into trouble."

"Trouble! Hap LeClair, I'll give you trouble!" Piper put a box of tissues on the table near Molly, who took one and blew her nose. "My Molly has never in her life—"

"We like to keep it that way," Hap replied stiffly, clearly a little offended. "And if you'd a been there, you wouldn't accuse me of overreacting. That bus was rocking, lit'rally, from the goings-on inside. Young thugs out in the parking lot shouting and shoving. Whole thing a haze of smoke, music so loud you couldn't tell what was playing—"

"They broke into Jacques' sake," Molly broke in. "They started doing shots—"

Piper, rummaging through the cupboard for one of Cassie's herbal teas, turned. "Shots of sake? You don't do sake in shots!"

"Mom, forget the sake—that isn't the point—"

"No, the point is that Jacques Marquand thinks it's funny to set things up and disappear." Piper, not waiting for the water to boil, splashed it into the mug and dropped in a teabag. "My daughter is not going to be a rat in his maze, not if I have anything to say about it."

Hap, his eyes going from mother to daughter, was looking increasingly uncomfortable. "Seems the two of you have things to sort out. Why don't I leave you to it…"

Neither Piper nor Molly paid any attention. "Molly, you were supposed to be here," Piper said. "You've got a houseful of people here who were expecting you."

"I thought I'd be back…"

Piper took a sip of the tea to check its temperature, then put the mug in front of Molly, taking her daughter's hands and wrapping them around it. "This is his dry run for your party, Molly. He's going to do the same thing."

"Mom, why do you always assume the worst?" Molly held the mug, her tears were subsiding. "He didn't mean to leave us hanging."

"Of course he did—but that he would dare involve you…"

"Mom, please, don't say anything!" Molly sounded panicked. "To Jacques, or Dad—"

"It'll be in tomorrow's Daily Union." Piper glanced at Hap. "Police blotter. Daughter of local publisher—"

"No names were taken," Hap said. "Just an incident report—unruly crowd dispersed."

Piper smiled a strained thank you and leaned down to kiss the top of Molly's head. "Won't you join us, Hap?" she repeated. "Cup of coffee? Tea?"

"Thanks, Piper, but I'd better get back. Time for Marquand to move his bus…"

Piper nodded a goodbye and started to turn back to Molly, but Hap paused on his way out the door. "By the way. Saw your post."

Piper half-turned back, looking at Hap questioningly. "When you're serving baked goods with your coffee," he said, "let me know. You owe me a cupcake."

* * *

Alone at last, in the privacy of her third floor bathroom, the silence felt strange. Funny how rarely she got to experience silence and solitude nowadays. Today had been long and eventful—but every day was long, when you started at three in the morning; every day eventful, when your house was filled with an absurd number of people.

Piper opened her phone and jabbed in a number, holding it to her ear with one hand while she turned on the taps of the big old claw-footed bathtub with the other. The hot water sputtered and spurted, brown with rust, then cleared and settled into a steady stream.

The ringing on her phone cut off: "Marquand."

"Jacques, it's Piper."

"Piper, my dear, how nice to hear from you. Do you have any dirt for me today? The bits you drop about Coral are wonderful."

"No, Jacques, I'm not calling with 'dirt'. I'm calling about this latest mischief of yours. The chief of police was in my kitchen—"

"No—really?" Jacques laughed. "Wonderful—how do you do it? I haven't had one in my kitchen in years. The sterility of life nowadays— politics, publishing, broadcasting, what are you going to do? I knew I could count on you to rekindle that old fire. I can see you now, Riverboro's rocks clutched in your anarchic fists, making your stand—"

"Do you never stop?" Piper closed the drain with a rubber disk and reached for her bath salts. "I'm not calling to report a revolution. I'm calling to ask you to dial it back with Molly and Donny."

"Donny? Donny? I was with you till Donny. Who's Donny?"

"Donny is Jake's godson, that's who he is!" Piper tried not to let amusement creep into her voice. It would only encourage him. "Remember Jake? Your son? Jacques, you know who Donny is, don't play those games. And you told him you'd put him on TV, and you are going to break his heart. I won't have it. And I won't have you dragging Molly into your schemes, either."

"Piper, darling, it won't break his heart. Donny's tough. He'll be fine.

And Molly's a woman—"

"A girl," Piper corrected.

"—who must know by now not to trust men. Her own father—"

"Jacques, leave Dan out of this. In fact, leave us all out." Piper, choosing a peppermint bath salt—bright and tingly, a birthday gift from Molly—tried to hold onto the thread of her complaint. "Jacques, Donny is only three."

"A great age to make his media debut," Jacques said. "I put Jake on the cover of *To the Barricades* when he was three, alongside Richard Nixon and John Lennon. You should run a retrospective in *Riverboro Rocks*: the best of those years. I can get you the images, totally authentic. That was before you could doctor your photos with Photoshop. You had to cut and paste—"

"You can't move people around like chess pieces." Piper floated a rubber duck—a gift from Donny—on the rising bath water. "Not my family. What are you trying to achieve?"

"You know me, I like to mentor the young," Jacques said breezily.

"Mentor someone else's young. Leave mine alone. You can't tell a three-year-old you'll put him on TV, Jacques. You just can't."

"Of course I can. And what's more, I'll do it. Wait and see."

"Yes, Jacques, we've all had experience waiting and seeing what you'll do. And what's all this about governors and captains of industry? This is Riverboro—"

"Piper, love, when I get through with this party it will be much, much more than Riverboro. People will be talking about it for years."

"That's exactly what we don't want. Too many people, and they'll be the wrong people, and you're setting them up to expect big names, and you know what will happen. That flash mob at the campaign bus—it was a trial run, wasn't it?"

"I'm doing you a huge favor, love. Get pictures, you'll have a story for your magazine that will send circulation through the roof. It's what you need. It'll shake things up."

"My daughter doesn't need to be shaken up more than she was. I know how you work, Jacques. You're leading up to the end of the month with a string of broken promises and this is going to be the biggest broken promise of them all. No governors, no captains of industry, no Jacques, just an unmanageable party—" In that instant it struck Piper what Jacques must be planning. "You think they'll trash the H.I.T. don't you? Delay the opening? Create a corporate muckup?"

Jacques chuckled. "What a media event that would be. You could sell advertising on the strength of it for a year. Make Riverboro rock! You can thank me when you're back in the black."

"And it won't stick to you, you won't even be there."

"Piper, you cut me to the quick. I wouldn't miss Molly's party for the world. What kind of man do you take me for? My word is my bond."

Piper rang off, feeling rattled. The way she and Jacques sparked off each other could be exhilarating. But Piper needed her life to be in control, and Jacques throve on the uncontrolled and uncontrollable. Entertaining, to be sure, but now it was cutting too close to the bone. It was affecting her, her life, her daughter, her business.

She stirred her bath distractedly, thinking ferociously about this problem. She was making too big a deal of this, she knew. She was getting too drawn in. Why should she play the game on Jacques' terms? What if she cancelled Molly's party? Called off the entire ordeal at the H.I.T.? Let Molly have a few close friends at home—or, better yet, at the River Place. Molly could snap a few photos to send to Jacques for her contest entry and that would be that.

Done and dusted. Having made the decision, Piper immediately felt better. Jacques was Jacques, and she wasn't going to let him spoil her bath evening. After two weeks without power, she needed a long hot bath more than almost anything.

Her phone rang. Piper flipped it open, checked the screen. Dan.

"Hello, Dan?"

Dan's voice echoed over the line. "It's Dan. Hello? Are you there?"

With Riverboro's cellphone reception, it always took a bit to get the conversation onto an even keel. "Yes, Dan, it's me. Where are you?"

"Downstairs in the living room. Leon's got a fire going. I'm going to head over the mountain with Silas and Brumi. They want to shop for components for the jukebox. The store's open till ten tonight. You want to keep an eye on Donny? We might be back late."

"And Coral can't watch him because…?"

"She's coming with us. She's been working hard and we thought we'd grab dinner. Molly's here with the Liars, working on the party. You and she can double-team him. " Piper started to speak, maybe to protest, but he steamrolled on. "I'll pick up your new keyboard while I'm out. Now I'm going to put the little guy on. Donny guy, here's Piper."

"Piper? Hi! Can we hang tonight, us two?"

Piper found herself beginning to smile. A bath would have been nice, but there was always tomorrow. "Sure baby, come on up. I've got a nice hot bath waiting for you with peppermint salts and a rubber ducky."

*   *   *

So now Molly, seemingly recovered from the Hap flap, was looking through costume ideas, and Donny, cozy in his feet pajamas, was in Piper's lap in the big chair. The tumult of the mob had subsided, in Piper's awareness, to a rather pleasant background buzz. Piper surveyed the room with charity, affection, and perhaps a touch of pride. What grist for her blog mill might tonight provide?

"I knew we could hang tonight," Donny said happily. He touched the tablet on his lap to bring up a screen. "Mommies and Dads can't hang every night. They need a break."

"Oh yeah, baby bro?" Molly asked, shifting aside on the window seat to make room for Colby. "Who says?"

"Daddy does." Donny spoke with the assurance that comes of having an infallible source. "It's been that way since the dawn of time." He looked up at Piper questioningly. "When is the dawn of time?"

Piper laughed. "When your dad was young."

Donny nodded, back on familiar ground. "He's an old guy now," he confided. "A Grand Old Guy."

"Is that what he tells you?" Piper stroked Donny's curls, still damp from the bath. "And what about your Mommy? What is she?"

"Mommy's a Sweet Young Thing. We've all got names. Molly's Big Sis."

"Really? And what," Piper asked, unwisely, "am I?"

Donny, either not seeing or not understanding his sister's frantic gestures for silence, replied innocently. "You're the Nutcase. That's what my mom says. I say so, too. Don't you love nuts?"

The soft chatter around the room ceased and everyone froze—rather like a game of statues, Piper thought with a kind of dissociative amusement. Pasco, who had snagged a couple of floor cushions from behind the sofa, stood with them clutched to his chest. Cassie, who had been reaching to take them from Pasco, was arrested mid-motion. Miranda, cross-legged on the floor, unpinning blue paper flowers from her overalls, stopped mid-gesture, her mouth opening into an "o" of shock. Only Peter, already lying on the floor, feet propped on the arm of the sofa, hands behind his head, continued in his relaxed pose, though his elbows gave a jerk of surprise.

Then everyone was talking at once.

"In the best way," said Pasco, loudly. He looked around as if wondering what to do with his cushions. "We should all be so nutty."

"Pasco's nutty," Cassie announced, wrenching the cushions from him and tossing them onto the floor next to the fireplace. "He thinks I can't do anything." She settled onto a cushion, swatting Pasco's helping hand away. "I'm pregnant, not ancient."

"I think we're all a little nutty." Miranda bent her head over her tissue paper, pleating a new flower with unaccustomed care. "Our brains are all a little scrambled, don't you think?"

Molly met her mother's eyes, her own showing both amusement and concern. Piper glared back. Even if she could have laughed off—barely— this unfunny appellation, the group's rush to defend her gave it power. Before anyone could dig them in deeper, she stepped in with a diversion. "Would you say zombies are crazy, Pasco?"

"Zombies don't have brains to scramble." Pasco, looking relieved, dropped down on the floor near Cassie. "They're already fried."

"Fried brains is the reason zombies are limited." Peter spoke upward into the air from his place on the floor. "How about we move on to robots?"

"What do you mean, limited?" Pasco demanded, boisterous from the barely-averted crisis. "You can't kick zombies to the curb!"

Cassie patted him comfortingly. "We'll have a zombie monkess," she promised. "She'll be so cute."

"He," Pasco corrected, tickling Cassie's midriff. "*He'll* be cute."

"I'm not kicking zombies to the curb," Peter assured Pasco. Everyone else might still be scrambling to recover from Donny's comment, but Peter had moved on, absorbed in his topic. "But we have to get ready for cyberization. A part-cyber human?"

"That's almost scarier than zombies, isn't it?" Cassie suggested. Pasco looked gratified by the thought.

"What's the difference between flash mobs and zombie mobs?" Colby put in. "The estimable Jacques Marquand—"

"The late Jacques Marquand," Miranda reminded him.

"Late? We should be so lucky," Piper said, a little crankily. "And speaking of Jacques, Molly, I wanted to talk to you about your party…"

"It's why we're all here," Molly said. "What about it?"

But Donny, almost imperceptibly, had grown heavier on Piper's lap. Looking down at the little boy, she saw he was slumping, his eyes closing, his head cradling on her shoulder. "Tomorrow," she said. "It's time to get Donny to bed."

Donny, not quite asleep, heard, and sat up straight. "I'm awake!" he declared, rubbing his eyes. "I'm wide awake!"

Piper laughed gently. "Bedtime, baby," she said.

"Please," he begged. "Just a little longer? Let's read. Can we read Molly's book? The one she drew, with Pikachu? Daddy says you have it."

"I'll get it down for you when you are older," Piper promised. "Little boys aren't so gentle with books."

"I am gentle," Donny said with indignation. "I am always gentle with books. And phones. And tablets. And jukeboxes. "

"Jukeboxes? What's this about jukeboxes? Do you mean the one Silas found in the barn?"

"I'm helping fix it," Donny said. "Silas says I'm a big help. He's fixing it up for Molly. To play at her parties."

Molly made a slashing motion across her throat. "Hey, ut-shay up-yay, baby brother, you're going to get me in trouble."

"You're not supposed to say ut-shay up-yay," Donny said.

Molly glanced from Colby to her mother, both of whom had their eyes fixed on her with identical looks of horrified disbelief. "Hey," she said defensively. "I don't know anything about this."

"You can't accept a gift like that," Piper told her daughter. "It's too big, it implies…" She trailed off.

"But isn't it our jukebox to begin with? Didn't it start out in the barn?"

"But I told Silas he could have it. So now it's his."

"Why can you give it to him but he can't give it to me?"

Piper could hear their voices growing tense. Clearly, the others could too. Miranda stood, reaching a hand down for Peter. "We should give these guys some family time. Come on, Peter and Colby, we've been here for hours."

Piper watched the three of them go, feeling flattened, deflated. Why did the moments of harmony have to be so fragile? Always that dark boundary to life's bright gleams, an inexpert mullion between the glass panes. If it wasn't Silas it was Colby. If it wasn't Colby it was the noise from the shed. And if it wasn't the noise it was—

Her thoughts were interrupted by the opening notes of *Eine Kleine Nachtmusik*—her ring tone. She flipped her phone open.

"Piper? Piper, it's Dan. Are you there? It's Dan," he bellowed, loud enough that even without the speaker it could be heard throughout the room. "Piper, I'm at Staples. I wanted to pick up your new keyboard. You know, for the one Sasha wrecked? They tell me they've closed the account. Did you know they did that? *Riverboro Rocks* no longer has an account with Staples."

And here it was, that feeling, as if someone was strangling her from within. The monks, the children, the room full of people, and panic rising.

Dan's voice echoed through the phone, throughout the room. "The bill hasn't been paid in months. The credit card is maxed. I can't get so much as a packet of paper clips or a ballpoint pen unless I pay cash. Do you have a clue about that?"

Piper found she couldn't speak; she could barely breathe. She had to get out of there, up to her office, away; she had to get away from the people, the eyes fixed on her…

"It isn't my fault, is it? I say, is it, Piper? I mean, was there some transfer I was supposed to do, from your account to the business account? Piper? Are you there?"

Then Lisette was on her feet, taking Donny and handing him off to Cassie and then taking Piper by the arm and gently urging her to her feet and leading her from the room. Dan was still booming out through the phone clutched in Piper's trembling hand: "Anyway, here's the thing, Piper, you know I've said this before, I told you way back in the spring, we're strapped for cash, we can't go on like this. We can't wait, we don't need to do this to ourselves. I've discussed it with Coral. We think it's best to declare bankruptcy."

November 14: Pawprints in the Paint

For those of you who haven't met him personally, Donny is my stepson (sort of), and he's in and out of the house at all hours. He is a great favorite of my monks, and especially of the women. They like to dress him up to look like one of them, draped in little white robes, and they've taught him some of their chants, which he sings in his sweet high voice, wandering in and out among them while they laugh and coo and take his picture. We have been tempted to shave his head—but perhaps that would be taking it a step too far.

Donny's best friend in the world (after his puppy, Ralph) is, he says, Sasha (my cat). Sasha must reciprocate the friendship because the patience she shows when Donny dresses her up or hauls her about is remarkable. Yesterday Donny was carrying Sasha around as he sometimes does, arms clasped around Sasha's middle, lugging her from room to room while the cat hung like a limp heavy sack, her paws almost brushing the floor.

Donny and Sasha staggered into the bathroom on the first floor. Why? He said they were looking for Ananda, who hadn't been there to see him in his robes. He wanted to make sure that he and Sasha got to say good-night to her. Earlier that day Brumi had been working in that bathroom, touching up the trim. A bucket of white paint was sitting in the middle of the floor on a newspaper mat, awaiting tomorrow's paint session.

I am sure you can guess what happened next—the collision; the tipped bucket; the cat shooting through the air to land in the spreading pool of thick white paint; the bundle of fur hurtling through the house, leaving white paw prints in its wake. Can cats get heart attacks? Poor Sasha must be close to one. Donny, who had bathed already, had to go back into the bath, while Lisette washed and dried his feet pajamas and Pasco and Cassie gave Sasha her own bath.

So now we have cat prints all over those wide pine floorboards. Left to ourselves, I think Dan and I would treat them as a decorating statement for years to come, but Leon and Brumi have already had their heads together about sanders and varnish and stain, and Lisette and Cassie have already assured me that it all is working out the way it is "meant" to, since the floors needed work anyway.

After all that, somehow I ended up on one end of the big sofa, Ananda established at the other (to keep me company, Lisette said), our feet pointing in toward each other, sipping hot drinks and wrapped in blankets while everyone else flew about and waited on us. Such unnecessary ministrations! Now I know how Ananda feels—though in her case it is her beauty that commands so much love and attention. In mine, they seem to think I need it. But I do not complain—far from it. With these monks there will hardly be a minor calamity or mere hiccup that isn't accompanied by pampering and petting; and so much the better, is what I say.

All this led to me sleeping in this morning, and by the time I got to my computer this morning (still without a real keyboard, for a host of reasons I won't go into now) the sun was beaming its first rays over the mountain and splashing down through my brand new skylight into my office to greet the day. Good morning!

Tags: Colonial floors, white pine, step families, found art for home decor

COMMENTS:

RiverCoral: Piper, don't you dare cut Donny's hair! What a ridiculous idea! Bad enough he got white paint on his feet pajamas. ☺

ZombiePatrol: It would grow back fast, though. And it would make for a great photo shoot.

RiverCoral: It's nothing but adventure at the Hadley House these days. Are all those paint and work things finally put away? The monks should go through and check that there isn't anything unsafe left lying around. ☺

PipersPebbles: Everything is fine. The monks have plenty to do without me directing them.

RiverCoral: How about the Hadley House group plans to spend a few hours a week here? We're adding new shifts to our volunteer rotation. ☺

Private Message to RiverCoral: Can't you leave any part of my life alone?

Private Message from RiverCoral: It will give them something outside themselves to focus on. Plus, I thought you hated having all those people in the house. I thought I was doing you a favor. ☺

Private Message to RiverCoral: Enough with the favors. And what do you mean, the Hadley House group? Are you talking about Molly?

Private Message from River Coral: Everyone could get involved. Miranda's Great Aunt Ani thinks Miranda should have something productive to occupy her. She can't be a kid forever. She needs to get a job. That's what Ani says. Miranda needs to set an example for Jilly, and stop obsessing on costumes and haiku and flash mobs and Japan and all. ☺

Private Message to RiverCoral: You're the one who got them started on the costume thing. Don't you think you're being hypocritical?

Private Message from RiverCoral: No, I don't. You keep saying you're worried about Jacques' influence. I thought I'd help. ☺

ImmaterialGirl: We have a leftover can of paint, robin's-egg blue. How about we use it to paint Molly's room?

PipersPebbles: Cassie, breathing paint fumes is not a good idea in your condition.

ImmaterialGirl: It's OK, the boys can do it, I'll just supervise.

PipersPebbles: Hold off for now. Leave Molly's room as it is.
AuntieP: I have some interesting news from the world of commerce. Hey! It's Thursday is preparing to do what they are calling a "soft opening." That means that while their official "Grand Opening" is to remain at the end of the month, they are beginning to serve food and beverages, to work out the kinks and see what people enjoy most about their menu and ambiance. Perhaps Molly's group would like to work there some afternoon.

PipersPebbles: Silas, make sure you get down there to get them organized with advertising and special offers to our readers.

ConArtist: On it.

(*Comments approved*)

* * *

"I think it's hilarious that the entire town is calling us 'the monks'," Cassie said, handing a plate to Piper and then offering her a selection of pastries to put on it. "Molly, your mom started that, you know. Before her and that blog of hers no one ever called us monks."

"You are pretty funny, Mom," Molly said. She helped herself to a cinnamon pinwheel and took a crumbly bite. "You say these things and half the time no one suspects that it's mischief. Cassie, these cookies are delicious."

"It's a good thing, isn't it, that I didn't decide to call the women 'monkettes,'" said Piper, swiveling in her chair to face her third-floor visitors and sipping her tea. "Or the whole lot of them 'monkeys.' I thought of it but decided it wouldn't be respectful."

"Thank you for that, Piper," hooted Cassie. "I have a feeling that however you talk about us is how the world will see us for years to come. I don't mind, though. I can see how it works." She set the pastries on the corner of Piper's desk and sank down to sit comfortably with Molly on the floor. "You pretend like you're dissing us when all the while you're making us look really good."

"Like she pretends she's praising the River Place and instead she's dissing it," said Molly.

"That Coral!" Piper waved a dismissive hand. "If it isn't Donny, it's *Riverboro Rocks*. She can't decide if she wants to tear down everything I do or take it over for herself. Now she's talking about having November Lies at the River Place two days a week. As if you already don't have enough to do this month."

"We all do," said Cassie. "November Lies is fun, but kind of overwhelming."

"A step at a time," Piper advised.

"Half a Lie is better than none," Molly added.

"Maybe," Cassie said. "But even half a lie is hard. I do think Jacques is a genius, or maybe psychic. He didn't even know I was pregnant, and he made me read that thing about babies and food, which are pretty much the only two things I ever think about nowadays. How did he know? But I don't think he took the queasiness into account. The stuff about cooking babies makes my stomach heave." Cassie shook her head despairingly. "I don't think I'm cut out to be a social satirist."

"Not everyone is," said Piper. "You have to be true to your own voice."

"That's what I think," agreed Cassie. "It's true that every single thing I start to write ends up being about food. What if I do recipes as part of my polemic? Like I could say: Jonathan Swift suggests we cook babies, but I say it's better to cook *for* babies, so here's a recipe for baby food. And then I put in the recipe and go back to the polemic."

"Sounds good," Piper laughed. "You could say: if you're planning to cater a protest, try these finger sandwiches."

"Don't talk about finger sandwiches," Cassie protested. "All this eating people! I swear I'll hurl."

Molly was laughing too. "How about recipes for energy drinks? People could take on their protest walks."

"The union of the political and the palatable," Piper said.

Cassie nodded enthusiastically. "That way if you were pregnant and interested in political change, you could read my polemic and be happy either way."

"I've read books with recipes in them," Molly said encouragingly. "Some have done really well."

"That's right," said Cassie. "Like that Mexican novel with all the chocolate?"

"You don't always have to change people," Piper reflected. "Sometimes you just feed them."

"Food can be good for change," Cassie said. "Food can make you feel peaceful, or angry. There are lots of things about food that people don't know."

"Or zombies," Molly added. "A world of stuff to learn."

"How to feed them?" Piper asked, bemused.

"How to kill them," Molly corrected.

"Pasco says that up here on the hill, we're good," Cassie assured her. "Zombies are drawn to light and noise. They go to where lots of people are. So they won't come here. Probably."

"We could turn out the lights," Piper said thoughtfully. "But what about Molly? She might be in trouble if she's at her dad's house when they come."

"Don't worry, Mom," Molly reassured her. "I'll make sure I'm here when the zombies attack. Can I bring Dad? And Donny and Coral and Ralph?"

"Dad and Donny can come," Piper said. "Coral and Ralph can stay where they are. Let them do good for the zombies."

"OK," Molly said. "But don't blame me when zombie Coral and her zombie dog break in to eat our brains."

"How will we know the difference?" Piper said.

"This is a great place to have a zombie apocalypse," Cassie said. "People are always talking about barricading themselves into malls to ride it out, but Pasco says that's a bad idea. Too many entrances. Too many ways for the zombies to get in."

"That noise from the shed," Piper said. "Do you think it's zombies? Trying the door?"

Molly shivered. "That's a creepy thought, Mom, even for you."

"I'm not the one who brought up zombies. Anyway, I'm not likely to get caught in a mall. I hate shopping."

Cassie nodded. "Best to stay in the house."

"That works out well for those of us with home-based businesses," Piper said.

"It sure does." Cassie reached for the tray and offered it to Piper. "Try the chocolate empanada? It's chocolate chips and puff pastry. I'm going to use the recipe in my polemic."

Molly stood. "I've got to get downstairs. Silas wants me to come with him to check out the H.I.T. I'll be back later, Mom, to fill you in. Also, I think Mr. Winchester might stop by later today or tomorrow. I asked him to come if he could."

"Mr. Winchester?" said Piper. "Who is Mr. Winchester?"

"He's my business teacher, Mom. You know, from school? You had that phone conference with him about student internships?" Molly bent to pick up the plates.

"Don't worry about that, let me take care of it," said Cassie. "You shoo now."

Molly waved a thanks and headed out, Piper calling after her, "Molly, why is he stopping by?"

Molly disappeared without answering. Piper turned her attention to Cassie, who was picking up the dishes and stacking them onto the tray. "Why is Mr. Winchester stopping by?" she demanded. "What's that about?"

"He's been asking about *Riverboro Rocks*," Cassie said. "Molly invited him to help."

"Help how? Help what?"

"Figuring things out," Cassie said matter-of-factly. "Picking up the threads of the finance end of things. Since it might be better all round to buy Dan out."

"*What?*"

"You know, since he's been spending more time on River Place projects. And of course," Cassie said, balancing the tray on her hip and opening the door with her other hand, "Dan's a really nice guy and all, but he isn't that good for you, is he?"

* * *

"They made some progress on the Hey! It's Thursday," Molly said. She peered through her barn sale eyeglasses over her plastic nose. Silas loomed behind her, his head small beneath the reaching horns of his Viking helmet. "They've got the booths and the bar installed, and the walls are all painted. Guess who was there?"

"Marty?" Piper guessed. "Scoping out the competition for the lunch crowd?"

"Nope. The little dude with the big truck," said Silas.

"From the barn sale," said Molly. "The one who bought all the leftover stuff? He's in charge of the soft opening."

"No! Did you ask him why he bought all that junk?"

"To raffle off at the opening?" Silas guessed.

"To build a big bonfire to celebrate?" Molly put in.

"To blackmail the entire town into eating at Hey! It's Thursday?" Piper added. "Eat here or we'll deliver all your discarded junk back onto your doorsteps?"

"This doorstep," said Silas.

"Since this is where he got it," said Molly.

"I knew it. There's no escape," said Piper. "Like zombies. That junk is coming back. It's going to haunt us forever."

Piper's List: Boys Molly Shouldn't Date
(Not for Publication)

4) Peter: hopelessly in love with Miranda

3) Colby: a player—or so he would like to think

2) Silas: too many reasons to count

1) Everyone else

November 15: Monkeys, Monks and the Zombie Apocalypse

Donny is a little monkey, and although he did have an accident on a ladder earlier this month, he still loves to climb. So yesterday when he slipped through Molly's hands and went running off, naturally the first thing he did was head for the hills—or, in this case, the highest place he could find.

The old Hadley House is a warren of nooks and crannies, a child's magical playground. On the second floor at the end of the hall is a window that overlooks the roof of the shed; and from that roof it is possible to clamber into the branches of the enormous oak that shades the house. I myself used to climb up into the tree from there when I was a child, and Sasha still uses the roof as a way up into that tree—or she did till recently, when she came plummeting through my skylight and crashed onto my computer keyboard.

I hasten to say that Donny was in no way in any danger at any time—so Coral, do not freak out. We watch him like a hawk up here at the Hadley House, and that window is always closed and locked. The only reason it was propped open yesterday was that Brumi had been out there repairing a leaky patch. He had lowered himself off the roof (you see it is low enough to do so, Coral) to check the leak from inside. So for that one moment, security, you might say, was down.

At some point Donny had heard me say that a noise out in the shed was bothering me. Who knows what went through his mind? Children are curious; children can be protective. Whatever it was, he gave Molly the slip and out through that window he went. It happens!

The entire house was in an uproar, but do you know who actually walked out on that roof to get Donny? It was Lisette! She was in Ananda's room, nearest that end of the house and closest to the window. And, cool as you please, she gathered up her white robes and she—in her sixties, in her jingly bangles and bracelets—stepped out through the window onto the icy peak of the roof and walked across, picked Donny up, and calmly carried him back. She handed him through and stepped in herself as if it were nothing, absolutely nothing. Then she took him down to the kitchen for a snack.

Those monks! So recently a hive comprising six similar (if not identical) cells, they do keep differentiating themselves from one another in interesting and surprising ways. Though why it should surprise me that individuals should individuate is not a question I feel I can answer today.

Cassie is adorable, and she is becoming my favorite. (Though should I admit it now that I am aware that they all read my blog?) She nurtures through cooking and feeding people, and is gamely trying to apply those skills in Marquand-esque ways, though I'm not sure she has the dissatisfaction with people and life that it takes to be a successful muckraker. Jacques, we can't all be gadflies! Some of us just live peacefully and take care of those around us.

Pasco has what he claims is a lifelong obsession with zombies. His first toy, he tells me, was a zombie doll, and when other kids were playing cops and robbers he was playing zombies and aliens. Now he is drawing us all into his net—much as you, Jacques, are drawing us into your November Lies.

With their lively playfulness, Pasco and Cassie will be big helps in this upcoming apocalypse. They are sure to keep our spirits up when we're (all) trapped inside the house. Though you don't stay in *all* the time. People have to foray out from time to time to stock up on food and ammunition—yes, ammunition. While I tend to sympathize with the gun control set, the zombie apocalypse is where the second amendment really kicks in. If you shoot a zombie in the head, it goes down for good.

The monks will be a comfort in the zombie apocalypse, if it is anything like an ice storm followed by a power outage followed by a flood. Not that we needed weapons for our recent challenges—in fact, there were moments when it was probably better that I, at least, had none. But there were deprivations to be endured, and my experience with my houseguests has indicated that, when the apocalypse comes, you want them at your side. I am going to send Brumi and Lisette out onto that shed roof to pick off zombies. (Note: Can monks shoot zombies? Is there a Zen of zombies? Is that proper Buddhist protocol? Must ask before it's too late and the zombies are upon us).

I am not sure what role Ananda will play. She is an otherworldly being, floating in and out of our gatherings, saying little but radiating her beautiful luminosity. Perhaps her role will be to inspire us to greater feats of heroism. Certainly she will do so for Brumi. If you could see the way he tries to anticipate her desires! As do they all: Cassie always has some amusing story to tell her, and Lisette is frequently by her side, their heads close together, murmuring and smiling, a beautiful picture of the old and the young.

I intend to still, in some ways, see the monks as a collective, rather than discrete units, as the idea of a hive of monks buzzing throughout my house fills me with pleasure. But individually or collectively, if an apocalypse is coming, I hope they will be here with me.

Piper's List (With Thanks to Pasco): Top Five Tips for a Zombie Apocalypse

5) *Stay out of malls.* Lucky there isn't one near Riverboro. They draw the refugees, who draw the zombies.

4) *Weapons are your friends.* You have them. Zombies don't.

3) *Stay fit.* Learn to sprint.

2) *Stockpile food.* Sam, don't send a zombie to deliver!

1) *Keep your spirits up.* The monks should help with that.

 Except for the weapons part, they sound like great tips for living.

Idea for today: Set up a page (www.RiverboroRocks.com/ZombieApocalypse) where readers can add their own tips. I can't promise anything, but I suspect the good ones might end up in Pasco and Peter's script.

 Tags: Zombie apocalypse, how to kill a zombie

COMMENTS:

 ZombiePatrol: When shooting zombies, make sure to pull the trigger all the way back. Guruji told us that.

 ImmaterialGirl: Um, Pasco, Guruji was talking about bows and arrows, not guns. And I think he was talking about our yoga practice? I don't remember him mentioning zombies.

 ZombiePatrol: Thanks for clearing that up, Cass. I never can remember if we're doing this stuff to get rid of the zombies or to turn into them. Either way, Piper, you can count on us to zombie-proof the house.

ImmaterialGirl: Shouldn't we baby-proof it first?

ZombiePatrol: It depends on which is coming first, the zombies or Pasco Junior.

ImmaterialGirl: Cassie Junior. Cassie Junior is coming first.

RiverCoral: I do think that big old house has never been appropriately childproofed. How can you expect a mother not to be worried when her child ends up on the roof? And let's not get started on the weapons thing. ☺

PipersPebbles: Let's not get started on the *toy* weapons thing, either.

SamKing: I knew you'd love that group from the Ashram, the "monks" as you call them. There's an energy about them, isn't there? It's a blessing having them here in town, and I hope you enjoy them while they are with you. I have an idea for them that I'd like to propose. Let's take a few minutes to talk next time I bring their groceries.

DrewHadley: What about when the food runs out, lol?

SamKing: King's Market is working with the local suppliers to make sure that the needs of the Ashram are met—all organic, of course.

AuntieP: He means in the Zombie Apocalypse.

WeatherOracle: To avert mass zombie-related starvation
A greenhouse garden might offer salvation.
The Hadleys and Hammonds could jointly contrive
To grow a few veggies, and thusly survive.
Though as for those Hamons—while good in a garden,

A whack with a shovel is hard to pardon.
PS: though the topic is trending calorical
A garden needs weather advice from an Oracle.

AuntieP: I do like the idea of the Hadleys and Hammonds uniting. Don't you, Harvard Prof?

HarvardProf: Cooperation will serve better than conflict in, if you'll permit the pun, weathering tough times.

AuntieP: I couldn't agree more.

HarvardProf: A century ago New Hampshire was mostly cleared land, but today it's heavily forested. On the one hand, the forested nature of the land would be supportive of hunting to stay alive during this apocalypse of zombies.

AuntieP: On the other, you wouldn't see the zombies from as far away.

ImmaterialGirl: Plus we monks are all vegetarian.

ZombiePatrol: Peter and I were thinking we could hold classes down at the River Place on how to survive the zombie apocalypse. It's a very subtle science. Post if you're interested.

TheGeekster: I'm in.

BookLover603: Me too…

AuntieP: You may count me in, as well.

(*Comments approved*)

* * *

"Molly, I'm puzzled," Piper said.

Actually, Piper was more than puzzled. She was haunted, harried, sick with worry. What was going on with her magazine, her finances, her career? Why were people talking about issues having to do with her, what were they saying, and what did it mean? It all loomed, growing larger by the hints people seemed determined to drop. Today, sitting with Molly in the library off the living room, looking through cover proofs and inside layouts, might represent an opportunity to clear it up.

"Puzzled by what, Mom?" Molly had a stack of costume jackets in front of her. She was hand-sewing emblems onto them.

"Something Cassie said. She seemed to think your father is leaving *Riverboro Rocks* to spend more time at the River Place. But he told me we'd have to close the company. File for bankruptcy. What do the monks have to do with this? And what business is it of Cassie's?"

"The monks aren't involved, and Cassie shouldn't have put her foot in it like that." Molly concentrated fiercely on her task, as she sometimes did when a conversation made her anxious. "I wish it wasn't my business either."

"Sweetie, it isn't something you have to worry about. We'll sort it out somehow, but when your Dad moves on, he needs to give some thought to what he's leaving behind."

Molly hunched her shoulders as if to fend off her mother's words. "I don't know where Cassie got the idea that he wants to leave. It's only he loves the kids at the River Place and the mission and all."

"Yes, he's always loved the River Place," Piper replied. "And we all know how that's worked out. If he wants to leave the company, he should say it straight out."

"Mom, I don't think it's like that. Look here, what do you think of this stitch, where I loop over the edge, will it be strong enough?" Molly held her project out for her mother to check. "It's not a big deal, him helping out at the River Place. Coaching some peewee teams, taking kids on outings."

"And now Coral wants you and Miranda and the others to 'help out,' as well." Piper blew a poof of air through her lips. "Miranda has had enough people pulling her this way and that throughout her life. Now, when she's starting to settle in with a real family structure and some creative things to do, Coral wants to stick in her oar. Typical."

"Is there anything Miranda could do for the magazine?" Molly seized on the change in topic. "You wouldn't have to pay her much."

"Maybe she could help Silas." Piper gave a sideways glance at Molly. "I think those two have a lot in common. What do you think? Would they get along?"

Molly shrugged. "They already do. They grew up together." Molly stitched quickly, stacking the finished jackets to one side. "Mom, could you thread a needle for me?"

Piper accepted the needle and thread. "And what about this Mr. Winchester person? Who is he?"

"He teaches my business class at school. Remember? He reads *Riverboro Rocks*. He offered to take a look at things."

"Because?"

"Because you've been blogging on about money problems—"

"I have not been 'blogging on'. I might have mentioned it once or twice—"

"So he read it once or twice. And he says home-based businesses are his specialty."

Piper handed the threaded needle back to Molly. "Your dad is the business manager. What could your teacher do that he couldn't?"

"Fresh eyes," said Molly. "Plus, it might make an interesting case study for the class."

"The class?" Piper demanded. "Now you have a high school class looking at my business?"

"Just the social media and online stuff. Our age group is good at that. But not today. Today it's just him."

"Today! What do you mean, today? Who said he could come, never mind today?"

"Mr. Winchester is great, Mom. Really smart. One of my best teachers ever. You'll like him. And he's not going to charge you anything. It's free. I thought you'd be excited."

"Excited! About someone I don't know meddling with my business?"

"Yes, about that." Molly gathered up the jackets. "And while we're waiting, could you help me sew buttons onto all of these?"

* * *

Piper didn't think she could bear to have one more new person in her home, but Matthew Winchester, when he arrived, did not seem threatening. Standing inside the doorway, computer backpack slung over one shoulder, he had an easy posture and a self-effacing air. The kind of guy who left some space in a room for you.

He followed Piper into the library and smiled a hello at Molly, who waved her fingers in reply. Piper found herself fluttering about nervously, offering him drinks, offering him snacks. He looked around, orienting himself, taking in the cozy room, the stacks of magazines, the pile of jackets on the chair. "Are those the costumes?" he asked. "For Molly's party?"

"You know about the party?" Piper asked.

"Of course I do," Matthew answered. "I love to see people take on ridiculously ambitious projects. I couldn't resist coming and seeing it all for myself."

"It all? What all? You mean the Lies?"

"The Lies, the party, the barn, the magazine—the whole nine yards. Everyone who reads your blog knows about them."

"And you're going to help me keep *Riverboro Rocks* going?"

"I'd love to try." Matthew sat down on the settee and opened his backpack.

"How?"

Matthew pulled out his laptop and set it on the low table in front of him. "Do you have any kind of budget? A business plan?"

"A budget? A plan? To do what with?"

"Just to look at. Right here," he said, pointing at this laptop. "It will be confidential. It will be painless."

Matthew Winchester was already wrong. Piper could feel a knotted pain in her stomach. "We don't have one. Not exactly," she admitted. "I have some reports on flash drive…"

"We'll start with them."

When Piper returned with her reports, Matthew flipped open his computer and turned it on, accepting the flash drive from Piper and fitting it into the port. "We'll start by taking a look at what comes in and what goes out, money-wise. Then we can start to figure out how to increase what comes in or reduce what goes out. Or both."

"Sounds basic."

"But that's pretty much how it works." With his computer open and a subject he could warm to, Matthew seemed to gain authority. "It isn't easy to find the right balance between getting and spending. Sometimes an outside perspective helps. It's why people bring in consultants."

Almost in spite of herself, Piper felt a flicker of hope. Maybe Matthew had the magic. Maybe he would find something she and Dan had missed. "What are we looking for?" she asked.

"Let's start with the losses," he replied. "We'll take a hard look at the negative numbers."

Drawn by the lure of her publication, Piper perched beside him on the settee. Matthew shifted his shoulder to accommodate her and she leaned in to look at the laptop screen with him.

And there they were—the numbers, her numbers. They represented the life of her publication, as pulse and breath rate represented a human life. They were so familiar, so dear to her. And looking at them with her, shoulders touching, was a stranger, someone she had only just met. Now he was in her house. He was looking at her magazine. It was strange, disorienting.

Why couldn't it be Dan who was here? Why couldn't Dan suggest they sit together, look at spreadsheets together, talk about what was coming in, what was going out? He was the business manager. Why didn't they do this anymore?

It had been so long since anyone had shown real interest in what she did. So long since anyone had wanted to meet about the magazine, to talk about the magazine, to look at the magazine. If suddenly there was to be a person, an amazing miraculous person, willing to take the time, to give the attention, why did it have to be a stranger? Why couldn't it be Jake? Or Auntie Polly? Or...or Sam? Or maybe one of the monks? Who was this

Matthew? He seemed rather bony compared to Dan, rather insubstantial. Piper caught a faint whiff of aftershave. Who wore aftershave? Dan never did. Why did Matthew?

Piper looked at Molly in sudden panic. But Molly didn't look up or catch her mother's eye. She sat calmly, sewing buttons on her costumes, ignoring the danger that Piper felt roaring all around her.

Matthew also seemed unaware of the rollercoaster emotions that his presence was triggering in Piper. He seemed to see only what was on his laptop screen, which he was narrating in a pleasant, neutral voice. "You've got some costs that are fixed, some that are variable, some that are negotiated," he said. "Let's look at each and see if any can be reduced."

Piper closed her eyes, feeling almost disembodied, listening to the rhythm of Matthew's voice. It flowed like a brook around her, low-key, even, unemphatic. It began to soothe her, to relax her. Bit by bit she allowed other perceptions to filter in. The faint scent of Matthew's aftershave—not so unpleasant, a nice light spice, you could get used to it; the warmth of his arm against hers, shifting as he pointed to line items on the screen or clicked the mouse to scroll down.

When she tuned back in, Matthew was looking at the line item for photography. "This is a big one," he was saying. "Why is it so expensive?"

Piper felt as if she had swum up from the depths of a silent pool. "It's one of our biggest expenses," she acknowledged, her own voice sounding strange in her ears. She paused, allowing her attention to re-focus, then continued more naturally, "It's what the magazine *is*. We buy original photos. They cost a lot."

"Can you get them someplace cheaper?" Matthew asked.

"We like our photographer," said Piper. "And we can't use stock photos—they have to be original, they have to be local. Readers like to recognize and identify places."

"Can you re-use pictures from your archives?"

Piper shook her head. "Lots of readers save every issue. They have them going back years. They'd pick up on it if we did repeats."

Matthew glanced at her. "Are you OK with this?" he asked. "Me sticking my nose in?"

Despite what had looked like complete preoccupation with his task,

Piper realized, Matthew had noticed something of her inner uproar. How did he do that? "Yes, of course," she said quickly. "Thank you for coming, where are my manners? I don't mean to seem resistant. I appreciate it, all this time you're giving me, all this effort you're putting in. No one ever comes and talks to me about *Riverboro Rocks*. I work alone almost all the time, so for me this is a treat."

As she spoke, she realized that what she was saying was true. What could be better than talking about *Riverboro Rocks*? And here was someone new, someone different, a presentable attractive male person, sitting here giving it his full attention. Yes, the magazine was sick, but she loved it as much as if it weren't. She felt like a mother, sitting by the bedside of a dearly loved child, watching a doctor take the child's temperature.

But is the illness fatal? Piper thought with a chill. *And what will I do if it is?*

Molly looked up from her sewing. "What about doing a best-of issue?" she suggested. "Using pictures from old issues?"

"That's not a bad idea," Piper admitted.

Molly smiled happily. "That way you could save photography costs at least once," she explained.

"Could you take it a step further, with a series of best-of issues?" Matthew suggested. "In different categories?"

"I think we could," Piper said. "Best of recipes…best of day trips… best of shopping—the advertisers would love that…"

"What about using more of the photos that readers send in?" Molly asked. "Like you're doing with the snowstorm?"

"It could draw in the community," Piper conceded. "There are a lot of questions about photo quality, about consistency, about curation that we'd have to deal with. It might save something, but these things are never as cheap as they seem at first look."

"What about Silas?" Molly asked. "He's cheap. And you said he's getting pretty good."

"Or maybe your advertisers?" Matthew asked. "Local businesses with professional-grade photography you could use?"

"Editorial integrity…" Piper began.

"However you do it, we're going to have you save at least one full issue of photography costs in a year," said Matthew, making the change on the spreadsheet. "Now, let's look at some of your other costs. Are there savings to be had in the printing? When was the last time you re-negotiated your printing contract?"

Rocking like a skiff on the endless ocean of afternoon, Piper bobbed on the crests and troughs of her magazine's finances. Editorial followed printing, and was followed by postage.

"It's not just the savings we want to look at," Matthew said. "It's also important to look at opportunities to increase revenues. But when you get to the point you can't sustain the losses, obviously the savings are the first thing to scrutinize."

"And are we there yet?" Piper asked. "Does all this make a difference?"

Matthew scrolled to the bottom of his spreadsheet to check the totals. "It's a start."

Piper felt deflated. All this work, all these hours, this whole afternoon working and looking at numbers and comparing scenarios and it was only a start. Matthew was a disappointment. He didn't have the magic.

But then Molly said, "Cool. All these changes from looking at a report."

And Matthew said, "The magic of spreadsheets. Gloria in Excel sheet deo."

And Piper laughed, charmed. "They call it float but it's sinking me," she said.

"A good pun is its own reword," Matthew quipped.

"Funny and true," Piper said.

"Puns are great," Molly added loyally, and Piper felt a surge of love for her daughter and pure happiness from the afternoon.

Because, after all, what a wonderful day it had been—the best in such a long time. Here she was with a new man, one she hadn't known practically all her life (unlike Dan and Jake and Sam and who else was there, anyway?); and they were sharing ideas about the magazine, they were finding ways to improve the business, they were making jokes and puns, and Molly was here with them and participating as almost an equal, and they were all talking and laughing together. This was what she had imagined, this was what she had dreamed, back when it all started; this was where she had imagined time and life would take her and Dan. The thought made her happy and exhilarated and desperate and sad, and she felt a pricking in the back of her eyes and oh God no, she was fine, just fine, and she said, really fast, "I used to be a banker but I lost interest," and they all laughed.

Because there was nothing wrong with Matthew; he was no Dan, but who was? He didn't fill up space like Dan, he didn't fill the room with the sound of his voice, he didn't laugh in such a big way. One minute she kind of liked him; the next she knew that no afternoon, however magical, could make up for what she had lost: no meeting, no magazine, no man was ever going to fill that Dan-sized hole in her. Matthew seemed to flicker in the changing light of her perceptions. But there was, increasingly, a feeling of easiness about him, and he did want to talk about the magazine. And he could work some magic with words, and anyway, what was she thinking? You really do need to get out more when every guy that walks in the door gets compared to your ex-husband.

But as they were ticking through the last line item, as Matthew was closing down his laptop and packing it into his backpack, he looked directly at her and said, "I wanted to tell you, Piper, that I am a big fan. Of your work, I mean. I've read *Riverboro Rocks* for years. From day one."

"Me, I'm totally impressed by anyone who's a teacher," Piper said, deflecting the compliment. "Taking a bunch of unruly teenagers and educating them can't be easy. Such a tangible thing to do. Very hands on, very engaged. Very out-there-in-the-world-ish."

"As opposed to numbers on a spreadsheet?" Molly suggested.

"Or words in a blog," Piper added. "You can do that in an office all by yourself. It's so much easier that way."

Matthew hoisted his backpack and stood awkwardly for a moment. Then he said, "Hey! It's Thursday is opening for drinks today. The soft opening your Auntie P mentioned. A free drink and snacks."

"Since it's Tuesday," said Piper. "What could be more appropriate?"

"I was thinking about going down," Matthew said. "To check it out."

"Great idea," said Piper quickly. "How I wish I could join you! Such a shame. You'll have to tell me about it after."

Matthew nodded, absorbing the rejection. He turned to go, hesitated once more, and then turned back. "One last thing," he said. "Why is Dan still drawing full salary? I ask because, going over the numbers, it looked to me as if you've stopped taking yours."

Piper suddenly wanted to go off by herself and rest. How she *hated* long goodbyes. "Theoretically we are both still drawing," she explained, starting to edge away, "but I volunteered to give up mine for a while. We can't afford both salaries at this juncture."

"And you agreed he should be the one to keep his…because…why?'"

Matthew had started to follow her back in and she stopped, to keep him at the doorway, to keep him on his way out. "It just made sense. Dan's got a son and a lot of expenses. I don't have as many, especially since the mortgage is paid on this house."

Matthew must have understood that it was time to leave, but he lingered, following his train of thought. "As far as I can see, Dan's contribution is less significant," he said. "You're doing the creative work. You're supervising the production. And you seem to have a lot to do with the ad sales as well."

"That's because I'm the managing editor," said Piper. "Dan is more in charge of the business side of things."

"Then where," asked Matthew, "is he now?'"

Piper's Index of the Men in her Life
(Not for Publication)

Number of men she has dated: 2

Number of years since she had a real date: 18

Number of times Dan swore there was nothing going on with Coral (give or take): 62

Number of times Dan admitted that there was something going on with Coral: 1

Number of years Dan has been with Coral: 4

Number of years since Dan left Piper: 3

Number of years since Donny was born: 3

Number of years Piper has been having panic attacks: 3

November 16: She Wishes for the Cloths of Heaven (or at least a Revenue-Positive Bottom Line)

Even those of us who regard magazine publishing as our personal form of Paradise must admit that the gods of publishing have not, lately, spread the cloths of Heaven under our feet. Following economic trends, people are buying fewer things, which means that businesses don't spend as much to advertise those things in magazines, and so it begins. Costs go up, revenues go down, print is overtaken by digital, yada yada yada. Why should *Riverboro Rocks*, mirror of our times, be exempt?

While I'm sharing my woes, I might add that my ad sales manager (Silas, you know him, don't you?) has told me he's a con artist. A. Con. Artist. What am I to do with that information?

Maybe now would be a good time to talk about all the things we're doing to make *Riverboro Rocks* a magazine you have to have. We start with the print magazine. Classic local content! Then we have the blog, the social media, the forums and reader-submitted content. Next come the great new ideas we've introduced: the book group, the zombie page, the reviews page, the swap page. Never a dull moment!

A gardener once told me that when a tree is stressed it will often produce an unusually large amount of fruit—to increase the chances of seeds being cast and taking root and growing into new trees.

My magazine is stressed, and I am casting seeds. Some might take root. Some might blossom. Some might grow. But each seed contains within it a spark of life. All I need is time and, readers, your support. Share these posts (the ones that interest you) with your friends. Post your comments and updates, your recommendations and ideas. "Like" us on Facebook. Tweet the ideas.

And tread softly, because you tread on my dreams.

Piper's List: Top Five Convergences of Business and Poetry

5) *My object in living is to unite my avocation and my vocation.* (Robert Frost) The poet's formula for professional happiness: finding reward in the right work.

4) *Whatever your hand finds to do, do it with all your might.* (Ecclesiastes 9:10) This one goes Robert Frost one better as it requires us to create the reward in any work.

3) *Some rob you with a six gun and some with a fountain pen.* (Woody Guthrie) Which does this comparison romanticize: the outlaw or the banker? Which does it vilify?

2) *Who steals my purse steals trash.* (Shakespeare) I don't know about you, but this is certainly true of me!

1) *Money is a kind of poetry.* (Wallace Stevens) And poetry, Stevens also said, is the supreme fiction. Would that make money the supreme fiction?

Tags: WB Yeats, horticulture

COMMENTS:

ImmaterialGirl: What I love about poets is how they can turn things around. Like our power outage. It started as a state of emergency and turned into a blessing.

PipersPebbles: Gaiety transfigures all that dread.

WeatherOracle: The gaiety will turn right back to dread;
                  High winds, a Tempest lie ahead.
                  Your storm-tossed ship is not yet shorable—
                  You heard it here, from Weather Oracle.

AuntieP: I am lately finding the contributions of Weather Oracle somewhat discouraging. Drew, if it is your dad can you ask him to cheer us up from time to time?

DrewHadley: I'll do my best, Auntie P, but you know my father, he marches to his own drummer, lol.

BookLover603: I would seriously love to meet your ad sales person… Silas the con artist. The rainmaker or trickster of story and myth… Silas, are you out there? Do you make magical things happen?

ConArtist: Sometimes it does seem as if there's something pretty magical about those cons. But it isn't because of anything I do.

PipersPebbles: Do you have any cons that might save our sorry butts? Because at this point I'd stoop to almost anything.

ConArtist: I don't get why you think of cons as stooping. They can be pretty cool.

TheGeekster: Is your specialty the long con or the short con?

ConArtist: I'll do both, but the long ones can get grueling. Some seem to last forever...

(*Comments approved*)

Piper's List: Top Five Reasons Molly Shouldn't Date Silas (Not for Publication)

5) He is too bald for her

4) He is too tattooed for her

3) He is too old for her

2) He has no educational or professional aspirations

1) He is a con artist

* * *

"Mom, you will not believe it," Molly said, leaning against the door and laughing. "Silas and I stopped by Hey! It's Thursday to check out the scene. And oh my God!"

"Oh my God what?" Piper demanded.

"The junk," said Silas.

"Junk?"

"From the sale," gasped Molly. "Coral's Peter Pan costumes—the pirates, the Indians—are displayed on the walls. Aunt Polly's beat up old birdcage? It's hanging near the salad bar. All the town's junk is out for all the world to see!"

"They used the town's junk to decorate the restaurant?"

"They did. A montage of ticket stubs from local concerts, faded covers of back issues of *Riverboro Rocks*, that cracked aquarium set up with moss and rocks."

"Old bike," Silas said helpfully.

Molly snorted with laughter. "Yes, the rustiest of the bicycles is fastened to the front of the bar. The half set of old china is in a glass-front display case."

"The croquet mallets?" Piper asked.

"In an umbrella stand by the door!"

"Auntie P is going to *die* when she sees her birdcage set up there," said Piper.

"And for Coral? Peter Pan lives on," said Silas.

"I knew we'd never be free of that junk," Piper said.

* * *

The library was crowded. Way too crowded.

Piper glanced behind her into the living room: no escape that way. The living room was filled with students and monks, tapping away at keyboards, whirring away at sewing machines. Silas was moving from group to group with his camcorder, talking, interviewing, filming.

In front of her, in her library, the scene was a blur. Piper stood poised at the door, calming her impulse toward flight, struggling to make sense of the noisy shapeless melee. Gradually her eyes started to differentiate: Matthew. Molly. Colby. Jilly. Some other high school students she knew.

Molly's business class.

Molly detached from the group and came over to her. Matthew stood and joined them. This, Piper told herself, was *not* a problem. She turned to Matthew with an assumption of ease. "Welcome," she said. "I see you've brought the class."

"I hope that's OK." Matthew sounded worried. "Molly said it was OK."

"Consider yourself at home," said Piper with all the hospitality she could muster. "We have plenty of room. And these kids are hardly strangers. Half of them are here all the time anyway, with November Lies."

"That's what I said, too," said Molly. "I knew you wouldn't mind. Mr. Winchester said we could compare some city and regional magazines, and you've got all the back issues of *Riverboro Rocks* here."

"Of course I don't mind," Piper managed.

"That's great, just great," said Matthew. But he said it too heartily.

And there it was, the other side of that quiet inward life of the writer. You wrote in the quiet of your office, in the privacy of your home, but then you sent those words out into the world. Then people read what you wrote, and then you saw those people. And then you were exposed and vulnerable.

Because here was the thing: there were simply too many people in the house. Piper felt trapped in the midst of them, like one of those tragic cavalry soldiers in *The Charge of the Light Brigade*. How did all these people end up here, in her house—people to the right of her, people to the left of her, people in front of her? Someone had blundered.

Of course she minded.

"I guess I'm something of an introvert," Piper admitted.

"Like most creative people," Matthew said. "But you'd never know it by coming here."

"I've got to…" Molly said. She gestured to the group of students. "We need to…" She edged her way back to the group and disappeared into it.

"I'm sorry," Matthew said. "It's kind of a mob scene, I see that now. I should have called, or maybe kept the kids in the classroom. I thought…"

How different today was from yesterday! Yesterday the three of them had worked toward a common goal. Today the illusion of togetherness, the playfulness and high spirits and hope: all had vanished. Now Molly edged away and Matthew felt bad and Piper felt choked, and it was all because of the people, all these damned people in the house and nowhere to hide.

But then Matthew tilted his head, indicating a quieter corner of the room. He made a "carry on" gesture to his class. Colby caught it and nodded reassuringly. Matthew put out his arm, careful not to touch her, and gently shepherded Piper toward that pool of privacy. Piper felt herself begin to relax.

"Your blog is picking up momentum, isn't it?" Matthew said. "I think it's taking root as a new Riverboro tradition. I love your sly sense of humor. This morning's comment about Silas was very funny."

"Thank you…" Piper tried to remember her post. What had she said? How had she been funny? She didn't remember being funny.

"I see him at the cons from time to time."

No way. "Who—Silas? You know Silas? You...participate in his cons?" A prickling dread seemed to gather around her, press in and seep into her body. Not a full-fledged panic attack, thank God. Not yet, anyway. Still, it was almost as bad: that creeping hollow conviction that everybody knew something that she didn't. One of the reasons it was good to work and live with fewer people, to stay away from large groups, was that you didn't get these kinds of feelings. At least, not so often.

But now, with people swarming all around like this, it was all coming back. Matthew and Silas, in cahoots? What was going on?

And she had a horrible feeling that she was beginning to know. Silas went to cons. Matthew went to cons.

Molly went to cons.

"Conventions," Piper said. "You go to conventions. Costume conventions. Japanese conventions. Anime conventions."

"Only the local ones," Matthew said, seemingly unaware of her distress. "I'm not such a junkie that I'll go way out of my way for them. Also, I don't go in costume. I'm not that hardcore."

"But Silas...is more serious?" Draw the breath down into the lungs, let it out. "The costume...is that his art? For these conventions...these cons?"

"He draws caricatures, that's his main thing, but his costumes are pretty amazing too. Of course Molly's costumes are always the best, she's got a genius for them, doesn't she? But Silas—that's some dedication, taking it as far as permanent body art."

This can go either way, Piper thought, breathing. *Either I can laugh merrily and pretend I am having fun. Or I can never, ever live this down my whole entire life.*

Because, in defiance of all expectation, Silas wasn't a scammer, a cheat, a shyster, a thief—a con artist. Who knew? He was an artist. He worked at conventions. Did he know how she had misinterpreted his screen name? Had he set her up? Oh if he had she would murder him. If he had done that, it really was a con. And she was a dupe, a sucker; she had been scammed. How could he do that?

Today was a disaster.

"Molly has asked me to come with her from time to time," she managed. "To these...cons. I didn't...I never...this whole Japan cartoon thing...it's usually her and Coral..."

"Of course it does have its roots in Japanese pop culture, but I think it goes way beyond that," Matthew said. "Those costumes will make a great portfolio for Molly, if she wants to go on to design school. And who knows? There could be a career in there for her. This party of hers—organizing her entire group to participate—it's pretty impressive."

At that moment, Piper hated Matthew; she hated Silas; she hated Coral; she hated Dan. Why was Matthew telling her things about her own daughter, things she didn't know? This had started with that trip to Japan, the one Piper had been meant to take, the one Coral had taken in her place.

Most of all she hated herself.

"I always mean to go but there always seems to be something else going on," she said. "So much to do. So hard to do it all."

"The cons are a real experience," Matthew said. "People dressed like comic characters, like videogame characters. Dancing, acting, roleplaying. Definitely a strange scene."

"I now wish I had gone," Piper said. She half meant it—what fresh hells, what depths of humiliation could she have spared herself? What had she written in her blog? How could she backtrack from it? Could she pretend it had all been a joke?

Of course she could! Matthew thought she had been joking; Matthew thought her words had been playful. So would her readers! She could tough this one out. She had to.

"I won't be surprised if Molly's costume party captures some of that vibe," Matthew was saying. "The prep part certainly does. The excitement and buzz is almost like the real thing."

"The story of my life," Piper replied. "What I don't go out for seems to come to me. Whether I like it or not."

"You'll get an even better taste of it at the party," Matthew continued.

The conversation was starting to feel like a minefield of topics waiting to explode, a game where the bombs tick down faster than you can defuse them. "What's your costume going to be?" Piper asked quickly.

"What do you suggest?" Matthew asked. "Someone in uniform, maybe?"

"We women are supposed to go for the guy in uniform, isn't that so?" Piper rattled on. "Like men are supposed to like the kick-butt warrior princesses. How about you be a UPS driver? You can show you're tough by wearing those brown shorts in a New Hampshire November."

"I suppose I could dress tough," Matthew said reflectively. "As it's a Lie. What about you? Will you be the kick-butt action heroine? And do warrior princesses go for UPS drivers?"

"I haven't decided yet," Piper said, thinking it might be time to go back to the students. There was no greater irony, from Piper's perspective, than the idea that sanctuary was to be found in greater numbers. But any port in a storm.

She was turning away, but Matthew put out a hand to stop her. "I've been wanting to tell you," he said. "I remember you. From high school."

"Really?" Piper hesitated. "What class were you in?"

"I was a class behind you."

"I don't—"

"You wouldn't. We were a pretty non-memorable class."

"A heinous class," Piper supplied.

"I wish. If we were heinous, you'd remember. No, we were completely unremarkable."

"Ah, then. No wonder I can't place you."

"I used to see you in the cafeteria. You were always with Sam King."

"I wish I could remember you," said Piper.

"Why would you? We never talked."

"Who was your girlfriend?"

"Girlfriend? Nobody. Didn't have one."

"Oh, wait, I've got it! You were that quiet guy that was with Bradley Bennett, right? Used to eat those huge salads at lunch?"

"*What?* No. No! That was Chuckie McDougall. I couldn't have been gay; I didn't have the clothes for it. I was just another socially awkward boy that didn't know how to talk to girls. Perpetually condemned to admire from afar."

"You've spiffed up since then," Piper suggested.

"I try. Who doesn't want to leave their high school selves behind?"

"And now you're back as a teacher," Piper said. "In charge. The big cheese. Your time has come. And not only you—all the bright misfits from high school. Out there running things now."

"The geek will inherit the earth," Matthew said.

* * *

When Matthew re-joined his students Piper retreated to a chair to watch until she could breathe easily again. Matthew seemed to come into his own as he directed the students' efforts and answered their questions, interacting easily in a way Piper found hard to fathom. He really seemed to like the kids, and they seemed to like and trust him. Was he showing off for her? Or did he lose himself (or find himself) in his work, much as she did? Either way, she found herself watching him with appreciation, even admiration. Even in a stranger's home, working on an unfamiliar project, teaching was clearly Matthew's milieu.

Silas lrooked in. "Ad sale," he said to Piper. "Riverboro Madrigal Group, three time placement, quarter page, non-profit rate." His eyes found Molly, sitting on the settee on the other side of the room. She had been filling out a strategy form that Matthew had handed out. Colby had taken the other seat on the settee and was leaning toward her, saying something. "Trouble," Silas said.

Piper followed his gaze. Silas was right: Molly looked furious. Her entire face was squinching in on itself the way it did when she was about to completely lose it. Her voice was rising; Piper could hear it from across the room.

"You have got some nerve!" she cried. "What do you mean, 'Nowheresville'? Riverboro is nowhere near Nowheresville! What have you ever done, to think you're from Somewheresville? Do you even know where Somewheresville *is*?"

Colby looked worried, as well he might. "Molly, wait. I only meant—"

"And what's with 'hashtag Riverboro'? Stop saying 'hashtag Riverboro,' as if you're too good for us!"

Colby tried again. "Is Riverboro a country town? Sure it is, " he began. "Is it therefore hick? Not at all. I was just saying—"

"Just saying! Just saying! Hashtag Colby—Colby is just saying! Is Colby a poser? Of course he is," Molly continued, mimicking Colby's habitual turn of phrase. "Does that mean we're taken in? Well I'm not. Find someone else to say things to! You think you're so...so..." Molly began to trail off; she looked as if she was struggling not to cry.

Piper started toward Molly, but Silas was ahead of her, taking out his phone and clicking to his text messages, scrolling down as he crossed the room. "Hey, Mol, can I steal you for a sec?" he asked. "Gotta problem. With my Lie."

Molly glanced over, momentarily derailed, her eyes going from Silas' face to his phone. "What—"

"Main guy says: I love you. Main girl says: What do you mean, it's less than three?" Silas took Molly's wrist and drew her up and away from Colby. "Like: what to do?"

"Hey," Colby said, standing. "Wait a sec—"

Silas gestured him quiet with one hand, holding his phone screen for Molly to see with the other. "Not now, dude," he said. "Got to get this solved. Urgent."

Molly looked blankly at Silas, still blinking back angry tears. "What…?" She took his phone and studied the screen. Silas waited as her attention focused. "I see what you're saying," she said finally. "She's reading the symbols literally, instead of as emoticons." She allowed Silas to draw her away, move her toward the other room.

"But…" Colby protested.

"What's the hero going to do?" Molly asked, her attention fully shifted. "Could he turn it into some kind of play on the concept of family?"

"It could get algorithmic," said Silas. "Wheels within wheels."

They started out, heads together over the phone. Molly was saying, "They're using the same language to say different things. You could use that to build the meaning. Si, this could be really good, but really hard."

"The mystery subplot is a challenge," Silas acknowledged, handing Molly her coat. "How 'bout I buy you a cocoa and you help me work it through?"

Molly looked back at the group. "I don't know…" She hesitated. "Mr. Winchester, is it OK if I go?"

"Hey man," Colby sputtered. "Not cool. You can't…"

Matthew waved them off. "Got it covered," he said. "Thank you, Silas."

"No problem," said Silas. "Let's go."

November 17: The Circus Animals Return

How many of you, my readers, have ever been to an anime convention?

These "cons," as we call them, take place all around us, several times a year, and they are truly *the bal masques*, the *commedia del arte* of the 21st century. If you stop by a con you'll find characters from the folk literature of our day, roleplaying, miming, posing in *tableaux vivants*. The mummery, the pageantry, the epic tales and heroes' quests, the juggling and fencing and acrobatics, the mystery and morality plays happening right here in our midst—brought to us courtesy of the geeks and the nerds.

As you now know (because I told you about it yesterday), we at *Riverboro Rocks* participate in this magical world. Our own Silas of ad sale fame is the Arlequin who delights us with his playful and quirky drawings, the Tatterdemalion who sketches on his own body images drawn from the imaginative worlds found in the stories told.

At Molly's request he drew a sketch of me yesterday using a photo as a model, and he sent it to me by text message. The me he drew is so evocative—those big cartoon eyes and a sweet angelic face, but when you look closely there are devil horns and a devil tail. I thought to be offended, but in the end I succumbed to its charms: he had truly changed me into something rich and strange. So Shakespearian of him! How about I post it here, and you share it with your friends? It will bring people to the blog and if you like Silas' art you can commission pieces of your own. Soon everyone will want their own Silas Pickering, revealing their hidden angels or demons in the most innocent of ways.

And speaking of epic tales and heroes' quests: Matthew Winchester, business teacher at Riverboro High, has come riding into town. Bad guys beware!

He and Molly and I have gone over revenues and expenses for hours and hours over the past couple of days; and while the tale the numbers tell is bleak, the hero has in any case arrived on set. As heroes do when times are darkest.

He (along with his entire high school business class) has put me on an austerity plan, and it is one that is intended to put *Riverboro Rocks* back on sound footing.

As an independent publisher, I am likely falling into errors common to our sort: spending more than I need to, failing to recognize potential economies, that sort of thing. Matthew is taking all this in hand. He intends to straighten things out in his fierce, implacable business-school way.

For example: I have set up quite a number of pages and projects over the past weeks in what is, perhaps, a slightly manic way. This all seemed to me simply brilliant when I was doing it. But each project, each page, requires resources. Even reader-generated content requires a measure of curation. Someone has to sort, weigh, accept and reject; someone has to motivate and create interest. And I am spread too thin.

So while we are all still here, Riverboro and larger interested community (extending, according to my site stats, throughout the state and even, thanks to what is picked up by Damn Lies, to other parts of New England), please check out the various pages that we have set up over the past weeks: November Lies; Riverboro Recommends (the information on this page is going to be the basis of an app); Riverboro Reads (our book group); Riverboro Reveals (our page for the costumes people are going to wear to Molly's party); Riverboro Recycles (for swapping whatever junk anyone has left after the Great Barn Sale); Riverboro Recipes; Riverboro Remembers (our page for historical vignettes); Riverboro's Resolutions; Riverboro Rides Out the Storm; and, most recently, Riverboro Survives (the Zombie Apocalypse).

If any engaged reader is interested to work with the (somewhat-volatile) personalities who own this magazine and curate content for any of these pages, please get in touch. Of course we can't afford to pay you, but these pages will be by, of, and for the town and we'd love to have townspeople get involved.

Otherwise, Matthew has decreed that pages without volunteer curators must come down, as they demand resources we simply don't have.

Piper's List: Top Five Matthew-Mandated Austerity Measures

5) Reduce the total number of editorial pages per issue (Note to advertisers: the more advertising pages we sell the more edit pages we can print, so on your heads be it…)

4) Cut the number of four-color pages in half; replace with one-color (Note to readers: I barely managed to keep him from cutting us back to newsprint so be grateful)

3) Reduce the quality of the paper in the classified ad section of the magazine (Note to readers: many publications use a bulkier and less glossy stock in that section of the magazine; the quality of paper we have been using till now is overkill)

2) Raise the price of advertising for the advertisers getting both the print and the site links

1) Get rid of most of the new online forums or get outside help to manage them

Tags: Anime conventions, publishing models

COMMENTS:

Private Message from DanTheRiverMan: Matthew has decreed??? Who the hell is this Matthew guy to decree anything? What is going on up there? And what do you mean, the hero of the magazine? What's that?

Private Message to DanTheRiverMan: If you don't like what I said in my blog you're going to hate what he has recommended regarding your salary.

MollyHH: Silas' cartoons are called chibis, by the way. It's the style he uses.

BookLover603: I love Silas' chibis…I want one too. I'd want a halo… or maybe devil horns…something like that for the big reveal…

SamKing: You know, Piper, your monks might be able to pitch in to help with some of those projects of yours. How about putting one of them in charge of some aspect of that site? Pay them on commission only.

Private Message from RiverCoral: Piper, that's such a great idea of Sam's! And here's another: what if you got Andy Hadley to help you with the garden page? Unless he's too busy, between running his farm and predicting the weather? ☺

Private Message to RiverCoral: If you're trying to trick me into revealing who the Oracle is, you'll find out when Dan and the rest of the world does. You might as well stop guessing.

Private Message from RiverCoral: You mean you're going to let the whole world know when you tell Dan and me? What about the sanctity of the secret? We'd never tell anyone who the Oracle is! ☺

Private Message to RiverCoral: There's no "we" about it. I hired the Weather Oracle, and I'm now thinking that we should let the town know who it is.

Private Message from River Coral: But so much of the mystique comes from the mystery! ☺

Private Message from RiverCoral: I hate to say it, Piper, but this sounds an awful lot like a power trip. ☺

DanTheRiverMan: It's good to see the town getting involved, and Sam, having the monks help is a great idea. From the time we started this magazine, Piper and I have seen it as a collaboration with the townspeople—a living, dynamic expression of who we are here in Riverboro. It couldn't make both of us happier to see this concept come to fruition.

AuntieP: I love the concept of curation of the historical page. Although I don't know that I could do it alone. Might there be another reader who is willing to help me on it?

ConArtist: Brumi and I might be able to manage a music page for the site. The anime page too, if you're going to go there.

AuntieP: For the historical page I'd need someone who was good with history, and interested in history, and who'd have a good sense of what is appropriate to include and what is not.

PeterWriter: Pasco and I will manage the Zombie Apocalypse page.

We're thinking of turning it into a blog format with comments instead of a forum.

ZombiePatrol: Because a forum is a free-for-all, and there is a right way and a wrong way to deal with zombies. It's important to provide leadership.

AuntieP: I don't think that the historical vignette page would take too much time. I would collect them and organize them. I only thought if another person—a scholar maybe—was willing to look them over and give an opinion on their authenticity, it would be helpful.

ImmaterialGirl: I could manage the Riverboro Recipes page, as long as you don't expect too many recipes with meat in them. No babies either, at least not in the recipes.

AuntieP: If there isn't anyone out there who can help, I will certainly take this on alone.

HarvardProf: My apologies, Auntie P, I just came online. I would love to help you curate that page. I have quite a backlog of historical tales of my own, and when you have some time we can go over them and compare notes.

AuntieP: Why thank you, Harvard Prof, that is very generous of you. It being Sunday, the library is not officially open today. If you'd like to meet there, say after church this morning, we can begin to go through some of the stories we have and organize them into a proper form for this page.

HarvardProf: After which I would be most honored if you would allow me to treat you for lunch.

(Comments approved)

* * *

Damn Lies
By Presidential Candidate and Weather Apologist
Jacques Marquand

A rising star in the field of weather forecasting shines in the New Hampshire skies. Several weeks ago, *Riverboro Rocks'* Weather Oracle, long a favorite with his audience, and a frequent guest on the pages of this blog for his catastrophic couplets and mind-altering misses, anointed a successor. This bright new talent tries to trump his teacher in iconoclastic iambs and wild weather wisdom. His first few predictions dovetailed, somewhat startlingly, with what people laughingly refer to as Reality—a terrible letdown to my Damn Liars. In fact, in a syncopated stroke of unfolding untruths, this poetic prognosticator, this phantom foreteller, this Delphic divinator, is flummoxing his followers with an accuracy in his augury that has no antecedent. Chalk it up to beginner's banalty, and look for long years of meteorological myths and climatological cock and bull.

Who is the man behind the mask? Weather Oracle, we call upon you: reveal yourself! Divining the truth at Molly's masquerade will bring the paradox to an unparalleled peak, elevating the event to a true Wintry Whopper. Piper Hadley, we beg you: unveil the Oracle!

* * *

If it were possible to race into the future, to get ahead of the curve, to find a comfortable place to sit and observe and look back on it all, this is what one might see:

Dan and Leon going down to the Ashram's flooded building with Sam King and the insurance adjusters to assess the damage and get a quote for the repairs;

Pasco and Cassie heading off to the Mushroom with Molly to work on planning the party;

Brumi and Silas bound for the music shop to talk about jukebox repair scenarios;

Lisette and Ananda setting off together for a doctor's appointment.

The house was almost empty again, like in the old days. Piper and Donny had the whole big house to themselves and the whole long afternoon to look forward to spending together.

Such a cozy afternoon it was going to be! In Riverboro, tucked in among the mountains and the trees, it wasn't often that the wind audibly howled, but today it was singing around the house, rattling the glass in the windows. Piper loved the sound.

Donny didn't.

"Why does the wind blow so hard?" he asked. "It sounds like screaming. Does the wind scream? In here it's safe. It's safe in here, right?"

"It is," said Piper. "And you know what we're going to do? We're going to pick out some music for Silas' jukebox today. What do you pick, Donny?"

"Kids' songs are my favorite," Donny said. "I like to listen to kids' songs."

"I bet you don't listen to much classical at home," Piper said. Here was a project, here was something special for her and Donny. Piper would play him classical music; she would give him crayons and colored pencils and he would draw what came into his head. Donny would come often to listen. He would grow up to be a great music lover, maybe a musician himself, and he would tell Dan and everyone, "It was Piper who got me started."

That's a project they'd never do at the River Place, Piper thought.

"Let's get cleaned up," Piper said. "Then we'll go into the living room and put on some music. I've got something I think you'll like."

Donny turned to face back in the chair and slid to the floor. He took his soup bowl off the table and carried it to the sink. Then Piper heard it. The Sound.

It was the sinister, creaking, creeping sound coming from the shed. And she and Donny were alone in the house.

Who was it? Did they know that she and Donny were alone—alone and vulnerable? Were they coming for them?

"Donny," she whispered. "Do you hear that noise?"

"Yes," he whispered back. "The branch is making noise."

"Branch?" Piper said aloud. "What branch?"

"The branch out there," Donny said, still whispering. "The one from the big tree. Where I went out the window."

"That noise is a *branch?*"

"It scrapes the roof. The roof I went out on."

"The branch that Sasha uses to get into the tree?" Piper asked.

"Yes. It got hurt in the ice storm," Donny said.

Piper almost laughed from the wave of relief that flooded her. Sasha's branch! Piper herself used to clamber on it. Now it bent to touch the roof of the shed.

"There's a lesson in that," Piper told Donny. "Though I'm not sure what—"

But as she was speaking, so was nature. A roaring howl—that would be the wind. A loud, creaking groan—her branch, Sasha's branch.

She and Donny froze for an interminable moment. Then an enormous *crash!* seemed almost to explode inside them, it echoed all around them, and her house, the Hadley House, was buckling and caving under an impact, collapsing, it seemed, onto them, broken and rent.

Piper, screaming, threw herself across the child, shielding him with her body. Donny was screaming too. What had happened?

Plaster from the ceiling rained into the kitchen. Part of the kitchen wall was buckled in. Outside the kitchen door an enormous branch—actually the whole top of the tree—lay across the shed roof, caving it in across the stacks of cordwood lining its back wall. Through the shattered window on its back wall, Piper could see the splintered tree swaying in the wind.

Donny was white with shock. "What happened?" he whimpered, over and over. "What happened?"

Piper stood, gathering him into her arms. "It's OK, Donny love, it's all going to be OK," she soothed. "It's over. It was a big noise, wasn't it? A huge noise. What a shock to us both!"

"It was a shock," Donny sobbed, clinging to her. "A really loud shock."

"A huge noise," said Piper. "A tree fell on the house." *I have to pull myself together,* Piper told herself. *I have to be strong. For Donny's sake.* "We're OK now," she told him. "It's all over. Wow! What a noise!"

She forced a laugh and was relieved when Donny gamely echoed it.

She hugged him to herself, drawing comfort from the warmth of his body. "Donny, baby, I have an idea. How about we start a list?"

"A list," Donny repeated. "How about we start a list? What goes on it?"

"How about all the people we need to call on the phone? Insurance people. Carpenters."

"Mommy. Daddy," Donny added.

"That's right," Piper affirmed. "We need to call your parents. And guess what? The other people we need to call are all the same people your father is talking to right now, down at the Ashram! We'll call him up and ask him to bring all those people here."

"Yes, call Daddy," Donny said. "He'll come up. He'll come right up."

"That's right, Donny," said Piper. "He'll come right up, and he'll bring the very people we need. Was there ever anyone luckier than us?"

Piper flipped open her phone with hands that were still shaking. She hit number one on her speed dial. Voice mail picked up and she said, her voice catching, "Dan? When you and Leon finish with the insurance people and the carpenters at the Ashram, could you bring them all up here? Donny and I are fine, but there has been an accident..."

* * *

"We're doing great, aren't we baby?" Piper asked a little later. "Your dad is going to come sort us out, and in the meantime it's you and I and we're A-OK. How many people could say that after a tree fell on their house?"

"How many people?" said Donny.

They were huddled together on the sofa, talking about the crash, using the same words, the same phrases, over and over. There were picture books in their hands but they were unread, unopened. "Such a loud noise it was!" Piper would say. And Donny would echo, "Such a loud noise."

Now Piper said, "We're lucky, aren't we?"

And Donny echoed, "Lucky." But this time he added, "What's that nasty smell?"

Then Piper smelled it, too: smoke and the acrid odor of electricity, an electricity that had slipped its surly insulated bonds and run amok, an electricity gone terribly wrong.

She ran to the doorway to the kitchen and saw it: Fire. Flames. Licking up the kitchen wall, dancing crazily, making their own crackling roaring sound audible in the roaring of the wind. Beautiful and terrible, the dark and dangerous side of humanity's old friend and older enemy.

Piper picked Donny up and fled, deeper into the house. Where to go? What to do? Not upstairs, that would be crazy; *never* go upstairs in a fire. The library? A dead end; there was no exit from the library except back into the living room. It was a trap, a death trap.

They had to get help. They had to call 911.

"It's an emergency!" she shouted into the phone. "A fire. Come right away!" The operator was asking questions. Why? "Yes, Hadley Street," Piper said. "Yes, yes, the old Hadley House. We need someone now! Yes, it's a fire. A fire in the kitchen. Can someone come?"

"I'm sending help, they're on their way," said the dispatcher. "Is anyone hurt?"

"No, but the fire is getting bigger. I can see it from here."

"A fire truck is on its way," the dispatcher repeated. "Get out of the house and wait at a safe distance."

"I have a three-year-old here with me!" cried Piper. "I can't take him out of the house!"

"Ma'am, you both need to get out of the house right away," said the dispatcher. "'Don't wait to get anything. Don't carry anything. Just go."

"He'll freeze!" Piper said. "It's November! His coat is in the kitchen, where the fire is!"

"Ma'am," said the dispatcher. "I need you to take that child and walk to the nearest exit. The EMTs will have blankets. You can go to a neighbor's house. But now, right now, get out that door."

* * *

How does it happen that life changes so suddenly? How is it possible to have a business and a career and a magazine and a whole grown up life: a daughter and an (almost) stepson, a house full of monks (or not), and a daily blog read by (sometimes) several hundred people; and suddenly you are in a cold drafty mudroom at the far back of the house with a three-year-old and you are clinging to one another shivering and murmuring to one another "It's OK, it'll be all right," and "Daddy will come soon."

And then the sirens and the shouting and the tramping and the doors slamming; and there is Dan shouting "Donny!" with real panic in his voice, and there is panic in Coral's and she is screaming "Donny! Baby! Where are you?" And they are standing at the mudroom door looking at you accusingly, as if you had done something wrong—you who had taken a child, not your own, and kept him safe—and they are sweeping him up and away from you, out of your arms, and now he, who has been so brave, is sobbing.

And Coral is saying "It isn't safe leaving him here with her, I won't leave him here again, not without Molly, not unless Molly is in charge"; and Silas is saying "Ms. H? Can't you leave the house?" And you wonder if there will ever be anyone, anywhere, who cares about you as much as Dan and Coral care about Donny, to come screaming into a house looking for you and taking you to safety.

And then Molly is there saying, "Mommy, Mommy, are you OK? I was so worried," and "Shut up, Silas, we can talk about that later," and leading you back into the main part of the house, where there is now, in fact, no fire, and not much of a kitchen, either: just a sodden, blackened, dripping wreck of a room and a black pit where the dishwasher used to be.

November 18: These Fragments I Have Shored

One reason I love my endangered magazine, my plucky frigate tossed on the massive sea of expense, with waves of debt crashing over its bows, has to do with the often-documented but nevertheless true power of words, of narrative, of art in general, to transform and ennoble.

Of course, Riverboro, never was there a more worthy subject, one that hardly needs a writer to glorify it, than this town. But here is what I have discovered, as writer and editor over the years: the transformation from the sluggish matter of the earth to a new, soaring, impalpable, imperishable being isn't happening between the reality of life and the writing of the word. It happens between the writing of the word and the reading of the word.

Riverboro, our town, often seems to me to glow from within, lit by its inner brilliance; by the living consciousness of its 6,000 precious souls; by their yearning, and striving, and growing, and creating. It doesn't need—you, my readers, don't need—me in the isolated workshop of my tower office to re-imagine your being in terms any more lofty than the life you live every day. You are each a bright thread in the skein of light that is our existence: more real, more alive, and more beautiful than my words about you will ever be.

But something does happen between the time I put words on paper and the time I return to read them. In that space, in that gap, something is made manifest.

We writers love to compare it to God him-or-herself creating creation, and there is power there for sure. But it is a paltry power compared to the power of people to choose, with that awful daring, to live their lives day by day; to earn a living and pay the rent; to bear and raise children; to connect in whatever way they know to the spirit within.

To get up in the morning and walk out the door.

Tags: TS Eliot, James Joyce

COMMENTS:

AuntieP: Piper dear are you all right? I'm going to bring a bundt over for you this afternoon. You should stay in bed a day or two.

SamKing: I'm sending up a batch of groceries for all of you today. I got in 50 pounds of basmati rice for the monks and a dozen butternut squashes, plus some new herbal teas. And it sounds to me as if you need a nice hot cup of coffee. I'll send up today's special, Blueberry Cheesecake light roast.

(*Comments approved*)

* * *

Piper didn't think she had ever been so tired.

And there was an intervention pending, she could smell it. She could feel it in the silence around her that muffled her interactions with people, and the way they looked at her, and the solicitous way they ran to get her things and asked her, so gently, to come to the living room to discuss things.

She even knew who was going to be part of the intervention. It was going to be Molly, and Dan; Silas, and maybe Lisette or Leon—though if those monks dared meddle, here in her own house!—oh, they would regret it. They were going to bring Jake in. And she had a feeling they were going to bring in other people too: Auntie Polly, Miranda's Great Aunt Ani. She wouldn't put it past them to bring Coral Lane.

What was the point? She knew what they were going to say. And she was just too tired to hear it.

"I think I'm going to bed," she told Molly. They were having lunch in the living room, takeout from the Japanese place at the plaza. Piper would have preferred to eat at her computer while she worked, but Molly had wanted to have lunch together. At least it was bearable, here in the living room. The monks (thank God for those monks) had scrubbed and aired it that morning. Through the doorway, the kitchen hunched black and charred and foul-smelling, but here, at least, it was free of ashes, free of smoke. The scent of aroma oils came from diffusers placed throughout the room, dispelling the acrid odor that the fire had left.

Piper was having her lunch in the big chair. Molly and Silas sat on the sofa, shoulders touching. Even now it was two against one; their body language said it all. The monks had discreetly vanished. Who knew where they were? In their rooms, perhaps, studying arcane literature or drawing pentagrams on the floor with the residual ash from the fire.

Piper continued, "This ordeal you've got scheduled? Let's put it off for another day."

Molly looked up quickly from her sushi. "Mom, please. Don't be difficult. Do you want to meet sooner?"

"Molly, there's no point. What are we going to accomplish?"

"It isn't…" Molly began, then trailed off and looked at Silas for help.

Silas had been watching, saying nothing. Now he spoke. "You don't go out? At all? Since when?"

There was a moment of loud, prickly silence. Piper wondered if she should lose it, or scream, or tell Silas it was none of his damn business.

But she was just. So. Tired. "I think it was…I don't know…it's been a while," she said. What was the point of denying it? "Three years?"

Silas blinked. "But—" He fell silent, perhaps puzzling through the sleight-of-hand that made him feel as if he'd seen, or just missed seeing,

Piper around town over the past three years.

"It was right after Donny was born, Mom," Molly said. "Right after Dad moved out."

"Yes," Piper said wearily. "Then."

"What happened?" Silas asked. The women looked at him.

"I mean," said Silas, "Donny was born and you stopped going out? Just like that?"

Molly glanced at her mother. "Mom started having panic attacks. She was so upset. About Dad and Coral and all. It probably didn't help that Dad said there wasn't anything going on—with Coral, that is. That Mom was wrong about him and Coral. So sometimes she'd be out in a place and she'd see something, or hear something...and she'd panic. Isn't that right, Mom? Isn't that what happened? You'd start to panic?"

"Yes, Molly," Piper said. "That is what happened."

"Then you wouldn't want to go back to that same place, right, Mom? The place you got panicky." Piper nodded, and Molly went on reflectively, putting it together for herself as well as Silas. "Dr. Jake said that people can start feeling like the place is what made them panic, so each time they have an attack, that's one more place they can't go—he wasn't talking about you, Mom," she added quickly.

Piper scowled. "No, he just happened to be talking to my daughter about panic attacks," she said.

"He was talking to Dad. I was eavesdropping. You know I like to—"

"Didn't we ever teach you that eavesdropping is wrong?"

"No, Mom, you didn't. And how am I supposed to figure things out if I don't listen in? You stop going out, but no one admits it, and one minute Dad's with you and the next he's with Coral, but still taking care of you, and I'm just out of middle school, and suddenly there's a baby brother and Dad's moving out, and we had planned that trip to Japan for years and years and you were saying we should all go without you—"

"That's what they told you?"

"Dad said you wanted to stay closer to home.."

Molly's voice was beginning to tremble. Silas put his hand out to calm her and spoke to Piper. "You never said anything," he said. "I come here every day. You never said a word."

"I thought you might have noticed," said Molly.

"How is this anyone's business?" Piper said sharply.

"Mom, we care about you, we want you to be healthy."

"Nothing has changed. I am as fine today as I was last week, and last month, and last year. And please stop exchanging glances with Silas, Molly, I am sitting right here."

"It's just, no one explains, no one acts like it's weird or strange, we all carry on as if nothing is wrong—"

"And nothing is. I manage quite well, thank you very much—"

"And Dad still working here, and bringing the stuff you need, and all the business meetings taking place in this house—"

"You have only been behaving as anyone would who is in a family and makes accommodations for family members. And the same is true of your father."

"I thought you went out sometimes. You pretended like you did. You talked about things as if you'd been there. It made it seem like—anyway, I thought you could if you had to—"

"But now?" Piper asked quietly.

Molly looked at Silas again, then away quickly. Silas was sitting back, watching with a neutral expression. Molly said, very hesitatingly, "After the fire...I know you would have taken Donny out...if you could..."

The total injustice of it all took Piper's breath away. "Of course this all tracks back to Donny, and Coral, and Dad. *Coral* doesn't want me taking care of Donny anymore. Well, isn't that too bad. Let her take care of her own child. *Coral* has a life so important helping other people she can't take care of her own son. And now she isn't going to *let* me take care of Donny." Her voice was getting shriller, she could feel it climb toward a scream, and she closed her mouth and took a deep breath.

"I," she said, "am the victim here. I am the person wronged. I have spent the last three years being the good guy. Smiling and taking care of Dad's other family. Pitching in for Coral, helping to raise Donny, accommodating your father as he comes and goes. And now I am being punished."

"Mom?" Piper could see that Molly was fighting off tears. "No one is punishing you."

"No?" Piper said. "Tell me about this meeting, Molly. People are coming, aren't they? People who know me, people who know us. What's on the agenda? A nice meet and greet, a gathering to make sure that Piper is all right after the fire, after she protected Donny, after she was trapped and traumatized? Or maybe the family is coming for a work party, pitching in to get the shed fixed, to get the kitchen fixed, to cut back the dangerous branches on that tree?" Piper gave a harsh, humorless laugh. "No, not any of that, I'll bet. The agenda is me, isn't it? How I put Coral's child's life at risk? How I am inadequate? It isn't going to be about how they can help, is it? It's going to be about how *I* need to change."

"But what about me?" Molly was sobbing now. "How was I expected to know what was going on, with Dad, or Coral, or Donny, or you? Why you didn't come to my stuff anymore, why you stayed and worked all the time? And was it my fault, and was I supposed to pick sides? How could you expect me to figure everything out for myself? How could I do that? Can't you think of me, Mom? Can't you?"

And there was Piper, housebound and neurotic, but still the mother, and there was Molly, confident, beautiful, and almost all grown up—but still the daughter. Piper put her sushi down on the floor by the chair and put out her arms, and Molly came and curled up with her on the chair, and Piper rocked her daughter as if she were the child she once had been.

November 19: The Kindness of Strangers

Thank you, Riverboro, for the outpouring of help and support that has come in the wake of the fire at headquarters.

You have brought salads and soups, casseroles and cakes and cans of cat food, bushels of apples and baskets of avocadoes. We have been flooded with offers of help to rip out the kitchen and put something new in its place. Local businesses have sent groceries and dry goods and takeout foods, tarps and tacks.

Special thanks to:

Marty's Café
King's Market
Aroma and Incense
Mt. Fuji Asian Eatery
Riverboro Hardware

Neighbors have offered us places to stay.

That last offer is certainly tempting, as there is a hole in the kitchen wall (the tarp is a great help there), black soot coating my walls and floors, and insurance adjusters, electricians, and carpenters coming through at all hours measuring and noting things down on clipboards. (Thank you

Ready Electric and Perry Insurance for the quarter page ad placements). But I have decided to stay put. Nothing upstairs has been harmed and the living room—thanks to the monks—is back to a habitable state.

At least a dozen people have offered to take in the monks.

Riverboro, perhaps I have been talking up those monks too much. Or maybe I have overstated any reluctance I might have felt to have them in my house. But the monks are settled in. They are not going anywhere.

That is, unless they want to. Perhaps they'll get a better offer, with a kinder landlady and less home maintenance involved.

But until then, here they are and here they stay.

Tags: Marty's Café, King's Market, Aroma and Incense, Mt. Fuji Asian Eatery, Riverboro Hardware, Tennessee Williams

COMMENTS:

ImmaterialGirl: Piper, we don't want to go anywhere. We love it here, and we love you.

BookLover603: If we're going to read *Streetcar*, can we do *Zoo Story* too?

MollyHH: It's a zoo story at the Hadley House between the monks and the Liars and the handymen all over.

BookLover603: I keep wondering what the Oracle has to say about the fire…

DrewHadley: My dad came down with a cold from all this bizarre weather. He still hasn't admitted to doing the forecasts, lol, but if it's him he might not feel up to it.

AuntieP: His ill health might also explain the disgruntled tone of his recent forecasts. Tell him I'll bring him hot soup, and I want to talk to him about these negative predictions of his.

DrJake: Donations of winter clothes and bedding came in to the River Place earmarked for the Ashram. I'll bring them up today.

(*Comments approved*)

* * *

Jake was coming today. He was bringing donations for the monks.

Piper didn't know whether to look forward to the event or dread it. Jake would know what had happened with the fire. That was inescapable. The whole damn *world* probably knew.

How would he look at her? What would he say? He would try to make her leave the house. And she *would* go out—but not now. It was too cold now. She could bear it if it were spring, or summer, with the trees filling out overhead and the warm sun wrapping you up. She could stand it all then.

Today it was twenty degrees outside. Normal New Hampshire winter weather. She would not go out in it. Jake had to understand. She was drawing the line.

But she couldn't stay upstairs. She had to face him. She had to see what Jake would reflect back to her when she saw him. So she went down.

Jake was standing in the library with Dan. He heard her steps and turned and smiled. Piper smiled back, her heart lifting. Jake looked…normal. She hadn't thought that he would look normal. She'd thought he would have changed since the fire, that he would be different, look different, reflect her image back to her differently. But this was the Jake she knew—handsome and warm, with a special welcoming look for her.

If, after that horrible fire, after her abysmal failure to properly care for Donny, people could still look at her and be normal, still greet her as if she were an ordinary person, maybe it would be alright. Wouldn't it?

Of course it would.

Or…not. Because Jake was speaking to Dan in a low voice, an urgent-sounding voice. Piper caught something about "perhaps in principal" and "doctor/patient confidentiality" and "conflict of interest." She frowned. What were they up to?

"I am taking all of your excellent points into account," Dan was saying in his confident, carrying voice as Piper came to join them. "Nevertheless, you know and I know that we have to do something. Furthermore, I am the person who has been taking fiduciary responsibility for these sessions, as both doctor and patient are well aware. So I think I do have something to say about it."

And there it was. The truth.

The unlovely truth, so often best ignored, so rarely ignorable forever. The truth was that Jake didn't come because he wanted to. In the last three years he had never done so. He didn't stop by to say hi, to check up on her, to find out how things were with Dan. For three years she had been living, alone and frightened, in the house on the hill, and Jake hadn't come. Not once. Not until he started to get paid.

By Dan.

"Something to say about what?" Piper asked, and she hated herself for the way her voice quavered.

Jake made a motion but Dan said, "Piper, Dr. Rosen has been kindness itself, the soul of kindness and accommodation, coming to Hadley House for your therapy sessions. Coral and I have spoken about it at length since the incident with Donny and the fire. When a person allows her perceived limitations—limitations to which, to put it bluntly, we have all been pandering—when she allows those limitations to put a child's life in danger, I think that even you will agree that it has all gone too far. The steps we have taken to accommodate you have not made anything better. In fact by the look of things we have made the situation considerably worse."

Dr. Jake tried to speak, but Dan carried on, "Like every other doctor in this day and age, as a rule Dr. Rosen does not make house calls. For you—for us, actually; by that I mean for Coral and me—he has made an exception in your case. But from this moment there will be no more exceptions. It is clear to us—that is, to Coral and me—and in fact to anyone in town or in the world for that matter who reads your blog—it is clear to us that these sessions are something that have great importance to you. Let us hope that this fact will work in your favor. Let us hope that the change we are making today will serve as motivation for you to take the next step—in fact, the first step, the step out the door of this house."

Piper gasped in indignation, but Dan continued, "We have been talking about it, the doctor and I, and as of today, you will be leaving the house and going to his office for your therapy sessions—same as any other patient would do."

Piper's Index of Last Times (Not for Publication)

Last Time to Step into Mt. Fuji Asian Eatery: Piper's 35th birthday dinner.

(Dan pouring wine, speaking of visitors from outer space, of new technologies, of 21st century conspiracies; his voice changing, growing louder, deeper, more resonant: why? Piper turning to look over her shoulder, to follow his gaze, to see Coral coming in with Jake; Coral standing, staring at Dan, lips parted, radiant. And the restaurant itself shifting, transforming, no longer cozy and safe, now looming, now terrifying).

Last Time to Step into the River Place: Movie night for the elementary school children.

(Molly and Dan setting up the movie, setting up the screen; Coral joining to say something; laughter, heads together, a group of three; the seed of aloneness living somewhere inside Piper's heart growing like a mutant devouring plant, choking off breath, choking off life).

Last Time to Step into the Riverboro Public Library: the annual Hadley presentation.

(Auntie Polly showing the Joshua Hadley Civil War Diary, speaking of heroism, speaking of war; Coral Lane turning, coat swinging open, belly jutting, unavoidable, smug: surely nothing to do with Piper? Then why this peculiar twisting inside; why this sense of her own familiar world as no longer hospitable, no longer habitable?).

Last Time to Step Onto the Hadley House Front Porch: Donny's birth.

(Walking out the door, destination King's Market; hearing the phone's muffled ringing in her purse; clicking it open; listening to the voice at the other end saying words, inevitable, anticipated, life-altering words; turning back into her house, into her cocoon, her last remaining refuge).

November 20: Don't Cry for Me Riverboro (I Can Do It Myself Perfectly Well)

All right, world, you win.

I am a divorced woman with teenaged daughter, abandoned by her husband for a much younger (blonde) woman. I have not set foot outside in over three years, and whether I want to or not I am completely unable to do so. I have no career except as editor of a floundering magazine which has been losing money for most of this fiscal year and which is, I have known for the past five months (yes, Silas, since summer began) unlikely to survive.

This house that I can't leave? There is a very real possibility that I will have to leave it. Permanently. That the nasty world of debt and taxes and home repair and electric wiring will cause me to take, as Dan so poetically (or so he imagines) calls it "that first step"—the step out my front door, out of my safe haven into that big, terrifying and chaotic world.

The fire in the kitchen has created damage that insurance may or may not cover, but the massive code violations of the wiring are going to have to be repaired if the house is to remain habitable. And even that might be a moot point if I am unable to keep up with my property taxes—which is, in fact, the case, given that I am unable, of late, to draw a salary from the magazine.

My so-called friends are turning from me—supposedly for my own good. (Ha, ha.) And the one person who (I thought) actually needed me—ironically, the son of the woman who has taken my place—that person I am no longer allowed to care for without the supervision of my teenage daughter.

I can't keep up the charade any longer.

No, I am not going to kill myself. I am braver and stronger than that. I will continue, somehow, from day to day in this life. But for now I am going into my room and getting into bed and pulling up my comforter and going to sleep.

(DRAFT—DO NOT PUBLISH)

* * *

"Mom? Dad got you coffee and scones. I brought some in."

"Thank you, sweetie. Please leave them on the table. I'll have some later."

"Dr. Jake is here. He was worried when you didn't do your blog this morning."

"Please tell him I'm sleeping. I can't see anyone now."

"I'm on my way to school. Will you be OK?"

"Yes, don't worry, I'm fine. Have a wonderful day."

Nothing could be more engulfing, more comforting than bed. Why not stay here? It was the ultimate indoors, the cozy cocoon of inside, where all the demands of interaction and keeping going fell away.

* * *

"Mom?"

Piper stirred.

"Mom, I'm here. Have you been in bed all day?"

"Mmph. Molly. Is school out?"

"Mom, can I get you anything? You haven't touched your breakfast. The coffee's cold. Can I make a new pot for you? Or some herbal tea?"

"Maybe later, Molly. I'm going to sleep a little longer."

The light in the room was changing, getting softer, flatter. Molly came back in. "Mom? Dr. Jake is back."

"Please thank him for his concern. Don't worry about me. I've been working too hard. I need a rest."

"He'd like to see you. Can he come in?"

"No, no, no...Please, Molly, tell him to let me be. I'm going to sleep a while longer."

"When should I tell him to come back?"

"I'll call him if I want to see him. Some other time."

"Mom, Dr. Jake is concerned. So am I."

Piper turned over and brought Molly into focus. She didn't want to worry Molly or upset her. Molly was important. And Molly cared about her. But Piper had to, she *had* to be left alone. Molly couldn't be expected to understand that.

But Jake should. "Molly, why must he torment me? Can't I catch up on my rest? I don't want to see Jake. I don't want to see him now. I don't want to see him ever again."

"Not *ever*? But, Mom...but...why?"

"Because I'm finished with that. It's over. It's my choice. I've made it. It's final."

Molly stood, looking vulnerable, her face, her eyes the same as those of the baby Piper had brought home, the child she had raised. Piper was tired, so tired. But she needed to reassure Molly.

"Molly, sweetie, why don't you climb in with me? Take a nap before dinner."

"If I do, will you get up with me?"

Piper's eyes were starting to close. "I don't know. Maybe."

Molly hovered for a moment, undecided. "I need to tell Jake. I need to tell Dad."

"You do that," Piper murmured.

* * *

It was full-on dark when she awoke the next time. Piper had to go to the bathroom; she had to eat. She was also wide awake.

She slid her feet into her slippers and headed downstairs.

Now here is the thing about filling your house with people. There is always, always someone around. You can creep through your darkened house at two in the morning, silent as a cat (and now Sasha was padding beside her, saying "mraow?"), but when you get downstairs someone will be up. You will see a lamp burning in the living room; you will see a monk sitting on the sofa; and despite the destruction in the kitchen, a pot of milk will be sitting on a hotplate and a plate of toast will be buttered and a bowl of sweet oranges will be waiting on a tray.

"Up late," Piper asked, "or up early?"

"For me, early," Leon said. "Same as for you." The strong New England cadence of Leon's voice sounded un-monk-like to Piper's ear; she smiled at the contrast between his otherworldly appearance and his very secular-sounding intonations. Leon added, "We're taking it in shifts."

"Shifts," Piper said. "For what?"

"We wanted to have someone up. To wait for you when you were ready."

"Were you afraid I'd hurt myself?"

"Oh no," Leon said. "Not that. Not you." He poured and handed Piper a mug of hot milk. "We want to be here for you."

"Keeping vigil." Piper felt inside herself for annoyance or indignation and found neither. Instead, she felt oddly comforted.

"In a way." Leon passed her the toast. "It's my very good fortune to be the one up to see you. I've been wanting to have our talk."

"Our talk?"

"The one where I was going to be smart enough and lucky enough to say the perfect thing at the perfect time. You mentioned it in your blog."

Oh. Right. "And are you smart enough?"

Leon shook his head. "Definitely not. I'm hoping for lucky."

Piper settled down beside him on the sofa to sip her milk. She offered the toast back to Leon and he helped himself to a piece and bit into it contentedly.

"Why," Piper asked, "do you all wear robes?"

Leon nodded. "That's good. A nice easy one to start with. A soft-ball. So here you go. One: these robes are comfortable to wear around the house. Two: they give us a sense we're a team. Not distinguished from one another by what we wear. Three: they support our sense of peacefulness and coherence. Four: they remind us that our vocation is different from that of the people around us. How am I doing so far?"

"Very well," Piper poured hot milk into a second mug and offered it to Leon, who took it. "I suppose that's also the reason you shave your heads?"

"Actually, no," Leon said. "At our ashram in Vermont, we've got members who haven't cut their hair in years."

Piper raised her eyebrows; she waited.

"Ananda is ill," said Leon.

Piper looked at him blankly. She must have misheard. Ananda, sick? No. "But it isn't serious," she said.

Leon waited quietly, allowing the information to process.

"It has to be a mistake," said Piper. "Ananda is the picture of health."

"Is she?" asked Leon.

"She is," Piper insisted; but even as she said the words, understanding was flooding in. Ananda's frequent absences from the group. Her doctor visits. Her thinness. The circles under her eyes. How easily she tired. How the monks hovered nearby to help. How they settled her in, wrapped her in blankets, ran to get her things. Piper had told herself, had told the world, that it was because Ananda, waif-thin Ananda, was beautiful. She had insisted it was because of Ananda's beauty.

Only it wasn't. The attention, the deference, the marking Ananda out as special: it wasn't because Ananda was beautiful. It wasn't even because Ananda was good.

It was because she was sick. Very sick.

How could I not have known? Piper thought. *How could I not have put it together? Why didn't I—*Aloud she said, "God. Do I ever think of anyone but myself?" And then: "Oh crap. That was about me, too."

"Tough to avoid, isn't it?" Leon said, sipping his hot milk.

"Why didn't anyone say?"

"We didn't want to worry you. And Ananda doesn't want more attention going to it than is strictly necessary. She doesn't want to be all about her illness."

"Will she…?"

"Ananda recently finished her chemo."

"Her chemo." Piper said. "Going to the doctor. Throwing up at night. Losing her hair. I feel so blind. So stupid."

"We think she's getting stronger," Leon replied. "We hope and believe, God willing, that she can beat this. Lots of women do, more every day. The wonders of modern science."

"And maybe the wonders of your lifestyle?" Piper suggested.

"Yes, we're hoping that something about our lifestyle has made her strong enough to ride this out. Pasco and Cassie thought it might be better to stay away from chemicals and radiation and drugs. All the allopathic stuff. They thought the way we live would tide Ananda through. But Lisette and Brumi insisted we try everything. They are both so afraid of losing her. We all are."

"What about Ananda?" Piper asked. "What does she want?"

"Ananda's scared," Leon said. "And she's worried about Brumi. She doesn't want to leave him alone. And if she's forced to, she doesn't want him to have any regrets. So she follows his lead."

"And you all cut off your hair…" Piper's hand went up to touch her scalp at her hairline. "To support Ananda."

"That's right," said Leon. "We didn't want to mark her out."

"It seems to have worked," Piper said. "For me, anyway. It seems so obvious now."

"Only because you know."

"I should have known. I should have asked. I am selfish, self-centered, incurious and horrible. I can't believe I didn't see it."

"It's what Ananda wanted," Leon said. "It's what we all wanted. I'm sorry to blindside you. We should have told you before."

"No, no, no. It isn't your fault. I'm just upset—I thought—it's a shock. But you all, your hair. What a wonderful way to support her. And you know, you all look beautiful this way. Your faces look…ascetic and pure."

"I agree," Leon said peacefully. "I'm going to miss it myself, when everyone else's hair grows back. Now that Ananda's done her chemo. For the moment they all look like me."

"Not a bad thing," said Piper. They were silent, sipping their milk, nibbling their toast. Then Piper spoke again.

"I can't leave the house," she said.

"I know," said Leon.

"Can you tell me how to fix that?"

Leon sighed. "I think maybe our Ananda story shows we don't have all the answers. I wish we did."

"Aren't you supposed to?" Piper gestured at his robes. "Isn't there some…some responsibility for answers in this kind of thing?"

"It could be we just spend more time asking the questions," said Leon. "But you make a fair point." He stopped for a few moments in thought. Finally he spoke again. "OK. Here is something I can tell you. Our whole lifestyle, the way we live, is based on this one idea: Turn within."

"So, from a monkish point of view," said Piper, taking a piece of toast, "maybe it's not such a freakishly bad idea to stay inside?"

"From our perspective, it's not an issue of physically going outside or staying in," Leon said. "You step out the door, you don't step out the door. Inside, outside—it's still you."

For a few moments Piper was quiet. When she spoke she said, "I'm trying to think how this is helpful."

"I'm sorry," Leon said humbly. "I would like to help."

Piper waited to see if he would say more.

The moment stretched.

"I find the toast and milk very helpful," Piper finally said, and, as Leon brightened, added, "Tell me more."

"OK. OK. Think of it like this: life, the world, has two sides. The deep ocean, its surface waves. The blank canvas, its colors. The tree, its roots. The whole world like that. And mostly we only notice the one side, the obvious visible side. But if we were to turn around and look, we would find the other side."

"The other side. The other side of what?"

"Everything," Leon replied.

"And what is it, this other side?"

"It's huge," said Leon. "You mentioned in one of your blog posts about a glint of light on the wave of an ocean. The other side would be the ocean, and this side would be that wave. If you're the glint on the surface, the wave seems huge. But from the perspective of the ocean, the wave is tiny. From the point of view of the wave everything is separate. Unrelated. On the surface, every single thing we see or do or experience can trap and isolate us, like a prison. But if we turn around and look the other way, the walls disappear. The ocean is totally connected. That's the other side."

"And you have to turn—"

"Actually, you can get to the other side no matter which way you turn—whether you turn out or you turn in, it's there. But going out is the long way of getting to something that's closer than anything."

"Sometimes we have to take the long way to come back correctly," Piper mused. "That's what Edward Albee said."

"Was he a mystic?" Leon asked. "I don't know him."

"A writer," said Piper. "A playwright. Sometimes it happens, does it happen to you? Everything starts squeezing in and squeezing in? It all seems to cave in on you. Like you can't breathe."

"That's not *quite* the experience—"

"And it would be wonderful if it would spit you out the other side. Like if you went down a whirlpool, and at the bottom it twirled you out the other side. Whoosh! You're free."

Leon was watching Piper, looking worried.

"I like it," Piper decided. "The other side of everything."

Leon looked relieved, and they went back to munching their toast companionably. *I should leave it at that,* thought Piper. *It gets us both off the hook.* Yet some impulse made Piper ask, "What is the other side of Ananda having cancer?"

But Leon answered readily enough. "Cancer is something Ananda has. It's not who she is. And having her with us, fighting this disease, we remember that we're body and we're spirit, both. Each is the other side of the other."

"And if she dies?" Piper pressed.

"Then that boundary, that beautiful boundary that we call Ananda, but which is only her body, will be gone," Leon said sadly. "What's happening with Ananda reminds us that a monk's life isn't about turning away from the happiness of the world for the austerity of the spirit. It's the opposite. Every happiness that we find in the world comes from that huge reality spilling through the boundaries. The monkish lifestyle is meant to make those boundaries more..." Leon's hands moved in the air as he sought the word. "... porous. To let that huge reality shine through."

"That isn't bad," said Piper. "For a beginner."

"I don't usually talk so much," said Leon. "Lisette is better at that. I'm more the chop-wood-carry-water type."

Again they fell silent, and the peculiar heavy silence of late night pressed in around them, broken only by the sounds of teeth crunching on toast. In repose, Leon looked less like a Buddha and more like a basset hound, his eyes pouchy, his jowls jiggling as he chewed. And yet it wasn't Piper's imagination: he did radiate a certain peace.

Actually, peace wasn't the exact word for it. What Leon radiated was kindness—a kindness that appeared to be bone-deep. Piper suspected it was a characteristic of his nature before he became a monk, that it would be his if ever he left his ashram to do other things. She was suddenly very happy that she had come down on his watch.

"And me not being able to go out?" she asked. "What is the other side of that?"

Leon put down his toast and looked directly at her. His face relaxed into its customary smile lines, and Piper felt something she didn't often feel.

Safe.

She felt safe. Sitting there in the night, munching toast and talking to Leon, Piper felt a sense of safety reach up and surround her like a warm bath. She relaxed into it, basked in it. She had no idea what Leon might say, but this she did know: Leon was not going to attack her. He was not going to hurt her. He was not going to shine a light on what she ought to do or should have been to him or to others, but had somehow failed to do or be.

"I can't describe your reality for you," Leon said, "I can only tell you what I see. And I don't see someone who only lives in this house and never leaves it. I see someone who is involved in everything that happens in Riverboro. Someone who observes and reports. Someone who influences, who makes things happen. Someone who has people she loves, people who love her.

"I look at you and I see someone big, someone powerful, someone with a range of influence I would describe as mighty. Staying here expresses something about you. What is that something? I don't know. Maybe you don't either. But just like Ananda's illness isn't Ananda, staying inside doesn't say everything about you. Far from it. It's something. But it's a very small part of who you are."

"Maybe I should be a monk," said Piper. "Then I could just go inward."

"We go in," said Leon, "but we always come back out again."

November 21: I Blog, Therefore I Am

Sometimes I feel so insubstantial. I wonder where the *me* exists, or of what it consists.

My writing gives me structure and purpose. I sit at my makeshift keyboard and put words on the screen and I read them and think: here is someone. Someone with identity.

Someone who weaves a shimmering web of hope with her words. Someone who assigns meaning to books, and poetry, and sights, and icons, and random conversations with houseguests.

Someone who looks for someone to save her. Who will do so?

I know the answer. A child would know it. No one can save me. No one has put me here, and no one can take me out.

A New England poet once threatened that the sky would fall on the soul that was flat; that the points of the compass would crush the heart that was narrow.

My soul is flat. The sky is caving in on it.

When Dan and I were first married and so, so young, we took a road trip across the country. Those days of freedom—playing the car radio and singing along to the songs while the road unspooled to the horizon. The wide fields, the tall mountains, the broad sky, the ocean glinting in the sun at the end of the road. The sense that anything and everything was possible.

I live 60 miles from the ocean. It has been many years since I have seen it.

How did I get from there to here? How will I find a way forward, or back?

Leon told me (I think) that however one behaves, whatever one creates, is a kind of beam from within. No more, no less.

Maybe he's right. Perhaps, as another poet says, divinity does live within me. Perhaps somewhere deep within is some imperishable bliss. But what I experience is more that grieving of loneliness, that sense of myself as the river, seeking for seas it will never find; that island solitude.

I have lost and continue to lose much of that which was precious to me. As it ebbs away, what remains?

(DRAFT: DO NOT PUBLISH)

Private Message from DrJake: Piper, I would like to talk with you. When is a good time?

Private Message from ImmaterialGirl: Good morning Piper. I hope all that sleep perked you right back up. If you don't want to come down, PM us. We'll bring something up to you. I'm making a paella, it's going to be super tasty—can I bring you a bowl?

Private Message from AuntieP: Piper, we miss your blog. When are you going to start posting again?

Private Message from ConArtist: Coffee? Sam's got Malted Milk Dud Mocha. I could bring some.

By email from RiverboroMiddleSchool: Dear Ms. Hammond. We use your blog to learn about writing and journaling and the internet. We read it every day. Will you post tomorrow? There are only two other sites we're allowed to look at and both are really boring.

Voice-to-text transcription: Hi this is Dan. And yeah I spoke to Jake. And yeah if everything is all right. Then we'll go from there. Anyway let me know all things are doing. And if it works. Yeah so that's all. Bye.

* * *

Back in bed, Piper snoozed but, much as she wanted to, she couldn't recapture yesterday's oblivion. She sat up when Molly and Cassie tapped on the door to offer a warm drink and a bowl of Cassie's paella. It was delicious—fragrant and full of bits of vegetables and surprising bursts of spice. Molly and Cassie sat on the edge of her bed and talked to her while she ate.

"Vanilla is my secret ingredient," Cassie was saying. "For the drink, I mean. I didn't use any in the paella. But I'm going to put vanilla in most of my recipes. In fact, maybe I'll name my polemic Vanilla Something or Something Vanilla."

"Plain Vanilla?" tried Piper.

"Vanilla Lies?" suggested Molly.

"Do you know plain vanilla is itself a Lie?" Cassie said. "Because vanilla is anything but plain. Pasco says that if I ever start carrying a flask, you know like people do in the movies and all? That's what will be in it. Vanilla. Then when people take out their flasks and tip them into their coffee, like in the old private eye books and all? I'll tip mine in and it will be vanilla."

"Hmmm," Piper said.

"And since vanilla has alcohol in it, I'll be staying in the 'spirit' of the thing." Cassie sketched out air quotes to emphasize her pun.

"Always important," Piper murmured.

"Of course, I would have to wait till after the baby comes," Cassie continued. "No alcohol, no caffeine, no meat—"

"Unlike the rest of the monks?"

"No, you're right, we don't do any of that stuff anyway. Can you imagine how easy it is for a monk to be pregnant? We've already given up all the things you have to give up for the baby." Cassie was gathering up the dishes. "I'm going to take these down. Don't worry, Molly, I'll take care of clean up."

"Thanks, Cass," Molly said. "I'll see you back down there. Mom, is there anything else I can get you?"

"Stay here a minute, Molly." Piper adjusted the pillows in her bed and sat up straighter. "I want to talk to you."

Molly looked wary, but sighed and waved Cassie off. Cassie vanished through the door, carrying the dishes.

"Come sit here." Piper patted the bed beside her, "I've been thinking—"

"Brooding—"

Piper ignored the interruption. "Your party."

Molly looked startled. "My party? I thought you were going to want to talk about Dad. What about my party?"

"I don't think we're going to be able to do it, darling," Piper said gently. "Not on that scale. Not open to the world, not at the H.I.T. I'm concerned about the liability."

She glanced nervously at her daughter. Molly's brows were drawing together ominously; she seemed to be clenching her teeth. "We'll still have the party," Piper rushed on. "Just not so big. We'll have a select group... all your closest friends...and do it at the River Place...make it special..."

"The H.I.T. is special!" Molly cried. "You said so yourself! You said you were impressed! Why do you have to make such a big deal of everything? If you're going to worry, why do I have to suffer for it?"

"It's not to make you suffer, it's to make things easier—"

"This *is* easy!" Molly interrupted shrilly. "The H.I.T. is going to *help*. Changing makes it hard! Why do you have to make things so complicated?"

"It isn't me, it's all those other people—"

Tears of frustration were leaking from Molly's eyes and running down her face. "So people are hard for you. But not for the H.I.T. Restaurants *like* lots of people! Plus, I promised Jacques—"

"Jacques! He's the king of complication. Did you see his latest post? He's already setting up shots—probably sake—"

"*Camera* shots, Mom, for the media coverage—not sake—"

Piper felt a rush of heat to her face. Damn Jacques for ensnaring her in his ambiguities! She rushed on. "He'll stir up trouble—frame it as a people's revolution—and won't be there to take responsibility—"

"He'll come—"

"He didn't come to his own party on his own bus—"

Molly had shifted away from Piper, tensing in anger. Piper closed her eyes to try to calm herself. She couldn't allow Jacques and his Lies to come between her and her daughter. She needed for Molly to buy into this change. "Molly, think of how nice a party will be at the River Place. You can decorate it the way you want—Cassie will help make the snacks, and so will I—"

"Oh, will you?" Molly spat. "And will you be there as hostess?"

Piper recoiled, feeling slapped. "Molly, how could you?"

"Mom, just because you're afraid, you can't use that against me!"

Piper strove to control her voice, to speak calmly. "And you think I do that?"

"I didn't used to. But since the fire—and all that anger and rage that came out—"

"And exactly what anger and rage might that be?" Piper asked carefully.

"*You* know. Coral saying Donny couldn't come unless I was here to supervise, and you refusing to see Dr. Jake and going to bed for two days, and Dad saying Dr. Jake couldn't come here and you'd have to go see him at his office. All that kind of thing."

"You think all that has something to do with your party?" Piper asked incredulously. She pulled up her knees and put her arms around them protectively. "Do you think I would disappoint you just so I could get back at your dad?"

"No, that's not what I meant!" Molly pulled up her own knees in an unconscious imitation of her mother. "It all gets so tangled—the way you two depend on each other, the way you try to control each other—and if you thought Dad wasn't stepping up about the party—is it normal," Molly burst out, "expecting so much of each other, being divorced and all?"

"Who's to say what's normal and what isn't? Although," Piper couldn't stop herself from adding, "if we are going to talk mutually enabling relationships, someone should take a closer look at Jake and Coral."

Molly frowned. "What do you mean?"

"I mean, despite what you might think, your father and I might not be the poster children for dysfunctional relationships. Everyone knows your father broke my heart. But have you ever asked yourself: whose heart did Coral break?"

* * *

"I thought it would be good for you to remember those devil horns you've got," Silas said. He had inked out another version of his sketch of Piper; in it, Piper's horns poked through the rings of her halo and knocked them askew. "I put a pitchfork in there for you, too."

Piper was amazed and somewhat horrified to find herself choking up. "That's lovely of you, Silas," she said, trying for a playful tone.

Silas seemed to understand. "It's how all of us in the con world deal," he said.

"With…pitchforks?" Piper asked.

"Or hero capes or whatever."

"People hiding in the world of make believe, do you mean? Or would you say they are expressing some sort of inner empowerment?"

"Empowerment," Silas confirmed. "Inner superhero."

"The possibilities for metaphor…"

"Epic," Silas agreed.

November 22: Where Motley is Worn

Thank you, Riverboro, for your messages of love and support the couple of days I was offline. As many of you guessed, my absence was related to the fallout from the fire. So much to do, and I felt I needed to rest.

In the interim, Hey! It's Thursday, while still readying itself for its official grand opening, has opened its door to serve drinks and snacks. I would encourage anyone who donated anything to our barn sale ten days ago to drop by there. I'll say no more; but if you are looking to see a junk-to-jewels style transformation, look no further than right here in this town.

This alchemy will set the tone for the get-together that Molly and a few of her closest friends are planning for Tuesday after school. We're shifting the venue and scaling back the guest list, but this transfigurative magic still drives the November Liars and gives that group its sense of purpose. I have seen them working into the night, lit by the glow of their own feverish creativity, transcendent, luminescent as they forge a weapon or hot glue a totem or sketch out a tattoo or a scar. The money they will spend! Contact lenses to make their eyes glow red, vampire teeth for their incisors, wigs to make their hair straight or curly, long or short, red or black or blonde.

And the sacrifices they will make for this whimsical art form of theirs! Peter had Lisette cut off his hair, sitting on a stool caped in plastic while his shorn locks dropped to the floor around him—all that lovely hair! All to fit the profile of the character he was playing. Why, I asked, didn't they use someone who was already bald? Silas, or one of the monks? Let Peter play one of the hairier superheroes or villains and save someone else the expense of buying a wig? The answer was simply: because Peter is the one who is playing that character. He will shave his head, and someone else will wear a wig, and each person will play the character he is meant to play. End of story.

Speaking of hair, the monks have started to grow theirs out. It is their prerogative, but oddly, I feel a sense of loss. Still, with a couple of days' growth on their heads, they do look amazing—so striking that I am half-tempted to shave my own head to get the same effect.

Lisette's hair is coming in white, and it makes her look very distinguished. Brumi looks as if someone has shadowed his head with a charcoal pencil. Ananda, who seems to be emerging from her room more, looks like a model with her stubble of yellow hair; though I was getting so accustomed to seeing her bald that her lack of hair only accentuated her beauty—nothing to hide those striking features, those brilliant green eyes.

Leon, sadly, will not be growing in any hair, unless it's a very little around the sides.

Serious work is due to commence on the kitchen on Monday. We'll be seeing carpenters, painters, and, above all, electricians in and out of here until the kitchen rises like a phoenix from its ashes to cook anew.

And here is a piece of amazing, wonderful, and if-I-keep-it-to-myself-I-will-simply-burst news: the insurance coverage will pay for rebuilding the kitchen—*and for the work it will take to bring the wiring up to code*. I'm not sure how that whole thing was managed, but Sam King was working on the logistics with the insurance company, the price quotes for the work, and the town offices for the code specs. Brumi and Leon were involved, too, as qualified hands to help with the carpentry and the wiring.

There are not enough words in the world to express the thanks in my heart for that, but: thank you, Sam King. Thank you, Leon and Brumi. I truly don't know how we would have managed without you. (And as a note of thanks from *Riverboro Rocks*, we are offering King's Market free display ads for an entire year).

So now I am back to blogging, and I apologize, Riverboro Middle School, for taking a Monday off. If I ever take another break I will try to make it happen on a weekend. I have an idea for you. Why don't members of your class take turns guest-blogging? I'll set up a separate page for you and we can set up a schedule for you to submit your work. We'll link to it from this blog and from the main site and from Facebook, too.

And bit-by-bit we will have every group in Riverboro represented somewhere on the site and in our companion pages in social media. We'll be one big virtual community supporting and reflecting and amplifying our real, genuine community; and if we don't see each other every day in person, we can visit with one another here and give one another comfort and encouragement, and cheer each other on as we accomplish ever-greater things.

Tags: Riverboro Middle School, New Hampshire building code

COMMENTS:

DrJake: Welcome back, Piper. It's good to see your observations again. The way you have created an entire community, almost an entire world, online is an amazing feat. And I'm fascinated by what you say about this online world supporting and reflecting the actual world.
(*Comment declined*)

ImmaterialGirl: Welcome back Piper! It's so good to see you here again. You like our hair? We've been thinking about keeping it shaved—it makes us feel sort of hive-y, like you said. But it's easier to take care of when you don't have to shave it all the time and as spiritual people we don't want to spend so much time on physical appearance.

BookLover603: I like the bit about the motley…some kind of Yeatsian rebirth thing here? And the idea of wisdom coming from fools and jesters…and con artists…I would love to meet yours…

PipersPebbles: Silas will be at the party Tuesday. You know we are changing the venue? But since you are now one of our own, I'm sure we can manage a special invitation for you to come and meet him. He's single, you know!

AuntieP: I plan to attend Molly's party, if I am still invited, but hesitate to go without costume. I do have a very old Star Trek officer's uniform from my "trekkie" days, but I fear it might not provide the requisite amount of social commentary.

MollyHH: Auntie P, of course you are still invited. Mom, there is NO CHANGE IN VENUE, so could you please not go telling people not to come to my party? Now we're back to square one on getting people to come! Please, everyone, please come! We'll have something special for you. Jacques said so! And Auntie P, Star Trek was nothing but commentary. Please do wear the costume and come. Mom, are you trying to wreck my party? You're going to wreck it!

AuntieP: Now, Molly, your party is going to be fine. You don't need the whole state to come. The core group is fine. Maybe one of them wants to wear an old Klingon outfit? I thought to donate these costumes to the barn sale but decided to keep them for nostalgia's sake. And it is ironic that from what I hear if I didn't keep it to wear myself I might have found it on the restaurant wall. Is anyone in Piper's audience interested in wearing it?

HarvardProf: Auntie P, if the costume is large enough to fit me I would love to accompany you to the party, wherever it may be, dressed as a fellow "trekkie."

AuntieP: We can show by example the importance of overcoming boundaries, even galactic ones, to come together as allies and friends. Hadleys and Hammonds, Klingon and Federation…

(*Comments approved*)

* * *

Ananda wasn't feeling well.

This is what you get when you let new people into your life, thought Piper. *More reasons to be worried and upset.*

She tapped on the door to Brumi and Ananda's room. Lisette peeked out. The room was darkened and Ananda was lying in the bed. "Would you like me to sit with her for awhile?" Piper whispered.

"Thank you," said Lisette softly. "Brumi has gone out to get her some things to make her comfortable. Some herbs, something to eat. I'm going to make tea."

"What should I do?"

"Sit with her. Don't talk unless she starts it. Talk softly. One of us will be back before long."

Piper slipped into the room.

She could see in the dim light how changed it was from only a few weeks ago. The twin beds had been moved somewhere—probably to the barn—and been replaced by a futon on the floor, heaped with throw pillows and colorful blankets. Warm-colored area rugs were scattered on the floor, and the light fragrance of aroma oil permeated the air. How different, a lived-in room from a vacant one.

Piper sank onto a floor pillow near the futon, murmuring a greeting to Ananda, who smiled weakly and put out her hand. Piper took it. How thin and fragile it seemed—had it always been like this?

"Do you mind the cat?" Piper whispered. Sasha had slipped in with her. Ananda shook her head no. Sasha, purring extravagantly and in complete disregard for any code of quietness, climbed onto the futon next to Ananda and began kneading the bed with her paws. Piper watched Ananda anxiously but the younger woman smiled faintly and reached out her hand to stroke the cat. "I like it when she comes to visit," she said in a voice barely above a whisper. "Sasha is a good name for her. Have you always had a cat?"

"Sam and Felicity gave her to me when she was a kitten," Piper replied softly. "It was after…Dan had moved out. They thought I might get lonely. Sam has always looked out for me. He was my first boyfriend."

"Yes," Ananda whispered. "I read it in your blog. Tell me about that."

"We were like one person. We grew up in each other's homes, with one another's families. We used to slip into his family's market after hours and help ourselves to salads and cold cuts out of the deli case, boxes of cookies, cartons of milk. We'd sit on the floor and have a picnic right there. We'd go night swimming at Abbey Pond on the full moon. We'd make granola in his oven and take it up the mountain for a snack, but we'd end up using most of it to lure the birds and chipmunks to come eat out of our hands."

"Sounds like a dream."

"To us it was just life. His graduation picnic was typical—the town park, the same set of people we had known all our lives. Except, Sam's dad told us, Jake and his dad were going to come too. That was such an honor. Jacques was notorious for *To the Barricades*, and seeing Jake again was going to be a treat. He had gone off to Dartmouth and we hadn't seen him for years. And, we learned, Jake was bringing his college roommate and best friend—a Hammond relative."

"Big doings in a small town?"

"Poor Sam didn't stand a chance. We were kids, fresh out of school. Dan and Jake seemed like grown ups. They had already done their 'On the Road' year in a conversion van and spent two years in Boston with Jacques, teaching performance art to the homeless. That was before Jacques started to dabble in state politics. Before, as Dan would say, the aliens took him up."

She smoothed the blankets over Ananda. "I'm tiring you out."

"No. You are telling a story and taking me out of myself. Thank you.

Tell more."

"The story is of a young woman choosing between two men: one who seemed limited, one unbounded. She went with the one who seemed to offer a bigger world. And she became trapped in her own house."

"And the other?"

"The other one had exactly the life expected: he ran his family grocery, he lived above the store. But something was going on inside, wasn't it? Something that made him go out and find a group of monks and bring them to his town." Piper shook her head, turning over the concepts in her mind. "It's ironic, isn't it?"

"And surprising?" Ananda asked.

"Though maybe it shouldn't have been," Piper reflected. "Sam was always doing little things for other people."

"Sometimes the little things end up being the big ones."

"They do," Piper agreed. "And what kind of fate ties us back together?"

"Karmic connections," Ananda whispered. "Look where they've led. You made choices with Dan that led to Molly coming into your life. You started a magazine. And Dan made choices that brought you Donny, and even Coral. And Coral brought us to you. So now you've got us, and that connects you back to Sam and Felicity too."

Piper, following Ananda's words, felt her story changing, morphing into a brilliantly threaded tale of interwoven connectedness growing layer by layer until something new and wholly unexpected was glimpsed. And Piper's own life, moments ago so fettered, seemed to open up into the vastness of possibility.

Piper's Index of Donny Moments
(Not for Publication)

Eight Weeks: Molly is on Donny duty, walking him around in a front carrier. Why won't the baby stop crying? Molly makes an emergency stop at the Hadley House, in a panic, in tears. Piper unstraps the screaming baby from his carrier, unwraps Donny's diaper. Why hasn't Coral shown Molly how to change him? Piper sends Molly to King's for an emergency stash of diapers and wipes; Donny can have an air bath on a blanket on the floor while they wait. Molly hugs her mother gratefully, but Piper shrugs—it's what mothers are for. While Molly is at King's, Piper suggests, better let them know to start keeping the Hadley House supplied with diapers and formula.

Six Months: Dan stops by with Donny riding high in his arm. Donny sees Piper, breaks into a smile, and leans toward her, arms outstretched. Piper receives him, and he burrows into her neck like a sweet-smelling kitten. What is it that Piper feels? Whatever it's called, it's a little like heartbreak.

Eleven Months: Somehow a supply of toys and a crib have become a part of the aesthetic of the Hadley House living room. Molly does her homework here while Donny plays nearby. Piper is watching a video clip of a town meeting. Donny crawls to the TV, pulls himself up, turns around, and teeters toward Piper. His first steps! And it is Piper who is there for them.

Two Years: Donny has entered the terrible twos with a vengeance, melting down into a tantrum about once a week. His preschool isn't sure how to handle it. Neither, it seems, is his mother. What's the big deal? You gather him up, keep him safe, let him cry it out. It takes an experienced mother to know these things—something Coral most definitely is not. Maybe Donny should come to Piper, rather than going to preschool, those two mornings a week?

Thirty Months: Coral is scheduled to attend an out-of-town conference. Why, Piper suggests, doesn't Dan go too? Donny can stay at the Hadley House with Molly and Piper. Surely he is old enough for a sleepover, and it will be good practice for Molly. Molly and Donny review their supplies. Favorite snacks? Check. Favorite videos? Check. Favorite pillows, favorite blankets? Check and check. Pup tent in the living room, to all pile into together? Check!

Three Years: Piper has dressed Donny up in his new cowboy outfit and strapped on his six shooter; she has put a cowboy hat on her own head. They are gearing up for their game of pretend when Dan arrives to take Donny home. Donny looks at his father and his face crumples. Sobbing, he crawls into Piper's lap to kiss her a tearful goodbye. Piper wants to be triumphant, to show Dan, to show Coral. But she can find no triumph in the boy's tears. Because, reluctantly, inescapably, and irrevocably, Piper has fallen in love. With Donny.

November 23: Pay No Attention to That Woman Behind the Curtain

I feel I owe apologies to my readers, beginning with my daughter. I also feel the need to explain and justify a decision I have recently made. It has to do with Molly's costume party, her project for November Lies. She had very cleverly worked out an arrangement with our Hey! It's Thursday to hold it there, and we had invited all her friends, and all of you, my readers.

Jacques Marquand, our dear friend and November Lies founder, thought he'd help us out by giving the party a little nudge in his readers' awarenesses. With this in mind, he introduced it to his entire readership, which as we all know is many times the size of mine. This of course changes the scale entirely and brings to mind horror tales from my own childhood having to do with open-invitation parties.

If you've ever seen a teen movie, you're sure to know what I mean. Parents go out of town, and the word spreads: Party! Total strangers come from miles away, bringing drinks, drugs, destruction. Eventually the police show up, or the parents return home unexpectedly, but not before the damage is done.

Back when my Auntie P was young there was a house, right here in

Riverboro, that had parties like that *every night*. Come one, come all! Everyone welcome! Eventually, almost Biblically, the house burned to the ground, and whether they salted the earth where it had stood I do not know and wouldn't venture to guess.

The story has a punchline: Guess who lived in that house? Our own Jacques Marquand, his wife Aurora, and their little son, Jake. I was raised on that story—Jacques himself has told it to me more than once. So when Jacques, who now has a bigger following than he could have dreamed of back in those years, gets involved in party planning, alarm bells go off in my head.

And that is why, dear Riverboro, we are trying to moderate this party affair. You will thank us when you see what a civilized event it will be. Molly is cross about it, and I'm sorry for that; but Molly, it is still quite an achievement, pulling this whole thing together, and it's sure to be a big winner in the November Lies competition. Just a shift in location (for you in the immediate group who are coming, we'll let you know), a more limited guest list, and we'll make sure to get lots of pictures to post here and on Jacques' blog.

Meanwhile, I hope you'll all come to the Riverboro Public Library for the Hadley Scholarship Day. It isn't quite the same as a house party, but it is, in fact, open to the public—everyone in the public, and there will be cider and doughnuts, courtesy of King's Market and Marty's Café.

There has been much shouting and finger pointing, of late; much moaning and gnashing of teeth; and much of it has been based around the fact that I personally—unlike other Hadley family members—do not, in fact, get out much. Or at all. But this Friday I'm getting out, and I expect to see you all.

Auntie P wanted me to come and speak—words being my thing, as you might say. I felt impelled to refuse. I operate behind the scenes. I, like the Wizard of Oz, am the person behind the curtain; I, like the Artist as a Young Man, forge my words alone in the dark smithy of my soul.

But Molly will speak, and she will present the scholarship that day. And I will be there to support her.

I'll see you there!

Tags: Hadley Day, Riverboro traditions, Riverboro Public Library, spiced cider, doughnut recipes

COMMENTS:

Private Message from DanTheRiverMan: Piper, don't be ridiculous. There has been no shouting, no finger pointing, no moaning, and definitely no gnashing of teeth. Why do you have to tell the world there has been?

Private Message to DanTheRiverMan: It's more metaphorical; or rather, an external depiction of internal perceptions.

Private Message from DanTheRiverMan: *Your* internal perceptions. Why must you drag the rest of us into it?

Private Message to DanTheRiverMan: I didn't drag you into it—that's *your* internal perception.

Private Message from DanTheRiverMan: Piper, I have offered you nothing but support, and I very much look forward to seeing you at the library for Molly's talk. You appear to want to atone for your capriciousness about the party, and while I have a hard time keeping up with the ping-ponging cause-and-effect in your life, I wish you the best.

MollyHH: Mom, this is so unfair! It's going to ruin everything! And how can you decide yourself like that, without me or Dad or Coral?

And how can you compare a party in a restaurant with a teen house party? You've got to see the differences!

PipersPebbles: The differences aren't the problem. It's the similarities that worry me.

ImmaterialGirl: How about a monk party, tomorrow? It's Thanksgiving and we don't even have to invite anyone to get a crowd—there are so many of us here already. We don't have much of a kitchen, but since we can still use the oven and range we thought we'd cook up a big one-pot meal and have it in the dining room together.

SamKing: I would like to bring up a vegetarian turkey roast all cooked up and ready to go as my contribution to the feast.

PipersPebbles: Will you join us for it, Sam?

SamKing: We'd love to, but have family commitments. But Felicity tells me she'll send along her mashed sweet potato casserole.

AuntieP: Your Grandma Tini used to do hers with mini marshmallows, remember?

PipersPebbles: Would you like to join us for dinner, Auntie P?

AuntieP: Why thank you, dear, but I have invited one or two new friends from this blog to join me at the condo. I sent them Private Messages and was pleased to get acceptances. I look forward to seeing you and Molly at the library the following day.

ImmaterialGirl: And what about the Weather Oracle? Will he come in off his farm and join the people? His fans want him to step out from behind *his* curtain and show himself.

PipersPebbles: Oh, I don't think so. Prophecies and their originators are best veiled in mystery.

BookLover603: In one of his posts, Jacques indicated that the Oracle would unveil his identity at the party...he said we should all come to find out...

PipersPebbles: You see what I mean? That's why his blog is called *Damn Lies.*

WeatherOracle: The secret dark of my identity
                  Is guarded close with due solemnity.
                  To unmask in a masquerade
                  Confusion brings to the charade.
                  It mocks the true disguises worn
                  And lands the farmer deep in corn.
                  Though you might find the Lie deplorable,
                  Don't look to meet your Weather Oracle.

MollyHH: My party will be deplorable? I knew it!
(*Comments approved*)

* * *

Damn Lies
By Presidential Candidate and Weather Talent Scout
Jacques Marquand

My November Liars labor like miners in the subterranean caverns of the unconscious, crafting their collective conundrums. A story awaits a telling, a plot prepares to unfold, and the first submission will be screened in only five days in Riverboro. Piper Hadley is poised to become the new Mistress of Lies, as in a masterly move she has secured our insecurity. Whither will we wander? Are we to be all dressed up with no place to go? Fallback location is the Hadley Haven, the grand Victorian on Hadley Street—you can't miss it. So if the H.I.T. turns partiers away, you have a warranty of welcome from *Riverboro Rocks*.

* * *

Could it get any worse? Disaster didn't begin to cover it.

Piper sat on the edge of the sofa, watching Molly pacing the living room in tense circles. "Mom, how could you?" she was wailing. "You told everyone not to come. It's going to be a flop!"

Molly had called for her troops to rally at the Hadley House. The downstairs was in full multi-tasking mode, the costume stations set up. Matthew, inexplicably, was present, reading something on his laptop screen, looking absorbed. Was he a costume consultant now? Miranda, her mouth full of pins, was fitting a blazer across Jilly's shoulders. Lisette, exuding a kind of purposeful calm, was taping a chart to the wall.

And Molly was mid-meltdown.

"If no one comes—"

"—we'll have to fall on our swords," Miranda finished cheerfully, around a mouthful of pins.

"Lucky they aren't that sharp." Peter swooshed a crudely-cut scimitar through the air. "Since they're made of cardboard."

"Mom, we *can't* have the party at the River Place. Coral won't let us bring weapons if they don't look fake. We can't even spray paint them."

"What does she think we're going to do," Peter grumbled. "Start an uprising with plastic lasers?"

"Come the revolution, all our weapons will be painted," Pasco said.

"People will come." Piper said. "Your friends will come."

"Jacques blog wasn't such a big deal. How can you let it ruin everything?"

"Jacques needs to mind his own business," Piper snapped.

Molly interrupted shrilly. "He was trying to *help*—"

"—and as for Japan, your father—"

"Mom!" Molly screamed. "You don't understand! This is important! Dad knows—"

"And now we're at each other's throats. Jacques loves—"

Matthew made the kind of sound a teacher makes to get the attention of the class. Then he waited. Gradually the cacophony subsided and, one by one, people turned to look at him. "Jacques' post," he said, gesturing to his laptop screen. "People will come."

Piper and the others looked at him blankly. Matthew looked serious and, watching him, Piper began to feel that things could, perhaps, get worse after all. "What?" she demanded. "What about it? The Oracle—?"

"Not the Oracle," said Matthew. "The warranty of welcome."

"A warranty of welcome? What warranty? What welcome?" Piper had, admittedly, only skimmed that morning's post. It took energy to parse Jacques' ramblings—energy she didn't always have. Now the shiver in her skin, the pressure behind her ears, told her she had let her guard down. Things could get worse—they could always get worse.

Matthew began to read, and, as he did so, Piper's perceptions started to splinter. She heard Matthew's voice, followed the meaning, until he spoke the words, "you have a warranty of welcome at *Riverboro Rocks*." Then the room disintegrated, his words disintegrated, and all Piper could see or hear was a disconnected chaos of visual and auditory fragments. She must have made some gesture, some noise—she must have said or done *something*— because the buzz in the room seemed to move, to center around her. Faces zoomed in and out of her vision. In a ritual that was becoming familiar, someone was putting an afghan around her shoulders, someone was pressing a cup of tea into her hands. Lisette was at her side, stroking her hair and rubbing her hands.

What was she doing, why were they paying attention to her? How to seem normal, what was normal? "I'm fine, it's all fine," she managed. She drew in a breath, tried to wave people away. "A warranty of welcome. To here. This house. To Jacques' *entire blogging audience*." She tried to laugh. "There you have it, Molly. We'll be wishing for that flop by the time this is all over."

"I'm sorry Mom," Molly said shakily. "But it isn't my fault, I had a place for the party and you called it off. What was Jacques supposed to do? He's bringing the governor!"

"He's not bringing the governor," Piper said. "Neither of them are coming. But he's made good and sure that hundreds of people *will* come— here." Piper took breaths, rubbing the knot in her stomach. The room was starting to cohere again, its pieces falling back into place. Still, all of Piper's dread, her near-constant anxiety, was gathering itself and focusing on the upcoming event. So many years of phantom dreads, phantom anxieties, swept away by this looming peril. She tried for another laugh. "This gives a whole new meaning to social anxiety," she said with a forced lightness that sounded, even to her own ears, borderline hysterical. "We are literally going to be barricaded in this house while the hordes gather outside, preparing to invade."

"A party apocalypse," said Miranda, sounding awed. "Didn't I call that one?"

"It's like a horror movie." Piper found she was actually wringing her hands together like a cliché personified. "Jacques is the dark avenger, directing his minions. And we're sitting in the house on the hill, awaiting our doom."

"It's our zombie apocalypse come to life," Pasco said, a little too cheerfully. "Party-going zombies."

Miranda turned Jilly to face her, tugging the sleeve of the blazer down and stretching Jilly's arm out to check the length. "Maybe people will get so confused they'll stay home," she suggested.

Jacques Marquand loomed in Piper's awareness, no longer as a loveable old friend but as a sinister force, moving his fell troops toward her, towards her destruction. Everyone was still acting so normal. Why couldn't they see? "What are we going to do, how are we going to—"

"Re-direct." Silas interrupted her rising tones, his voice calm and firm. Her eyes flew to his.

"Re…" Piper trailed off.

Silas gave a single, firm nod. "Back to the H.I.T."

"I think we'll have to," Matthew agreed. "It gives a context to set limits."

"But how?" Piper cried. "Jacques told everybody to come here!"

"We still have time," Miranda said. "We'll get him to announce the original location."

And you'll announce it too, Mom," Molly said pleadingly. "On Piper's

Pebbles."

"We'll put it on the Daily Union's community calendar," Lisette said.

"The more we mention it, the more people will hear about it," Piper said despairingly. "We're back to the original problem. People are going to trash the H.I.T.! What are we going to do about that?"

"Muscle," said Silas.

"Right. Bouncers!" Pasco agreed. "Big brawny men, keeping order."

"We don't have any!" Piper said. "Bouncers? Brawny men? We don't have a budget for that. There are only three policemen in this entire town!"

"Us," said Silas.

"Us? Silas, you're scary, but you're not that big, and there's only one of you—"

"Monks," Silas elaborated.

"Monks?" Piper was flabbergasted. "The *muscle*?"

"You don't think we can handle it?" Pasco countered. "We can be the muscle. Why not?"

"Because you're—" Piper glanced at the others for support. Matthew looked thoughtful, Silas amused. Miranda, arrested in the act of pinning the hem of Jilly's sleeve, looked transfixed. But Molly looked hopeful. Piper tried to picture the monks, with their white robes and serene countenances, summoning the ferocity to keep the hordes in order. "Because you're monks," she finished lamely. "You're supposed to be peaceful."

"We'll be tough," Pasco said confidently. "We'll have all the power we need."

"How is that possible? Do you mean because of your practice?"

"Not our practice," Pasco replied. "Our costumes. Remember?" He lifted a plastic bow. "We're superheroes."

* * *

Feeling as shaky as a convalescent, Piper made her way into the kitchen. Matthew followed. "Anything I can get you?" he asked. While Piper sank into a chair at the table, he rummaged in a cupboard and found a couple of mugs. Piper watched as he measured coffee into the coffeemaker on the counter.

"Why?" she asked. "Do I look frayed?"

"Not in the least." Matthew poured coffee into the mugs and handed one to her. "You're holding up amazingly. It can't be easy."

Piper clasped the warm cup in front of her in much the same way Molly had clasped her tea the evening Hap LeClair had brought her home. "Everyone thinks it's me," she said in eager gratitude for Matthew's validation. "Being unreasonable, freaking out. They can't see this Jacques thing for what it is. He's throwing in something for everyone—protests and costumes and drinks and governors and Japan—everyone is dazzled. But there is a serpent in every garden, and never more so than in Jacques'. Why does he have to promise Molly that trip? Doesn't he know how crushing that must be? To me?"

"He might not," Matthew took a seat across from her. "I don't. How crushing is it?"

"Crushing enough. Who wants to disappoint their kids? And even if I wanted her going back to Japan, Jacques is not the man to chaperone a bunch of teens. Trust me on that. But Molly—she won't hear it. She thinks if she gets it right, every detail perfect, she'll win that trip. Why does she have to throw herself into things like that?"

"Following the example of an adult role model?" Matthew suggested.

Piper was doubtful. "I don't think so. Coral likes costumes, but—it's different. I can't think of an adult in Molly's life that acts like that."

"No grown up who takes on many projects and gives them her all? No grown up whose days are immersed in creative work? No grown up who takes joy in a beautiful outcome, regardless of its commercial value?"

Piper felt herself growing pink. "Me?" she squeaked. "Do you mean Molly is like me?"

"Of course. Isn't it obvious?"

"That is so flattering," said Piper. "And so scary. On so many levels."

"But so true," said Matthew.

* * *

Lunch was a deli spread of breads, cheeses, tapenades, and hummus. When Piper returned Molly brought her a plate.

"Yours looks austere," Piper commented. The plate in Molly's other hand held only rice crackers, hummus, and a few grapes.

"This is for Ananda. She's dairy- and gluten-free for now. She's coming down to see the costumes. You stay too, Mom. We're going to suit up and model them."

The next hour was a flurry of putting on costumes and wigs, applying makeup, doing hair, painting on scars, cries of "I dropped mustard on my tunic!" and "Who took my bear?" and "Where is my other earring?" and "I can't get this contact in!"

Ananda and Piper were settled on the sofa to watch it all, like special guests, like pageant judges. "We're the silent witnesses. Kind of like you monks," Piper joked to Ananda, adding, "Do you feel up to this?"

"Oh yes," Ananda said. "I love sitting comfy and watching it all swirl around me."

Silas was doing video interviews. He moved his station near the sofa so Piper and Ananda could watch as people took it in turns to explain their costume details, pointing out a special piece of embroidery or a tricky bit of sculpting, describing the harrowing process of creation.

"I spent two hours forming this, and it fell apart in the oven. I was in tears, but then Lisette suggested I try a different clay…"

"It was too thick, the thread kept breaking, so I had to do this part by hand—you can't tell, though, can you?"

"I thought I would pass out from the smell of the spray paint, we had to open all the windows and it was, like, fifteen degrees outside."

In the middle of the afternoon, Piper heard Dan's signature thumping and stamping. Her eyes went to the door; unconsciously she reached out for Ananda and clutched her hand. Ananda gave hers a reassuring squeeze.

Then Dan appeared, carrying Donny. He whispered something to his son, pointed at Piper, and set Donny down. Donny made a beeline across the room and climbed on Piper's lap to greet her.

Piper clung to him for a few precious moments. "I missed you, Donny," she whispered.

"I missed you too," he whispered back.

How long since she had seen Donny? Less than a week. But it had been a week marked by feelings of abandonment and fear of loss, by the replaying of old scenarios in which Piper was punished for her inadequacies by the loss of a child. Now, holding Donny, she felt that old mix of attachment and loss and relief and joy. She closed her eyes and felt herself almost disappear in the swirl of emotions and the uproar around her and her one still point, Donny, clinging to her with his light rapid heart beating against hers.

Then Donny straightened his body to be let down. Piper forced herself to release him from her arms with a kiss on the cheek. Her eyes followed as Molly and Cassie bore him off to dress him as Link, a little hero in an altered and updated Peter Pan costume. He reappeared clad in green, tiny in a sea of big people who were by now decked out in full pageantry, and was taken to Silas for his interview.

Throughout the room costumed people were taking exuberant or pugnacious stances, leaping and landing. Piper was startled to see Lisette, wearing a sari and declaiming: "Let there be calamities!"

"No!" Piper cried, feeling a clutch of fear.

Leon, who had joined the company for lunch, looked at Lisette with deep affection. "Because they make us remember God," he explained. "But not here. Not now. She's playing a great queen from long ago."

Molly and Jilly appeared before Piper, each wearing identical short red wigs, identical blue blazers, arms linked—twin boys. "We have to practice the body language. That's why everyone is jumping around like this," Molly explained, adding, "Mom, tomorrow is Thanksgiving. Can I come here?"

"You mean for dinner?" Piper's eyes found Dan. He gave a small negative shake of his head. "Molly, sweetie, we'd love to have you but you're supposed to be helping with the community dinner at the River Place."

"I always help with that dinner." Molly sounded like a mutinous child. "I want to come have dinner with you and Cassie and the others. Why can't I?"

Piper looked at Dan in appeal but he had turned away to say something to Brumi, though still listening, by the set of his shoulders, to the outcome with Molly. "Molly," Piper said, somewhat helplessly, "they count on you down there, you know that."

"No one my age does that kind of thing," Molly protested. "It's for kids and old people—it isn't fair."

"Yo." Silas lowered his camera and started over to them. "Mol. Need help at the do?"

Colby, who had been watching sharply, came leaping across to join them. "I'll help too!" He quickly relaxed into a slouch like an acrobat correcting a landing and added more casually, "Count me in."

Molly looked from Silas to Colby in amazement. "You'd do that? Both of you? Si, don't you have plans already? Pasco said he invited you here for dinner."

"We'll come up after," Silas said.

Molly was glowing. "*Thank* you Colby. Thank you Silas! We're serving at one. We should be through clean-up by five. Then we'll come up here with the leftovers. OK?"

Dan's shoulders relaxed, satisfied. Molly flung an arm around each of her friends, beaming at them happily. Colby and Silas glowered at each other. Then Silas turned away to focus his camcorder elsewhere.

Piper gave a small sigh.

November 24: Where Two or More Are Gathered

Happy Thanksgiving, Riverboro. What are your plans?

Today I plan to eat my midday meal with six monks. Although they have been with me now for almost three weeks, we do not, as a rule, eat our meals together as a family would. What with one thing and another—fire and flood and work and breakdowns—we haven't set up that kind of shared schedule. And, as Cassie says, we don't have much of a kitchen. But the dining room has been opened up and aired out, and all that lovely wooden cabinetry has been oiled and is shining, and Granny Hadley's enormous wooden table (which hasn't been used in years) will be set with Grandma Tini's heirloom china and we will give thanks together.

And I wonder: will we "go round the table"?

How many of you did that growing up? Going round the table, saying what you are thankful for? There are always a few (usually the men) who complain, but even they feel uplifted by it.

Today I'd like you, my readers, to go round the table, metaphorically speaking, and write what you are thankful for in the comment section below. I'll start:

I am thankful for my brilliant and beautiful daughter, Molly, who will be enjoying her Thanksgiving dinner with her father's family, as she always does, but will stop by later to spend the early evening with me.

I am thankful for my (almost) stepson, Donny, who will be starting on Mozart soon (if we can organize for him to be here somehow. Maybe Molly can bring him for his lessons?).

I am thankful for my magazine, and my monks.

And I am thankful for Sam King. Because Sam King is organizing something which is a pure miracle for me and for my home. And today I want to share that thing with all of you.

The Hadley House (also known as my home) is going to have a new role in town for the immediate and foreseeable future. It is going to be the location of the Riverboro Ashram. The monks will live here. They will teach their classes and sell their goods at their center by the river, but they will live and meditate and chant and pray (or whatever it is they do) here.

They will have the second floor of this big old house, and I will have the third, where my office and bedroom are now. They will pay some rent to help with taxes and expenses, and it will help financially. And they will fill my house with their presence and it will be a great solace to me. When I want to be alone I will leave them and go upstairs, and when I want people around me I will go down to the main living area, and someone will be there.

Thank you, Sam, for interfering for good in these human affairs.

And welcome, monks.

Tags: Thanksgiving traditions, stepfamilies, everyday heroes

COMMENTS:

SamKing: Felicity and I are thankful to you for providing in this way for the "monks". It's important to us that they continue to have a home in Riverboro, and we credit you with making it happen.

ImmaterialGirl: I'm thankful for Ananda's improvement. She has had a rough month and it's amazing that we had all these challenges, with no power and no heat and no bathrooms and having to move and stuff getting wrecked and all that, right when she was feeling the worst. And now she is finishing her chemo and starting to feel better and there is nothing on this earth that makes me happier than seeing color come back into her face.

PipersPebbles: Cassie I didn't know, most of the time, that she was even sick. I am so sorry I didn't give her, and all of you, more support in this difficult transition.

ImmaterialGirl: Piper, that's crazy. You have been our good angel, opening your home to us and making us comfortable and giving us the run of your place. I swear without you I don't know where we would have been. We all love you and thank you from the bottom of our hearts. And if I say any more I am certain I will cry.

RiverCoral: I'm so thankful for the good works we're able to do at the River Place, and the role we play with the monks as well. For those of you who don't already have plans, or a family to spend Thanksgiving with, we're doing a community dinner mid-day. We're having real (non-vegetarian) turkey and stuffing and cranberry sauce, and like every year Molly and Dan and I will be there helping out. This year Donny will help too, and two November Liars, Silas and Colby, and if any more of you November Liars want to come help, we can always use more cooks and servers. See you there! ☺

BookLover603: I feel as if I've made such an amazing group of friends through this blog…so many people that love to read. I hope we all meet in person one day…

DrewHadley: My dad seems to be getting over his cold. It means he'll cook dinner today, lol.

AuntieP: Is he going to start predicting weather again? I will be thankful for that, with the understanding that he forecast sunshine now and then.

ZombiePatrol: Being the macho man that I am, I don't get all girly and mushy like you ladies do. But I'm happy for Cassie and the baby. I've got his ultrasound picture in my wallet. He looks like a tadpole, but I'm told he'll grow out of that awkward phase. He's looking forward to meeting his Auntie Piper, and hopes she'll teach him Mozart.

ImmaterialGirl: Her. Auntie Piper is going to teach her Mozart. And since when are you macho?

The Geekster: Don't forget to say thanks for the Hadley House—Riverboro's new zombie fortress.

ZombiePatrol: I was going to mention that.

ConArtist: And the jukebox is done. It looks so fine.

(*Comments approved*)

* * *

"No texting at the table, Pasco," Lisette reproved.

They were gathered, for the first time, around the big table in the dining room. Lisette had created a centerpiece with pinecones and branches. Leon had lit a fire in the dining room fireplace. Piper kept looking at it apprehensively, but it looked as if the chimney was drawing properly.

"I'm not texting," Pasco protested. "I'm checking Piper's blog for comments. She's got over two hundred of them. Seems like everyone in town is going round the table."

"That blog is mega popular," Cassie said. "Everyone I know reads it."

"This is the first time we've had so many comments, though," Piper said, pulling her gaze from the fireplace. "Why are these people online? Why aren't they having dinner with their families?"

"Which brings us back to you, Pasco," Lisette said. "Put the phone away."

"Fascist. You're worse than Guruji." Pasco snapped his phone shut. "Silas texted. He and Molly are up to their armpits in soapsuds. Dish detail." He helped himself to meatless turkey and offered the platter to Cassie. "What that guy will do for love. No pride, no shame."

"As it should be," said Ananda, scooping a modest serving of sweet potato casserole onto her plate. "If Molly asked him to fly off the roof he'd be diving into the air." She looked around at the group. "What? It's what any man would do if he had romance in his soul."

"Romance in his soul?" Piper asked, holding out her glass for Lisette to fill with sparkling cider. "This is Silas we're talking about. Does he even have a soul?"

"Of course he does," said Ananda. "He is a pure romantic."

"I'd dive off the roof for you," Pasco said, nuzzling Cassie. She pushed him away, laughing.

"Have you *met* Silas?" Piper asked, rhetorically.

"It takes a very romantic person to commit himself to body art," said Leon.

"Or a completely insane one," said Piper, taking a roll and passing the basket. "At least he hasn't tattooed himself with Molly's name." She intercepted a glance between Brumi and Lisette. "Has he?"

"He got a Pokemon," said Brumi.

"In her honor," said Lisette.

"I hesitate to ask *where*?" Piper asked.

"Over in Nashua," said Pasco innocently. "The day they went to Best Buy for jukebox parts."

Cassie giggled and Piper said, "Where on his *body*?"

"On his left shoulder blade," said Lisette.

"So Molly would want him to take off his shirt," added Cassie.

"I guess we should thank the Lord he didn't get it on his butt, then," Piper muttered sourly.

There was a stunned moment of silence, then a muffled snort from Brumi. Piper glanced over. Brumi looked purple and strangled. Actually, they all did. Leon's sides were going in and out in silent paroxysms; Ananda was making cheeping sounds high in her throat; Cassie sounded as if she were hiccupping; and Lisette was leaning over, face in hands, her shoulders heaving.

Pasco gave a loud, involuntary "Ha!" and the group around the table dissolved into helpless shrieks. Piper clutched her stomach and gasped, tears of laughter streaming down her face.

* * *

Silas trailed into the living room, following Molly and Colby. Molly and Colby looked glossy and shiny, almost brother and sister with their dark hair and eyes. Colby guided Molly in with a hand on the small of her back and took her coat, straightening her collar, smoothing her hair. Silas slouched after and stood awkwardly near the door, tattered and unkempt, looking, by comparison with Colby's finished good looks, like a discarded trial human being.

"An inconvenience to miss family Thanksgiving? Maybe. A privilege to help the less fortunate? Absolutely," Colby was saying. "We should do it every year."

"I already do it every year," said Molly. "I guess it is pretty special."

"It's an antidote to the commercialization of Thanksgiving," said Colby sagely. "I learned about true poverty when I went to Africa with my godfather. He showed me life in its simplest form. The best man I ever met."

"I thought the late Jacques Marquand was the best man you ever met," Piper murmured. She caught Silas' eye; he gave a what-are-you-gonna-do tilt of his head, and she felt an unexpected surge of affection for him.

"Silas," she said, "that jukebox of yours out in the barn. Molly was wondering how it was coming along. Why don't you take her out and show it to her?"

"Great idea," said Colby. "I'd like to have a look at it too."

"Yes, of course; but Colby, Lisette has been wanting to talk to you about those Jacques Marquand performance pieces. Could you spend a few moments with her first?"

Lisette started forward and took Colby's arm firmly. "Yes, I'm dying to hear about those monkey protests. I read about them in the *Globe*. Were the monkeys part of the protests, or were the protests about the monkeys? And what did they mean by monkey juggling? Did he actually juggle the monkeys or were the monkeys doing the juggling? I'm starting in on the dishes; come sit and tell me all about it."

Reluctantly Colby allowed Lisette to tow him along into the kitchen. "And were they riding tiny motorcycles?" she was asking. "Or was it little bicycles? The reviews mentioned 'bikes' so I wasn't sure…"

Silas and Molly followed them out, heading for the barn. As they left the room Silas turned to look back at Piper, and she wondered why she had never noticed how sweet his smile could be.

* * *

"I thought," said Matthew, "that if I brought a couple of pies, I might get an invitation to join you."

He stood just inside the door, a pie in each hand. At the sight, Piper was surprised by a springing sensation in her stomach. It was something she hadn't felt in a long time. Tall, geeky, high-school-teacher Matthew had come to see her on Thanksgiving. It made her feel popular. It made her feel sought-after.

It made her feel wonderful.

"Your timing couldn't be better," she said, gesturing him in. "We'll have it by the living room fire."

Pasco and Cassie converged on Matthew, zeroing in on the pies. "We love pies!" cried Cassie. "Cassie Junior loves pies!"

"Pasco Junior," said Pasco. "He's a pie junkie. What did you bring?"

"A pumpkin and an apple," said Matthew. "My mother made them. To get me in good with the Hadley House crowd."

His mother, thought Piper. Why didn't that sound pathetic? The idea of Matthew telling his mother about her and her group, the idea of his mother sending him along with pies, sent another surprising flutter through her.

Lisette took the pies. "I'll cut them up and bring them out. Brumi, could you get the dessert plates? Leon, forks and napkins?"

Soon Matthew was perched on the sofa, balancing pie and coffee on his knee, Piper seated next to him. She felt like she was on a date; she felt as if he were a young man come a-courtin'. She found something very attractive in his easy awkwardness. It was, she thought, an unpretentious, I've-come-to-terms-with-my-inner-geek kind of awkwardness. Could she work something about it into her blog?

"I read the news about the monks in your blog this morning," Matthew said, as if picking up on her thoughts. "Instant family."

"Or reality TV show," said Piper.

"I checked it before I left my mom's house." Matthew cut his pie with the side of his fork and offered the first bite to Piper. "You have almost three hundred comments. So far."

"What about you?" Piper, feeling like a teenager, accepted the bite. "I didn't see a comment from you. You're not The Geekster or anything like that, are you?"

"I wish," Matthew said. "I'd comment if I could think of a clever screen name."

"Does it have to be clever?" Piper asked. "You couldn't log in as 'guest'?"

"The other commenters have set a high bar," Matthew said. "It's amazing, isn't it, how people can capture something important about themselves in so few words? It's like tweeting: my life in 140 characters."

"Like a bumper sticker," Piper said.

"Or a vanity license plate," Matthew added. "Something else I never could master. I'd need at least a paragraph to capture the essence of me."

Piper felt she was starting to get the hang of Matthew. He was *funny*. You didn't know it right off because his delivery was so low-key. After Dan, low-key took some getting used to. But there was something appealing about it. *I can do low-key,* Piper thought. *It'll make a nice change.*

"So, a whole paragraph?" she teased. "All those words—what would be in it?"

"My hopes, my dreams, my desires..."

"Sounds more like an obit. Matthew Winchester, former resident of Riverboro, dies at eighty three..."

"Ninety-three," said Matthew.

"A hundred and three," said Piper. "Why think small?"

"Lover of spreadsheets and numbers..."

"Con goer," prompted Piper.

"Will one day write a book revealing how mathematical principles apply to human interactions," Matthew continued.

"Which will be required reading in high school and college business classes," Piper supplied.

"How did you know?"

"Lucky guess."

"Maker of bad puns."

"I would say maker of good puns," said Piper. "Though puns are presupposed to be bad."

"A man who, like any good geek, owns a souvenir pencil mug from the original TV series of Dr. Who," Matthew said thoughtfully.

"No, really? I've always wanted one!" Piper exclaimed.

"A man who now knows what to get you for Christmas..."

"Member of a particularly heinous high school class," Piper reminded him.

"Though he held the exalted role of Dungeon Master, thereby distinguishing himself from lesser mortals."

"Now I remember you! You were with that group by the window. You guys were so weird. You played every lunch hour."

Matthew shook his head. "Weird, maybe, but a different group. We played after school. At lunch I had other fish to fry."

"That's right," Piper said, remembering. "You spent your lunch hours admiring from afar."

"Gazing soulfully at a girl who didn't know I existed."

"Stalker boy," accused Piper. "You're lucky you didn't get arrested."

"I used to sit near the doors," Matthew said. "So I could make a quick getaway."

"A man after my own heart," Piper said. "With the getaway."

"It was you."

Piper was getting ready with her next line; this threw her off. "What?"

"I was in love with you."

For an appalling moment Piper thought that the catch in her breath might be the start of a panic attack.

"Me?" she asked squeakily. "But…why?"

"Only because you were beautiful, smart, lively, playful, and funny," Matthew replied. "I can't think of any other reason."

"Oh," said Piper.

"You still are," said Matthew.

"Oh," said Piper.

"And I still am."

"Oh—"

"I hear you are going out tomorrow."

"Oh…"

"I'd like to take you. Or come with you. Or see you there."

Finally back in control of her breath, Piper smiled. "I'll keep watch," she said. "You drive the getaway car."

* * *

Piper thought she would collapse with fatigue, so she didn't protest when Lisette shooed her off to her room much later.

"The kitchen is sparkling," Lisette said. "The usable parts, anyway. I put Colby and Silas on it. If either of them stayed much longer I'd have had them scouring out the oven or up in the rafters hunting for cobwebs."

Colby and Silas, each having failed to outwait the other, had finally started off, leaving Molly to say goodnight to her mother.

Molly followed Piper from bedroom to bathroom and back again as Piper brushed her teeth, washed her face, and put on her nightie. When Piper crawled in under her comforter, Molly perched on the edge of her bed, still talking.

"Colby does have good social skills," she was saying. "You should have seen him with the old people and children. Helping them to their seats, asking if they needed anything, laughing at their jokes. They loved him."

"The suck up," Piper murmured from deep in her blankets.

"I know, right?" Molly laughed. "It isn't his fault. His parents treat him like all that and a bag of chips. He's always trying to live up to their image of him and prove how special he is."

"He'll come into his own." Piper, snug in her bed, her daughter close by, felt too vast a sense of well-being to summon anything but a sleepy universal charity. "He just needs time to grow up."

"But people love Silas too. When Silas talks to them they feel special."

"Because it's surprising someone who looks like that can put two words together," Piper said.

"Or doesn't hit them first," added Molly.

"I suppose Colby would be considered a good catch," Piper mused. "He's good looking, smart, has a certain degree of charm…"

"A poser…" added Molly in the same musing tone.

Piper laughed softly. "He's aiming for cultivated sophistication. When he gets there, women will be all over him."

"They already are," Molly said, "at school. They see his potential."

"And you?"

Molly kissed her mother and got up to go. "I see his potential too," she said, pausing by the door to switch off the light. "But I guess I'm the type that goes for tattoos."

Piper's List: The Top Five Reasons Why, OK, Maybe Molly Could Date Silas (Not for Publication)

5) He really likes her

4) He isn't that physically hideous

3) He is not a player

2) He probably couldn't be a player even if he tried

1) He is, after all, a Con Artist

November 25: In the World and of It

I have a date for Molly's talk today.

Someone has asked me out: a smart, handsome, fully-employed teacher from the high school. A mentor to the young, an inspiration to his students, a candle in the darkness, a help to the helpless.

Matthew Winchester.

He will come at ten, and we'll sit and have a cup of coffee (or maybe decaf tea). And then we'll go.

Silas will be there to take pictures, and Auntie P will get transcripts of the talk. So I could stay right here, as I often do, covering the whole thing from my office aerie. But this time I will not. This time I will be there with my daughter and my aunts and uncles and cousins, with people I have met and people I have not. I will be in the world and of it.

So I expect, Riverboro, for all of you to come too. Perhaps I will meet those of you I have not yet seen or met: HarvardProf and The Geekster and BookLover and all you others who have dropped by my blog in the early morning and throughout the day.

The world awaits.

Tags: Overcoming social anxiety, Riverboro Public Library, Hadley Meet the Public Day

COMMENTS:

BookLover603: You go girl! I'll be there as your greatest fan…I'll bring a copy of *Riverboro Rocks* for you to sign.

RiverCoral: Piper don't you think you are getting your hopes up excessively here? I know it's a good thing to set up some accountability, but don't you think this might backfire? And to do it at the same time as your first date since…well, you know… ☺

PipersPebbles: Since you ran off with my husband?

RiverCoral: I did not *run off* with your husband. For heaven sakes I'm still right here! And I'm concerned about you, is that so strange? ☺

PipersPebbles: It's beyond strange. It's chilling. With help from you, who needs horror movies?

The Geekster: Catfight! Pile on!

HarvardProf: Deep breath, ladies.

Private Message from DanTheRiverMan: Coral, Piper, the tweets and shares are going through the roof. You might want to take this offline.

MollyHH: See you both at the library!

BookLover603: Enjoy your date…

ZombiePatrol: Don't let the zombies eat your brains.

PipersPebbles: Thank you for the encouragement, Pasco.

(*Comments approved*)

* * *

Piper dressed with care. Her first date in—well, decades. Her first time out of the house in a while, too—all in all, an important day. She put on a swingy skirt and a pair of dress boots and a peach angora sweater. She was tempted (since she got ready early) to change several times, the way people do, to find the perfect outfit, but she knew she looked good and decided to stick with a win.

Molly looked in. She had Donny with her. He hugged Piper. "See you at the library?" he asked. "For Molly's talk?"

"I'll count on it," Piper told him.

Molly hugged Piper too. "Good luck," she told her mother.

"To both of us," Piper responded.

After Donny and Molly left, Piper went to her office to look over an article that had just come in. Then she went downstairs and opened the door for Matthew, who was looking fine in khakis and blazer, handsome and intelligent, the perfect date for one's re-entry into the wider world.

Piper made tea for them both—herbal, non-caffeinated—and as they drank it they talked about the magazine. And then it was time to go.

At the door, Piper was about to leave and she remembered that she needed to run upstairs and turn off her computer. And so she powered down and re-joined Matthew at the door; and she thought, maybe she should have a warmer coat, as it was nippy out there. So she did go back and got one and that was good, because it was nippy.

On the way back through the ruined kitchen to the shed door she stopped to give some extra kibble to Sasha, who was likely to miss her. And then she ran to the second floor to tap on Ananda's door to make sure there was nothing more she needed.

By this time Pasco and Cassie were hovering about in the kitchen, making shooing motions with their hands and saying things like, "It's OK, Piper, we'll take care of it," and "You'll be back soon, she'll be OK," and "Ananda will keep an eye on the house so let's go," and "If we don't leave now we'll be late."

And Matthew was standing by the door looking uncertain and Silas looked in and said something to Pasco and Cassie. They conferred for a moment and then said to Piper, "We're going now, with Silas. Do you want to walk with us?"

And Piper leapt up from where she had sat, just for a moment, at the table in the kitchen and said, "Of course I do." And she walked to the door with them, cool as you please, and at the doorway she said, "You go on ahead, I need to visit the bathroom one last time," and they headed on out. And Matthew stood and waited and she came back down and he said, very calmly and softly, "Molly's talk is starting."

And Piper said, "Oh! It just takes a minute to walk down. Maybe she'll see we're not there and wait a few minutes for us."

And Matthew said, "She waited half an hour. Silas texted. She's starting."

And Piper said, "Well then, if we leave right this second we'll be there before she even starts the Q and A." And Matthew nodded, watching her.

Then Piper said gaily, "So what are we waiting for? Let's go!" And Matthew stood and waited and she said, "Just that I need to check the fire before we go, that it's burned down." And she went and checked and it turned out no one had built one yet, so it was all good, and she came back into the kitchen. And Matthew was sitting at the table and it was noon.

Matthew looked at her and she saw in his gaze compassion, and fear, and even a touch of despair—or could it be what she saw was what was in her own eyes, reflected back to her? She said, "Molly's talk is over, isn't it?"

Matthew nodded.

So Piper sat down at the kitchen table and cried.

November 26: Who Will Buy?

Is there anyone out there, in my reading audience, who might be interested in owning a much-loved regional publication? As I have decided to put *Riverboro Rocks* on the market.

I realize I haven't been doing a good job of preparing the market for a sale till now. Complaining about how we are losing money! Saying we are teetering on the brink of financial ruin! Well surely you know, prospective buyers: that was all in fun. In truth I have this money machine, this cash cow, and now I want to sell it so I can spend more time with my family.

Isn't that what people always say after they are ousted from their jobs? And *Riverboro Rocks* is in its own way ousting me.

Riverboro Rocks is not bringing the opportunities, the adventures, the confidence, or the financial success I once believed it would. Much as I appreciate Matthew Winchester's austerity plan, I spent yesterday going over the numbers—yet again—and while I am sure better times will come, while I am sure that my plucky publication has what it takes to be a financial success, for me, for now, it is taking rather than giving. If it had the resources, the backing, the financial wizardry and economies of scale that a better publisher, a bigger company, could give it, it could shake the cumbersome mud from its wings and fly. I am a child with a pet I can no longer care for; a mother putting a much-loved baby up for adoption; a woman seeking a divorce for the happiness of her husband and family. I do it for the sake of the publication, deeply though it may cut.

I know a solution exists. I know someone exists who can find it. But for me, it is what Russia was to Churchill: a riddle, wrapped in a mystery, inside an enigma. So Riverboro: if there are among you any aspiring publishing magnates, business tycoons, captains of industry, now is your opportunity. Buy now, before the price goes up.

Tags: Magazine for sale, magazine publishing, how to publish a magazine, Winston Churchill

COMMENTS:

Private Message from DanTheRiverMan: Piper, shouldn't you have spoken to me about this? I own half the publication. Does this have something to do with your inability to go to Molly's talk yesterday? Are you lashing out because of that? Or trying to set up a distraction from that? Either way, this is not a decision you can make unilaterally.

Private Message from RiverCoral: Piper you get up to some strange things locked in your drafty house up there but this is the limit. Dan and I are half owners! And how can you sell a magazine by saying it's tanking? No one does that! ☺

Private Message from DrJake: While this decision might be appropriate, be careful that it is not based on some impulse rather than a long-term business reason.

ACaptainOfIndustry: While this is not the usual way of putting a business on the market, I'd like to have a look at your books and start a due diligence. I'll be in touch separately.

(*Comment declined*)

* * *

"This is a novel approach to catalyzing a confrontation," Dan said. They were gathered in the living room—Dan, Jake, Molly, Silas, Piper, and Matthew. Dan had wanted to bring Coral, who as his wife (he said) did have an interest in the magazine, but Piper had been adamant. They met without Coral or they didn't meet at all.

"But to paraphrase Mark Twain," Dan continued, "those who make peaceful confrontation impossible make violent confrontation inevitable."

When, thought Piper, *had Dan become so pompous?* For the first time in her recollection, his words made her feel sick. Literally sick, as if she might lose her lunch. It was so much a part of Dan's nature, his joy of expression, that she had never before seen it as pretentious or grating. *Still,* she thought, *that was then, this is now.* Now she wanted to scream and rail and lunge at him with her fingers crooked into claws. A violent confrontation indeed.

Instead she murmured, "Are you planning on becoming violent?"

"I entertain the hope that violence, both overt and covert, will be shunned by all," said Dan.

"Let's lay down some ground rules then," said Piper, and felt a sense of grim satisfaction at the flicker of surprise that passed over Dan's face. Dan didn't expect her to lay down ground rules. He didn't expect her to stand up to him.

Dan's expectations were going to have to change.

"*He's* out." She indicated Jake, who dipped his head in acquiescence.

"I understand that you are angry, Piper," said Jake. "And I think you understand that I am not the real target of your anger."

"*I'll* decide who my targets are," Piper replied icily.

Dan shook his head. "I'm afraid he's in. To ensure the smooth flow of communication, I have asked Dr. Rosen to join us as a mediator."

"He can't mediate," Piper said. "He isn't impartial. He's your guy. As you made so explicit, you're the one who's paying him, aren't you?"

"Piper, that was for your treatment. I'm not paying him to mediate. I've invited him here as an experienced professional whom we both, by the way, have known for years. Whose friendship we both have enjoyed for years."

"He's out," Piper repeated stubbornly.

"Dan," Jake said. "I can't mediate if both parties don't accept my participation."

Piper was astonished at winning her point so easily. *That'll show Dan,* she thought triumphantly. *I'll rattle his cage today.*

"And why, exactly, is Molly's high school teacher in this meeting?" Dan asked.

"He's helping us with the numbers," Piper said. "I thought that's what we were here to talk about. Looking at the numbers. Seeing what we can and cannot do."

"Is that what the meeting is about? I thought it was about you selling the magazine."

"Right. Selling the magazine, which is not making it financially. Selling the magazine, which is floundering."

"So this very public blog post of yours that you are selling the magazine was exactly what it seems to be—a plea for attention, a cry for help."

"No, Dan, it wasn't. It was about putting the magazine up for sale."

"Which you are not authorized to do. As the magazine is not wholly owned by you."

"Hence, our meeting here," Piper said.

"And now you have your entire group gathered at your whim. How not to see that as a ploy? Like your refusal to leave the house."

Piper glanced quickly at Matthew, then back at Dan. "Some days I get too busy," she said.

"Right," said Dan. "And some days you need to move people like chess pieces."

"I'm not moving anyone like a chess piece. I just don't want Jake."

"Because he's not yours," Dan said.

"If you like. Because he's not mine."

"My move, then," Dan said. "A piece for a piece. Your piece takes out mine; Dr. Rosen leaves and the high school teacher leaves too."

"The high school teacher has a name," said Piper. "And when did you get so mean?"

"Hardly mean," said Dan. "Just keeping the field fair. Saying those things we've both known but never expressed."

"The masks are slipping," Piper said to Matthew lightly.

"I think that also has hardly begun," said Dan.

Piper looked at him in genuine surprise. "Was that some kind of veiled threat?" She felt a flicker of fear. What might Dan do? What further act of abandonment was he capable of? "Or perhaps, as you would say, 'hardly veiled'?"

"Mom, Dad, please," said Molly uncomfortably.

Silas added, "Dudes. Walk it out."

Molly and Silas looked worried. Jake stood, indecisive, seemingly torn between leaving and staying. Matthew, abstracted, was paging through some documents having to do with the magazine, seeming more concerned with the puzzle of keeping it alive than with the interplay of personalities.

But Dan looked genuinely angry. And Piper, watching him, felt as if she were standing on a field of ice, a massive Arctic ice floe with a vast, icy ocean underneath. And she felt as if that ice was beginning to crack and break and rifts were appearing all around her and under her feet; and they were beginning to separate, and her piece was floating off in one direction and everyone else was on another piece, floating away all together, and she had to stay on her piece all alone in the middle of a vast, dark, cold sea.

"I'll walk it out," Dan said. "I'll walk to my lawyer and hand this whole thing over to him. I'll see you in court, Piper. Oh, but wait," he added nastily. "You won't be able to make it, will you?"

He turned and headed for the door. "I'll let you know what happens."

And Piper screamed at his retreating back, "Take the whole damn magazine! See if you can run it! See how long it lasts!" And she picked up a copy of *Riverboro Rocks* and hurled it at his head...

...then turned to look at the circle of shocked faces staring at her, and Sasha who crouched, hissing, under the sofa.

Piper's List: People I Should Have Married Instead of Dan (Not for Publication)

4) Sam King

3) Jake Rosen

2) Matthew Winchester

1) Anybody else

November 27: Dear Dan

Today I write to say goodbye to our fragile, mutually-supportive and mutually-destructive life together. Goodbye to what that life has warped into over the past three years as we have huddled here in the shadow of what we have become, waiting for the other shoe to drop.

You think, and you have said, that I have used my fears to control you and to punish you. Perhaps you believe that you deserve to be punished. Perhaps the simple fact that I am still here, living in the town in which you started your affair, and then started your second family, and then left your first—in that order—is punishment enough. Perhaps it shadows the pure clean joy you would like to take in your new wife and your new child.

What you see as vengeance—those increasing fears and dependencies that began to dominate my life—I see as my reaction to the loss of my emotional safety. Don't you think, from my point of view, that the fears that have kept me indoors for the past three years would be too high a price to pay for getting back at you? Too high a price for keeping you around?

Especially since the next thing you did was to turn my new fragility, the result of the loss of my marriage, into a further loss. Because the second thing I lost was my custody of Molly. To you.

Can I ever forgive you for that? Your desertion had rocked me to my core. Probably you were right that at that time, that finite period, I was in no condition to care for a child. Such an irony that the man who caused the breakdown came to me with that solution. You would care for Molly in your home till I was on my feet again. We'd sort it out.

How could I have missed the fact that if you could betray me in marriage, you could also betray me in parenthood? You say I am punishing you, but from where I stand, it looks as if it is you who are punishing me. And for what? For failing to keep your attention; for failing to be more alluring to you than Coral; for failing to cause you to honor the bonds of matrimony?

So when Molly was only fourteen she moved from my home to be with her father. And his new wife. In the house by the River Place.

In a stroke, you took everything. That trip to Japan was symbolic of our life as a family, of our hopes and plans as a family: paging through the guidebooks, imagining the adventures we would have, dreaming of the future when we'd go into the big world together.

The day I saw Coral pregnant, smug and triumphant, though unmarried—at that moment I knew our Japan trip was never going to happen. How did I know? She was with Jake at the time; Jake ought to have been the father. But somehow I knew, deep in my gut, though I pretended to myself I didn't.

You told me, and you told Molly, that I needed to stay close to home. You told us that people move on, that we needed to adjust, that as the adults you and I had to help Molly. I had to let her strengthen her bond with Coral. And you said that since I was fearful of going out, Molly shouldn't have to pay the price.

So you went to Japan with Molly. And Coral.

You said it was for the best—for Molly, for me. Maybe you thought so. But you were wrong. You were wrong about Japan, and you were wrong about Molly's custody. In taking Molly you took the only thing that mattered to me, other than you—and the magazine.

Today you are trying to take the magazine as well.

And I say: take it. Sell it yourself if you want to. Or try to keep it going without me. Good luck with either. It's been a long time since you've shown an interest in it. Yes, you've come to work. You've brought coffee and wood for the fire and started the generator. But Silas is selling the ads and no one is looking after the books. So, in any case, I have concluded after going through them myself.

Dan, is this about money? I've given you most of what I have for Molly's child support. Unlike me, you have continued to take your salary. What can I give you that I haven't already?

Or is it about power? Perhaps on some level you are afraid of me, in the way that men are afraid of emotional women. What dark Dionysian horror might play out, they seem to think, if the dam of self-control bursts, if the thread connecting women to the sunlit world of male reason is broken?

And I think you have always been afraid of my voice—my written voice, that is. What might I say if I chose to use that voice, to really speak? What if I decided to tell my story to the entire town?

Today we discover the answer to that. Because I have written this blog. My last blog for *Riverboro Rocks*. And contrary to precedent, I am going to publish it.

As it says in the song: you should have known.

Tags: Dysfunctional families, Taylor Swift, divorce settlements, female poverty subsequent to divorce

Private Message from DanTheRiverMan: For Christ's sake, Piper, what are you trying to do? Do you think this is going to help matters? God this is one for the books. Take down that post or I'll have my lawyer slap a cease-and-desist on it.

COMMENTS:

DanTheRiverMan: Piper, don't you think you're overstating these issues? I know that since your meltdown the other week it has seemed to you that people have been working against you. But we have a long history of publishing *Riverboro Rocks: The Voice of Our Town* together. I know you know that our readers are also your well-wishers and are right behind you, cheering you on and hoping for your full recovery.

(Comment declined)

Private Message to DanTheRiverMan: Dan, don't try to play those games. You think you can manipulate public opinion through my blog? Don't you know that I can decline comments?

Private Message from DrJake: Dan forwarded me your Private Message. He asked that I speak to you about it—concerned that you are taking over the public dialog and not permitting him to tell his side. I can imagine that it is empowering to have the final say as to what will be published. But to start a dialog it's important for all parties to participate as equals and to listen to one another. Whatever your history, it seems in all fairness that both voices be heard equally.

Private Message from RiverCoral: I swear to God, Piper, you are such a bitch. I mean it's no wonder Dan left you to start a new life. Who can blame him? Don't think you're going to be seeing anything of Donny going forward. I wouldn't want you to have an influence on him. ☹

DrewHadley: Auntie Piper, you can't give up the magazine. We all count on it, the whole town. I know you can work this out with Uncle Dan. Please try!

TheGeekster: Hey, if this Dan dude ends up with the 'zine, will he be doing the Zombie Apocalypse spin-off page? Or does that stay with you?

BookLover603: What about the book group?

PipersPebbles: I think those are things we'll have to leave up to the lawyers.

(*Comments approved*)

* * *

Damn Lies
By Presidential Candidate and Tabloid Blogger
Jacques Marquand

The fate of one of New England's most respected regionals hangs in the balance today as co-founders and former spouses Dan and Piper Hammond drag their dispute into the public eye; click here to link to editor-in-chief Piper Hammond's sizzling screed on the subject. Apparently the bitter disagreements of years, exacerbated by pecuniary complications, are culminating with the sale or the closing of the magazine—or will Dan Hammond keep it alive single-handedly? Could this be a Machiavellian maneuver by the ever-resourceful Piper to recruit readers? All southern New Hampshire is likely to be riveted by this spectacle. *Pipers Pebbles* has been a sumptuous source of surprises, and today we add the question: is this to be Piper's final post? The politics of marriages, past and present, are imponderable.

* * *

So this was how ugly things could get.

Piper got up from her computer and went downstairs. The living room was, for once, empty. Donny's basket of picture books sat in its usual place near the big chair.

Piper crumpled paper and laid kindling and a couple of logs and built a fire. When she had gotten it burning nicely, one after another she fed in Donny's books. Then, before anyone could come in and strike up a conversation, she retreated to her office again. She had a sick sense that she had committed an act that was both violent and irrevocable.

A check of her blog post showed that additional comments had started pouring in. Everyone, it seemed, had something to say—more people were posting comments than had ever read her blog. The blog was getting *thousands* of hits. Readership had been growing, sure, but this was exponential. It was crazy.

So this is how to build readership, Piper thought. *Start a nasty public fight with your ex-husband. You'll go viral in a morning.* She tried to keep her righteous anger burning, but she was starting to cool down. Without that shield of anger, she was starting to feel embarrassed—actually, more than embarrassed: ashamed, humiliated—by the number of tweets and shares her post was getting. But in for a penny, in for a pound; might as well be hung for a sheep as for a lamb. She was going to hold her head high and tough it out.

Messages were pouring into her email inbox, which beeped continually as new messages were downloaded. Piper saw one from Jacques Marquand. She clicked it open.

Piper, she read. *Magnificent blog post. You are a gorgeous triumphant bitchgoddess and have got to keep this going. What say we set up dueling updates, he-saidshe-said, a face-off between you two? You both can have your say and your supporters can weigh in on either side. We'll create a points system. For national visibility I'll host it on Damn Lies.*

Piper hit the delete key and another message appeared, also from Marquand.

No, really, unbelievable. Pure gold. You've got to tell your story on my TV show. This is the most robust thing to come out of New Hampshire in years. A mother's love, a magazine's struggle for survival. It'll represent all dualities: heart against mind, Mars against Venus, zombies against aliens. Check with Dan to see if he's in, will you?

Another day Piper might have smiled, might even have felt grateful to Marquand for suggesting ways to spin this. Piper's sense of mischief often resonated with Marquand's. Another day she might have even been tempted to do the face-off page, if not the TV show.

But today the spark was gone. She didn't have the energy to blow on that flicker of mischief and fan it into the flame of action. She closed her inbox.

She toyed with the idea of going back to bed. But: been there, done that. She felt exhausted, but bed wasn't the answer.

So…what? She could go out—or at least, into her living room—and face the world. But oh God, those monks. Peaceful and serene, they'd never countenance the kind of *losing it* that went into putting up that blog post.

What had she done?

Whom could she face?

What should she do?

Piper sat and stared into space. When Dan had left, and shortly thereafter taken Molly, she had thrown herself into her work. It had created structure, purpose, and direction. Today she didn't even have that. She had lobbed the biggest bombshell of her career into the center of her own life and blown it up from within. If she hadn't posted that blog for the world to see she might have been able, somehow, to put things back together with Dan. That was impossible now.

Even at this point she couldn't entirely suppress an impulse to keep doing her work. Was it really over? If she stopped, she wouldn't meet her deadlines, and the slope down which she had begun to career would get steeper, the final crash more inescapable. How hard it was to walk away. But she couldn't—wouldn't—give in to the pull of work.

What, then? Facing other people was a no. Working was a no. Going back to bed was a no. Going outside was not an option. The only thing she could think of doing, the only apparent option—a miserable one—was to stay right here in her office. Oh God oh God oh God.

Piper sat in her chair and folded her hands in her lap. Something had to happen. She would wait here until it did.

Since it was early in the morning, it was unlikely anything would happen soon—nothing concrete, nothing real-worldly. They might post a comment on her blog, but she wasn't checking. So be it. She sat. She breathed.

She waited.

She dozed in her chair.

Her cell phone rang—a possible something. She glanced at the screen. It was Jake. She let voice mail pick up. She knew what he would be saying—that wasn't something happening.

A private message flickered on her computer screen. She glanced at it—Dan. She clicked it closed. She knew what he would say—that wasn't something happening.

She heard monks moving around downstairs and thought for a moment she would like to hear their messages of support, of transcending the self, of mastering the self, of forgiveness, of how the universe is perfect. Or whatever their message might be. She didn't exactly know the message but she thought she knew its general outline. It was good, it was important even. She did want to hear it—later. After something happened. The monks weren't the something happening (probably).

She could feel life gathering itself. She could feel Something getting ready to happen. It would be Molly, she thought. It would be Molly, and maybe Matthew Winchester. It would be new, it would be fresh, it would be different. It would include her daughter somehow.

It would change her life.

She knew, she could *feel* that it would happen soon. And it did: a tap on her door. Piper turned to it, waiting for her Something to walk in. "Come in," she called. The door opened.

It was Coral Lane.

Coral Lane, whom Piper hadn't willingly seen in years; Coral Lane, still small and blonde, but not as thin as she had been—well, she'd had a baby, hadn't she? She was starting to look the way some fine-boned blondes can look when they've put on weight and their skin starts to redden. Though in fairness the redness could have something to do with the situation, the meeting, the conversation they were about to have. And anyway, Coral was still pretty, all things considered.

Piper had often fantasized about the things she ought to say, could in justice say to Coral. The points she might make, the digs, the snide remarks at her expense.

But there was no doubt in her mind, not the tiniest whisper of a doubt, that Coral was the Something that was due to happen. So she sat and waited for Coral to sit down too, in the wing chair, and for a moment they sat and looked at each other.

And while she sat and waited, something did happen. Or more precisely, something did not happen. Something that was, by its absence, so big, so significant, so remarkable, as to count as life-changing.

Piper was not having a panic attack.

Maybe the events of the past day had broken her down to a more fundamental level and she was moving at that level and it was beyond panic. Maybe she had found her voice with that blog post, or taken her stand (three years late) with Dan, and with that she had found an inner strength that protected her, raised her above anxiety attacks. Maybe it was the peaceful influence of the monks, permeating the house.

Or maybe she was too damn tired to react to Coral Lane.

Whatever it was, the realization that she was not having, was not going to have an attack spread through her like delight, like a pure radiance, like bliss, starting deep in her stomach and bubbling up through her body and settling in her very bones.

Part 3

My Dome of Many-Colored Glass

One of the main problems with letting go of your magazine was when you awoke in the early morning—or, alright, the middle of the night—you didn't have a project to work on. You didn't have a blog to write.

What you did have, if you were very lucky, was a houseful of monks. And maybe, if you were even more lucky, one of those monks would be awake, downstairs, keeping vigil.

And most fortunate of all, that monk might be Leon. Leon the starter monk; Leon the one without the answers. Leon who could make you feel that you, floundering among the debris of mistakes made, a life poorly lived, still had something to offer even to someone who lived the life of the spirit day after day.

If you were very, very lucky, Leon might be waiting with hot milk and toast.

"I hoped you would be here," said Piper. She headed right to the sofa, to the same seat she had taken the other night, and settled in next to Leon.

"I had a feeling," the monk said, pouring her milk out.

"Because of this morning's blog post?" Piper reached out to take it.

"And all the rest of it."

They were silent for a moment, contemplating the sheer immensity of all the rest of it.

Piper broke the silence. "What is going to happen?"

In what was already beginning to feel like a ritual, a comforting ritual that might repeat itself year after year in early morning conversations, Leon picked up the plate of toast and offered it to her. "What do you want to happen?" he asked.

"What difference does that make?" Piper took her toast, held it in her hand, looked to Leon in expectation of his answer.

"Every difference," Leon said. "Because if you aren't clear on what you want, life can't help you make it happen."

"Life is going to help me get what I want." Piper's voice was flat with skepticism.

"Maybe, maybe not," Leon said. "But it's a lot harder if you don't know."

"All right then," said Piper. "Here goes: I want none of this to have ever happened. I want Dan to have stayed in love with me, to have stayed faithful to me, to have lived here with me and run the magazine with me and raised Molly here in the house with me. I want Coral Lane to have never been born or at least never come to Riverboro. I want my old life back."

"That might be difficult," Leon acknowledged. "Even for a force as all-powerful as life itself. What about going forward?"

"How is it possible to know what you want when you've mucked things up so badly?" Piper asked. She reached over Leon to put her toast back on the plate, unable to take a bite even for ritualistic purposes. "I have blown things up so irretrievably that there isn't any way of picking up the pieces and putting them back together. I don't even know what it would take to fix things."

"The end of the second act," said Leon.

"What?"

"That's what Pasco calls it when things are worst. The end of the second act. When things are really, really the pits."

Piper thought of Matthew, Molly, Sam King...she could see plays within plays within plays. Plays that seemed light and bright compared to hers. Her play was dark and shadowed.

Her play was at the end of its second act.

"Coral came to see you," said Leon.

"She did," Piper acknowledged.

"And...?"

"And I didn't melt down. Victory."

"You mean you didn't have a panic attack?" Leon looked at her keenly. "That does sound like victory."

"Coral says she wants to start fresh," said Piper. "She wants a reset. Why wouldn't she? She gets to keep Dan, and her family, and her job, and her life. She wants to wipe out the bad feelings and start new."

"And you?"

"It's what I've been trying to do for three years," said Piper. "Haven't I?"

"But?"

"But this. Here we are. Or here I am. No money, no family, and I can't walk out the door. So much for trying to keep the peace."

"You spoke up for yourself on your blog," Leon reminded her.

"I suppose I did. For all the good that came of it," Piper said bitterly.

"Something happened," Leon said. "You moved things forward."

"Or back," said Piper. "I am beside myself. That damned Coral Lane. That God damned Coral Lane." Feeling increasingly agitated, she stood up and began pacing back and forth on the worn Persian carpet in front of the cold fireplace. "She thinks she can mince in and say, 'can we start over?' Yes, we can start over if you give back my family. If you give me back the last three years of my life! Sure, let's rewind the tape and record it differently."

"Is that what you told her?" Leon asked.

"So then she's all, 'This isn't good for Donny, this isn't good for any of us,'" Piper mimicked. "It makes me so mad when she drags Donny into it! Like I haven't turned myself inside out for Donny over the past three years. Who does she think she is?"

"Did you say that?" Leon asked.

"And all the stuff she spouts about Dan! 'Dan needs this, Dan wants that.'" Piper flung her hand into the air to punctuate her words. "How can she? I know what Dan needs! I know what Dan wants! I was married to him, I was raising a daughter with him when Coral Lane was in middle school!"

"Did you—"

"And she goes, 'Do we have to *do* this, Piper?' I hate it when people say that! 'Do we have to *do* this?' Yes, Coral, we have to do this! You know why we have to do this? Because I say we do! I want to do this! And for once, we're going to do what I want to do. For one God damn time, we're going to play the game I want to play!"

"What did she say," Leon asked, "when you told her all that?"

"I didn't," said Piper. "I didn't say anything. I just listened." She turned to the empty fireplace. "It's cold in here." She picked up newspaper and began opening and crumpling it, throwing it into the fireplace.

Leon set his milk down and stood. "I'll get wood." He disappeared out through the kitchen, and Piper heard the door to the broken shed swing open and shut. A minute later Leon was back, his arms piled high with logs. He dropped them by the fireplace. "What does she suggest for her reset?"

"The usual. Get together. Again. 'Talk it out.' Like that's going to change anything." Piper took some branches from the kindling basket and layered them on top of the paper in the fireplace "When I wrote that post, I thought I'd be getting the last word. But you never do get the last word, do you? No one ever gets the last word. Do you know Jacques Marquand emailed me within minutes of that post going up? He wants us to keep this whole thing going. He wants us to ratchet it up."

"You don't want that," Leon guessed.

"I was actually tempted," she admitted. "It sounded...funny."

"Seems weird." Leon knelt to stack logs neatly on top of Piper's pile of kindling. "Of Marquand, I mean. Trying to capitalize on your misery."

"Jacques likes conflict." Piper sought to explain. "He thinks it can turn into a creative tension that brings out higher truths. It's like his dialectical imperative--you use opposing viewpoints to get at something fresh and new. You hold it all in your heart, the good and the bad, and you don't judge, and it creates a dynamism that produces something we never could have conceived of in a more linear way. So he likes to stir the pot."

"And you thought if you did as he wanted, if you ratcheted up the quarrel, you could make the whole thing more, what, progressive?" Leon asked.

"No, of course not." Piper waved off the idea. "I thought I could *win*. I'm better at words than either Coral or Dan. It's my superpower. I could trounce them on that battlefield."

"But you decided to rise above it?"

"I guess."

"And where does that leave you?" Leon leaned back on his heels. "Back where you started? Or somewhere better?"

"Somewhere worse, I think. Because now that Jacques' involved, he's going to put Coral on TV."

They looked at each other for a moment. Then Leon said, "I heard that. That Coral was planning on going on TV. It doesn't make sense. Isn't his show about politics?"

"Oh, you know. Marquand. The personal is political. It all ties in."

"I suppose," Leon said dubiously. "So he asked her on TV to tell her side of the story. I guess he thinks he's leveling the playing field? You already told your side, on your blog, so now it's her turn?"

"No." Piper felt on top of the mantelpiece for matches; she struck one and held it against the paper. It caught. "He emailed me. He wants me on the show too."

"But you refused? Because you can't leave the house?"

"He offered to come film the whole thing here."

"And you said...?"

"No." She and Leon stood back to watch the blaze strengthen and spread. It caught at the kindling, which began to crackle and burn. "I'm done fighting. Let them have what they want, be what they want, do what they want, say what they want. I'm walking away."

"Walking to where?"

"Maybe not so far. It depends." Piper curled her fingers into her hands, glanced at Leon nervously. "I'm thinking of becoming a monk."

Leon turned from the fire to look at Piper. For several moments no one said anything, and Piper became aware of the loud ticking of the living room clock and the crackling of the fire in the curious muffled silence of the very late night.

"What?" she finally said defensively. "Isn't that good? For you, I mean? Don't you guys need converts?"

"Maybe good, I don't know." Leon set the screen in front of the fire. "I'm not the one to ask. But I wouldn't have put you down for this, not if you asked me."

"Why not? I'm flexible. Physically, I mean. I can sit in lotus. I'm introspective. I never go out. I stay in the house. I would think I'd be a natural fit."

"Maybe you are, it could be, maybe." Leon brushed off his hands and returned to his place on the sofa. "I'm not one to discourage you.
People come from all over for this. From all walks of life. And who knows? It might be the right thing. You should talk to Lisette."

Piper followed him back to the sofa. "You seem skeptical," she said, settling in and drawing her feet up under her.

"Not skeptical, no, I wouldn't say that. Surprised, yes. I wouldn't have thought—well, staying in the house isn't a good indication of whether this is for you."

"From what I understand you didn't have much of a vocation when you started," Piper pointed out. "And it seems to have worked out for you."

"But I have Lisette."

"Last time we talked, you spoke about going in." Piper was beginning to feel defensive. Was it possible that even the monks didn't want her? They took anyone, she thought, everyone! Would even they turn her away? She continued urgently, "You talked about the other side. If it's a choice between this misery we call the world and a monkish inner peace, why shouldn't I go monk? Like you?"

Leon said nothing. He refilled her cup and they sat in silence. Finally he said, "I think there's another side to it."

"Of course you do," said Piper.

"There is a story in my tradition, a story of a great war. A huge war between powerful people. A war that had heroes on both sides."

"Allegorical. Metaphorical," Piper said, to show she was a quick study. "The battlefield of life. So they found that peace was within, and fighting was the wrong approach. Right?"

"They did not. They fought to the death. The field was soaked in blood. Many brave men perished. Many beautiful things were destroyed."

"But afterward they realized they were wrong. They should have taken a more inner-peace-ish approach."

"Well, no. Not that either."

"What, then?"

"In the story there was a hero on one side, a great man. On the other side, his relatives, his cousins, his grandfather and his teacher. And the hero decided not to fight. He talked to God about it. He told God that he would rather let his relatives win the war. That way there would be no bloodshed."

"What did God say?"

"To pick up his bow and fight."

"No way! Why?"

"As you say, the story is symbolic. It tells us that any action that we undertake does have to come from that place of peace. But acting from peace doesn't mean we don't act. It's tricky."

"Tricky!" Piper cried. "It's crazy! How does it help figure out what to do?"

"The God in this story was a piper, like you," Leon said. "He played the song of life. He showed the hero how to reconcile peace and power, inner and outer. The one side and the other."

"But what does it mean for me?" Piper asked. "To monk? Or not to monk?"

"I can't tell you that," said Leon.

"Of course you can't," said Piper resignedly.

"I would if I could," offered Leon.

"Of course you would," said Piper. *Time for bed,* she thought, standing up again; but Leon was smiling kindly, and she stopped to return his smile before leaving the room.

November 28: Coral's 15 Minutes

Challenge accepted, Cameron Diaz: I have partied with monks, or at least one monk, in the middle of the night. I have come, in fact, from a real bacchanal with hot milk and toast and deep conversation, and I learned that I must act as I feel to be right, and not care one bit about what happens as a result of it.

At least I think that's what I learned. My midnight sessions with Leon seem to leave me with more questions than answers. I know he would say it is because he is not a good communicator, but I think it might be because he is an excellent one.

He told me (I think) that I have to stand up and fight. That's what Leon's hero did, and that is what I have decided to do as well. No handing over what I have spent my life building. The catch—there's always a catch—is that there is no guarantee what will happen as a result.

Today I am more popular, or perhaps more notorious, than I have ever been. *Damn Lies* brought me thousands, at this point *tens* of thousands, of hits; and thousands of the visitors have signed up with their email addresses. If I am going to fight, it gives me more to fight for. Leon's archer hero was told to pick up his bow and fight. And if the pen is mightier than the sword, perhaps the keyboard is as mighty as the bow. So I am turning to mine (still broken from Sasha's fall, but that's another story) and taking my stand.

In doing so, I am acting as I feel to be right.

What does NOT feel right is that Coral Lane now wants to go on TV to talk about our private business. So maybe I've said a word or two about it—privately, here on this blog, just between you and me. Coral wants to do it on TV! Coral and her resets—Coral and her fresh clean slates. Right. That lasted about a minute. Jacques offered her time on his TV show and Coral is leaping to take it. Such a surprise. *I* said no—I told Jacques no—he even offered to come to my office to get my side.

I thought that would be the end of it. You can't go on a he-said/she-said unless both sides are represented. Plus, what's Coral got to do with it, anyway? This is between Dan and me. We started the magazine and we, if anyone, will end it. Dan, I am told, tried to talk Coral out of this caper, by the way. He said it would make everything worse (obviously), and she said (apparently) how could it get any worse? So now he's going on TV to keep his trophy wife happy. It makes me want to spit nails.

Well go ahead, Coral—do your worst. Put on your prettiest dress and go on TV and have your say. Tell the world your side of the story. See what good it does for you or your family or anybody.

But don't expect me to lie down and let you roll all over me. I have claimed my voice and I am going to use it. I, like the hero on the battle-field, am picking up my bow to fight.

Tags: Campaign Only Network, Jacques Marquand, the Bhagavad-Gita

COMMENTS:

RiverCoral: For God's sake Piper you are being so unfair. You have your say every single day on this blog, and now thanks to Jacques people all over the *world* are reading it. Whenever Dan or I try to defend ourselves you decline the comment. You can't pretend you're taking the high road by not saying your side of the story on TV when you take shots at us here all the time. ☹

RiverCoral: And how can you say that you are just now starting to stand up for yourself? Look back at your blogs since the beginning of the month. The very first one was you picking on me for trick-or-treating. And you haven't let up since. ☹

RiverCoral: Plus, a ton more people read *Damn Lies* in print than watch it on TV. Which means that since Jacques links back to your blog, like, every day, you have more readers than will watch the TV show. And you say anything you want on that blog—why can't I say something too? ☹

PipersPebbles: Like what? What can you possibly want to say to the entire state?

RiverCoral: You'll have to tune in and watch, won't you? ☹

(*Comments approved*)

* * *

Damn Lies
By Presidential Candidate and Aspiring Mediator
Jacques Marquand

With votes pouring in from all over the world, the overwhelming majority are siding with Piper Hadley Hammond, editor of *Riverboro Rocks* and damsel in distress trapped in her fairy tale tower. For those sympathetic to conspiracy theorist and Riverboro Do-Gooder Dan Hammond, a respected figure for many years, the opinion is that Piper's version of events is not likely to be objective. Expect the balance to shift this afternoon at five o'clock when the Other Woman, Coral Lane, joins us to tell her side of the story.

* * *

The problem with reclaiming your voice, the problem with becoming an overnight sensation, is how quickly you lose control of the dialog.

Piper had told Coral to do her worst. She had approved Coral's comments on her blog. She was allowing Coral to tell her side of the story. Not that she had any choice, with Coral even now prepping, no doubt, for her moment of fame.

It was as if she'd unleashed a tsunami of public opinion. Messages were pouring in from all over the world. Her email wouldn't stop dinging; her phone wouldn't stop beeping. Piper scrolled through her messages, trying to get a feel. The messages were supportive, they were bitter, they were angry, or loving, or simply weird. Most were predictable: you heroine; you bitch; we're on your side; I'd like to f*#k you; you are the voice of women everywhere; you are a disgrace to your gender. There were also the inevitable pictures of naked women's torsos with Piper's face photoshopped on.

And there were stories—many, many stories. Funny, brave, outrageous, poignant. Stories of people trying to keep their businesses, keep their marriages, cope with their children or their parents, live their lives; stories of people who were at the end of their own second acts, trying to struggle through to their own other sides.

A man wrote in from a town in Vermont. "The man isn't always to blame. We want the same things that you do. We want our families, our children. Years ago my wife left me with two young children. I worked two jobs to support them. I missed my opportunity to go back to school. I worked days at a gas station, nights tending bar. She didn't want anything to do with them until they were teenagers. Now, surprise! She wants to turn them against me. She tells them I was always out at the bar when they were growing up. She tells them I never went to their games. I will spend Christmas alone this year. How is that fair?"

A woman Piper knew from a popular Mommy blog wrote: "I hear what you're saying, I've been there. Men can never be trusted. They will never love their children as a mother does. How many mothers abandon their children compared to the fathers that do? How many mothers could hurt their own children? And don't get me started on stepfathers. The storybook wicked stepmother is an angel compared to a whole world full of real-life stepfathers. Read the statistics. Do the math. Draw your conclusions."

Some wrote in defense of Coral. One said: "You get on your high horse, you play the role of woman wronged, but there is another side to that. I have been the other woman and let me tell you it is no picnic. It is nothing but stolen moments, and lonely days and nights, and children without a father to point to openly. Coral Lane is a lucky woman and Donny is a lucky boy. Good for Dan for acknowledging them. Leave them alone, let them be. You and Dan raised Molly together. Now step aside and let Coral and Donny have their turn."

Stories came in from faraway countries. A woman wrote: "If you lived where I do your life might be at risk for speaking out. I take a risk writing to you. Whatever your problems, please remember that."

A woman emailed Piper from prison: "You should thank heaven you got out of that marriage when you did. You have no idea how much worse it can get. I was one of the many women who could not get out, until finally I took drastic action. I will live the rest of my life in a jail cell but I do not regret what I did. I am more free now than I have ever been."

So many people wanting to tell their stories, so many stories to be told. I need to tell these stories, Piper thought. *I need to help these people tell their stories.*

From a local email provider came the following: "I know how quickly life can change—for the worse, and for the better. Like you, I know what it means to be imprisoned. Like you, I know how much it hurts to lose a child. I don't think I'd be alive today if people hadn't believed in me, hadn't given me a chance. One of those people was you. It makes me sad that you feel beleaguered and alone, but it was brave of you to share your story. Maybe you will inspire others of us to share ours. Maybe through the telling we can help other people face what they are facing. We all come out of the woods at different times. I wish we all came out together, so we could all stand in the sun together."

Even without the signature, Piper recognized the address; she recognized the story.

It was Miranda's.

Piper knew she had done so little, so pitifully little, to help Miranda.

The gratitude the younger woman showed humbled Piper. *I will do something,* she resolved. *I will help these people tell their stories.*

Jacques called around noon. "Listen, darling, I know you don't want to come out of your tower to go in front of the world on TV. So here's the deal. Coral will go on the show today. Tomorrow you and I will do a phone interview. Audio only, and you can give your response to Coral, how's that? I'll call tomorrow around six in the evening."

What would she say, she wondered. Dan hurt me. Coral hurt me. Life is hurting me. I don't have the power to command the life I want. I've said it; what more can be said?

But she was a warrior now. No shrinking, no retreat. "All right," she told Jacques. "Today Coral can have her say. Tomorrow, I'll provide the rebuttal."

* * *

"No," said Piper. "No, no, no, no, no."

"A no," Silas, slouched against a wall at the side of the living room, said helpfully.

"Mommy," Molly pleaded, sounding unexpectedly young, "why not?"

"Because it's completely inappropriate! To the point of being crazy. It's inconceivable to me that anyone would think it a good idea."

"We all do," said Molly. She gestured at the monks who were filing into the room to take their places: Pasco carrying his laptop, Brumi a large TV monitor, Cassie with backjacks to set on the floor.

For just an instant, these people, usually to Piper's eyes so helpful and benign, seemed to flicker into something malevolent. She actually shuddered and took a step back toward the door. Molly tightened her grip on her mother's arm and Silas moved over to join them. Piper felt a queasiness in the pit of her stomach, prickles in the back of her eyes. "No," she said.

Brumi set the monitor on a coffee table and knelt to connect it to the TV; Cassie was setting cushions on the floor. In their purposeful actions, Piper thought, they looked like the neighborly townspeople in the story, cheerfully tossing their smooth rocks onto a pile in the town square. The rocks they would use to stone her to death. "I will not do this," she said.

"Mommy, come sit here for a moment, see, right on the sofa," Molly said. "I'll bring you a cup of tea. We invited the group. Everyone will be here in a few minutes."

"Molly, why? Why would you do that? How could you imagine that this would be what I want?" Piper felt tears, three years' worth of unshed tears coming on. She felt that if she began to sob nothing in this world could make her stop. Was her own daughter against her now? "You can't ambush me like this. Who is coming?"

"Only the core group, Mom. The family, the monks, Silas. No one else. We asked Matthew to come over after," Molly said wheedlingly. "And Jake."

"Everyone is coming to see Coral on TV," Piper said flatly. "To see me humiliated publicly. To see Coral flaunt herself in front of the world and give 'her side of the story.' Can't they see that Coral has no side to this story? She has a role, not a side! This is intolerable. I'd like to *kill* Jacques Marquand!"

Leon and Lisette came in with plates of Indian sweets, picnickers at a public hanging. They set the plates on tables, then Leon gave Lisette a steadying hand while she lowered herself onto a backjack cushion. She crossed her legs neatly under her and Leon sank creakily beside her, sitting with his legs out in front of him.

Cassie and Pasco were lining up next to Leon and Lisette, facing the TV like members of a theater audience. "We wanted you to have your group around you for the show," Cassie said over her shoulder to Piper. "We didn't want you to be alone for it."

"See, Mommy?" Molly said. "We're here to support you."

From the kitchen came the sound of the shed door banging, feet stomping, then Dan and Coral appeared at the door, Donny between them holding their hands. "The whole show was done and in the bag by six this morning," Dan said. "We had Donny back in time for preschool."

"*Donny* was on TV, too?" Piper's voice rose to a squeak of indignation.

"He promised Donny a TV appearance, Piper, and you gave him hell for it. Jake gave him hell for it. So Jacques called Donny personally and asked him to come on TV."

"Jacques Marquand says he's my god-grandfather," Donny piped. "He says I'll help him change the world."

"Oh for God's sake—"

"Oh yes, Jacques says he'll go far," Coral said with satisfaction. "And he says I'm a natural, and Dan, too. He's going to have us back to talk about our work at the River Place. He might do a show where we bring some of the kids on to tell their stories."

"He's desperate for content!" Piper said. "He'd have Donny's *puppy* on if it would fill the hour!" She tried to get up, to leave the room, but Molly pulled her back and Brumi was fiddling with the volume and Marquand appeared on the screen.

"Funny you mention Donny's puppy—" Coral began, but then, on TV, Marquand was speaking and everyone turned to watch.

"The town of Riverboro, nestled in southern New Hampshire, is home to artists, writers, and a popular local magazine, *Riverboro Rocks*. It also is the scene of a desperate struggle—the struggle of that magazine for its survival. Today we'll meet the Hammonds, one of Riverboro's founding families. The Hammonds are going to tell us about their award-winning publication, and about the bitter infighting that has sprung up as the family struggles for its control and its future. Let's welcome Coral, Dan, and Donny Hammond."

And out came Coral, Dan, and Donny.

Coral on screen, abetted (Piper thought bitterly) by the network's professional makeup artists, looked delicate and pretty; she also looked very young. Dan, wearing a flannel shirt open at the throat, seemed like a pure New Hampshire Yankee. *And he's from Pennsylvania,* Piper thought. *The poser.*

But what they had done with Donny was the limit. He was dressed in his cowboy outfit, and strapped in a little holster to his side was his toy six-shooter—the one Piper had given him, the one Coral had complained about. One of his hands was tucked in his father's big one; the other held the end of a leash. At the other end of the leash was his black and white puppy, Ralph.

Unbelievable. Not enough to come on TV, the three of them. Not enough to bring their son, fair and rosy-cheeked like both his parents, clearly the much-loved son of a married couple. They had to bring the dog. The dog, who bumbled out onto the stage, cocking his head and wagging his tail and stealing the show—except he wasn't. Because who could tear their eyes off Dan and Coral and Donny? The three of them, so assorted in size, so similar in coloring, so united in body language, looked as if they belonged together.

They looked like a family.

A family that, on screen, sat on chairs in a semi circle, their puppy at their feet, and looked at a flamboyant man wearing a buccaneer hat on his gray curls. A family that, right here in Piper's living room, watched themselves on screen as if this were a normal thing to do, as if they were having an outing, as if they were at a theater matinee (which in a sense they were). Piper gazed at them, incredulous. Could anyone in the world, in the entire universe, be so cruel? It was like they were setting a new record, achieving new heights of what people could do to torture one another. For a few moments her sheer disbelief obliterated her every other perception and she just marveled.

Then her attention reverted to the screen. "Dan Hammond, you started *Riverboro Rocks* with your first wife, Riverboro's Piper Hadley, almost twenty years ago," Marquand was saying. "I remember your launch; you interviewed me for one of the very first issues. What do you remember about those early years?"

Dan's smile flashed. "A lot of investment, a lot of hard work."

"But that was a better time for magazine publishing, wasn't it?"

"It was, in some respects, but starting a magazine has always been risky." Dan reached down and snapped his fingers to the puppy. Ralph ambled over and Dan scooped him up onto his lap. "Most don't make it past their first couple of years. It's a miracle that we've continued publishing these past two decades."

"How did you manage it?"

Now, the room had quieted; the rustles and murmurs had ceased. Everyone waited to hear what Dan would say.

"We borrowed money from our families to keep it going. I sold shares of some funds I inherited." Dan patted Ralph; Donny scootched his chair over nearer to Dan and reached out to pet the dog too. "I picked up extra work. Back in the beginning it was mostly odd jobs, evening stuff. I did deliveries for the market a couple nights a week."

How did this end up being all about him, Piper wondered? *He* did this, *he* did that. You'd think he was the big hero of the magazine. And he's using that dog to make him look like a good guy, a family man, an animal lover.

Although she did remember, now that Dan was talking about it, those extra projects he had taken on to bring in much-needed cash when Molly was small. That carousel horse they had bought for her, the one they'd sold in the barn sale—Dan had made the money for that gift, the year he had helped Andy Hadley repair his old stonewall. Three days he'd spent in the hot sun, and three nights Dan had come home, sunburned and exhausted, but with money in his blistered hand. They'd used it to pay that month's utilities bill—a challenge then as now—and to buy the carousel horse. It had made Molly so happy.

"Then maybe five years ago I picked up some work at our community outreach center, started to teach evening classes there," Dan continued. He met Coral's eyes; they smiled warmly at one another. "Coral worked there."

How could they? But Coral was turning pink and looking at Dan as if he were some kind of Northern god that had gathered her into his embrace and his life.

"Did you ever think of giving up on the magazine?" Jacques asked.

Dan turned back from Coral to answer. "I would have done so many times," he said. "But Piper loved *Riverboro Rocks* almost like a family member. She poured her heart and soul into it. She was editor, art director, production manager. Not a word went into the magazine that she didn't read and judge worthy, and many times she wrote the words herself. She battled for that publication night and day. So every time I thought, 'we can't go on like this, we can't keep this magazine afloat,' I would look at her and think, 'we have to. Somehow, we have to'."

"And you did," Jacques said.

"We did," Dan agreed.

"But at a cost?"

"Everything comes with a cost," Dan said. "Life comes with a cost. You don't know if things would have been different if you had done something else. You don't know if they'd have been the same."

"You seem like the kind of guy who will do a lot to keep his women happy," Marquand said. "Rumor has it that you didn't want to come on the show today." He turned to Coral. "Now Coral, the story seems to be that you don't have much to do with the publication, but you were the one who wanted to come on the show, is that true?" Coral nodded, and Jacques asked. "Why is that?"

Because she gets to flaunt her husband and son in front of the cameras, thought Piper. *Because she gets to have her fifteen minutes of fame. Because she gets revenge against the ex-wife.*

"I thought the exposure would be good for the magazine," Coral answered.

"For the sale?" Jacques asked. "Because it is going up for sale, isn't that right?"

"We're sorting that out," Coral said. "But either way, going on TV should help, right? Maybe someone watching will want to read the next issue, or buy advertising, or buy the whole magazine. Who knows? Getting the word out has got to be good, no matter what."

"Ooooh, that's good," said Cassie. The monks stirred about, murmuring agreement. The Dan in the living room smiled proudly at the two Corals, the one in the room and the one on screen. Piper thought she'd puke. *She's always wanted to be part of this,* she thought. *She's always wanted to be on the magazine. Does she think she can to force her way in like this?*

"You heard it, New Hampshire." Jacques turned from his guests to look directly into the camera. "Read *Riverboro Rocks*, buy an ad, buy the whole damn magazine." He turned back to Coral. "With only a few moments left, is there anything else you'd like to say?"

"Just one thing," Coral said. She turned and smiled at Donny, who pulled his little six-shooter out of its holster and handed it to her. She took it in her left hand and, with her right, grabbed Ralph by the scruff of his neck and lifted him up. She pointed the toy pistol at the dog and turned to the camera.

"Advertise in *Riverboro Rocks*," she told New Hampshire, "or I'll shoot this dog."

As the screen faded to black, Jacques could be heard in the background, laughing.

* * *

Here is what Coral said: We are not in a good place. We are not in a place we need to be. We need to get to a new place.

And what Coral needs, Piper thought. *Coral gets.* Whatever place they were going to get to, it was certain to revolve around Coral. Right now the uproar in the living room was all about Coral. Everyone crowded around her, babbling congratulations and praise; her phone was buzzing and Dan's was ringing and calls and texts were pouring in from friends and well wishers who had seen the show and couldn't *believe* that thing with the dog.

Piper stood and walked to the fireplace to stand by herself. So Coral had won. She had gone on statewide TV, having announced her intention to do so on Piper's own blog. She had been aided and abetted by a Piper who had believed that if this whole thing came out into the open, she, Piper, would emerge triumphant. Well, Coral had proven herself more clever, deeper and more devious. She had set up expectations of an all-out confrontation; but not once, not once in the entire show, had she or Dan spoken against Piper. Not once had they stated any kind of case against her.

And that, Piper realized now, was far more devastating, far more powerful than any attack. It put Coral and Dan into a position they never could have battled themselves into: it put them in the right. And that, by implication, put Piper in the wrong.

So Coral had carried the day. It left a bitter, ashy taste in Piper's mouth; it poured misery all down her spine and into her stomach. The atmosphere in the room—*her* room, *her* house—was festive, party-like. People bunched in groups, talking animatedly. Jake, who had arrived a few minutes ago, was deep in earnest conversation with Coral. Donny, elated at seeing himself, his parents, and especially his puppy on TV, was perched in the window seat with Molly. Pasco and Cassie stood leaning against the back of the sofa, talking and laughing. Ananda had watched the show upstairs on her laptop, but she came down to join the party. Brumi was setting up cushions on the floor for her, propping them against the wall, settling her in, tucking a shawl around her. Dan, typically, had left the room. Now he was out in the kitchen making pots of tea to serve the group.

Piper stood alone near the fireplace, huddled in on herself, stewing about the TV show, stewing about the dog, stewing about the gun—the gun! Oh, it was all emblematic—that Coral had used the weapon *she* had provided—Piper chewed on her misery.

Dan came in with the tea, followed by Lisette with stacks of cups and Matthew, still in his parka. "Looks like we're all here," Dan boomed. He set down the tea and went to stand with Coral. Quickly and quietly, Lisette began to pour the tea and hand it around. And everyone turned and looked at Piper. She glowered back at them.

Dan cleared his throat, started to speak. Piper interrupted, speaking over him, their voices canceling each other out. And into the opening that this created, Donny spoke.

"Where are my books?"

Donny was looking at the basket that usually sat by the big chair, filled with his picture books, empty now. He turned to gaze at Piper, and everyone waited for her answer.

Piper could hardly bear it. Everyone was waiting, everyone expecting an answer that made sense. Piper didn't have that kind of answer. In burning Donny's books, she had crossed a line she had never crossed before. And so what? That wasn't what she cared about.

What she cared about was Donny. That he would think her action was meant to hurt him.

And here was the problem with conflict: the collateral damage it caused. How could it be contained?

"Donny, your mom," she tried to explain. "She wasn't going to let you come…" No one said anything. No one stepped in to help her out. And Piper almost shouted into that waiting silence, "What good are the books if Donny isn't here? I'm not the one who made that choice!" Piper stared into blank uncomprehending eyes. "Can't anyone see that? Why am I always the bad guy—with Donny's books, or that fire, or that pestilential trip to Japan—can't any of you ever take my side?"

Then her voice was lost in the uproar. "You don't mean—" "Piper, we all—" "We never—" And over it all, Molly screaming, "How can you say that? How can you say we're pestilential?"

It was Coral who interrupted. "Stop, no, that's not what she means. Molly, she doesn't mean it like that. She doesn't mean you're not loyal, she doesn't mean you're not a good daughter. Isn't that right, Piper? You don't mean that. Molly, shush, it's just that your mom feels isolated. She feels like no one is here for her. But that's not true, Piper. Matthew is here. He's here for you. Come on, let's change the seating. Piper, come sit on the sofa. Matthew, you sit next to her." Pointing and nudging, Coral began to move people around. "Piper, Matthew is your ally. I'd rather you think of us all as your allies. I'd rather you see us all as here for you. But if you won't, let Matthew be the one person on your side. He came just for you."

Matthew came and sat by Piper. "It's true," he whispered. "I did come just for you." He squeezed her hand.

Molly, her sobs subsiding, came and sat on Piper's other side, curling into her. She didn't say anything, and neither did Piper, but Piper began to feel an unwinding, a loosening of that tight thing twisted up inside her. She felt her breathing ease.

And then Donny let go of his mother's hand and walked over to Piper and climbed on her lap and put his arms around her. "I'm on your side too, Piper," he said.

Here is what Donny said: Let's go to that place my mom wants to go. Maybe my books are there.

Donny started to slide off her lap to return to his mother. Coral made a motion, shook her head. "Stay with Piper, Donny. You help her feel better."

Piper stiffened, offended. She had an impulse to put Donny down on the floor and send him back to his mother. Who did Coral think she was? But Donny was an innocent. The wars should not be fought on the fields of the children. She hugged the boy and said softly, "That would be lovely, Donny. I'd love to see that place." She half smiled and added, "As long as it's in this house."

Dan cleared his throat. "Piper, that's the point—"

And, for the second time, a surprise from Coral: "Dan. Please. It isn't helpful. Piper is doing the best she knows how. Like all of us."

Who was Coral to try to insinuate herself into this battle? What did it have to do with her? But Piper could feel Molly's breath coming fast and shallow, her body tense. Donny clung to Piper. *The children,* Piper thought. *Scale it back. For their sake.*

Coral turned to look at Jake. Jake nodded. "Coral's right, Dan. You and Piper have a complicated set of mutual expectations, mutual rewards and punishments. It doesn't all go one way. And it can't be turned off like a switch."

"Medication—"

"Dan, you said allopathic drugs are a conspiracy of pharmaceutical companies," Coral said anxiously. "They make money undermining our health. Remember?"

Dan, I'm not going to start taking drugs because you don't like my habits," Piper spat. She felt Donny tense again and turned her face to murmur soothing words into his hair.

"Habits! This goes way beyond—"

"Dan," Coral interrupted, "you and Piper go round the same circles over and over again. Let someone else get a word in edgewise. Molly, don't you have something you wanted to tell your mom?"

Here is what Molly said: Mommy, the Japan trip was supposed to be for you.

Piper shook her head. "Molly, I know your father told you that, but—"

"I don't mean the one when I was fourteen," Molly said. "I mean this one."

Piper frowned. "This one? What one?"

"Jacques' trip, Mom. The flash mob. The November Lies reward. I thought if I could win, Jacques would take us both. I thought it might tempt you out. I thought we could have an adventure together, you and I. To make up for the other one."

Piper turned to look fully at Molly. Molly was looking at her hopefully, beseechingly. Piper found herself remembering Molly as a little girl. She remembered a time when, for one reason or another, voices had been raised—Piper and Dan fighting, or maybe scolding Molly for some minor infraction—it happens. And Molly had gone to her room, and taken some coins from her allowance, and wrapped them in a bit of paper, and brought it to her mother and presented it as a gift, as a peace offering. Now Piper felt the deep shudder of a sob rising in her as the piercing joy and desperate grief of life came together in the person of her daughter.

Piper put her arms around Molly and held her, Donny burrowing between them and squeaking, "Sandwich!" She put her face in Molly's hair and heard Dan's voice in the room, its resonant timbre creating a river of sound, and Coral's higher note sparkling and skipping on its surface, and the voices of Jake and the monks moving around them, creating rhythm and balance. The words were indistinguishable but the sound was a symphony, harmonic, balanced, crystalline, a structure of people and words and awarenesses creating a place for Piper to let go and be.

And then a new voice came in, like a new theme in the symphony, a pleasant light tenor, not loud enough to overpower the others but somehow, for the moment, the lead note in the flow of voices.

Here is what Matthew Winchester said: Have you thought about changing your frequency?

The voices in the room quieted. Piper turned her head, startled to remember that he was with her. Matthew blinked owlishly. And, once again, Piper wanted to cry.

Because what did Matthew have to do with it? What did Matthew have to do with anything? What did he have to do with Molly, or the panic attacks, or Japan? What did he have to do with Dan? When Dan was in the room, no one else seemed to exist. All Piper's attention—all anyone's attention—was on him. How could Matthew, who was quiet, who was unassuming, how could he compete with that? How could anyone? Dan was exciting, he was infuriating, and what did that *freaking* Coral Lane have to do with it? This was between her and Dan and dear *God* it was hell but it was real and it was theirs and it was no one else's business.

Yet somehow, now, everyone's eyes were on Matthew. Piper half-turned toward him. Donny shifted on her lap, settled in again. On the other side of her, Molly adjusted her position to maintain her physical contact with her mother.

"What?" Piper asked.

"You don't have to stay monthly just because you've always been monthly," Matthew said. "It's a fairly standard fix."

Piper blinked. What about Coral, what about Donny, what about all these *issues*? It was as if none of it mattered, as if he hadn't even heard. As if they had been engaged in social chitchat and now it was time to come to the point.

"What," said Piper, "are you talking about?"

"The magazine," said Matthew reasonably. "You said you wanted to talk about the magazine. So here's an idea: publish less often. Publish every two months, instead of once a month. Publish four times a year. You can save a lot of money on production costs."

"We'd save even more money if we didn't publish at all," Piper snapped. "We'd save *all* the costs. But we wouldn't *make* any money either." She glanced at Leon and added, "It's like leaving the battlefield." Which, she reminded herself, she had already done. She had closed the magazine; she had given it to Dan; she had put it up for sale—she had done all three of those things in the last thirty-six hours, thirty-six of the most exhausting hours of her entire life; and if, like Rasputin, the magazine was still alive after any one of those assaults, it should certainly perish under the weight of the three.

Yet, as if Matthew were a doctor suggesting one last desperate measure, she couldn't completely suppress an impossible, unreasonable spike of hope.

"If you can sell the same number of ads for one issue as you now do for two," Matthew explained patiently, "then each issue becomes more profitable."

Dan spoke. "How could you sell the same number of ads? If you have an advertiser with a full-year buy, you can't charge him for twelve issues when you're only putting him in six."

"If you could show him that more people read each issue, you could raise his per-issue rate," said Matthew.

"Why would more people read it?" Coral asked.

"It's out there longer," Matthew explained. "It gives people more time to pick it up. Plus, there would be more content in each issue, so more reasons to read it."

"We've talked about changing the frequency," said Dan. "But we need to maintain the relationship with our readers. Out of sight, out of mind."

"People count on us," said Piper.

"That was before Piper started her blog," Matthew said. "Now you connect with your readers every day online. Some recent posts have gone viral. People all over the world are reading them. You won't disappear from sight."

"But..." Piper trailed off. What was going on? Dan was talking about the magazine as if it were still alive. Coral was talking about it as if it were still alive. Coral had asked, on air, for readers, for advertisers. Could there be something left to talk about?

She turned to Dan. "Dan, isn't there *anywhere* you could get more money for us? For the magazine? An infusion of capital—maybe some Hammond family money—?"

Coral started to speak, then closed her mouth. Piper thought she knew what Coral was going to say: the Hammond family money had started the magazine. The Hammond family money had taken years to pay back.

The Hammond family money had been diminished in the process, as the interest paid on it was low.

The Hammond family money was Coral's now. Coral's and Dan's.

And it was Molly's and Donny's, too. If either of them were to go to college, they'd need what was left of that family money.

It just wasn't there for *Riverboro Rocks*. It wasn't going to be the fix they needed. Not this time.

Here is what Dan said: Silas, do you think with fewer issues you would be able to sell more advertising pages for each issue?

Piper felt as if her world was tilting, its edges crumbling. Dan was looking at Silas, at Matthew—not at her. He was weighing solutions that didn't have to do with Piper's talents, Piper's limitations.

In doing so, he was breaking a pattern that had defined their entire adult life.

What would happen to her, to *Riverboro Rocks*, if Dan turned away? What would happen to her identity, her presence in the community, if she didn't publish a magazine every month? If she weren't Piper Hadley Hammond, brilliant, surprising, the forger of her town's identity, the chronicler of its day-to-day, who would she be? An abandoned woman stuck in a house.

"It isn't a magic bullet," Matthew continued. "There have to be other revenue-enhancing and cost-cutting measures."

"What measures do you suggest?" Dan snapped. "We're cut to the bone as it is."

"Not quite to the bone," Matthew corrected. "You're going to want to take a look at the compensation packages. Yours in particular, Dan."

And suddenly all eyes were on Dan.

"Why mine?" Dan asked.

"Because yours is the biggest."

"And what is the point," Dan said impatiently, "of having a company, of investing to build a company, of spending years of your life on a company, if there is no, as you call it, 'compensation package'?"

"Oh, I think we can salvage a small compensation package for you, Dan," Matthew replied imperturbably. "You can cut your hours to, say, ten a week? And adjust your compensation accordingly. Since you'll be participating more in a consulting capacity and less as a full-time employee, it might be possible to edge up the hourly compensation for you and still realize savings for the magazine. It will take financial pressure off the company and create a basis for positive growth."

He's good, Piper thought with a surge of admiration. *He plays the geek card well. Deaf to the nuances, immune to the emotional temperature of the room. Nonchalantly talking numbers. A good ally.* She smiled brilliantly at him. He flicked a glance in her direction and she caught a glimmer of a returning smile. Then he was back to the spreadsheet, talking net; talking gross; talking bottom line, key employee, deferred compensation. He was tapping the spreadsheet with his index finger, pointing out numbers printed in red, numbers printed in black.

And Dan was listening; Dan was following; Dan was nodding. And when Matthew paused, Dan turned, not to Piper, but to Silas again.

"Si," he repeated, "can you keep up the volume of ad sales with fewer issues to sell?"

Here is what Silas said: Dunno.

Everyone looked at Silas, waiting for him to say more. Silas looked around at the expectant faces and shrugged. "Maybe," he added.

Piper smiled. She felt very light. "Embrace the uncertainty," she said. She was rewarded by a ripple of laughter from Cassie and Pasco, and was suddenly happy that the monks were at the meeting.

Then people were chatting and moving about and Brumi was refilling teacups and Cassie went out into the kitchen and got some granola cookies and started handing them around. It seemed that the meeting was over.

Donny, sensing the drop in tension, fell instantly asleep on Piper's lap. Coral crossed the room to join them. Molly got up to make room for her.

With her daughter gone, Piper's side felt cold where Molly had been pressing. Molly went to join Cassie and Pasco on the floor where they were arguing about baby names. Coral took the seat Molly had vacated.

"Piper, I need to know what you would do if you needed to get Donny out of here," Coral said.

"What are the odds that the house would catch on fire again?"

"What were the odds it would the first time?" Coral countered. "I'm not saying this to hurt your feelings, Piper. Honestly I'm not."

"You're saying it because you want to allow Donny to spend time here again," Piper said. "With me as the supervising adult."

"He misses you. And it's good for him to have grownups in his life besides Dan and me. And Molly isn't always around to come here with him. But I need to feel safe about it. Does that make me a bitch?"

Piper was thinking about her answer when Matthew spoke. "Buddy system." Coral and Piper stared at him blankly, so he continued, "You get a buddy. Someone to back you up. Put them on speed dial. Or pager."

"But—" said Coral.

"Piper should have a buddy anyway," said Matthew. "Especially if the monks leave. If anything happens she's going to need someone to turn to."

"Who would—" Piper began.

"What about Auntie Polly?" said Matthew. "Or Coral?"

"Coral!" Piper sputtered. "You mean Dan?"

"No, I don't mean Dan," Matthew said firmly. "But someone nearby. How about me? I'll do it."

"But you're new," said Coral, and Piper nodded, for once in agreement.

"Sam and Felicity King." Matthew was ticking them off on his fingers. "Jake. Piper, most people don't have so many people who would be on call for them. Do you know that?" Matthew continued ticking. "Leon. Lisette."

"Cassie. Pasco." Cassie called from across the room.

Brumi added, "Ananda. Brumi."

"Molly," said Molly.

"You're a teenager," said Coral. "And what if the back-up is out of town or unreachable? What if they don't get here fast enough?"

"Coral, you're never going to be able to take all the risk out of a situation." Even as she spoke, Piper was aware of the oddity that she should be the one saying this. But she continued, "You can't keep Donny in a bubble."

"He'll never make it in the zombie apocalypse if you do," said Pasco.

Here is what Cassie said: Do you think it's possible to survive a zombie apocalypse long term?

Coral stood up. She lifted Donny off Piper's lap and settled him on her shoulder. "I'll talk to Dan," she promised.

And then—there were no end to the surprises of this day—Piper stood, too, and put her arms around Coral and Donny and closed her eyes. "Thank you," she whispered. Because she knew, as any mother would, that it was only necessary to win Coral over. The rest would take care of itself.

Coral smiled happily. *Oh God,* thought Piper. *Now she thinks we're friends.* But she smiled back and patted Coral. Because Donny was what mattered here. And then she sat down quickly and sighed in relief.

Matthew slid his arm around her. "How'd I do?" he asked.

"You were brilliant," Piper said fervently. "Just brilliant. How did you learn all that stuff about magazine frequencies?"

"How does anyone learn anything?" Matthew replied. "Long years of business school. Plus, I looked it up online."

"You can learn everything online," said Brumi.

"Like how to survive a zombie apocalypse," said Pasco.

"So you *can* survive it?" asked Ananda.

Here is what Brumi said: You can if you get rid of the zombies.

And Ananda beamed at him as if he'd just said the most brilliant thing in the world.

November 29: The Best of Blogs, the Worst of Blogs

No one who has been following this blog consistently will be surprised, I imagine, at almost anything that happens here.

These posts have taken such a personal turn I hardly know if I should be talking about my life now, or blogging about our town (as was my original intention in starting this blog). This blog was not meant to be my diary. It wasn't meant to be the record of my inmost thoughts. And it was not (until recently) meant to be a way of setting the record straight from my point of view on any topic on this planet.

The setting straight thing does seem to have its pluses, however. As a direct result of the public brawling of the magazine's co-owners, our site traffic is way up, there isn't a copy of the current issue to be found for love or money, and I'll be joining Jacques Marquand as a guest on his internet radio program today, and maybe in the future as well. And although the future of *Riverboro Rocks* still "hangs in the balance," as Jacques would say, at least the co-founders are communicating with one another, and looking at various options and scenarios. And like the fellow says, there's no such thing as bad publicity. We take what we can get.

Jacques and his publisher have started talking to me about doing a book. Jacques calls his publisher A Captain of Industry, and the two of them go back a long way. Jacques claims he was planning to introduce him to me at Molly's party (as if either Jacques or I is likely to be there). This Captain tried to post a comment on my blog the day I put the magazine up for sale, but we were all in an uproar then, and I declined the comment.

After I refused the comment, the Captain got in touch with me through Jacques. And regardless of this man's relation to industries of any sort, I think he should be called the Captain of Conversation. Once we got started, there was no stopping us. We talked on and on—it is always difficult for me to resist someone who shows a true interest in my publication. He got me talking about the people who were sending me their stories, those ordinary stories made extraordinary in the telling. I told him I wanted to give these people voices, to allow them to tell their own stories. My Captain of Conversation led me from story to story, from telling to telling. The upshot is that the Captain has asked me to edit and curate these stories for an annotated collection, which he has committed to publish.

Each story expresses something personal, significant, and relevant for many women (and a few men) whose challenges far exceed mine. Some of the challenges are small yet universal. Others have global import. Their telling has been catalyzed by the events in our little town, and so the stories will be filtered through our local lens in the re-telling.

The advance on this book deal will not be insignificant. It could give our magazine a stay of execution well into the coming year. After that, who knows? As we begin to act in a more civilized manner, Dan and I, all this excitement may begin to die down. But let us gather our rosebuds while we may, which is now; and perhaps one book will lead to another, and so our dreaded demise might be forestalled indefinitely. In the meantime, if you are a venture capitalist looking for a regional dot com, or a Hollywood producer with a large checkbook, or even another Captain of Industry (or the same one), take a look at our current site stats. They will blow you away.

Having gotten so far off track, it's hard to think how to get back on without at least addressing some of the issues that I brought up in my recent posts. I've had hundreds, or maybe at this point thousands, of phone calls, text messages, and comments on the blog page, and I have not approved most of those comments for posting. I didn't want to keep adding fuel to the fire. Plus, I wasn't logging in very much (though I do admit to peeking now and then, just to see whose side was getting more support in this intra-familial fray).

And today I think that if I approve all those comments from my previous postings, it will start the whole uproar all over again. I wouldn't want to do that, but I can't resist excerpting just a few.

Piper's List: Top Five Responses to the Recent Uproar Here at *Riverboro Rocks*

5) Piper, you are the voice of Riverboro Rocks, and without you there is no magazine. Now as to that comment, it might seem self-serving, but I had to use it, as it was by a long shot the most-repeated observation of all my commenters.

4) Unbelievable that you would do this to your partner and ex-husband, and if I were married to you I would (insert threat/expletive/other disgusted comment here). I had to put that one in to balance the scales but it was also the type of comment I got a lot of from my good readers.

3) I am a lawyer, please get in touch with me as I specialize in this sort of thing. A remarkable number of comments with this theme; or, along similar lines:

2) I am a lawyer and don't say another word about this on the record until you get to court. I guess those lawyers hadn't picked up on the bit about how I am unlikely to make it to court, as I can't leave the house. However, I am grateful to all my lawyer followers.

And one of my readers said:

1) Piper, I am a huge fan of your work. Will you marry me?

To which I would reply: Of course, if you can save my magazine and fix my life and sweep me into a happy-ever-after that includes Molly and (maybe) the monks, and if you are relatively good looking and have all your hair. And lots of money.

Oh, and be prepared for a scalding blog post, should things go awry

Tags: Blogging as memoir, blogging as correspondence, blogging as art form, divorce lawyers, publishing law

COMMENTS:

HarvardProf: I am a lawyer and if there is as little money in the publication as you have consistently indicated there is, then it isn't worth anyone's while to take this to court. Here's my advice for free: if there isn't anything to fight over, walk away from the fight.

RiverCoral: Hi Harvard Prof! We're actually not fighting quite so much now, and we're looking for ways to resolve this in a positive manner. So it looks like we won't be needing any lawyers for now! Isn't that right, Piper? No lawyers? But thanks, Harvard Prof, for the free legal advice. ☺

TheGeekster: So does this mean you are going to keep publishing the magazine?

PipersPebbles: We're working on that. For the moment, Dan has stepped down as publisher and will be taking a part-time consulting role. There is some discussion of dividing the company—Dan to take the print publication, and I to keep the online property—but there are many things that would need to be hammered out if we were to move in that direction, as many of our resources are used for both print and online.

RiverCoral: Dibs on the Weather Oracle! ☺

PipersPebbles: Right, Coral. You don't even know who the Weather Oracle is.

RiverCoral: Time for you to tell us then! Just remember the Oracle started with the print magazine, so he gets to stay with it. ☺

PipersPebbles: Dan has always poked fun at the Weather Oracle. Why should the Oracle stay with him?

RiverCoral: You know that Dan loves the Oracle more than anyone! ☺

DrewHadley: Hey, this is starting to sound like that scene from the old days where they cut the baby in half, remember? Please don't do that to my dad, he needs both halves in one place, lol.

TheGeekster: Could you share the Oracle, so he does some stuff for print and some for online?

RiverCoral: If we ended up splitting off the print magazine from on-line we'd have to share some of the debt too. The person with the online part would get off scot free otherwise! ☺

BookLover603: It sounds enticing…to start fresh, unencumbered with debt…and there is a big upsurge online. The wave of the future…

DantheRiverMan: How is this turning into a townwide referendum? We're not throwing this open to debate.

TheGeekster: I feel like a kid whose mom and dad are fighting. The kid isn't supposed to be involved, but whatever happens affects him.

BookLover603: That's how I feel, too, Geekster...Dan and Piper have to keep publishing...for their fans...

ImmaterialGirl: Piper will keep publishing—won't you, Piper? Don't give up! Especially now that everybody has started to be friends again. Knock wood and all.

WeatherOracle: That Unim will be most E Plurible—
                 No doubts from sunny Weather Oracle.

ImmaterialGirl: Is everyone ready for Molly's party? It's tonight!

ZombiePatrol: Will there be zombies?

PeterWriter: There will always be zombies.

BookLover603: This month's blog made a community for me...so many friends and kindred spirits...

AuntieP: Meet us at Molly's party, Book Lover, to keep the community spirit.

BookLover603: I'd love to come...

ImmaterialGirl: Weather Oracle, are you up for a party?

WeatherOracle: Weary of weather prognostication;
                 Fearful of founders' litigation;
                 Hopeful of hostilities' cessation;
                 I think we need a celebration.
                 So roll back the carpets from the floor-acle
                 And save a dance for Weather Oracle.

HarvardProf: I'm sure the ladies will be delighted. Auntie P and Book Lover, I hope you each will honor me with a dance.

BookLover603: I'm not actually a lady, per se…more like a guy.

TheGeekster: Oh wow. Are you interested in zombies?

BookLover603: I'd like to learn more about them…

TheGeekster: I'll look for you at the party. How will I know you?

BookLover603: I'll come as the undead…

(*Comments approved*)

* * *

Damn Lies
By Presidential Candidate and Radio Host
Jacques Marquand

Riverboro continues to anchor the most exciting corner of our state as we await the word on the as-yet undetermined destiny of *Riverboro Rocks* and its mascot puppy Ralph. Will the publication and the puppy survive or perish? Only the antagonists, and the advertisers on whom they depend, can answer. Join us today for Piper Hadley Hammond's version of events, available on local radio, by download, and by podcast.

* * *

Lisette was coming out of Ananda's room, and for an unguarded moment she looked terribly, terribly sad.

Piper stopped. "Lisette. Are you OK? Is Ananda?"

"A hard morning," Lisette replied with a tired smile. "Nothing unusually serious. We're good."

Piper paused for a moment in the second floor corridor and then made up her mind. "I'm going downstairs for breakfast," she told the older woman. "Come with me?"

In the kitchen Piper poured hot water over a licorice teabag for Lisette and placed it on the table, then poured herself a cup of coffee. Lisette spooned yogurt over granola and fruit and set the bowls on the table.

What to say to someone facing what Lisette had to face? Piper felt tired and sad. These monks—they had been going to bring her peace and even salvation. That's what she had believed in some corner of her mind when they first arrived. Instead they had brought into her house sadness and illness, perhaps even death. Shouldn't they have warned her first? Shouldn't she have been allowed to choose?

She felt immediately guilty for the thought. It was selfish, monstrous of her to feel that way when Lisette and Ananda had so much to bear.

"Should we bring anything up to Ananda?" she asked penitently.

"No. She's resting now. I'll bring something to her later."

"Is it…" Piper hesitated.

But Lisette replied reassuringly. "She's tired. She didn't sleep well last night. She'll feel better after she gets some rest."

"How do you do it?" Piper asked. "What could be more painful for a mother than the suffering of her child? How do you stay so brave? Is it your practice?"

"I don't always feel brave," Lisette replied. "Sometimes I feel that what is happening is part of the powerful flow of life. It pulls us along and we can only surrender. And if we do it will all somehow work out. Then other times I fear that I will lose my daughter. And if I do, I won't be able to go on at all."

Piper was horrified to hear a quaver creep into Lisette's voice and jumped in quickly. "What do you mean, the powerful flow of life?"

"Things you can't change," Lisette replied. "Things you have to go with."

"To me that feels like powerlessness." Piper stirred her yogurt, chasing the granola and banana with her spoon.

"Me too," Lisette acknowledged. "Sometimes. But sometimes it can feel like power."

Piper wanted to know, more than anything now, if Lisette saw Ananda's sickness as part of the flow or against the flow. But she didn't dare ask. Instead she asked, "What about the fire in my house? Was that the flow?"

Lisette gave a little shrug. "It was, anyway, something you couldn't have done anything about. But it was odd, for me."

"For you?" Until that moment, Piper had been thinking of the fire only as a part of her own story. But of course, she realized. *Everything that happens is, for each person, a part of their story. Like Ananda is now a part of mine.* "Why is that?"

"I was away from the house during the fire," Lisette said. "I was at the doctor, with Ananda." She paused and Piper nodded, encouraging her to continue. "Years ago, another house that I loved caught fire. I would have been there that day. Except I had an appointment at a doctor."

"Weird," Piper said.

"Weird," Lisette agreed.

"But why?" asked Piper. "What does it mean?"

"I don't know," said Lisette. "For me, maybe, something I haven't worked out? An opportunity to get something right that I might have gotten wrong before? Some strong impression playing out on the field of life?"

"There are no coincidences," Piper said wisely.

"Or, who knows?" said Lisette. "Maybe there are."

Lisette rose from the table to turn the flame on under the kettle. When it began to rattle she poured hot water over her teabag, still in the cup. Piper watched her moving around the kitchen, bangles jingling, already so at home that Piper almost felt like the guest. "I wish I could handle things the way you monks do," she said. "I don't know what I'll do if I ever have to face real adversity."

"You will deal with it with grace and courage, as you do with everything in your life." Lisette poured coffee into Piper's cup and settled down across from her again. "One of the things that draws people to you is your talent for turning your trials into stories. You pull the bright thread out of a dark weave."

"Then the letdown. When they learn about the real me."

"Who feels let down?" asked Lisette. "Do you mean Matthew? What did he say?"

"I guess I do mean Matthew," Piper admitted. "He hasn't actually said anything. But he fell for me in high school. And I'm not that carefree girl he remembers."

"I don't think many of us were carefree in high school," Lisette said. "However we might remember it."

"Years ago, Matthew saw me across a cafeteria and thought I looked hot. And now he thinks he's in love with me."

"And you don't believe he is?"

"I fear that a world of disappointment awaits him."

"I don't think so." Lisette said. "How could it? He's already seen you in your worst moments."

"He doesn't seem to notice them," said Piper. "Does he get that I'm the prime neurotic? Does he see the real me—crouched in here like an animal in a cage?"

"A lioness," said Lisette. "The real you—beautiful, fierce, and free."

"You had me until the free." Piper looked at the older woman with a surge of unexpected affection. "If you're ever up at night," she said impulsively, "up and alone and thinking about things, come upstairs and see me. I'll make you a cup of tea and we'll talk. Because you know I'll be up anyway."

For a terrifying moment Piper thought she saw tears in Lisette's eyes. But then the older woman smiled. "Naturally Matthew loves you," she said. "How can he not? He's a moth to your flame."

"I just hope it doesn't fry him," said Piper, standing to collect the breakfast dishes.

* * *

Early in the afternoon, Piper, wearing a pair of cutoffs and an over-sized man's shirt, her hair tied up on top of her head, was in Molly's room. She had pushed the bed into the middle of the room and spread newspapers all over the floor. Now she was pouring paint from the can into the roller pan. The paint was robin's egg blue.

Jake looked in. "Need some help? Or is this something you have to do yourself?"

"Jake," Piper greeted him. "Thank you for coming."

"I was happy you asked me. It was a big step."

"Let's not start right in talking about steps," Piper said. "It exhausts me. It makes it all seem daunting. It makes it seem like work."

Jake took off his blazer and draped it neatly on a bedpost. "In that case, I won't call what you're doing now a step, either."

"Why should you?" Piper felt a sudden tightness in her throat. "I'm painting Molly's room. The walls were dirty." She dipped her roller into the paint and rolled it across the wall. The streak of paint it left was bright and clear. "God," she said. "It shows how dingy this room was getting. Jake, let's not make a big deal of this, OK? It's not my life. It's a room. No more, no less."

"Finding encouragement in small signs," Jake said, smiling. "Part of my job description. You've made some great progress here already—on the room, I mean. You hardly need me at all. Do you have one of those gadgets to edge the paint around the trim? I'm the master of that."

"You'll get paint on your clothes," Piper protested, but she handed him the edger. "The edging is the hard part." She turned back to her wall. "I didn't call you to have a session. Or to help me paint. I just wanted..." She trailed off.

Jake dipped the edger in the paint and carefully ran it around the window frame. "To normalize things?" he suggested. "Get an old friendship back on track?"

"Is there a friendship?" Piper asked. "To get back on track?"

Jake glanced at Piper, eyebrows raised. "I hope so," he said. "It's because of our history that Dan asked me to step in. He thought it would be easier for you to talk to someone you already knew. I thought it was a good idea, in the circumstances. I wanted to help." He turned back to the window, running the edger neatly along the frame. "The anger transference—that's pretty normal. It's OK."

"It's not—it wasn't—" Piper puffed a breath out, giving up, and turned back to her wall. "What about you, Jake?" she asked. "You must be angry too."

"Me?" Jake looked at her in genuine surprise. "Angry? At what? At whom?"

"Coral, of course." Piper stepped back to study her wall. "Can you do the ceiling trim over here?"

Jake stood, brushed off his pants, and moved to the outside wall. He set a wooden chair near it and climbed up on it so he could apply the paint without stretching.

Piper continued, "Weren't you in love with Coral? The two of you always down at the park on the swings, sneaking into the pool at night, planning bonfire evenings, like a couple of teenagers."

"Coral does have a way of making adults behave like children." Jake, running the edger quickly and neatly along the ceiling, smiled reminiscently. "She'd organize games for Molly and her friends and somehow we'd all be playing too. Remember that Halloween party she threw for the kids at the River Place? Monster tag, kids creeping in and out of the building, and we ended up in the midst of it all, running around laughing with the rest of them. I think it's why Coral's so good in her role at the River Place—she's still half kid herself."

"Half kid with no idea of responsibilities, of consequences!" flared Piper. "How can you defend her? You were dating, and next thing you know she's pregnant but it isn't your kid? And Jake is out and Piper is out and Dan is in? How does that happen?"

"Piper, this isn't about me. It isn't about Coral. It's supposed to be about you."

"Because of the way I came out of it. That's all on me, and I get that, I do." Piper spoke calmly, but found she was pressing the roller too hard; her strokes were getting shorter and sharper. She relaxed her grip on the roller and smoothed out the paint. "But Jake, I'd like to understand what happened. To understand the parts that had to do with other people, the parts that weren't all about me."

"All right. Fair enough. Let's talk it through." Jake turned from his work, stepping down off the chair and sitting on it, thinking. "Coral and I...we weren't ever in love. Not really. You remember what I was like, what I've always been like—the stodgy one, the stick in the mud. When Coral included me in her games and excursions I felt more interesting, more playful than I actually am. That set the tone of our relationship. We were more sidekicks than lovers."

He paused, remembering. "I never expected a lot from Coral. And she clearly didn't take things seriously with me. Maybe we were a convenience to one another. Both waiting for something else. Someone else.”

“Then Dan came along.”

“It wasn’t ideal,” Jake acknowledged.

“That’s an understatement, isn’t it? But you—*you* seem fine with it. If I were going to try some psychology of my own—” Piper broke off.

“You would say I interpret abandonment as love?” Jake spoke without rancor. “Because of my relationship with my dad.”

Piper was contrite. “I know you don’t like to go there, Jake.”

“No, it’s OK,” Jake said. “We are none of us free of our childhood influencers. And Piper, if it does any good now, after all the time that has passed, I’m sorry. It never occurred to me to leave the River Place. And if it had, I wouldn’t have done it. So much good is done there, for the whole town. It isn’t Coral’s. It’s all of ours.”

“Yet you dropped *me* like a hot potato,” Piper said resentfully. “Till Dan got you up here as my resident shrink—barely four weeks ago.”

“I didn’t realize you were housebound,” Jake said. “Dan and Molly never said. It seems incredible now. It was an amazing sleight-of-hand, that illusion that you were out and about among us. I thought you were avoiding me.”

“You? Why would I avoid you?”

“We tend to make everything about ourselves, don’t we? You could have needed some distance. Maybe you blamed me. Maybe you thought I should have seen it coming and warned you.”

“That would have been nice,” Piper muttered.

“Then things started to come back to normal. You keep seeing people—Coral and Dan—and old friendships weather these things.”

“I don’t get it,” Piper said. “How could you face her every day? After what she did to you?”

“You face Dan every day.” Jake climbed back up on the chair, resumed edging. “And if it weren’t for how things turned out, I think you and Coral could have been good friends. You two aren’t so different from one another.”

“Spare me.”

“I can see it,” Jake insisted. “You’re both bright, energetic, creative people.”

"Men." Piper gave a short laugh. "Take any two women they get along with, they always think the women will like each other. Trust me, I am nothing like Coral."

"Look at what the two of you have done with Donny—you've put aside your enmity for his best interests." Finishing the section of ceiling, Jake stepped off the chair and knelt to get the floor trim. "He's a bridge between you and Dan, you and Coral—you and Molly, even."

"Molly." Piper's throat ached and she blinked back tears. "When your kids are young, you can write their story for them. But Molly has her own story arc now, and she's writing in new main characters. Silas or Colby, Miranda or Jacques...who knows? I can't choose for her anymore. I can't even be a main character. I have to become a supporting character in her story."

"It's hard," Jake sympathized. "I suppose that's why each of us needs to keep our own stories fresh."

Piper nodded. "I shouldn't have taken it out on you. I just—"

"Didn't want to take it out on Dan?" Jake suggested.

"I suppose that might be part of it. But it isn't how I saw it. Or see it. Good or bad, friends or not, I wanted something with you that was separate from Dan." Piper waved a self-deprecating hand. "Tough to achieve when Dan's paying you. But I wanted it to be that you were coming here because you cared about me."

Jake looked up, pushed his hair from his eyes with the back of his hand. It left a smudge of paint on his forehead. "I get that now. I should have before."

"I wanted to at least create an illusion that we were friends, or maybe more. I wanted you to participate in that illusion."

"And the illusion would be...for Dan?"

"For everyone. For me. Like a game of dress-up. You know you are playing but you still get into it. Dan blew that fantasy sky high with all that talk about who is paying whom."

"No surprise, knowing Dan, that he would be less than delicate about it. I should have anticipated that it would be hurtful to you. I'm sorry."

"Apology accepted." Piper looked at Jake, kneeling in his ironed pants and button shirt, hair falling into his eyes, painting her trim, and felt regretful and sad and comforted. She dropped the roller back into the tray.

Jake joined her; together they began to gather up the newspapers from the floor. "I used to think that I could erase the boundary between in here and out there by publishing," Piper said. "And after that, it was the monks. They brought the big outside world in here to my house. I thought they would change everything."

Jake held open a garbage bag for Piper to stuff the papers into. "And now?" he asked.

"I still have to think that things will change, don't I?" replied Piper. "What else can I do? Allow myself to believe that I'll never set foot outside my front door again?"

"Is that what you do believe?" Jake bent to put the top back on the paint can.

Piper lifted a shoulder. "It didn't exactly go swimmingly on Friday, did it? My outing to the town library to see my daughter speak?"

"Perhaps it was too much at once," Jake said. "The date, the announcement, the crowds, the expectations."

"I got that. From Coral already." Piper wiped her hands on a rag and handed it to Jake to use. "She thinks I was setting myself up for failure."

Jake accepted the rag and wiped his own hands. "And what do you think?"

"Obviously, I would have thought I was setting myself up for success."

Jake let the silence hang for a few moments. Finally Piper said, "Now that I crashed and burned so spectacularly, it will be even harder to do it. To go out."

"Next time," Jake said, "instead of trying a date, or a town event, or a trip to the library, how about this: one step out the door? One step out, into the shed, out the kitchen door, then back in. And the next day, maybe, two steps."

"Jake, do you honestly think I haven't tried that?"

"I know you have. And I also know, Piper, that you never give up on anything you try until you succeed. I have seen what you can accomplish. I know you can accomplish this."

"Maybe," Piper muttered dubiously. She and Jake paused at the doorway, looking back into the room. The blue walls gleamed; Piper felt a glow of satisfaction for a job well completed. She turned to smile at Jake, her full, playful, mischievous smile. "Jake," she asked, "are you going to charge for this session?"

"Only for the painting," he replied.

* * *

By the time Jacques called that evening, Piper felt she had already gone through a week's worth of drama, between her morning conversation with Lisette and her afternoon one with Jake. Plus, she was physically tired from the painting. But the thought of spending time on the air with Jacques energized her. She had been thinking about what she wanted to say; it had built up in her and here, she thought, was her opportunity. *It's a medium,* she thought. *A different one, suited to a different kind of expression. I can do this. The media is my world. It's where I belong.*

"We're live on the radio, and we're also recording for replay later." Jacques' voice crackled over the phone line. "I have Piper Hadley Hammond of Riverboro here with me. Piper, you've seen your former husband on TV with his new family. They talked about founding *Riverboro Rocks,* and about the challenges it faces today. Now it's your turn. What's next for the Hammonds?"

Piper started to speak, easily and naturally. "Thank you, Jacques, and everyone listening. There's something special about a magazine, isn't there, Jacques? You published one, years ago, from the point of view of the countercultural movement. Compared to that, *Riverboro Rocks'* sphere is small."

"Small but mighty," Jacques suggested. "Like its publisher."

"And reflecting a point of view. I've been thinking about that a lot lately—how point of view will shape a story. What a story becomes, depending on point of view."

Jacques laughed. "I think you've shown us all the power of point of view," he said. "I'll bet there were plenty of people who weren't pleased to hear yours."

"You know what they say, Jacques. Journalism is writing what somebody else doesn't want printed."

"The rest is all Lies?"

"The rest is all Public Relations."

"Same difference," Jacques said. "Now tell us your point of view about your ex's TV appearance yesterday. Do you have a counter point you want to make?"

"I actually don't, Jacques—not today. Today I'm thinking about all the work people have done for your November Lies: my daughter's costume party and my ad sales guy's con art and all the Lies people tell. Aren't all these Lies really points of view? Specific truths, reflected through the perception and awareness of specific people? Aren't *Damn Lies* and *November Lies* celebrations of individual approaches to universal truths?"

"Sounds good to me, I'll take it. So what you see as a betrayal by Dan and Coral could be some kind of deeper truth from their point of view?"

"Do we have to talk about Dan and Coral? Let's talk about my daughter's party. Early this month we posted some of Molly's costume ideas. We asked people to submit their own ideas, their own stories."

"What responses did you get?" Jacques prompted.

"One young woman cannot interpret the tones of voice or facial expressions of other people. She lives in a world of her own, a world from which she has difficulty connecting with others. She will come to Molly's party disguised as a robot. She says she has often dressed in this costume and finds it to be liberating and also effective for developing bonds with other people.

"An older man wrote that he had been afraid to propose to the woman he had been dating until he dressed in a superhero costume and was able to sweep her off her feet."

Jacques cut in. "Let me remind our audience, Piper, that you will be curating these and other stories you have collected for a book—and following your lead, that's not a bad name for it: Points of View. But let me ask you a question. Is there a downside to this costume thing?"

"Some younger people wrote that their costumes seemed to bring out their inner partier; one even ended up in the hospital because of a costume evening that turned wild. A child wrote that when her parents dressed up in costume it was hard to get their attention; they seemed to tune her out. A woman wrote that she only felt real when she was in costume; the rest of the time she felt as if she were floating through life with no substance, no reality at all."

"So kids, don't try this at home?"

"Molly's party will be a safe environment," Piper laughed. "Even the monks will be there."

"Going as themselves?"

"They could, couldn't they? Maybe they'd say that reality is a costume worn by the Infinite, or that life is a costume party thrown by God."

"Or that God puts on a mask because we couldn't bear to see His real face?" Marquand encouraged.

"Or Her face," Piper said. "But we're getting philosophical now, aren't we?"

"You mention monks, I get philosophical," Marquand said. "I'm that kind of crazy guy. So what is your message today?"

"Put on a costume and head down to Molly's party," Piper said. "It's at the H.I.T. Do not, repeat, NOT come to the Hadley House! But go—and soon. It's starting. Molly and Donny are showing me their finished costumes, and the monks are abuzz putting the finishing touches on theirs. Don't miss it! And Jacques, you had better get going, you promised you'd show up too."

"So I did, so I did."

"You'd better not pull one of your famous no-shows," Piper threatened. "You disappoint my kids, you'll have me to answer to."

"Say no more, I'm going! I think we in New Hampshire have learned what it means to have Piper Hadley Hammond to answer to. Will I see you there?"

"I will be there in spirit," Piper said.

November 30: Three Chords and the Truth

They straggled back from the H.I.T. in groups of twos and threes, the heroes and harlequins and robots and zombies. They stood at the corner by the library saying goodnight and laughing, last hugs, last kisses, then turned to go off in their different directions, humming bits of the songs that blasted out at the party.

I watched from my window.

The party was a great success by all accounts. Or, I should say, by both accounts—one being Molly's and the other Silas'. They stopped by after the party to fill me in; and since the teachers at the high school had given an (unofficial) OK for students to come late to school, we curled cozily in my office for the debriefing, untroubled by the lateness of the hour.

The big news, related by a breathless Molly and supported with many brief nods and grunts from Silas, was Jacques Marquand. True to his word (for a change) Jacques (now going by the self-bestowed title of Father of Lies) actually made an appearance. Given his normal attire he could hardly be said to be in costume, but he looked presidential in a tricorner hat and general's outfit. He did not bring the governor—what a surprise—but he had with him a junior staff member from the Capital, and insisted, oh-so-innocently, that he had never said the governor, he had only said "a gubernatorial guest."

He and his team kept starting dances with groups of party-goers, and getting people to lip synch with the music and improvise skits. Silas filmed it all, and Jacques has asked for the footage, and promised to use excerpts on his blog and on TV. Of course Jacques isn't going to pay him (when does he ever?), but Silas will get full credit and a link to his own professional website, which he's now inspired to set up. A coup for our Silas.

Then Jacques commandeered the podium, facing the crowd, and called Molly to the front, where he publicly congratulated her on being the first to complete her Lie. He presented her with a certificate that said she is a true Liar and leader. Molly is over the moon. Her father and brother and stepmother went on TV without her; now she and her party will get TV time as well.

He announced (I could *kill* that man) that Molly, Silas, and Miranda should plan on Japan, and that Molly is to bring a supervising adult along. I am going round the bend about this, but I can hardly say which part of it annoys me more: do I insist that Jacques keep his word and bring Molly along? Or insist (to Molly) that there is no way she is going on that trip? I feel like I go round one bend and ricochet back to the other. The indecision and confusion gives *me* the bends, so for the moment I'm at a standstill. I do not know what I am going to do tomorrow. Tonight I can only laugh at the irony and marvel at the glorious success of Molly's masquerade.

Dan was there as Paul Bunyan. He hardly had to do anything: just put on a flannel shirt and pair of jeans and work boots and carry a fake axe. Donny's puppy, Ralph, accustomed by now to the limelight, was dressed as Babe the Blue Ox. Coral had fastened horns to his head and put a yoke around his neck and he romped through the dancing, eating, mingling crowds of people.

And oh, the monks. They came as characters from the Bhagavad Gita, a martial epic that Leon has described to me. They barely had to do anything but wear their normal clothes and carry fake bows and arrows.

Pasco was the great hero Arjuna—although, being Pasco, he couldn't resist zombifying the costume with a bit of blood around the mouth and blank, rolling eyes. Brumi had colored his skin blue as the mischievous god Krishna, who advised Arjuna during the great war but gave his army to the other side. Cassie went as Arjuna's brave and high-profile wife. Lisette was Arjuna's mother—also, I am happy to report, very brave and very regal. Leon was a beloved grandpa who ended up (along with Krishna's army) on the bad-guy side in the fight. I found this sad to the point of upsetting, but I suppose it is a way of reminding us that there is another side to everything.

These epic heroes were prepared to do the evening's dirty work. I don't mean clean up—the H.I.T. (bless them!) took responsibility for that. Instead, they promised to keep order. They patrolled the party finding very little to do—in fact, the one scuffle they saw was between Silas and Colby. I don't even want to know what bubbled up, but Silas and Colby say it was cosplay. So my fears were for nothing, and I am glad to be proven wrong.

By the time Jacques arrived, the party was close to its scheduled end—justifying Miranda's identification of him as "the late Jacques Marquand." And at first he took no notice of Colby, who stood to the side and watched his hero recognize everyone but him. But eventually Jacques found a few minutes to spend with his "official" biographer. As a result of that conversation, Colby now thinks he'll take a year off after he graduates high school to work on Marquand's perennial campaign. I think it might be the start of a political career for him.

Matthew was there, I am told, as a UPS driver, who spent the evening searching the crowd for a warrior princess he must have known would not appear.

Scenes from the party can be found on YouTube and the *Riverboro Rocks* site. For the rest of my report, I will allow your yard sale donations, Riverboro, to tell the tale. Our town's junk continues to play its role in surprising and even poignant ways.

Molly's List: Items of Note at Hey! It's Thursday

5) *Podium used at check-in to the restaurant (and for Jacques Marquand's presentation):* an old school desk, carved with the names and initials of generations of Riverboro children and young adults. DH and PH are intertwined in a top corner; an (optimistic) con artist's rendition of the names Molly and Silas now grace it, as well.

4) *Strapped to the front of the podium:* a bent old shovel. This couldn't be the one that Ethan Hamon whacked Isaiah Hammond with back when they both lost the love of the beautiful Abby Ann…could it?

3) *Booth One to the right as you come in the door:* an old carriage seat, torn and mildewed and no doubt horribly uncomfortable—except for the mice that once called it home. But festooned with colored tissue paper and very much in demand as the booth of choice, as people filed by to leave their votes for Weather Oracle's identity in the jar left on the table for that purpose. I can announce now that no one at all guessed right, not even you, Jacques—so there will be no Damn Hints in your Damn Lies!

2) *Hanging from a coat hook till someone claims it:* a little green pouch for a tiny hero. Slipped out of the fingers of a sleeping Link as he was carried out of the restaurant, an hour past his bedtime, by his mother, the Princess Zelda.

1) *Uniform worn by the maître d':* a vintage Klingon costume from the original Star Trek. How did it migrate from Auntie P to Harvard Prof to the maître d'? That is unclear; but by mid-evening Jerome Hammond, no longer in costume, danced on the bar, elbow patches flashing, as elves and high school hosts and star ship officers applauded madly and cheered till their throats were raw.

November Lies pulled an all-nighter last night. Though Molly's party is over, the contest continues, and projects remain to be finished. I went down this morning in the dark to find members sprawled about in their clothes, asleep, and Peter still up, pacing and muttering into his tape recorder. He looked like a college-age revolutionary giving voice to anarchic beliefs—which I'm sure is exactly what Jacques Marquand would have wanted.

I think they intend to do the same thing tonight. I suppose I will end up with a houseful of sleep-deprived teenagers who will spend the day asking for cups of coffee and creating strange new works of protest and art.

It makes me happy to think about it.

When Molly was a kid we made a picture book for her. We used to read it together in the evening before bed. When she got too old for it, I packed that book away to save. I intended, I suppose, to muse and snooze over it when I grew old and gray and full of sleep.

And now this is what I think: while I am, for the moment, sticking so close to home, then what I can do is to focus on those close to me, the people who need me, the people who love me. The people I love.

I think it's time I got the book out again. For Donny.

This blog has ended up being a more faithful record of my private life than I ever intended it to be. Now everybody knows that, in the Hadley/ Hammond family, somebody done somebody wrong. They have seen how a family, and a business, has been brought to the brink, and peered into the chasm, and retreated from the brink. That an ex-wife's optimism masks a deep despair. That she has arrived at the place where the ladders start—that foul rag and bone shop of the heart.

But you know what? All that is small potatoes. When it comes down to it, who really cares? So someone can't go out, so someone left someone to be with someone else. It's the stuff of art, it's the stuff of life.

But it isn't the big stuff.

The big stuff is when you look out your window after meeting with family and business partners and well-wishers and monks, and you see your daughter and her little brother walking away, down the street together, hand in hand; and he is looking up and talking earnestly and she is looking down and responding. And you can tell from looking at their backs that he is very loving and very trusting and that she is very brave and very responsible, and that they are both very fragile and very breakable, too.

And you wish you could take back every single word or action or look or gesture, past or future, that ever could hurt them in any way, however small, however forgotten.

Forget the boyfriends and the husbands and the exes. It's the children who will break your heart.

Tags: WB Yeats, country music, how to prevent sleep deprivation, the many uses of caffeine

COMMENTS:

DrewHadley: I don't know who ended up doing all those weather predictions, but I voted for my dad. I really thought it was him. I should have known it would have to be someone with better psychic powers than his, lol.

AuntieP: Well, Drew, I voted for your father as well, and the indication that we are wrong is unsettling.

BookLover603: Go November Lies...I'm heading to King's to order a gallon of coffee for you...Think of me as the cheering crowd holding out cups of Gatorade.

SamKing: Today we're brewing Raspberry Coconut English Trifle. I suggest a pot of that and a pot of Breakfast Blend to cleanse the palate.

TheGeekster: The Breakfast Blend sounds good. Hey Book Lover can I meet you at King's? I need a cuppa after the big do last night.

BookLover603: Sure thing…you can hold off the zombies…

AuntieP: As soon as Jerome—I mean Harvard Prof—gets up we could all meet to go over some of our committee work. I have some ideas for your Riverboro Reads page, Book Lover, and I'd like your thoughts on a couple of nice vignettes I've turned up.

TheGeekster: Woohoo, AuntieP, you've got the Prof there with you? I thought I noticed some Klingon-Federation détente last night.

BookLover603: Not so personal, Geek Guy… AuntieP, see you at King's…coffee for all…

AuntieP: Hot tea for me.

RiverCoral: Piper, I thought I'd drop Donny off at the Hadley House after his preschool today. Would that work out for you? ☺

PipersPebbles: Thank you, Coral. I appreciate the vote of confidence—really.

(*Comments approved*)

* * *

Leon wasn't awaiting when, awakening in the heavy, dark morning, Piper crept downstairs. The lights were out, the darkness relieved only by the flickering light of the fire's last embers. A shadowy figure hunched on the couch, scribbling.

"Are you OK?" Piper whispered. "It's late to be working. Or early…"

"You do. You are," was the response. "Since you're up, you can help me. We're going to be hearing some wind soon. What rhymes with howl?"

Piper sank onto the couch. "Disembowel?" she suggested.

"That might be going too far…"

"Even for our Oracle," Piper agreed, "who errs on the side of the darkly terrifying."

"Anyway, I don't see it."

"Thank God for that. What a Hamon sees tends to materialize."

"Don't worry. No one is going to gruesomely murder a family member."

"A nice change. So how about some sleep? The monks have your old room, but Molly's at her dad's. Her bed is free."

"I'm not quite finished…"

"Time enough tomorrow. Go on now. Get some sleep."

"You too," whispered Miranda.

And Piper nodded. "I'll try," she said.

* * *

When full day came, hours later, Piper awoke to the delicious realization that she had slept in. A miracle, considering the racket that echoed throughout the house—banging and rattling and loud voices calling.

Donny was in the kitchen with Brumi and the workmen. "We're going to have to pull down this whole wall," Brumi said. "Take out the cabinets. Pull out the appliances. Get back to the wiring and start from scratch."

"Can I help pull down the wall?" asked Donny.

"I've got a section here that's all yours. You can pull off strips and put them on that paper. I picked a safe spot for him," Brumi assured Piper. "Nothing can hurt him in this patch of kitchen."

"What about November Lies?" Piper asked him. "Your music video?"

"Maybe next year," he said. "I can't let a big project like this get away.

"A business plan. Version 9.0."

"Will it work?" Piper took his coat and led him through the ruined kitchen.

"It wouldn't be much of a gift if it didn't, would it?" Matthew replied. "It should work. If all the parameters are met, if what is projected on paper materializes in actuality, it will work. So it's within the bounds of possibility."

He put down the spreadsheet and turned to look at Piper. "Do you want to take a look at the numbers?" he asked. "Or would you like to kiss me?"

"Now why would I want to do that, do you think?"

"Can't say," said Matthew. "As a thank-you? Or maybe because I am smart, handsome, fully-employed, a help to the helpless, a candle in the darkness…"

"A mentor to the young…"

"Still have my hair…"

"Can make me laugh…"

Matthew stepped closer to Piper. "And you," he said, "are beautiful, smart, lively, funny—"

"—neurotic—"

"Whom among us isn't?" Matthew replied. "And I am still in love with you."

"I can't resist a man who reads my blog," Piper said, and stepped into his embrace.

December 1: I Shall Set off for Somewhere

November is officially over. I have spent it working, blogging, and quarreling with the people closest to me.

Here is how the people around me have spent it:

Ananda has spent it fighting her illness. We hope and believe she is winning. She comes out of her room more frequently, and today she will join us to celebrate the end of a month of challenges, large and small.

Brumi and Silas have spent it restoring and re-wiring a jukebox. Molly instructed them to bring it in and set it up in the living room, and it does look fine. Silas drew a sketch of her dancing beside it, her face alight with laughter. I look at it and see my daughter, drawn with talent and seen through the eyes of love.

Molly created and inspired the November Lies group and shepherded them through the month; she organized Project Save the Magazine with her class; she threw the costume party at H.I.T. I have learned that one of her talents is helping those around her to succeed—a talent that is surprising and exceptional. I am impressed with her and I am honored to know her.

And Lisette—astonishing, extraordinary Lisette—has finished her book.

She is going to have it printed and bound and I hope I am one of the few, the Happy Few, the band of Liars, who will get a copy. I think the story of her project, along with excerpts, should go into the May/June issue of *Riverboro Rocks*. What do you think, Riverboro?

As for the rest of the November Lies group: they have spent this month creating polemics and manifestos and official biographies and subversive haikus. They have spent it opening windows to other worlds—worlds where zombies are taking over (or not); worlds in which communication and mis-communication takes place entirely through texting; worlds full of kitchens, and cooking, and recipes; worlds, perhaps, where house-bound women are stepping out their doors into the sun.

I will step into my sun. I might not do it today (but I might); I might not do it this winter (but I might); but I will step out my door and onto my porch and from there into the yard, and into the street, and into the world. And whether I am there or here, I will be the person that I am.

The person who can publish a magazine with or without a former husband; the person who can start a dynamic website and a (practically) daily blog; the person who has raised a beautiful daughter and will help nurture and protect an (almost) stepson.

The person who has created a space in her house and in her life to accommodate six monks—or at least six unique souls who are spiritual and creative and write and build and fix and recover from cancer and love and marry.

And have children.

A new soul is coming into our house in the spring. A tiny little monk(ey) who will learn from his parents how to tease and laugh and imagine and play. And from his uncles and aunties he will learn how to chant and pray and decorate a home to welcome the spirit of prosperity.

And from me he will learn how to love music and words and the impulse of creativity.

And how to forgive.

I build my dome of many-colored glass. It prisms the bright radiance of eternity.